ROSEMARY ROGERS

"THE QUEEN OF ROMANCE"
The New York Times Book Review

"THE CRÉME DE LA CRÉME
OF ROMANTIC ESCAPIST FICTION."
Newport News Daily Press

"A SUPERSTAR"
West Coast Review of Books

"HER NOVELS ARE FILLED WITH
ADVENTURE, EXCITEMENT, AND, ALWAYS,
WILDLY TEMPESTUOUS ROMANCE."
Fort Worth Star-Telegram

"A WINNER"
Green Bay Press-Gazette

"HER NAME BRINGS SMILES
TO ALL WHO LOVE LOVE."
Ocala Star-Banner

Other Avon Books by
Rosemary Rogers

BOUND BY DESIRE
A DANGEROUS MAN
DARK FIRES
THE INSIDERS
LOST LOVE, LAST LOVE
SURRENDER TO LOVE
SWEET SAVAGE LOVE
THE TEA PLANTER'S BRIDE
THE WANTON
WICKED LOVING LIES
THE WILDEST HEART

Avon Books are available at special quantity discounts for bulk purchases for sales promotions, premiums, fund raising or educational use. Special books, or book excerpts, can also be created to fit specific needs.

For details write or telephone the office of the Director of Special Markets, Avon Books, Dept. FP, 1350 Avenue of the Americas. New York, New York 10019, 1-800-238-0658.

ROSEMARY ROGERS

The CROWD PLEASERS

AVON BOOKS ◆ NEW YORK

This is a work of fiction. Names, characters, places, and incidents either are the product of the author's imagination or are used fictitiously. Any resemblance to actual events, locales, organizations, or persons, living or dead, is entirely coincidental and beyond the intent of either the author or the publisher.

AVON BOOKS
A division of
The Hearst Corporation
1350 Avenue of the Americas
New York, New York 10019

Copyright © 1978 by Rosemary Rogers
Published by arrangement with the author
Visit our website at **http://AvonBooks.com**
Library of Congress Catalog Card Number: 78-57656
ISBN: 0-380-75622-6

All rights reserved, which includes the right to reproduce this book or portions thereof in any form whatsoever except as provided by the U.S. Copyright Law. For information address Avon Books.

First Avon Books Printing: August 1978
First Avon Mass Market Printing: April 1980

AVON TRADEMARK REG. U.S. PAT. OFF. AND IN OTHER COUNTRIES. MARCA REGISTRADA, HECHO EN U S.A.

Printed in the U.S.A.

RA 20 19

If you purchased this book without a cover, you should be aware that this book is stolen property. It was reported as "unsold and destroyed" to the publisher, and neither the author nor the publisher has received any payment for this "stripped book."

Giovanni, con amore per sempre

PART ONE

THE
STAND-IN

Chapter One

ANNE WATCHED THE SNOW FALL, blown in white sheets across the dark garden to flatten itself against her windows. With the flickering light of a dying fire sending grotesque shadows dancing against papered walls, she had sat by the big windows and watched the blizzard outside—an impatient, slashing, fury of a storm that would no doubt bring down power lines and block highways everywhere.

It must be so cold outside, she thought with an involuntary shiver. *Angry* cold—nothing like the inert, unfeeling coldness in the very center of herself.

Cold—equated with unfeeling. *Damn! Why not say "frigid" and be done with it?* She had started using that word to herself long before Craig had ever said it aloud. In the very beginning, when he was still being patient with her, he'd been gently teasing, calling her "my little ice-maiden." He'd put her unresponsiveness down to the fact that he'd married a virgin, and he'd spent a lot of time at first in trying to help her "unwind and grow less stiff," as he'd put it.

Well, she *had* tried, at first. But when she drank more than she was used to, she only felt sick and dizzy. And when she'd gone with Craig to see a couple of those X-rated films all his friends were raving about, they only made her feel disgusted and even more stiff when he tried to make love to her afterwards.

"Anne! What's the matter with you? What do you need that

3

I'm not giving you? Goddammit, I'm your *husband*, you know!
Why do you freeze up every time I touch you?"

But she didn't know. She didn't even understand herself; how
could she answer him? It was an instinctive thing that none of
the marriage manuals she dutifully read had prepared her for:
something inviolate inside herself that didn't want to be
reached—or perhaps the recurrence of her childhood nightmare,
the one she always thought of as "The Dream."

She had a fear of the ocean, because of the Dream. Even of
flying over the ocean. And after a while Craig, with his demands, was like the ocean, trying to swallow her up. But that
was another thing she could never tell Craig. "Only a nightmare; I'm sorry I woke you up, Craig," she'd say, turning away
from him.

Poor Craig! Away from him she could think that now. He'd
tried too, she supposed. And it really wasn't his fault; it was
something inside of her—a feeling of having to hold close to
herself, not letting go, or she'd never belong to herself again.
Self. Warm place to hide in. Retreat.

Anne had learned to be good at that. At resisting when Craig
tried to probe and question and take her out of what he called
her frozen shell.

"How can I try to understand you when you won't tell me
anything, Anne? For God's sake, things can't go on this way,
and we both know it! You won't even try to make friends—
Melissa Meredith invited you to join her and the rest of the
girls at their weekly lunches, and you made some ridiculous excuse! And when we *do* go out together, you hardly say a word to
anyone. Dammit, Anne, they must have taught you *something*
at that damned finishing school besides manners and deportment and a few foreign languages!"

That was when, prodded to defiance, she'd said the unforgivable. "Your friends bore me! And their wives even more so.
Craig, I wouldn't know what to talk about with them, and you
know it. I know nothing of politics, of the latest scandals on the

Hill. And what's more, I don't care! Even about clothes—*you're* always telling me what to wear and how to do my hair. They make me feel stupid and ignorant, when *they're* the ones who don't know and don't care about anything outside their own little world! And I suppose I haven't learned to pretend yet—"

He'd pounced on that, of course—lines of bitter anger were etched in his narrow, handsome face. "So you haven't learned to *pretend?* I suppose that's some kind of a nasty dig at me, now you've finished tearing down my friends. Christ! You're damn right you don't know how to pretend! You won't even try, will you? Not even in bed. You just lie there like a piece of marble, not even attempting to give *me* any pleasure when I try to make love to you. Sometimes I wish I'd married a whore instead of an icy virgin!"

"Well, why don't you go out and get yourself a whore whenever you're in that kind of a mood? I understand the call girls on Capitol Hill do quite a business—your *friend* Melissa Meredith was whispering all the latest gossip to her coterie of friends that *you* want me to join—who's sleeping with whom, which congressmen prefer call girls, and whose wives have lovers. . ."

The storm blew itself out with the keening of the wind in the chimneytops, swirling around the house with a final swoop of frustration while Anne, shifting in her chair to tuck her bare feet under her, deliberately continued to let her mind run backwards.

That discussion had ended in a full-scale row, with her fighting back. Telling Craig she wasn't cut out to be a politician's wife, she didn't know enough and she didn't want to know, she didn't want to be another Melissa Meredith, whom everyone said would make a wonderful First Lady some day.

"So what *do* you want, Anne? What the hell do you do with yourself all day while I'm working my ass off in the office?"

"I—I read a lot. And I visit the museums and galleries and watch old movies sometimes. There's so much that they didn't teach me at those schools my father sent me to so I'd be safely out of the way. And as for what I want—I think I want most of all to learn more about myself, Craig. I want to find out about *real* life and living free, not living inside a carefully wrapped cellophane package. I'm twenty-one, and I've been in schools all my life that haven't taught me anything about life."

"You're not in school any longer, Anne. You're married to me—" Craig's voice had been carefully controlled, but she was too far gone to care.

"And you've made it seem like going back to school! You're always trying to teach me, don't you see? To—to guide me, to try to mold me to whatever pattern you expect your wife, Mrs. Craig Hyatt, to be cut out of. Don't you understand? I don't want to be just Mrs. Craig Hyatt. I want to be Anne Mallory Reardon for a change. Myself—a person in my own right."

Had that really been Anne talking? Almost screaming the words into his startled face? No wonder Craig's look of shock had changed into one of disgust, merging into an almost insufferable patience as if she really had been the stubborn, intractable child he'd accused her of being before.

After that had come six months of analysis. Really Craig's idea, because he wanted to save their marriage. Funny, sending her to Dr. Robert Haldane to "cure" her and help her "come to her senses" had been instrumental in breaking up her marriage.

Thank God for Dr. Haldane, who helped her see things as they were, in their proper perspective! Reluctant at first—wary and resentful—Anne had finally come to realize that the good doctor's only intentions were to help *her*. She had started by seeing him only once a week—and then it had become three times.

"You've always had decisions made for you, haven't you, Anne? Well, it's high time you started making them for yourself. Go out and try. I'm not saying that you might not get hurt in the process, but that's a part of living and learning, too, isn't it? Do, Anne. Don't just sit back and think about it."

Maybe she'd reacted so quickly because Dr. Haldane was only

reinforcing what she had already known inside herself. She was a kind of anachronism in this day and age. Less experience than the average sixteen-year-old. She'd never had a date, never gone to a football game or a prom, never ventured anywhere by herself until after she'd married Craig. The *Now Voyager* syndrome—she remembered seeing that old Bette Davis movie on one of her private excursions.

And that was really where the idea of going to Europe on her own came from. The last time she was there had been soon after she'd left the Swiss finishing school. Craig's parents, friends of her father's, had arrived to pick her up and take her with them on a world cruise. Craig had been along—handsome, adult, sophisticated—and she'd fallen in love almost at once, flattered by his attentions, made to feel secure and cherished by the fact that he respected her enough not to do more than hold her hand or kiss her gently and discreetly. Craig was an up-and-coming young attorney who meant to go into politics one day— at the time it had all seemed very exciting and challenging, like the idea of having their own apartment in Washington, and all the interesting people she would meet. All of whom turned out to be shallow, boring people. *Even Craig himself . . .*

This was the guilty thought she'd been trying to flee from all along. When they were no longer on shipboard or going on guided tours of the different ports, where having an escort of one's own was exciting, Craig was really like a stranger to her. His making physical love to her was a clinical thing, faintly unpleasant, that didn't in the least turn her on, or make her feel anything beyond a slight repugnance and a stern desire to fulfill her obligations as a wife. No bells tolling, no magic explosions that would take her beyond herself and transform her, overnight, into a woman.

After she had learned to trust him, Anne was able to talk to Dr. Haldane quite frankly about that aspect of her marriage. "Oh, I've read everything I could get my hands on, of course! I know I shouldn't be looking constantly for the Big O. And

7

Craig did all the right things. I mean, he was patient, he was gentle, he tried . . ."

"Perhaps he tried too hard. Or perhaps you were not really in love with him?"

She'd looked up at the doctor with surprise. "But love—I thought that was an old-fashioned thing to believe in! I thought I was in love with Craig, but I couldn't have been. There I go, contradicting myself again! I don't know—all the books I've read, everything I've heard—isn't 'love' a self-induced sense of euphoria? Brought on by romantic music or a romantic setting or a purely physical desire that can occur between two people sometimes? Although it seldom lasts, of course. But in this day and age, isn't companionship more important? Having things in common, sharing the same goals?"

"My dear Anne—you sound so solemn, like a good little girl who has done her homework." Dr. Haldane's eyes twinkled, and although he didn't smile, Anne had the impression that he wanted to. He waved a hand at her when she opened her mouth to speak. "Oh yes! I've heard it all and read it all many times over. This is the age of the liberated female who has the right to an orgasm every time she goes to bed with a man, and the right to do the chasing if she feels so inclined. And why not? Have you thought about taking a lover yet?"

Craig had wanted to be her lover. But he'd also wanted to keep her dependent on him. Maybe someday, sometime, the bells would ring for her. Craig just hadn't been the right person, and that was why she had left him, why she was here in Deepwood, in her father's house, waiting for her father so she could tell him she had left Craig and was planning on a divorce before she left for Europe. She had her mother's money from the trust her grandfather had left, which would be more than adequate. Freedom! Funny that she should be waiting here— that in order to see her father and tell him what she was going to do, she'd had to call his office and make an appointment. The impersonal male voice at the other end of the telephone had sounded faintly reproachful that she should interrupt her father's busy schedule with a request for his time. But in the end, after she'd been stubbornly insistent, she'd been told to wait—he'd be home by the end of the week. The voice had been remote and impersonal, like her father himself on the few occasions when they had met . . .

Well, she didn't really care what he might say; she was only here to *tell* him, that was all. Face him, tell him, and that would really set her free.

Maybe it was the silence after the howling storm that finally lulled her into sleep. When Anne woke up, her body uncomfortably cramped in the wing chair she'd been curled up in, the sun was shining again, reflecting off the snow that lay piled up in great drifts of silver-whiteness. After the howling wind last night, the air was still; the leafless branches of the trees seemed etched against the rich blue sky. Everything outside seemed sparklingly pristine, all new and fresh, while her room was still filled with the faintly smoky smell of last night's dead fire. It seemed suddenly important that she be outdoors, smelling the freshly laundered air and letting the cold whip color into her face.

Everything in her father's house was efficiently ordered—the staff directed by old Mrs. Preakness, and even a private generator in case of a power failure. Her room had stayed comfortably warm, and there was plenty of hot water when she turned on the shower in the bathroom. The towels, hanging on warming rails, were soft against her skin.

Anne showered quickly, then pulled on one of her oldest pairs of slacks, a baggy, bulky sweater, and a ski jacket. No makeup— Craig wasn't around to protest—and her long hair, baby-fine and straight, needed only a comb run through it and a scarf to cover her ears from the cold.

Anne glanced at her reflection in the mirror for just an instant, as she thrust her hands into fur-lined gloves. Pale face;

too little sun. Dark blue eyes with darker smudges underneath them. Silver-blonde hair worn straight and long. She grimaced at herself, wrinkling her nose. There was no one to care, or to protest. Craig had wanted her to look like a fashionplate—hair, makeup, dress, just so at all times. It was good to be her natural self.

Outside, a slight wind had sprung up. Anne squinted against the brilliant sun reflecting off snowbanks, and hesitated for a moment, wishing she had remembered to wear sunglasses. Then she shrugged, breathing the clean freshness of the air and wanting only to go beyond the big, electrically operated gates that had always made Deepwood seem more like a prison than a home.

She felt her heart lift when she heard the gates shut again behind her. God, it felt good to be *free*! And what was it she kept reading on posters? "Today is the first day of the rest of your life." Somehow, with last night and all the retrospection behind her, she *felt* that way.

Anne started to walk downhill—nowhere special to go, just feeling like walking for as long as she wanted to. She'd always been driven before; this time was different, almost symbolic of her new independence. Her legs carried her with long strides, muscles stretched with unaccustomed freedom.

The snowplows hadn't had time to get up here yet, but before she knew it she had reached the outskirts of town, moving automatically onto the cracked and uneven sidewalk, paralleling a low stone wall.

She noticed the poster, slapped carelessly against the stone so that one corner had come loose and flapped in the rising breeze. And would have walked past, not caring, not noticing, if the *name*, in big red letters, hadn't caught her eye.

Miss Carol Cochran, appearing in the first pre-Broadway tryout of—Anne, suddenly curious, had to smooth the end of the poster down and hold it to read the rest.

Bad Blood was the name of the play, and now Anne vaguely

recalled reading something about it in a magazine in Dr. Haldane's waiting room. It was always news when Carol accepted a role in a new play, and this one had been written by one of the theater's most promising young writers and was already slated to be made into a movie.

Most of the other names that followed Carol's seemed familiar. One, in letters almost as big as Carol's: Webb Carnahan. She'd heard of him too, she was sure of it. But it was seeing Carol's name that stopped Anne, bringing a sense of nostalgia.

School. The one before the Swiss finishing school. Boston, of all places, and everything so dull and proper and correct until Carol had arrived, turning everything upside down with her unsubdued, flaming beauty, her terrible grammar, and her uncensored comments on just about everything.

Perhaps the real reason they had become friends was because they were such opposites. Anne had been the wide-eyed listener, and Carol the doer. It was Anne who covered up on the nights that Carol sneaked out, when she needed "a night on the town." Carol had brought adventure into her life. And although Carol had lasted only a year at school, Anne had never been able to forget her.

"I won't promise to write, sweetie, because—hell, I never write letters anyhow, you know that! But one day, when I'm famous and rich, we'll look each other up and compare notes. Talk about old times . . ."

Anne still remembered the way Carol had looked that day, sitting on her suitcases on the steps while she waited for her stepfather to pick her up. Her eyes squinted against the sun with determination; her smile was wide and flashing. They'd be leaving for Europe the next day, Carol had said. "Europe! Will you think of that? For a high-class call girl, my mom really did good, didn't she?" And then she'd laughed, seeing Anne's face. "Shit, baby! Haven't I taught you to call the facts of life by name? And me, I'm going to do even better."

Since then, Carol *had* gone on to become rich and famous,

just as she had promised. But Anne had never looked her up. Craig wouldn't have approved of Carol, with her marriages and her flamboyant antics that always made the front pages. And *she* had been too busy fighting for her self's survival.

But now, today—it didn't really matter at all what Craig might or might not approve of, did it?

They'd probably be rehearsing right now in the old theater in the middle of town. She could slip in through the side door and watch Carol. It would be fun to see her again—to watch a Broadway play in rehearsal.

Hands thrust into the pockets of her jacket, Anne started downhill again, and now she was almost running.

Chapter Two

THE SIDE DOOR to the theater had never been locked, for as far back as Anne could remember. She didn't think it even had a lock. As a child, she had often wandered into the theater through this very door, walking softly down musty, shadowed aisles, clambering up onto the stage to pretend she was a star, giving her best performance. With eyes half-closed, she had made the theater come alive—chandeliers blazing with light, the worn velvet of the heavy curtains taking on a bright new opulence.

She hadn't been down here for years—but now the wrought-iron doorknob turned rustily and the door opened as it had before, so many times, allowing her to slip quickly inside. Fortunately, there was some kind of a gun battle in progress on the stage—the staccato sound of shots drowning out the squeaking of ancient hinges as Anne pushed the door shut behind her. She stood there uncertainly for a few moments until her eyes adjusted to the dim interior.

Forcing herself into a sense of daring, Anne walked softly along the carpeted length of the theater and slid unobtrusively into a seat in the back row. No one seemed to have noticed—there were people in scattered, tiny groups, sitting ahead of her in the front rows.

The action onstage captured her attention almost immediately. It didn't take her long to realize that it was one man, playing an obvious gangster type, white suit and all, who was making the whole scene come alive. He was supposed to have just killed someone, she surmised, and was arguing with an older man and a woman as he thrust a gun back into his shoulder holster. He projected an angry, animal emotion that made only him real and the other two actors just background shadows.

Involuntarily, Anne found herself catching her breath, unable to take her eyes off him as the scene progressed. He moved like a jungle animal—she was reminded of a black panther, darkly beautiful to watch, but just as deadly and dangerous.

I'm being silly! Anne tried to tell herself. *He's just an actor, like all the others.* She suddenly remembered seeing him in a TV movie some time ago. He'd played a young medical student, hooked on drugs, and she'd been caught by his intensity, thinking that he was really good; but seeing him today, in person, he impressed her even more. Not just impressed her—that was too shallow a word! He fascinated her, forcing her to keep watching him, not wanting to miss any little gesture or motion, like the way he would occasionally rake his fingers through his shaggy dark hair, or let the corners of his mouth lift in a menacing-sarcastic smile.

Caught up, Anne forgot why she had come here in the first place. She hadn't even thought to glance around the darkened theater for Carol until the lights came back on abruptly, shaking her out of her trance.

"Webb's damn good when he wants to be, isn't he?" The man's voice came from behind her, and then, as Anne involuntarily turned to look, his voice changed. "Hey—who are you? Don't you know you're not supposed to be here during dress rehearsal?" He seemed to loom over her, a big, burly man in a checkered wool jacket. "How in hell did you get in here anyhow? I could have sworn I locked those blasted doors!"

Her first reaction was to turn and run. Oh, God! Now everyone must be watching her!

Anne heard her own stumbling words as she stood up quickly.

"I—I'm sorry—I didn't realize—the side door is never locked, you see, and I just wandered in when I saw the poster . . ."

She blundered out into the aisle, and suddenly felt a strong hand close over her arm.

"You're not going to let Mike scare you off, are you?" said a man's voice. "He shouts a lot, but he doesn't bite. It's okay, Mike, this little gal is a friend of mine."

Stopped short in her headlong flight, Anne looked up unwillingly, and amber-gold eyes raked over her, making her want to pull away from his possessive grip.

"Hi, baby. Thought you'd never get here." His voice was warm, just as if he had been expecting her after all. The man he'd called Mike seemed to melt somewhere away into the background, grumbling sourly in an undertone.

Webb Carnahan. Anne remembered his name, and she felt that she might never forget his face as he smiled down at her; the smile seeming to lighten his otherwise somber face, etching lines at the corners of his eyes.

"Well, now. Seems like I caught myself a wide-eyed country gal." His voice, deliberately soft and drawling, rasped across her nerve ends. "What's your name, country gal?"

He might have rescued her, but he was making fun of her now.

"Anne. And I'm not . . ."

He would be, of course, the kind of man who ignored what he didn't choose to hear. "Annie, huh? It suits you. Annie Oakley!" He had not let go of her arm, in spite of her efforts to tug it away. And now, as Anne felt her face flush with embarrassment, she heard him laugh softly.

"My name is Anne Hyatt, and please—let me go! He—that man was right, and I shouldn't have come in here at all. It was good of you to rescue me, but I . . ."

She wished she had the presence of mind not to stutter and stumble over her words. But everyone was watching them now, and she felt isolated in the spotlight of their curious looks.

His eyes squinted down into hers, making her feel mesmerized in spite of herself.

"Who said anything about rescuing?" He laughed softly, just as if he felt the sudden racing of her pulse under the hard, determined grip of his fingers. "I'm capturing you, little scared Orphan Annie! You were a bad girl, sneaking in through that side door to watch us, just like Mike said. And you're like the fresh air outside. Just what I need. Come sit with me and watch the next scene, huh?" His smile curved wickedly, and the curiously helpless feeling that had come over her ever since he put his hand on her persisted—making his hand on her arm stronger than her will.

Front row center, and if he could ignore the curious glances and the whispers, then so could she.

He was the type of man who had always made her feel uneasy. Far too sure of himself and his easy power over women. Now she was painfully aware of him, feeling the casual brush of his arm against hers, not able to see beyond his eyes, which close up were almost gold, with strange dark flecks in them. Eyes that coolly assessed her even while his mouth still wore that slightly mocking smile.

"Hey, settle down. No one's going to bother you now. And it's warm in here, so why don't you take off that silly scarf? Here—hold still . . ."

With a casual air of ownership he leaned toward her, long fingers untying the knot and slipping the scarf from her head; tossing it across her lap before he lifted a thick strand of her hair.

"Cornsilk hair—you ought to be a shampoo girl. You live here, Annie?"

Studying her through narrowed eyes, Webb Carnahan caught the mixed emotions of her face. How old was she? Seventeen? Eighteen? Hard to tell, with her scrubbed, un-made-up face; the only color in her cheeks was put there by cold and embarrassment. Funny that less than an hour ago, he had been standing in the snow outside the same side door she'd crept in by—arguing with Tanya. And when Tanya had flounced back inside, slamming the door shut behind her, he'd looked back up the hill and seen a girl running down it, silver-blonde hair flying. She had the grace and slimness of a skier, even when she held her arms out unself-consciously to keep her balance. Symbol of openness and freedom. Girl-child out for a run in the first snow. With a feeling of regret, he'd returned to the musty, warm interior of the theater, Mike's grumbling, and Tanya's sullen glances.

Annie. He'd recognized her at once from the silver swing of her hair, the dark blue of her jacket that almost matched her eyes. He noticed the slight swell of her breasts and the clean purity of her profile, and it amused him to pretend he'd invited her to watch their rehearsal. It had also been in his mind to teach Tanya a lesson. If there was one thing he couldn't take, it was a woman who acted possessive and started to make demands, just because he'd bedded her once or twice.

Tanya was what the French would call *un type*, and he'd met her type all over the world—a sexy, well-endowed woman, only too aware of her attractiveness and sexuality. But now he found himself unwillingly intrigued by this girl-woman at his side. "Country gal," he'd teased her—but was she, in spite of her air of nervous naïveté and an outfit she'd obviously worn more for warmth than with an eye for fashion? Funny to find her here, in a town of old people. He'd joined the other members of the cast in grumbling when Harris Phelps, who was producing *Bad Blood*, had picked this town of all towns for their tryouts.

Thoughts flashed across the surface of his mind while he watched her face, the way she bit her lip, pulling her hair back from his exploring fingers with an unconsciously graceful toss of her head.

"Please don't!" she said sharply. And then, in a lower voice,

"Stop making fun of me. I should have known better than to come in here without permission. Only . . ."

"Only?" He repeated the word, his eyes looking intently into hers.

"I saw the poster while I was walking down into town," she said as coldly as she could, wishing he would take his eyes from hers. "And the side door to the theater has never been locked, as long as I can remember. So I—it was a spur-of-the-moment thing. I thought Carol would be here and I wanted to see her again, that's all. I suppose I should have called—"

"Carol?" She had all his attention now, only she didn't quite like the way his eyes narrowed at her this time, reassessing her. Or the sarcastic note that crept into his voice.

"Yes, Carol!" Anne repeated boldly, daring him to talk down to her again. "I went to school with Carol, for a year. We were friends, even if we haven't kept in touch." Why was she explaining all this to him, under the intense scrutiny of his yellow-gold eyes? She'd meant to put him in his place and make her discreet escape now that everyone else was watching the stage again.

And yet, when Webb Carnahan suddenly picked up her hand, deliberately pulling off her glove in spite of her futile tugging, lacing his fingers with hers, she knew she couldn't have moved for all the warning signals going off in her mind. She was suddenly more aware of this man's presence beside her than she had ever been of anyone or anything before in her life.

"So you're an old school-chum of Caro's, are you? Well, well! From little Annie Oakley to grand duchess, proper New England accent and all! Sorry Caro's not giving her all this afternoon. That's Tanya, her understudy, up there. Caro's our queen bee, you know. She's probably sleeping or having her hair done right now, but she'll be here for the opening performance this evening. Maybe you should come back then, if you really want to talk about old times."

His voice drawled at her—she couldn't be sure if he gave it a caustic tinge because he was speaking of Caro, or if he was just doing it to tease *her*. Why did he have to hold her hand? Anne felt confused—almost drugged by the strange pull of emotion inside her. Practical, rational self warring with another self she hadn't known existed until just now. Why had she taken off all her rings? A gesture of defiance; wanting to remove all symbols of ownership. But what did Webb Carnahan want with her? What kind of game was he playing?

"I really do have to go now," Anne said quickly, knowing she was just saying words, any words that would get her away from him and the warmth of his fingers through hers. "It was stupid of me to come here as I did without calling first. And since Carol's not here . . ."

"Forget Caro. You can call her later. Stay awhile, Annie, long enough to get warm. Your fingers are cold, and I bet your nose is, too." He touched it gently with his free hand and she almost flinched, resenting his familiarity and yet unable to fight the unaccustomed urging inside herself to stay, with him holding her hand. Startled at the turn of her thoughts, she wondered how it would feel to be kissed by him.

A word floated into her thoughts. *Chemistry*. Something she'd read about and scoffed at. *Chemistry*. Was that why she felt as if he'd invaded her and taken possession of her with the touch of his fingers? *Chemistry*. Was that why she responded to the coaxing timbre of his voice when he said, "stay awhile, Annie . . ."?

He was a stranger, and a man who was obviously used to getting his own way. She sensed danger in him, as well as a supercharged tension between them. It was there, an instinctive, primitive feeling that she couldn't trust him and, most of all, couldn't trust herself with him.

"Don't you have to go on again?" She tried to make her voice sound even. Sanity, that was what was needed!

He stretched long legs in front of him, taking his attention from her long enough to glance up at the stage before he looked back at her. "In about five minutes. You going to stay until we get through?"

"No! I have to get back home—I didn't tell anyone where I was going and they'll be worried. I—I'll call Carol when I get back. Is she staying at the hotel?"

"We all are. There's only one hotel in town, isn't there?" His voice was uninflected—she wondered in spite of herself what he was thinking.

Her name was Hyatt. *Anne Hyatt*—Webb was amused at the way she placed that slight emphasis on her first name, as if to show him she resented his calling her Annie. And she lived with her parents, probably—"they'll be worried . . ." No rings. He found her reticence oddly intriguing. And even more intriguing was the fact that she had gone to school with Carol. Private school, which meant there had to be money in the background. Old, conservative money, probably. So what? He couldn't see Anne and Carol as buddies, somehow. More surprisingly, he couldn't place Anne. She didn't fit into any of the categories the other women he'd known had fallen into so easily.

Webb found himself curious, wanting to question her; but there was the damned rehearsal to be got through, and she was like a shy seabird poised for flight. He wasn't used to doing all the running or pursuing—only once in his life before, and that was something he didn't care to remember, not even now.

"You coming back to watch the show tonight, Annie?" He didn't understand why he persisted, keeping her fingers trapped in his.

"I—yes, I think so. Please—I do have to go now. And they're looking for you . . ."

He didn't know, when he deliberately brushed her cold lips with his, whether he meant the gesture for Tanya, standing glowering down at them from the stage, or whether it was a promise he was making to himself. "Okay, baby. Run back to your rabbit warren. But I'll see you tonight, huh?"

* * *

The Crowd Pleasers

Afterwards, Anne couldn't remember exactly how she had made her way outside again. She welcomed the cold bite of the fresh breeze on her face as she knotted the scarf about her hair again. Ridiculous! She'd made a fool of herself, and she certainly wasn't going to see Webb Carnahan again. The hand he'd held still tingled as she thrust it deep into the pocket of her parka. He was so arrogant, so sure of himself! Precisely the kind of man she ought to avoid.

Chapter Three

CAROL'S VOICE SOUNDED SLEEPY at first, then slightly wary, finally, once she realized who was calling her, surprised and glad.

"Anne! But, sweetie, you don't have to apologize for calling me—I'd have been mad if you hadn't! I should have remembered that this dinky little town is where you used to live and called you up first. But the last I heard, you'd gotten married, and I'd pictured you with a brood of little ones hanging on your skirts by now! What on earth are you doing here? Isn't your husband one of those smart Washington lawyers who's heading for a State Department post? I saw his picture in *Time*, and I did think about writing or calling you then, but you know how I am—full of good intentions but too little time . . . tell me all about yourself!"

"Well," Anne started cautiously, "there's really not that much to tell, you know . . ."

Carol was still Carol, fonder of talking than of listening. Just as if Anne hadn't spoken she broke in, "Better still, baby, why don't you come on over and visit me? If you can stand the mess this room has gotten into, that is—but then, you know what an untidy bitch I always was, don't you? Listen, I don't have anything to do until the show opens tonight. I had this lousy headache, and Harris let me cry off from rehearsals. He's a pet, by the way, and you must meet him! But I feel just fine now, and I'm dying to see you—you will come, won't you, Anne?"

Carol, the queen, summoning her subjects . . . but it was impossible to resist the coaxing note in her voice, and Anne had to admit to herself that there was another reason for her calling Carol. Webb Carnahan. His golden eyes seemed to see right through her and her quickly thrown-up defenses, the brush of his lips, so casually bestowed on hers, sending sparks like electric shocks on her nerve endings. "Country gal," his voice a deliberate caricature of a Southern drawl. And then—"Annie, huh? Annie Oakley . . ." teasing her. How was it that he of all the men she had met made her feel as if her bones had turned to water?

Carol was unchanged, except that she was even more beautiful, more flamboyant. She played the Star to the hilt, and Anne could not help being impressed. Whatever Carol did seemed to be larger than life.

She was alone in her suite when Anne arrived, wearing a pale green negligee that revealed the magnificent body of which she was so justly proud. Her bedroom was a mess, a large, dog-eared copy of her play script tossed carelessly aside onto a desk that was cluttered with tissues and overflowing ashtrays.

Catching Anne's look, she laughed. "I warned you, didn't I? Anyhow it'll be all cleaned up by the time I get back from the theater tonight." She effortlessly mixed then poured out generous martinis without bothering to ask Anne if she preferred something else. "Sit down, pet. Oh shit—dump that stuff on the chair onto the floor, would you? And you can kick your shoes off; I can tell you still like to sit curled up in a chair with your feet under you." While she talked her eyes appraised—ran over Anne's body, her clothes, to return to her face. "You haven't changed much. Why haven't you cut your hair yet? You'd look great with a Sassoon cut, maybe just ear-level. And if you'd just use some makeup!" Carol sighed exaggeratedly before she added, "Darling, there's so much you could do with yourself! I mean, you have a really fabulous face—remember when I used to tell you you could be a model if you'd just make some effort . . ."

Carol really hadn't changed! Feeling more at ease, Anne merely wrinkled her nose. "And remember when I used to tell you not to bother? Honestly, Carol, I'm quite happy the way I am. I just want to be—comfortable." To distract Carol, she went on quickly, "As a matter of fact, that's part of the reason I'm getting a divorce. Craig wanted a wife who could be on exhibition at all times, without a hair out of place. And I decided that I just wasn't cut out to be another Washington wife . . ."

As Anne had guessed, Carol, who had always loved gossip, pounced on that.

"You're getting a divorce? Sweetie, you've got to tell me all about it! What was he really like? A bastard, I'll bet—aren't they all?"

After that, talking became easier. Carol questioned, and Anne explained; Carol listened with raised eyebrows, finally commenting, "Well! It's too bad you two were incompatible. I can't say that I blame you though; there's nothing worse than being bored!"

And then Anne fell into her old role of listener while Carol, pacing the floor dramatically, using her cigarette for emphasis, told about her life, so much more interesting than Anne's had been. Beginning with the scandal that had flared when her stepfather had divorced her mother to marry Carol.

He hadn't lasted long. Lots of men, lots of publicity. A great part in a movie that had everyone calling Carol Cochran the latest sex symbol. And then she'd shown them by really acting, taking parts where her sexiness was played down. After that, the stage, and Carol was good, really good, or she wouldn't have made it even with her men and their money backing her.

"They said I'd never make it in the theater," Carol crowed. "Well, I did, didn't I? Did you see *Masquerade*? And then the jealous bastards started shrugging, 'Well, she made it in a musical, anyone can do that.' But with *Bad Blood* I mean to show them I can also make it as a straight dramatic actress. And after that I'll make movies again, good ones. That's what I really prefer anyway!"

"I saw your name on a poster and sneaked into the theater to watch a few scenes from *Bad Blood* this morning," Anne admitted. She grimaced. "I was almost thrown out, but I was rescued by the bad guy. Webb Carnahan?" She hoped the questioning tone of her voice would fool Carol. Had she introduced his name casually enough? But she needn't have worried—Carol's emerald eyes had begun to spark with anger.

"Webb? That son of a bitch! I'm sure he and Tanya were having a blast! Which scenes did you watch?" Carol gave a strident, angry spurt of laughter. "Tanya's so bad it's unbelievable! I don't know why she was picked to be my understudy. And it's really gone to her head since dear Webb decided to make her his latest target. Did you say he rescued you?"

"Well, he said it was okay for me to stay and watch. And he was really quite kind, except that he talked down to me, you know? I didn't like that."

"You didn't like that . . ." Carol was staring down at her, green eyes narrowed, and Anne wondered if she had been too casual. But then Carol laughed again, this time quite naturally. "Oh Anne—you're priceless! But of course Webb wouldn't be your type, or you his. Oh—perfect! Here, let me get you a refill, sweetie . . ." Carol whirled about, came back stirring a drink with a skewered olive. "You could do something for me, and yourself too. I mean, it would tie in with everything you've been telling me, about wanting to find yourself and being yourself. You will listen to me, won't you, Anne? Because I just had the most marvelous idea . . ."

"No!" Having listened unbelievingly as Carol expounded her idea, Anne couldn't sit still a moment longer. This was wilder than any of Carol's outrageous schemes at school. "You're crazy—it wouldn't work, Carol. I'd be insane to go along with such an impossible plan!" Anne jumped to her feet. "You can't be serious. What would be the point? You might win your bet, but everyone would be mad at you afterwards—and at me, if I was foolish enough to do it . . ."

"But, Anne, stop sounding so stuffy and just listen to me! No one need know. I'd have to tell Harris, but I can talk him into it. And as for Webb—well, after I've won my bet that I can make him blow his lines, he won't say a damn thing either! His pride wouldn't let him. Besides, don't you want to get even with him? Come on, Anne! If you'd just *think* about it, you'd realize it's a fantastic idea."

Anne shook her head helplessly, recognizing the stubborn, pleading note in Carol's voice as she continued to coax and cajole. "Carol, no! It just wouldn't work—it doesn't make sense!"

"But it does, Anne. And you'd be doing me a tremendous favor too. Listen—it's the last scene—no dialogue, no lines to memorize. It's Webb's scene, and I want to take it from him. All you'd have to do is stand there by the window, looking stiff and frightened. That's what it says right here in the script. Can you imagine? *I'm* the star, and they give *him* the big dramatic scene at the end. I've been trying to persuade Harris to have it changed. Maybe this will convince him! Listen—the lighting will be dim; all the audience would see of you is a silhouette. We're just about the same height, and with one of my wigs on, no one would know the difference! All I'm trying to do is prove a point, and you can help me." Carol made a wide, dramatic gesture with her arms. "Where's your spirit of adventure, Anne? Can't you admit to yourself that it might even prove kind of exciting for you? Just think—you'll be playing me, the lead in a big Broadway play, for a few minutes—and that's all it would take. You'd be my stand-in. That overblown bitch Tanya would give her eyeteeth for the chance, only I don't want her to have it—we won't let her know. *Please*, sweetie? You're my friend—maybe the only real female friend I've ever had, because you've never been jealous. I remember you would always cover for me. Remember those times I'd sneak out the window and hitchhike into town?"

"That was different, Carol. What you're suggesting this time is—is absolutely crazy! What would happen if the union found out? I mean, there must be an actor's union that this Tanya belongs to. And—and I don't think I'd like to have Webb Carnahan mad at me." Saying his name again made her shiver, not understanding why. Thank God Carol hadn't noticed.

Carol was still determined to get her own way, and she waved aside all of Anne's carefully rational objections. "Why can't you look at this like—like a kind of therapy, Anne? An adventure. Haven't you ever felt adventurous? I promise you, there'll be no complications afterward. Just read the script—and it's only for just this one time. There's no one else I could *trust* . . ."

Carol was at her most persuasive. It was hard not to fall into the old habit of being the follower while Carol led. But it wasn't entirely because of Carol that Anne felt herself weakening. What would Webb Carnahan's reaction be when he found it wasn't Carol he was saying his lines to? An adventure—with no complications afterwards, Carol had promised. She had a fleeting image of Craig's face, if he could have known, and that decided it.

"Here—read this—you'll see there's nothing to it." Carol thrust the script at her. "And I'm going to call Harris right now, before you chicken out."

In spite of the sputtering, old-fashioned heater that was supposed to warm the dressing room, Anne felt as if she was freezing. Even the heavy robe that muffled her goose-pimpled body didn't help.

She sat perched on an unsteady wooden stool in the doorway, with Harris Phelps's arm around her waist for support, waiting for her cue to go onstage. Although she was grateful for his presence, Anne hardly heard his soothing flow of words, because she was watching Webb Carnahan through gaps in the elaborate set. Noticing the movement of his lips, the dark, almost sardonic cast of his features, especially when he scowled, most of all the way he walked, making it seem like the angry pacing of a trapped forest creature. For this scene he had shed his jacket and wore only a thin silk shirt, open at the throat. He lifted his arm once to run his fingers through his shaggy dark hair, and she could almost see the fluid, rippling motion of the muscles in his back and shoulders. All grace and motion. And it was crazy of her to be thinking like this, especially at this particular time . . .

Anne shivered slightly, but this time her tremor wasn't from the cold.

Harris Phelps must have noticed, because she felt his arm tighten around her waist. "Cold, Anne? I suppose you're wondering how we let Carol talk us into this bit of madness. But then—I'm sure you know as well as I how easily Carol twists her friends around her finger. I wouldn't be surprised if she's sneaked into one of the seats at the back just to watch what happens."

Good, let him keep on talking about Carol. Anne supposed it must have been a surprise for Harris Phelps when he'd arrived in Carol's hotel room expecting love in the afternoon with Carol and it had been Carol's friend who had stood there in the darkened room with just a pink-shaded light behind her, wearing Carol's wig and Carol's pale green negligee.

That had been the test. "Because if Harris takes you for me close up, then there's no way a theater audience could tell the difference, Anne! Don't you see?"

All things considered, Harris had been very decent about it all, even forgiving Anne's part in the masquerade, shruggingly letting himself be talked into going along with Carol's scheme. "But just for this one time, remember! And we can't let anyone else find out . . ."

"Oh yes—union rules!" Carol had made a face at that, but she'd been gleeful at getting her own way, and magnanimous once she had achieved it. "I wanted you two to meet, anyway. Harris, this is Anne Hyatt, and would you believe we used to be best chums in school? Before they threw me out, that is!"

Harris Phelps had been charming, but Anne had the uneasy feeling that he hadn't stopped studying her. Assessing her? Wondering about her, even if he'd been too much of a gentleman to ask questions? And how much had Carol told Harris after Anne had left?

If only she could switch her mood back to this afternoon's lightness, Anne thought now, wishing her eyes wouldn't keep following Webb.

This time Phelps followed the direction of her gaze and she felt, rather than saw, his frown. "Do you mind if I give you a bit of advice, Anne? Keep away from him. Most women find Webb fascinating, and he uses that fact to use them. He's got it down to a fine art. Loves them and leaves them when he's squeezed them dry. He's a damn good actor, of course, but he carries that role into real life. Somehow, I get the impression you're not used to that kind of man, dear . . ."

Did it really show so obviously just how inexperienced she was? Anne stiffened, searching in her mind for an amused, easy rebuttal.

"I can't figure you out, Anne Hyatt," he continued. "You're like a chameleon, taking on colors that dont' really belong to you. With Carol's wig and makeup, you look so damn much like her that even I find it difficult to believe you're not Carol. And yet you're such a contrast to Carol! So pale and silver-blonde and—shy. I'm right, aren't I? Why did you really agree to this little charade, Anne?"

"You already answered that yourself, Harris. Remember? When you said how persuasive Carol could be." Anne shrugged. "And it was an adventure for me, of course. My life up till now hasn't been half as interesting as Carol's must be!"

Harris Phelps sighed. Disappointment or exasperation? Anne wished he'd stop talking, stop trying to psych her out. She didn't want to think beyond going through with this and getting it over with. Then she'd make an appearance as herself at the party in Carol's suite after the play.

Chapter Four

HARRIS PHELPS WAS INTRIGUED with Anne Hyatt. He was used to another kind of woman—women who were flamboyantly beautiful and bold and very willing, especially when they discovered how rich he was. He was also used to hiding his real emotions under the mild façade he chose to present to the outside world.

Harris had inherited money, and had turned his father's millions into a billion or more of his own. He looked like—and was—an epicure who could afford his tastes. Of middle height, he kept himself trim with exercise, massages, and steam baths, and had a medical checkup once a month. He played passable tennis and excellent golf. His hair was carefully styled, and his small mustache added what he thought of as a debonair and slightly rakish look to his face. Only the Phelps nose kept his features from being classified as regularly handsome. The long, proudly curved nose belied the thin and sensitive lips; it was the nose of a robber baron, a strong and unscrupulous man used to getting what he wanted, no matter what the means. But most people who met Harris Phelps and listened to his incessant, almost gossipy stream of chatter passed him off as just another playboy with inherited money—and forgot to be cautious, which worked to his advantage.

Harris called himself a dilettante of the new school; in a bygone age he would have been called a patron of the arts. At the moment he was interested in the performing arts—motion pictures and legitimate theater. A hobby—and why not? He could afford half a dozen hobbies if he wanted to, but he needed the challenge. He had other ambitions too, but he was smart enough and patient enough to know that this wasn't yet the time to move toward them . . .

Anne was raptly watching the stage again. Gazing at her classically beautiful profile, Phelps caught himself wondering again what it was that really intrigued him so about this woman. She wasn't his type as far as mistresses went. He liked to be seen with long-stemmed, big-breasted women, especially those who were well-known in their own right. Like Carol Cochran. He was Carol's official man-friend of the moment, but that didn't mean too much; both he and Carol understood that the arrangement was nothing permanent, leaving them both free to look elsewhere. He knew that what Carol really saw was his money—but that was only fair, because Carol herself was just another trophy to him.

But Anne Hyatt—Anne *Reardon* Hyatt, Harris corrected himself—was something different. He'd seen her first as Richard Reardon's daughter—and he was one of the few men who knew what Richard Reardon stood for and the extent of the man's awesome power. But he'd begun to see her as a woman, see through to her deeply hidden potential, during the past hour that he'd been acting as chaperone and mentor.

So she was divorcing her husband and breaking loose from the confines of a rigidly protected life. He couldn't blame her. But was she really as virginal and untouchable as she seemed? No gossip about her in Washington circles; Harris recalled hearing from Melissa Meredith that Craig Hyatt's wife was a mouse of a woman! Of course, one learned to discount half of what Melissa said; she was a dyed-in-the-wool bitch. But he'd been surprised all the same. Anne Hyatt was no mouse of a woman, for all that she dressed conservatively and could look like a teen-ager when she didn't wear makeup. She had a lovely face, and an excellent, if slightly too-slender, body, and she gave the impression of having depth to her character. Hidden depth.

Or did she? She didn't seem to be able to take her eyes off Webb Carnahan, and not for the first time Harris wondered irritably why women always watched Webb. Something about him. Machismo? Carol had used that word to describe Webb once. "You wouldn't understand, Harris my pet, but that bastard has it. Damn him, it's in the way he holds his body, the way he walks, like a big cat—the way his nostrils flare when he looks at a woman he wants. Oh, I'm wise to him now, but can't you see what he does to almost every other woman that crosses his path?" Webb drew women to him like flies, but not this one, surely not! Anne wasn't Webb's kind of woman, she was . . . Harris's mind hesitated over the old-fashioned phrase and repeated it. She was a lady. That was it. Definitely not the type to be exposed to Webb's crude line of bullshit, nor the kind of woman, surely, who would allow herself to become a one-night stand. Besides, Webb liked his women sexy and wild, like he was.

The scene was coming to a climax. Soon the curtain would come down and there would be the usual frenzied activity that accompanied each change of set. And then it would be Anne's turn, and then it would be over.

She was afraid, suddenly admitting her fear to herself.

Harris had stopped talking, and she hadn't even noticed, until he helped her off the stool in the doorway, pulling the door to the dressing room shut, closing her in with him.

His voice was calm and soothing as if he understood her sudden panic.

"It's almost time, Anne. And we don't want anyone to see you up close, when they start shifting props. I'm going to pour you some cognac, and I want you to try to relax until they knock at the door to warn you that it's time. Don't worry— Carol usually sits in the doorway muffled up just like you are, and then she has a drink and stalks out there at the very last moment to take her place by the window. And that's just what you will do. This is a very short scene, and it'll seem even shorter to you once you're out there onstage. No one will ever know the difference."

"He'll know."

Harris, pouring cognac into two snifters, tried to hide his frown of annoyance. "Of course he'll know! But that's the whole point, isn't it? To play a trick on Webb. I guess part of the reason I agreed is that she's entitled to her revenge . . ." He shrugged.

Anne took the glass he handed her, although her fingers felt nerveless. "Revenge?"

"Of course you wouldn't follow the gossip columns, or those trashy movie mags. But Webb and Carol were what would be referred to as a 'hot item' at one time. They were even engaged for a short while. I suppose Carnahan saw the chance to further his career; Carol was a big star even then, and he was just beginning, with that TV series. It didn't last, of course. Soon after that, Carol married her third husband, Ted Grady. We both know that Carol's no angel, but Webb really gave her a rotten deal. Since then, in spite of my advice, they've had an on-and-off affair. I understand he's taken up with Carol's understudy these past few days . . ."

Suddenly, Anne didn't want to hear any more. To stop herself from thinking, she held the snifter to her nose, sniffing up the heady fumes before she sipped the cognac very slowly.

Harris Phelps watched her appraisingly. "You know, you're the first woman I've seen who knows how to drink good cognac. You've got breeding, Anne. Good bone structure, too."

She began to giggle from reaction, holding the glass away from her so she wouldn't spill liquor all over herself. The heavy woolen robe fell open, and under the negligee Harris caught a glimpse of her breasts.

"Good bone structure!" Anne hoped she didn't sound hysterical. She didn't dare look at Harris's face, poor man, and he was only trying to be nice to her! Her voice shook. "You know,

33

that's all anyone really notices about me. I've got nice bones. Like a—a—racehorse! I've never been told that I'm sexy, or beautiful, or any of the things a woman really wants to hear. Oh dear, I'm sorry! You were only trying to be nice. I don't know why I'm reacting like this—I think it's all just nerves!"

Someone rapped twice at the door and a male voice said, "You're on, Miss Cochran!"

"Okay, she's coming. Get the lighting all set," Harris called. He looked sharply at Anne, holding her arm. "You're sure you're ready? Here, let me take that glass." His voice was brisk and completely businesslike now, but the look in his eyes was unfathomable as he went on, "Try to remember that all you have to do is react. You rehearsed this scene with Carol—there's really nothing to it. You stand there, holding onto the drapes, and all you think about is that you want to look out there to see what's happening, but you're afraid."

"Yes." Was that really her voice? It sounded disembodied. "It's like going to the dentist, isn't it? Once you sit in the chair, you know that soon it'll all be over. Honestly, I'm okay now."

Harris's voice, as he guided her onto the set, was like a sea murmuring in her ears. Or maybe that was the sound of the shifting, coughing audience hidden out there beyond the heavy curtain.

Anne tried to make her mind a careful blank, to remember the times she had climbed onto this same stage, playing different roles for an imaginary audience. She had always been good at make-believe, and this time was no different. She was Carol Cochran, star! Not Anne—Anne was another person she could rediscover after this was over. Forget the fact that there were real people out there and think only that she was Carol playing a girl called Toni, who had just betrayed her lover to the FBI.

Without her realizing it, Harris had eased the heavy wool robe off her shoulders, leaving her curiously light in Carol's borrowed negligee. The subdued lighting came from behind her, outlining her body.

Don't think; react. Someone had said that to her a minute ago. Now she was standing by a window that wasn't really a window, clinging to a fold in the heavy drapes that half-obscured it.

There was a sound of miniature explosions, like firecrackers going off, and a dull whooshing sound that meant the curtains had opened.

You're on, Miss Cochran!

She stood very still, her body gone rigid with fear; it looked right to the audience, because fear and tension and a sense of waiting were exactly what she was supposed to portray.

More shots and shouting voices before the door burst open and he half fell in through it, his white shirt spattered with dirt and blood; a look on his face combined shock and pain and hate.

She was forced to look at him, and he made it all become real, as if it was actually happening, the printed words she had read on the pages of Carol's script.

She stood there—*Toni* stood there at the window, still rigid with fear, and something else, now that he was here.

He was coming toward her, and she took an involuntary backward step, one hand coming up over her mouth to stifle a gasp.

He went down on his knees, staggered to his feet again as he stumbled toward her, one hand outstretched, gasping, "Toni—damn you, why do you just stand there? Help me! You've got to—"

He almost fell against her, hands clutching spastically, ripping the negligee from her body while his voice, hoarse and pain-filled, almost screamed at her.

"Toni—Christ! They're after me, and you've got to . . ." And then, just as if he'd read something in her face, his voice changed, becoming stronger, full of shock and hate. "You! You set them on me, didn't you? Just—like you promised . . . bitch! You killed me, just like you said—you—"

He was dying at her feet, and she couldn't move. Tears started to her eyes and she couldn't stop those either, or any of her reactions, like the shaking that seemed to begin in her bones, sending tremors through her body when the dim light behind her reflected off the sudden widening of his eyes, holding her own gaze snared.

Ridiculous thoughts chased themselves around in Anne's head, as she looked down at him, almost mesmerized. *He didn't blow his lines after all,* she thought. *Carol will be mad. So it was all for nothing. And what will he do now, when he finds out . . . ?*

She didn't realize the curtain had come down until she heard the applause—starting with a smattering and rising to a roar.

Escape—but she couldn't escape. He'd trapped her ankle with his fingers, digging painfully into her flesh.

"No curtain calls for *you*, baby." His voice was soft, angry. "Just a lot of explaining to do."

Someone had tossed her robe from the wings, and Webb Carnahan, his face dark and menacing, had come easily to his feet, catching it and pulling it roughly about her shaking shoulders as he demanded, "Is this one of Caro's pranks? But you're going to tell me all about it, aren't you?"

There were people swarming all around them now, moving bits of scenery, and he lifted her off her feet and into the strong grip of his arms. Sheer instinct made Anne turn her face against his shoulder, and she heard his cynical laugh.

"Smart move, baby. We don't want anyone to know you're not Carol, do we?"

Not too many steps to Carol's dressing room. Anne winced when he kicked the door shut behind them, setting her none too gently onto her feet.

But his voice was deceptively quiet. "Now, suppose you explain what the hell this is all about?"

Where was Harris? Nobody here to rescue her from the consequence of her own folly. But she was a big girl now, wasn't she?

Defiantly Anne moved back and away from him, ripping the wig off her head as she did, and shaking her own hair loose. She observed with pleasure the look of amazement on his face as he recognized her.

"I suppose I should apologize. We—Carol and I, thought . . ."

There was a rapping at the door, and Harris Phelps's voice, sounding sharply concerned, said "Anne? Are you all right?"

With a swift, angry motion, Webb strode to the door and locked it, the sound in the sudden silence making Anne flinch.

Webb's voice mimicked Harris's. "Why don't you tell the man you're just fine and we have some talking to do?"

"I'm fine, Harris. Honestly," Anne replied.

He wouldn't want a scene, any more than she did. Or Carol. And Webb knew that, of course. He had folded his arms, and was staring at her with a quizzical smile.

"You sure follow direction well, Annie. I can see Carol's touch behind the scenes. Well—who wins the bet?"

She didn't want to face his eyes any longer, and turned away from him, seating herself in front of the mirror, ready to cream off the heavy makeup. "You do, of course. And now that you know all the answers, there's nothing more to talk about, is there? This was Carol's idea of a trick—a joke. And I went along with it. I'm sorry if it made you mad."

Why did he have to come and stand so close behind her? So close that she could feel the angry warmth of his body . . . ?

His fingers closed over her arms, lifting her up and turning her around, almost in the same motion.

"Are you really sorry, Annie? Show me. Or did Caro forget to warn you about the kind of unscrupulous bastard I am?"

Her startled, involuntary protest was strangled in her throat as her head was bent back by the hard pressure of his mouth on hers.

Anne felt her mind give way as her body took over. She had never known what desire was, but she felt it now, like a hard, grasping knot in her belly—a pain that had to be assuaged. And as her senses took over, her arms went around his neck; instead of trying to pull away she pressed closer to him, wanting . . . needing . . .

There was a couch on one side of the dressing room, and he carried her there, stripping off her robe before he stripped off his own clothing.

Unshaded lights blazed an outline of the mirror, and the whole world was outside the door, but nothing seemed to matter at this moment, this time.

Desire was a snake, gnawing at her vitals, slowly uncoiling inside her and filling her with sensations she hadn't known existed. All her reactions were purely instinctive, completely primitive. And if his mouth hadn't covered hers she would have screamed aloud when the moment of cloudburst came, the only reality that of his body over hers, filling her, taking her past naked desire to fulfillment, all without wasted words.

There was a wetness on her face. She didn't know it was from tears until Webb put his hand up and wiped them away gently with his fingers. She thought his fingers shook, but she couldn't be certain; her own body was shaken by tremors she couldn't control.

Anne kept her eyes closed—against the glaring lights, against any form of reality that might take her back to what she had been before—before this.

"Jesus Christ, Annie!" Webb's voice was an oddly harsh, forced-out whisper—she could still feel that fast cadence of his breathing against her, but he hadn't moved, and neither had she since that final explosion of physical sensation. All her senses gathered up into one tight, aching knot until it had become a starburst . . . No bells going off, but who needed bells?

"Did I hurt you, baby?" Gentler now, his fingers still touching her face, smoothing back strands of damp hair.

She shook her head no, wondering if she was ever going to be the same again—if, when she opened her eyes and looked at him, the way he looked at her would be different. When he moved as if to draw away from her, Anne realized suddenly that she was still clutching him tight, her arms locked around his body, her fingers like nerve ends that could feel every slight movement of his muscles rippling under the smooth, sweat-slippery flesh of his back.

She did open her eyes then, and he was staring down at her—not smiling with self-satisfaction as she'd half-dreaded, not frowning with the impatience of sated passion either. His look seemed to concentrate on her intently, as if he too didn't quite believe what had happened between them just now.

"Annie . . ."

Then the telephone, sitting squat and malevolent on the floor, began to ring insistently. She'd never know what he had been about to say or how she might have answered him.

Br-rr . . . Br-rr . . .

Webb swore violently under his breath as her arms fell limply from around him.

At least she could watch him . . . Anne had never thought a picture of a male nude particularly entrancing, but now she found that the sight of Webb's naked body, the self-assured grace with which he moved, striding to snatch up the telephone, carried its own excitement. She had never been so acutely aware of a man's body, and its beauty, its "fearful symmetry," as she was now. And he did fit those lines from Blake's poem—"Tyger, tyger, burning bright, in the forests of the night . . ."

She felt as if she was on some kind of a high—not satiated but strangely content, so that even the interruption of the telephone couldn't bother her. Not yet . . .

Webb had scooped up the phone, snatching off the receiver with an angry gesture. "Yeah?" And now he sounded mad, his voice turning hard. "Yeah, Harris. Sure, Anne's here and she's okay . . . That was real thoughtful of you . . . Listen, why don't you talk to her?"

He was thrusting the phone at her, forcing her to fight the lethargy in her limbs in order to sit up and take it.

"Anne?" Harris's voice sounded worried. "Listen, I didn't mean to desert you, love, but that girl Tanya had been drinking, and she was working herself up into an extremely unpleasant mood . . . rather than have her banging at the door and creating a scene, I thought it might be best to whisk her away. But I'm concerned about you. Are you sure you're okay?" He seemed to drop his voice slightly. "I know how nasty Webb can get when he's angry, and if I'd thought . . ."

Anne tried to keep the breathlessness out of her voice as she said carefully, "Of course I'm all right. I mean—we did have quite an argument"—involuntarily her eyes went to Webb, who was calmly pouring Carol's cognac into two glasses, giving her a silent, mocking toast with one when he caught her glance— "but everything's just fine now. I'm sorry—"

"You don't have to apologize, Anne! Listen, I thought I'd call before I came down to get you—you *are* going to show up at Carol's party, aren't you? She's expecting you . . ."

"Carol's party?" Oh God, she hoped Harris wouldn't think she sounded as bemused as she felt, with Webb's eyes, narrowing wickedly, traveling all over her body. Some kind of sanity came back to her, and she clutched at the telephone as if it was a lifeline. "Oh—oh yes! It'll just take me a few minutes longer to—to finish taking all my makeup off and change—"

She felt the receiver taken firmly from her, exchanged for a glass she could hardly hold with her shaking fingers.

"Listen, Harris," Webb said, "you tell Caro-baby that she owes me for the little trick she played on me tonight. And you don't have to come charging down here to rescue Annie—I'll bring her back in one piece. We've decided to walk back for the exercise, especially since it's such a nice clear night."

Chapter Five

WHERE WAS ALL HER DETERMINATION to make something of her life to satisfy herself—the bitter courage that had brought her this far along the path to freedom?

Anne paused at the open door to Carol's suite, hesitating—still torn between the ridiculous, impossible urge to turn and run from the loud music and the heat and the *people* in there, to run back to Webb, and the need to assert her independence of him by walking forward instead.

Harris Phelps must have been watching for her. He came forward and took her arm, his pale gray eyes sharp with concern. "Anne! I'd really begun to worry, and so has Carol. It's been over an hour . . ."

"I really *am* sorry, Harris!" She hoped her voice sounded as insouciant as she tried to make her shrug. "But we walked, and it was uphill most of the way."

"Where's Webb?"

"Oh . . . he decided to make an early night of it, I guess." Had she said it lightly enough? She forced a smile for Harris, trying to shut out the image of Webb's dark, angry face—the sound of the door to his room slamming shut.

How had they begun to quarrel? Had it been her own urge for survival that made her want to negate the powerful pull he exerted over her senses? The feeling of not belonging to herself as soon as he touched her had been frightening. Wasn't that what she had been trying to escape? And then, when he had

41

left her alone to cream off her stage makeup and get dressed, there had come the nagging memory of Harris's warning words . . . Webb's own obvious familiarity with the things in Carol's dressing room, with Carol herself. And Tanya, who had been so upset. What about her?

The walk in the cold, still night air with pinpoint stars seeming to pierce the midnight blue sky had been exhilarating—Anne had been able to forget almost all her misgivings with her hand held in Webb's as he tugged her along with him. Laughing for no real reason except to see how the steam from her breath etched itself against the stillness of the air. The slightest brush of his shoulder against her bringing back the memory of his body—naked, arrogant, claiming hers, and making her feel at last for herself everything she had read or heard about feeling.

He had made love to her again, the cognac warming her within while his lips and his hands made her flesh burn everywhere they touched. And it had happened again, the starburst of ecstasy starting from deep inside to send its fire through every nerve in her body while the only reality was the piston-driving strength and hardness of his body possessing hers.

Afterwards . . . Why did there have to be an afterwards, with all of its doubts and fears? Maybe it was the overheated hotel lobby with its chandeliers and the curious looks from the uniformed clerks behind the old-fashioned mahogany desk. And her own ingrained, instinctive shrinking as her mind took over from her senses.

Webb had wanted to skip the party. He'd wanted her to have dinner with him in his room; he'd wanted *her*. And that was how the argument had erupted as they stood before the door to his room.

"But I did promise Carol. And then you told Harris. Webb, why can't you come too? Just for a little while . . ."

"Just to make a polite goddamned appearance? Hell no, baby. I'm not in the mood. But if you're anxious to make the party scene and have fun with all your friends, you go right on ahead, huh? Hurry along—you don't want to keep good old Harris waiting, do you?"

"You want everything your own way, don't you?" she had stormed at him, surprising herself with her own vehemence. "You won't give an inch, and yet you want me ..."

For an instant, his face had turned somber, looking down at her.

"That's right. I want you, Annie. But not in a crowd. And not enough to put up with that shit." The jerk of his head indicated the light coming from the open door down the hallway.

The calculated cruelty of his last words only stiffened her determination not to let herself be dominated by his will. If he had only been reasonable . . . but he hadn't. He had been the one to drop the shutter between them, patting her face lightly as if it didn't matter to him one way or another.

"Run along then, Annie. Have fun. And maybe I'll see you around, huh?"

Then his door had closed in her face. End of chapter, end of episode.

Harris was holding her arm and leading her into the hot, overcrowded room, talking all the time as he did.

"I told Carol I'd bring you along as soon as you arrived, Anne. She's dying to know how that last scene went. Her last ex-husband turned up unexpectedly; that's him talking to her now, the tall sandy-haired man wearing that absurd-looking string tie. He wants to try for a reconciliation, although there's no hope of that! Carol's outgrown him, I think. And she can handle him—he's acting almost decently civilized for a change, in spite of the nasty jealous scenes he used to put her through while they were still married." Switching from one subject to another with hardly a pause, Harris said softly, "I suppose that's why I've never married. Jealousy is pointless and passé. I'm a romantic at heart, and I've always hoped to find a woman

I didn't need to be jealous of. Oh—there's the mayor. I can see he recognizes you. Listen—no one knows, Anne, so there's no need to be nervous. I can feel your arm tensing up . . . But remember that you're merely one of Carol's old school friends—you two got in touch, and she invited you to watch the play and join her here afterwards. Do feel free to relax. It's a good thing Webb didn't accompany you here, in a way. Knowing Webb . . ."

How well did he know Webb? Did anyone really know what Webb was like? If she was to go by Harris, or even Carol, by now Webb must have put her out of his mind. And yet it had been she who had drawn back! She hugged that thought to herself, even if it didn't give her any satisfaction at this moment.

"Darling!" Carol said reproachfully. "Where on earth have you *been*?" Carol's theatrical training made her emphasize certain words when she spoke. "I was hoping you hadn't changed your mind—you don't know how I'd been looking forward to having a little girl-talk with you—it's been such *ages*, hasn't it?"

Tonight, Carol was wearing a stunning Halston creation that showed off her figure and her justly famous breasts. She introduced Anne to Ted Grady very smoothly and without any embarrassment. "This is Ted, my ex. He's a very sweet man, but of course I've always been a bitch to live with, haven't I, darling?"

Grady mumbled something, obviously still concentrating on Carol, and Anne felt herself smile tightly, hoping her smile didn't look too much like a grimace.

"Anne—we've *got* to squeeze in some time together. But there are so many people I haven't even talked to yet, so I'll get that over with first, and in the meantime, Harris will help you circulate and get you something to eat, won't you, Harris? Ted, you're going to have to circulate too. And no jealous scenes, sweetie, or you'll have to leave."

How easily Carol handles everything! Will I ever learn, Anne wondered, letting Harris lead her on with her smile so fixed upon her face so that her lips actually ached.

Fortunately, no one seemed to notice. The local people there were polite, their voices tactfully incurious as to the reason for her presence there, although they all inquired politely after her health and her father's.

"And how's your father, Mrs. Hyatt? When will he be coming home again?" They did not question why she was here, with "the theater people," but their veiled looks were curious all the same. The sole representative of the *Deepwood News* did not question or approach her at all.

Harris introduced her to a few members of the cast whose names or faces were vaguely recognizable. A young, brown-haired man called Tony, who had been in that first scene she had watched that morning; an older woman, a character actress who had once been a star in her own right; and the director, Michael Fenwick, quietly dressed in a dark suit and very polite now, acting as if he was meeting her for the first time.

"I think you ought to have something to eat, Anne." Phelps led her to a buffet and began filling her plate without waiting for her reply. He also got her a drink—a very dry martini—and found her a chair to sit on. Why was Harris being so pointedly nice?

Anne forced herself to take a bite of cold turkey, while Harris, with a murmured "You don't mind, do you love?" sat himself on the arm of her chair.

God, it was stifling hot in here. And the music was far too loud. What was she doing here, when she should be in that room down the hall? Everything that had happened before seemed unreal, a half-forgotten fantasy. But every nerve in her body strained towards that closed door down the hall, all the pride and the logic that had brought her here seemed suddenly unimportant in the face of what she wanted, had really wanted.

The martini tasted much better than the cold food. Anne swallowed all of hers, and accepted another glass from a passing waiter.

"It won't help you to get yourself drunk," Harris Phelps said quietly, a peculiarly controlled tone to his voice. She looked up at him, annoyed, but he went on, putting a hand on her arm for emphasis, "You have a very transparent face, my dear. And you must learn, like me, not to let your feelings show too openly. Webb Carnahan isn't worth your regrets. I'm not asking what happened between you, but you must know he isn't your type. He's an amoral animal who's far too used to taking what he wants, and then . . . But you're different, Anne. You've got both birth and breeding, and you haven't been exposed to his kind. It's understandable, of course, that you would be intrigued by him. I was over-protected too, and I learned how to fight my way out of the cage I was in, just as you will, Anne. Only, if you must experiment, start with your own kind. Stay away from the barracudas."

Harris had surprised her. Anne found herself studying him once again. What did she really know about him? He was very rich, very powerful. A dilettante who could afford to indulge his whims by dabbling in theater and movies. Why was he acting so protectively towards her? She didn't need protecting. She'd had enough of that!

"Honestly, Harris, I . . ."

He shook his head, this time giving her a slight smile. "I know; how well I know, Anne! You must be tired of warnings and little lectures like the one I've just been giving you. I don't blame you for it. I too had my share while I was growing up. It was only afterwards that I learned for myself what my father was trying to warn me against. It's hard not to be able to trust other people, isn't it? To become cynical enough to wonder, every time you make a new acquaintance, what he might really want from you; or whether he would like you just as well if you weren't filthy rich. It's a rather lonely existence, isn't it? And

46

whether you like my saying so or not, there's a certain air of vulnerability about you, Anne. I wouldn't want to see you hurt."

"What are you two doing, hiding away here in a corner? Anne, sweetie, don't you like the food? Your plate looks as if you haven't touched a thing on it!" Carol's voice sounded reproachful, but her bright emerald eyes were curious as her gaze flashed from one to the other. "You're supposed to *circulate!* Harris darling, I thought I could count on you to see that Anne meets everyone. She needs to meet people, don't you, pet? And I've been dying to ask you how it went tonight. Was Webb very mad? Where is he, anyhow? The bastard—did Harris tell you about the scene Tanya tried to make? Although Harris is very good at handling things like that, thank God! And with Ted turning up, trying to get something on me so he won't have to pay up on our marriage settlement . . . ugh! Harris— he can't get away with that crap, can he? You'll have to give me the name of that clever attorney of yours."

It was amazing how quickly Carol could switch from one subject to another, and all without stopping to draw breath.

"I think you want to talk alone with Anne," Harris commented dryly, contriving to let his fingers caress Anne's arm as he rose to his feet. With Carol's coming he had changed too, his manner more brisk and businesslike as he melted into his "Harris Phelps, Producer" role. "Don't worry, Carol, I think Grady's making noises because he's still jealous and wants to get you back. If I find an opportunity I'll try to have a little talk with him. And if he does get difficult I'll see that you're well represented."

"Well . . ." Carol looked slightly worried. "I *would* appreciate your keeping Ted out of my hair. He's always been so jealous it was almost paranoid, and there were a few times he really scared me, you know, with all his threats. He used to say that if he couldn't have me no one else would. And I was almost paranoid by the time I walked out on him!"

The next moment Carol's brilliant, world-famous smile flashed as she reached out for Anne's hand.

"Come on, darling! Let's escape into my bedroom for a little girl-talk, shall we? Harris will look after the mob for a little while."

It was comparatively quiet in Carol's untidy bedroom, with coats and wraps littering her bed; Carol had to clear some space on it before she could sit down. The party noises filtered faintly through the door that Carol had pushed shut, and every chair was draped with clothes—obviously discarded while Carol was deciding what to wear tonight.

It was amazing, Anne thought, trying to postpone the moment of Carol's inevitable questions, that she didn't bring along a maid to keep things picked up.

Echoing her thoughts Carol said, "I always seem to make such a bloody mess! But then, I do like my privacy, and if you tip hotel maids enough they'll even pack for you. Darling, why on earth don't you sit down? Here, on the bed by me. Or you can shove that silly gown onto the floor if you like; I'll never wear it again!"

Anne didn't quite understand why she felt defensive, but she did. She shrugged, perching herself on the edge of the dresser. "This is fine. I haven't been doing my share of standing about all evening. And I feel guilty about dragging you off from the rest of your guests."

"Anne, do stop being so damned evasive! You make me wonder, especially since you took so long getting here! Webb— exactly what did he do? What did he say when he found out it wasn't me but you? Did he—"

"He didn't blow his lines, if that's what you mean." Anne was surprised that her voice could sound so dry and even. "But he *was* mad, and I had a lot of explanations to make."

"For over an hour, in my dressing room—with the door locked?" Carol's elevated eyebrows gave the lie to her exaggeratedly patient tone of voice, and Anne felt herself tense. "*Darling*—theater people gossip, you know! And poor Harris was almost frantic. He had to get Tanya away from there, or you might have had a really ugly scene to contend with, and I don't think you've had experience with that sort of thing. I persuaded him to try calling you instead of going back there to batter down the door or something equally dramatic. I think Harris has developed quite a *tendresse* for you, which isn't like him at all!"

"I like Harris too—he's been very nice." *Fight back, Anne*, an inner voice told her. "But honestly, Carol, this—this farce tonight was your idea, after all, and I was the one left to cope with Webb Carnahan and his anger—which was really quite justified, you'll have to admit! Why all the concern, suddenly? Did you think I couldn't take care of myself?"

Carol's first reaction of surprise made Anne feel good. "Touché, sweetie! And hooray for you, if you managed to keep Webb in line. It's just that I happen to know dear Webb very well—*too* well, in fact. And it would be just the dirty, low-down kind of thing he'd do, just to get even with *me*, to try to . . ."

"To try to—what?" Anne hoped her voice still sounded steady, and that Carol wouldn't notice how tightly her fingers gripped onto the edge of the dresser. She didn't like the way Carol and Harris between them had begun to make her feel.

"Well—you know, I think. And believe me, darling, I'd make Harris promise to stick right by your side. If I'd thought Webb might pull something like he did, I'd never have suggested what I did. It just seemed like such a wild idea! And I did so want to get even with him. But not at your expense—you do believe me, don't you? You see, Anne . . ." Carol wore a frown now; she bit her lip as if she was trying to choose just the right words. "I don't know if you really *do* see, because you really haven't had too much experience with the bastards of this world, have you? Or of sex as a game or a weapon. I guess when I was being selfish as usual this afternoon, I wasn't really thinking that you

49

hadn't been around enough to find your own weapons or learn how to use them. I think I was born street wise, and so was Webb. We recognized that quality in each other from the first. Oh damn, how am I going to put this so you'll realize I'm not just playing big sister?"

"If you're trying to say that you and Webb are . . ." Anne began stiffly. She wanted to say the word "lovers," but it was too bitter to pronounce. She should have known, or guessed, shouldn't she?

But Carol caught her up swiftly, so that she didn't have to continue. "That's just it, sweetie! Webb and I are almost too much alike, I guess. We both know the score. We started way back—God, further back than I care to remember! And since then, between his women and my guys, we've been an on-and-off thing—although for my part I'd like it to be over permanently!" Carol sounded vindictive; her emerald-green eyes narrowed as she almost spat out the words.

"I don't expect you to understand, Anne, but sometimes, sometimes a man and a woman can really have a sexual thing going. In the sack they can really groove, and it's the greatest fuck ever, but out of it, apart from those moments of hunger, they could hate and despise each other." Carol's voice took on a slightly exasperated note as she leaned forward urgently. "Listen, I can almost hear the wheels go round in your head. You're wondering if I'm saying all this because I'm jealous, and I'm not! I got over being jealous of Webb a long time ago—I had to, in order to make it. But I don't want to see you all torn up like so many others I've seen it happen to. Like Tanya, for instance. Christ, I lost count of the rest a long time ago! And didn't give a shit, either. But I feel responsible for you, sweets. That's the reason for all this"—Carol gave an expansive gesture—"which isn't really my style at all! I mean, I can remember that stubborn, stony-faced look of yours from the old days, and I'm not going to ask you any more questions or give you any more warnings. Little Carol has done her girl-scout bit for the evening and that's it!"

"Thanks," Anne murmured, not knowing what else to say. She knew what she wanted—another martini, to take away the sick, self-hating feeling inside of her, and the voice that cried "Fool! You thought you were being adventurous, and you let yourself be used as a weapon in someone else's game that everyone but you knows about, didn't you?"

She forced herself to shrug lightly. "You and Harris! All the warnings weren't really necessary, you know, but thanks anyway!" She pushed herself away from the dresser, glad to be standing on her own feet again.

Carol stood up too, stretching lazily, then turned towards the mirror to run a small brush through her hair. "Oh well. As much as I hate the thought, I guess we'd better go back out there and face the crowds again." Carol frowned as she fought her curls into perfect disarray. "You'll stay for a while, won't you? There are some really nice people I want you to meet."

Chapter Six

THREE MARTINIS LATER, Anne was wondering when she could decently make her excuses and leave. She should have forced herself to eat when she had the chance—now there were only nuts and olives to nibble on.

Harris had found her another chair to sit on—really a bar stool with arms. He had his hand on her knee, while she explained to him seriously, hoping she didn't sound tipsy, that she had always wanted to be able to go to college here in the States.

"Finishing school! My father is very old-fashioned, don't you think? What good was that? All I really learned was foreign languages, and things like manners and deportment. I told him I wanted to go to college, to be an anonymous face among other anonymous faces. I wanted to major in psychology. I had to write to him to tell him that—and you know what he said? He said, 'When you come back home, we'll see.' And then he sent Mr. and Mrs. Hyatt to take me out of school in Switzerland and take me on that world cruise I really dreaded. I don't get seasick, but I'm afraid of the ocean. And Craig was with them. He made me feel safe, and flattered of course. I kept wondering what he could see in me, what was interesting about me."

"But you are interesting, Anne. And you have a classically lovely face. I think any man would find you fascinating." Harris

Phelps's voice was soft and soothing, and Anne thought that after all, she did like him. He was understanding and seemed to enjoy her company. And she could be confident that he wasn't out to use her or exploit her. He was so rich that he could have his choice of women—any woman in this room, for that matter. And yet he chose her to sit by and talk to, neglecting even Carol. She didn't mind the slight pressure of his hand on her knee—Harris was a toucher, that was all. And his touch was safer than Webb's.

Webb Carnahan—actor. She would like to blot out every memory of him if she could. Forget. Never think his name again.

Recklessly, Anne began to sip at another martini, ignoring Harris's disapproving, questioning look and his hand, which moved almost imperceptibly upward from her knee to her thigh, massaging gently while he continued to talk to her.

"Are you really going to go through with a divorce, Anne? What are you going to do with yourself?"

"I'm going back to Europe, Harris. On my own, this time. I think I need to travel, and find out things. Travel is supposed to be broadening, isn't it?"

"You could stay here and go to college."

"Yes, but it's a little late for that now, isn't it? Anyway, if I stayed here, I'd always feel—watched. And there'd be too much pressure. I think I'll feel more free in Europe. This time I'll travel where I want to go, not where somebody thinks I should go."

"Where's that, Anne? I wish I could show you my Europe . . ." Harris broke off with a sigh of annoyance. "Damn! I think Grady is drunk enough to start becoming obnoxious. Wait for me, will you, love? I'm going to have to rescue Carol."

It must be getting very late. She ought to go back home and get some sleep—or at least call and leave a message with the electronic voice . . . Anne didn't know whether she felt sick or wanted to giggle. Imagine Mrs. Preakness's cold-sober New

England face if she came back like this! *Oh dear—I think I'm getting quite drunk. Maybe Harris will have to rescue me next. Or will he take advantage of me instead?*

Thank God Craig wasn't here to look disapproving and disgusted. Why was it that whenever she had too much to drink she always felt sick instead of happy or sexy like everyone else? Defiantly, Anne finished her latest martini, frowning down into the empty glass while she wondered if she should ask for another.

The glass was taken away from her. She looked up to protest, her head moving in slow motion, and was almost sober again with the shock of meeting Webb's eyes. When had he come up behind her? Why couldn't she react normally and tell him to go to hell, that she was only waiting here for Harris to finish rescuing Carol . . . ?

"You look like you've had enough, Annie. Why didn't you stick to something safe like ginger ale?"

He had no right to sound so sarcastic. Nor to pull her off her safe perch on the bar stool as if he owned her, so that she fell against him. He shouldn't be here at all—she had just blotted him out of her mind. Angrily, she struggled against the pressure of his arm, thwarted by her own treacherous senses as much as by his strength. "What do you think you're doing, anyhow? You can't just . . ." She finished on a note of desperation: "You haven't even asked me if I want to go with you, damn you!"

Abruptly, he swung her around so she was facing him, his hands rough on her arms, his voice hard and full of tamped-down fury that she didn't understand. There was a long scratch down the side of his face that she didn't remember. How—

"All right, damn you, Annie! Why do you think I'm here? I'm not used to asking, but I will, if that's what you must have. Come back with me to my room. I want to make love to you again. I want more time with you, Annie, so I can try to figure you out, and maybe try to understand at the same time what the hell kind of hex you've put on me . . ."

His voice, softening, roughening, made Anne suddenly oblivious of who might be watching them. Her whole body started to shake when he held her against him and kissed her.

"You can't pretend it isn't there for you too, Annie-love . . ."

She made one last-ditch attempt to save herself from complete capitulation. "Why me? There's Carol—and Tanya . . ."

"Shut up, Annie. There's you. And are you coming with me or not?"

He wouldn't ask her again. She knew that, and she went with him, her fingers laced with his; feeling herself taken over and not even caring any longer. The half-hearted protests she continued to make were the merest token, a salve for her pride.

"Harris—I promised him I'd wait . . ."

She caught a glimpse of sheened gold as Webb slanted dangerously lazy eyes at her. "You supposed to be Harris Phelps's date tonight?"

"No—but I—I really should thank Carol, too, I can't just walk off without . . ." Why couldn't she finish her sentences? She stammered like an awkward teen-ager and hated herself for showing her weakness so obviously.

She felt Webb's fingers tighten over hers for an instant and wondered wildly whether he would leave her now—standing there in the middle of the still-crowded room. But instead, surprising her, he gave a short laugh. "You're a well-brought-up kid, aren't you, Annie? So okay—let's go say good-night to Caro and good old Harris."

Lengthening his stride, he pulled her through the room of staring faces, and Anne became miserably aware of half-finished conversations and speculative whispers that followed them.

At the far end of the room, the three of them stood together —Carol, all spitting fury; the sandy-haired Ted Grady looking sullen as he rubbed nervously at the side of his unshaven jaw; and Harris, the calmest one, talking urgently in a low voice to them both.

Carol looked up first, those slanted emerald eyes widening

and then growing narrow. "Webb Carnahan, you—you—what in hell are you doing here?"

"Better watch your language, Caro-baby. You don't want to give your old man the wrong impression, do you? And you invited me, love—don't you remember?"

Suddenly, Anne felt caught again in an unpleasant game these two were playing with each other, and she didn't want to be here. Only Webb wouldn't release her fingers.

Ted Grady had given up rubbing at his jaw and was staring nastily at Webb, his pale blue eyes swiveling from him to Carol and back again.

"Damn it, Webb!" Harris said petulantly. "It's a damned late hour to make an appearance at a party, isn't it? You might have—"

But Carol didn't give him a chance to finish. "What are you doing here with Anne? Where's that Tanya creature?"

Webb grinned, but the smile didn't reach his eyes. He said softly, "I was wondering why she turned up in my room, Caro, but now I know. It was thoughtful of you to send her along to look for me, but after a few words she trotted off to bed like a good girl. Disappointed?"

He was deliberately baiting Carol, who seemed to realize it belatedly.

She sucked in a long, vindictive breath that sounded more like a hiss. "Why should I be disappointed? Tanya's always been able to take care of herself—and she does have long nails, doesn't she? You'll have to cover up that scratch for the performance tomorrow, won't you, Webb darling?"

"Hey, what the hell is this? What're you two talking about? And, mister, I'd like to know just how well you know my wife!"

"Mister—you'd better stay out of matters that don't concern you. Why don't you tell him that, Caro? Unless you're planning on a big reconciliation, that is."

"Ted—you keep out of this!"

Harris Phelps sighed. Webb was spoiling for a fight, and so

was Grady. And Anne looked white and scared and helpless. He felt sorry for her and coldly furious at Webb. Damn him—why Anne?

"You the guy all the gossip columns keep linking with my wife?" Grady said aggressively, thrusting his jaw out. "What the hell is going on between you two, huh? That's what I came here to find out. And let me tell you, you damn Yankee, back in Texas we've got ways of dealing with bastards who mess around with other guy's wives!"

"Stop it!" Carol gritted, stamping her foot with rage and exasperation. She glared at Webb. "I might have known you'd do something like this! Deliberately come here to create a scene . . ."

"But he came here to find me, and we only meant to tell you thank you for a—a really nice evening." Anne heard her own voice, sounding amazingly calm and clear. Now they were all looking at her, even Webb, with varying degrees of astonishment. She gave his hand a tug. "Webb, darling, hadn't we better be going? And Mr. Grady, I'm really surprised at your language, considering that you call yourself a Southern gentleman."

She stared unflinchingly at Grady until his eyes dropped and he mumbled some kind of reluctant, shamefaced apology under his breath. She was able, more boldly now, to smile at both Carol and Harris, who was watching her through worried gray eyes. "Thanks, Carol. I'll talk to you tomorrow, shall I? And Harris, thank you, for being so kind. Webb will take me home, now that he's here at last."

Anne didn't remember what Webb said to them after that, if he said anything. She was so angry that it was all she could do to stop her whole body from shaking. This was one time when all the years of practicing rigid self-control really paid off. She would wait until they were outside the door of Carol's suite, and then she would—she would—she'd let him see very quickly that he couldn't use her again. That she was wise to him and all his tricks. Actor!

There were spots of color in her cheeks that even the dim lighting in the hotel hallway couldn't hide, and her dark blue eyes looked almost black with rage as she snatched her hand away from his. Watching her, Webb Carnahan had to admit that he had given her more than enough reason for her anger. Little Annie had surprising depths to her character, and she had done a magnificent job of handling that scene back there when he and Caro had gone at each other's throats. It wasn't often that he found himself at a loss in dealing with a woman, and not for a damned long time had one so intrigued him. She was a quicksilver contradiction, not falling into any pattern he could recognize, and he felt a quick sense of regret that he would lose her before he had really found her.

They were standing out there in the hallway looking at each other warily, almost like strangers. Webb found himself wanting to touch her, to pull her closely against him, but his reason told him not to try. So he regarded her somberly, hands thrust into the pockets of his faded denim jacket, waiting for her to make the first move this time.

She made a short, angry motion of her head that tossed the shining silver silk of her hair back over her shoulders, one hand going up to smooth it. So she was nervous too. He noted it with a kind of pleasure, wondering why he continued to hold back.

"Would you mind calling me a taxi, please?" Her voice sounded distant and almost disembodied. "I think I would like to go back home now."

He made an angry, shrugging motion of his shoulders. "Sure. But they don't have phones in the hallways up here, so I'll have to make the call from my room."

"I think I'd rather go downstairs, thank you. You don't have to come with me—I can find my way perfectly well."

She started to walk past him, and he let his self-control drop, grabbing her by the arms.

The door behind them opened just then, freezing them both,

and letting out light and noise and the smell of cigarette smoke. Two people, a man and a woman, came out, letting the door close behind them. Tactfully, they kept walking past Anne and Webb, the man clearing his throat before he said, "Good-night, Mrs. Hyatt."

"Good-night." Anne felt her voice clog in a throat tight with unshed tears of rage and humiliation. And a sense of loss. Why did she have to feel *that*? Why didn't she pull away from Webb and ask Mr. and Mrs. Nordstrom if they'd mind giving her a ride back home?

"*Mrs.* Hyatt?" Now his voice was ugly with sarcasm. "Where are your rings, Mrs. Hyatt, ma'am? Or did you get bored and come looking for some fun and games?"

His grip hurt her, and she started to struggle against it. "You haven't any right to presume to judge me! And anyway I'm— I'm separated from my husband. We're getting a divorce."

"Yeah? And who's the lucky guy? The lucky *other* guy, I guess I should say." He laughed, a short, unpleasant sound. "You know, for a while you really had me fooled, Mrs. Hyatt. Little innocent Annie. But I should have guessed from the fact that you and Caro are such friends, shouldn't I?"

"I don't have to answer that! It's nothing to do with you. Will you let go of me?" She struggled impotently against him while his hands slid down to her wrists, imprisoning them painfully behind her back. They were playing a scene of their own now, both of them lost to control.

"The hell I will! And I don't think you want me to, do you, baby? You didn't try too hard to fight me off before, did you? And I never did care for spending a night alone."

"Don't, Webb—don't!" But it was no use. Anne felt her own weakness as his mouth came down to capture hers—hard, punishing, hurting. She felt her teeth cut her lip and tasted the bitter-salty taste of blood before her mouth opened blindly under his.

Like a spark igniting a forest fire, the flame burst out of bounds and took hold of them both.

"Damn you for a witch, Anne—damn you!" She thought she heard him whisper that against her bruised mouth before he lifted her in his arms to carry her off like some ravishing pirate. She was dizzy and dazed, hearing only vaguely the bang of the door as he kicked it shut behind them, locking her in with him.

The bed was a shambles, covers rumpled and trailing on the floor. Tanya? But she mustn't think that—didn't want to think about it as he dropped her down on it. Just like a ship, it seemed to rock under her.

"No—please, not yet, not like this . . ." Anne didn't know if she said the words aloud or only thought them. Had he made love to Tanya before they had their fight? She didn't really care—and that was the most shocking thing of all. The lights in the room went off, and the blackness pressed like stifling black velvet against her eyes.

The feel of his hands came out of the darkness before her eyes grew used to it, and she felt the length of his body as he lowered it beside hers on the bed.

He was tender with her now, as he hadn't been earlier, and strangely, Anne thought she could understand why. Here, together in the dark, they could begin as if they were strangers again—not having to watch and gauge expressions, merely feeling, touching, tracing, with fingers at first, and then with lips.

She didn't know and didn't care what happened to her clothes as he took off each garment one by one. She undressed him, fingers fumbling until he became impatient and helped her. And then he held back—teasing her, tormenting her until she cried out to him, torn between anger and frustration—hardly understanding her own needs until he made her aware of them. And even more aware of the feel and the different textures of his body—roughness and smoothness, hardness pulsing in her hand, and finally motion inside her.

Just long enough to make her experience the familiar-unfamiliar eruption that came from inside again; then, while she was still gasping with reaction, he set his mouth against her like a seal, a brand of white-hot fire that took her beyond anything she had ever experienced before—his hard hands holding her thighs apart while she went from one peak to another, losing all capability of thinking, knowing only feeling, wanting, until he filled her again and she tasted herself against his roughly demanding mouth.

When the world stopped spinning she fell asleep, like dropping off from a precipice into an endless dark canyon.

Chapter Seven

THIS MORNING WAS DIFFERENT from any other morning she had ever known. Was it only yesterday that she had awakened feeling all cramped from sitting curled up in a chair all night?

Watery sunlight insinuated itself into the room through drawn curtains, falling across the bed; and the room was filled with the hunger-provoking odors of coffee and freshly fried bacon.

Anne's eyelids felt heavy—she had a sense of disorientation at first, as she opened her eyes, and then wrinkled them shut against the light.

"It's morning, love. Close to afternoon. Here—swallow these."

Memory rushed back when she saw Webb's yellow-gold eyes watching her.

Obediently, Anne swallowed the pills he handed her, washing them down with a drink he handed her.

"Only B-12 and E, Annie-love. No need to look so apprehensive." His voice sounded noncommittal and detached, like the look he bent on her. Trying, belatedly, not to think, the champagne-and-orange-juice drink tasted good. A mimosa— wasn't that what the combination was called? Anything to take her mind off the present. But he wasn't about to let her off easily.

"You'd better eat some breakfast too. Since you were so sound asleep I went ahead and ordered what suits me."

There were eggs under a silver cover, and fresh-baked buttered muffins. The eggs were soft-scrambled and faintly flavored with dill. Sitting up in the bed as she took the plate Webb thrust at her, Anne realized suddenly that she was ravenously hungry. And if she could concentrate on eating, that would serve to postpone thinking and remembering how she had got here, and what had taken place before she'd fallen asleep—or passed out. There would be a time for regrets and for self-searching—God, what would Mrs. Preakness be thinking? Would she have sent a search-party out, or would they know already?—not now. Not yet. It was much better not to think. Take another mouthful of these really delicious eggs—bite into a crusty, buttered muffin that Webb handed to her without a word. Don't wonder what he was thinking!

He had pulled on a pair of faded, pale-blue levis, and he ate much faster than she did, pouring coffee for her after he had finished. And still she couldn't read any expression at all on his face—not even in his eyes when they rested almost impersonally on her naked breasts. How could you know someone so closely in a physical sense, Anne wondered, and yet not know them at all? Last night he had been half-satyr, half-man, and today he seemed nothing more than an indifferent, polite stranger, urging more food on her when her appetite suddenly waned.

"Have some more, Annie. You look like you could use feeding up."

She flushed, pushing the plate back as she shook her head, suddenly miserably aware that she wasn't nearly as well endowed as Carol, or even Tanya. Was that what he meant?

Webb wished she didn't look so vulnerable and so young, with the color coming up to stain her cheekbones—pale-red wine in a goblet of translucent alabaster. She made him feel like an executioner, and he wasn't used to the feeling. And yet, damn her innocent blue eyes, she'd been playing games all along. A better actress than anyone would have thought, to look at her. And she could even blush . . . His eyes narrowed at her, and he didn't know why he felt angry. What the hell, she was fantastic in bed; there were no inhibitions under that little-girl exterior. But she was Richard Reardon's daughter. He mustn't forget that. Suddenly, angrily, he found himself wanting to strip away all the pretenses she'd surrounded herself with from the first, just as his senses urged him to strip away the sheets that were modestly draped across her slim thighs.

Reardon's daughter. Kept under wraps by her father's choice of a husband. So far as he knew, no one had ever realized that Reardon had a daughter, a vulnerable spot in his armor. Reardon the King-Maker, as one daring Washington columnist had dubbed him. But then, very few people dared mention Reardon, who was strictly a behind-the-scenes figure, head of a shadowy organization so secret that it didn't even have initials. The only reason Webb knew was because he had once been a part of it, one of "Reardon's boys," until he'd grown wise and much more cynical. One of the few to get out from under and survive, and that only because of Ria, who hadn't survived. Ria, who shouldn't have been involved at all.

Why now, of all times, did he have to remember Ria, after all the years he'd spent carefully trying to forget her, wiping her memory from his mind by using every other woman he met as just another cardboard image to hold up between himself and the clean, innocent reality that had been Ria before he'd screwed everything up and Ria had died to prove it? Even now, his mind slewed away from that thought. Reardon had been responsible. Cold-blooded, computer-minded bastard, living in a rarified atmosphere where people became pins on a map, to be moved around or discarded at will.

He hadn't let himself remember for a long time. But Anne had brought back the memories and the hatred. The time when all he'd thought about or planned was killing Reardon. And here he was with Reardon's hidden-away daughter.

What in hell was he doing, anyhow—making excuses? For Anne, or for his own mixed-up feelings for her? Anger, mostly at himself, made Webb's voice harsher than he intended it to be; almost jeering.

"What's the matter, Annie? Not hungry anymore? Or are you starting to worry about what your husband might do if he knew where you were right now?"

Her shoulders grew rigid under his sudden attack. But the color that now flamed in her face was from anger this time. "That's really none of your business. In any case, just to set the record straight, he's my soon-to-be ex-husband. Why do you keep bringing that up? I'm sure you've had more than your share of experience in playing around with other men's wives."

"Not when the particular wife also happens to be Dick Reardon's only daughter. Christ, Annie!" Temper flaring, he stood there frowning at her, one hand running through his dark hair. "You crazy or something? I can't figure you out. What are you out to prove? Thumbing your nose at daddy in his own home town or trying to make your soon-to-be ex-husband jealous? Just another bored Washington wife looking for kicks?"

"What are you getting at? What were you looking for, Webb? Amusement to pass the time in another boring small town? An easy, uncomplicated lay? Maybe we were both looking for the same thing—and found it!" Anne stood up, not caring that she was completely naked under his suddenly intent gaze. She could feel her body shake uncontrollably with a mixture of rage and humiliation. And all she wanted was to escape from him—from his sarcastic, accusing voice and his searing amber-gold eyes.

It was hard to be distant and dignified and look for her scattered clothes at the same time. He lifted one eyebrow as she said coldly, "Thank you for breakfast. And for letting me sleep in. But I think I've outstayed my time, and I really must be getting back now. Don't you have rehearsals or something?"

"Or something . . ." he said dryly. Maddeningly, he just stood there looking at her while her eyes hunted the room for any trace of the garments he'd all but ripped off her body last night.

She began to wish she'd wrapped the sheet around herself. Damn him, why did he just stand there looking at her, making her feel ridiculous? Finally, she was forced to look back at him, and found him grinning mockingly at her.

"I'm just a tidy kind of guy, Annie-love. And I didn't want the room-service waiter to have reason to gossip. Didn't think your daddy would like that. So while you were sleeping I hung your clothes up. Lots of closet space here."

So he was determined not to help her. She didn't care! "Thank you. That was considerate of you. If you'll tell me where . . ."

"Annie, I wasn't being considerate. Just careful. Just making sure you couldn't escape too easily."

"You . . ." She felt as frozen as her voice sounded, standing there petrified while Webb began to strip off his levis unconcernedly, making her, here in the sunlit daytime, even more aware of his body. The lean, compact strength of him, with the muscles moving smoothly under his California-tanned skin—tanned all over; no white patches to show he'd ever worn bathing trunks. The tight curl of hair on his chest and at his groin. And—she could not help noticing too, however unwillingly, that he wanted her. Nor deny to herself that just the sight of his naked body with its beautiful symmetry could make her catch her breath with a strange sense of excitement that started in her belly and spread, liquid mercury that made her loins ache.

"Hey, shampoo girl—want to take a nice hot shower before you get dressed?" His voice was suddenly husky, almost cajoling. "And look—I'm sorry, and you're right. It's none of my goddamned business who you are or what you are."

Before she realized what was happening, he had seized her hand, and once more she was lost to reason. And now he was concentrating on her and not who she was or what she was. Her hair streamed wetly down her back, strands clinging to her shoulders and breasts, and he pushed them aside as he soaped her all over, lingering between her thighs.

"Is this what you look like when you're caught in the rain? My God, Annie, you're beautiful!"

The small bathroom turned steamy, and the soap dropped and was forgotten as they touched each other, exploratively at first and then more boldly. Easier to forget all the things that stood between them outside of this time, this moment.

Like Richard Reardon, shadow-father. A private, almost legendary figure who had already outlasted several presidents and was likely to outlast more. But he'd always stayed out of the limelight. The Watergate affair and all its nasty aftermath hadn't touched him; maybe it was true that was because he had too much on every leading politician for anyone to dare try to involve him. Reardon was a whispered rumor, a name hardly anyone had ever heard of outside a very few closed circles.

And yet, Webb, who moved in a very different world, seemed to have known. How? Being her father's daughter, in spite of the lack of communication that had always existed between them, made her very vulnerable. It was an unspoken knowledge she had grown up with, and Craig had voiced it soon after they married and moved to Washington, where he had his law practice.

"You have to be very careful, Anne. I promised your father I'd look after you. There mustn't be any breath of scandal—not that I think you'd be that sort, darling. But I hope you'll be guided by me in your choice of friends."

God—he'd sounded like a Victorian husband! But it had been some time before she'd realized that, or even dared think it.

Anne felt as if her sanity had been returned to her too late. And she was able to begin to think rationally only because Webb, tossing his wet towel carelessly onto the floor, had gone into the other room to look for some clothes to wear. She was still trying to dry her hair, almost relishing the pull on her scalp as she rubbed long, wet strands between the folds of the towel.

"Wet silk . . ." he had said, the touch of his fingers a caress. But how much of what Webb said was acting and how much was real? She didn't know why he had come looking for her, to bring her here, any more than she understood why she had come—and stayed.

Be careful—be careful! her mind warned her, but wasn't it almost too late for that? What had happened to the carefully closed-in, inviolate part of herself that not even Craig had been able to reach? Anne felt curiously lost—and afraid. All the more stubborn because of it. *Play it light, stay cool.*

With a gesture of conscious defiance she tossed her towel aside on top of his, then walked back into the bedroom with what she hoped was careless insouciance.

Webb was already dressed, and her clothes were in a neat pile on the bed. She didn't want to look at him and see the way he watched her as each garment she pulled on became another layer of her defenses against him—and against her own weakness.

There didn't seem to be anyone in the hotel besides the desk clerk, who barely looked up as they came downstairs.

Outdoors the icy wind whipped color into Anne's pale face. Apart from the wind, the other moving thing on the street was a snowplow. The muffled-up man driving it waved to Anne and she waved back. She thought he turned his head to watch as Webb, suddenly impatient, dragged her along uphill with him.

They stopped at the electric gates in the high stone walls covered with skeletons of ivy; beyond the gates, a tree-lined avenue led to the house. Anne was out of breath, leaning against the warmth of his body, held in the curve of his arm.

"So this is the castle of the king where the orphan princess with silver-silk hair hides out . . . Do you always hide behind high walls, Annie? Where's your No Trespassing sign?"

"Well, where's your Danger, Sex Maniac at Large sign, then?" she retorted.

He threw back his head and laughed, and when he looked back down at her, his eyes were teasing instead of mocking.

"Poor baby. Is that what it seemed to you? Let's see—we've done it in the theater and the hotel—how about right here against the wall? Think the electric eye will be watching us?"

She laughed when he backed her up against the wall, but then she felt the hard urgency of his body against hers. "Webb!" She wished he wouldn't hold his mouth inches away from hers, tantalizing her, while he held her face immobile between his gloved hands.

"It's your fault, Annie-love. You're a New England witch, and you've put a hex on me. You make me want to rape you, to find out if you'd fight or not . . . and then again . . . when you close your eyes that way, I think I'd rather make love to you. Over and over and over . . ."

Was it Carol or Harris who had warned her? "When Webb chooses to exert his charm, few women can resist him. He knows that—and he's had lots of practice . . ."

But his lips were brushing hers between his murmured words, and when his mouth closed over hers at last she clung to it greedily, responding fiercely to his kiss while her body tingled with sudden warmth. Who cared for warnings? Her eyes were open, she wanted nothing but this—an affair of the senses, a lover who made her feel like a whole woman, able to respond like a woman.

Confused thoughts spiraled close to the surface of her mind but never quite got there while she gave herself up only to feeling. The texture of his hair under her fingers, cold air against her face, and heat everywhere their bodies touched as she pressed more closely against him.

"Christ, Annie!" he whispered at last. "Whose dumb idea was this? I should have kept you in my room and thrown your clothes out the window so you couldn't escape . . ."

He had a feeling that he didn't like—that she was escaping, and using him. From her husband? Reardon? He couldn't imagine Reardon emerging from his nerveless, coldly calculating citadel long enough to fuck a woman and make a daughter. It had probably been for the sake of the "ordinary man" image he wanted to project to the world.

But the hell with Reardon. This was Anne, Reardon's daughter, he was holding in his arms, feeling her trembling, wanting her again in spite of himself. And it had been his idea to bring her back home—to see her politely out of his life.

He'd made up his mind to that last night, after she'd fallen so deeply asleep it was almost as if she'd passed out. She obviously wasn't used to drinking too much. She hadn't heard the shrilling telephone that had awakened him from the beginnings of sleep.

Harris—checking up on Anne, his voice solicitous. And then Carol, her voice no longer furious as it had been earlier, but dripping sweet sarcasm. "Darling Webb—I know we've had our differences and always will have, but I really wouldn't want to see you tarred and feathered and ridden out of town, or whatever the modern equivalent is! But Anne is Richard Reardon's daughter. And she's married to Craig Hyatt. *Time* magazine had a piece on him not too long ago—lawyer grooming for politician, you know the story. I know they're separated or something right now, but you know how that goes, don't you?" Carol had given a malicious chuckle that made him want to strangle her. "Washington gossip says she's a nympho—that's why Reardon kept her under wraps . . ."

"So you talked her into doing your scene, Caro?"

"Therapy, darling, therapy! She's been seeing a psychiatrist for years, to cure her of her little problem. And I must admit I thought it might be fun to throw you two together, especially since we'd made that bet! I didn't think you'd . . ."

"I know just how you think, Caro." His voice, dangerously soft, caused a silence at the other end. He could almost imagine Caro sucking in a breath, green eyes narrowing as she prepared for her next barbed retort. And he hadn't wanted to hear it. Anne stirred in her sleep just then and he felt the silkiness of her hair against his thigh. Damn her! He didn't know how to deal with her, but he knew Caro too well. Two of a kind—they used to laugh about that in the early days, when their affair was still white-hot.

"Look Caro, I'll talk to you tomorrow. And I'm touched by your concern, but right now all I can think about is getting some sleep."

He could hear her voice, rising, sputter, "Webb, you bastard . . . let me warn you . . ." as he hung up on her. He unplugged the phone as a precaution before he settled back on the bed, lying there for a long time, frowning angrily into the darkness before he could finally get to sleep.

So much for Carol. All he'd meant to do was feed Anne breakfast, make love to her again if he had a mind to, and send her home to daddy with a pat on the bottom for good measure. Reardon would know he'd screwed his little girl and kept her out all night. If small-town people gossiped as they were supposed to, the whole damn town would know; and that would be the tiniest part of the payoff of his debt of hatred and revenge.

For Ria. He hadn't wanted to think about Ria for years. He didn't want to remember the clean, sweet reality that had been Ria before Reardon had stepped in and Ria had died trying to prove she was a patriot, prove that she could share in the part of his life he'd always kept separate from the life they'd shared. Life and loving—Ria had been both. And after there was no more Ria, every other woman he'd met and used was a cardboard cut-out to hold between himself and her memory.

Why remember that now? Ria, and the less cynical part of himself, had been lost a long time ago. Reality today, right now, was Anne, who reminded him in some crazy, indefinable way of Ria. But Ria had been transparently innocent—Anne was not. Damnit! He had to shake himself free. Kiss her again, making his kiss light and meaningless this time, and walk back down that hill to town without turning back.

He'd forgotten what he had said to her, but just as if she'd sensed the dark turn of his thoughts Anne put her lips against his throat. He wanted to keep on kissing her, postponing the inevitable, and he didn't trust his own reactions.

Webb put his hands in her hair, pulling her head back.

"Damn you, Annie! What are you trying to do, incite me to rape? You'd find the snow makes a cold bed; and your daddy might not approve, besides."

Why hadn't she learned to keep the hurt from showing in her eyes? Wide, dark blue eyes like an ocean to drown in. "Why do you keep throwing my father in my face? Why can't anyone see me as myself? Are you afraid of him, Webb?"

He had his excuse now, if he'd needed one. He moved away from her with an only half-smothered curse. "Shit yes, I'm afraid of him! Who isn't? I'm just an average, ordinary guy, princess, and he's spit up bigger and stronger men like so many orange pips. I shouldn't be playing around with you and you shouldn't be playing around with me." He made his voice deliberately cruel, trying to blank his mind to the suddenly frozen look on her face. "Not that it wasn't fun, baby, but as much as I'd like to keep you around for a while, my survival instinct is stronger than all the other instincts you bring out in me. I was a ghetto kid, baby. Chicago. My father was a crooked Irish cop and my mother was Italian—Sicilian. I grew up with the streets for my playground, and that's where I learned about survival. That, and a lot of other things you wouldn't like to hear about. A whole different world from the one you've been used to. Didn't Harris and Caro tell you what a bastard I am? I'm not your kind, and you're not mine. So"—this time his voice took on a kind of controlled fury that made her wince—"what in hell are we doing here together?"

He suddenly brought his hand up to her face, letting his fingers slip down its contours as if he was trying to memorize her by touch, not really knowing why he had to, for one last time.

Anne jerked her head away, thrusting her cold hands into the pockets of her jacket as she forced herself to stare back at him defiantly. "Why do you ask me that? I haven't demanded ex-

planations from you, Webb—or anything else! You don't have
to—oh, damn! Good-bye and thanks for the experience. It
doesn't really have to be put into words, does it? Not that you
needed to . . ." Now she only wished he would leave her
quickly, severing her free with one swift knife cut.

It was almost ironic that the gates should soundlessly slide
open just then. A long black car was driven out, to come to a
skidding halt and back up.

"Anne! I was on my way to look for you. We've all been
worried since you didn't call last night. Where . . ."

Oh God, why Craig of all people? She could have faced her
father more easily at this moment. When had he arrived? Why?
And why now? Not that she should worry about what Webb
might think, but . . .

Anne heard Craig's voice change, sounding colorless. "Oh hi!
Sorry I didn't see you at first, but I've been concerned . . ."

Classic confrontation, almost like one of the old movies.
Husband and lover—*ex*-lover, hadn't Webb just made that
clear?

Damn, damn! Shreds of stilted dialogue passed over her head
while her face burned and she hated them both for different
reasons. They made her feel like a puppet pulled in two different directions.

"Can't say that I blame you . . . I thought for sure Annie
had called home . . ."

Annie! How dare he? She had the feeling he was spoiling for
a fight again, as he had been last night, only Craig was far too
civilized to rise to the bait, of course. But Craig had no right to
be here either, or to be concerned about her.

Anne heard her own stiff voice performing pointless introductions, then Webb was refusing Craig's offer to give him a ride
back to the hotel. He was acting, a deliberate Western drawl in
his voice.

"Shoot, no, thanks all the same. I enjoy walking. Just wanted
to be sure I got Annie here back home safe. Promised Carol."

She wanted to scream at them both, *Stop it, stop it! Stop*

playing your goddamned male roles over my head as if I didn't exist! But in the end she decided it was Webb who needed putting down most, and she'd show him that she could act too.

Ignoring Craig, she put her arms about Webb's neck, kissing him lightly. "Mmm! Thanks again, darling, for being sweet enough to walk me all the way here! And be sure to give my love to Carol, won't you? Tell her I loved the party . . ."

His yellow-gold eyes looked like mirrors with sunshine reflecting off them.

"It was a real pleasure, sweetheart. And I'll be sure to tell Caro." He disengaged her arms with more controlled force than was really necessary. "Hyatt? Nice meeting you. See you around, Annie."

Webb had already started walking downhill when she realized that Craig was holding open the door of the black Mercedes for her.

Unshed tears that she could never let escape made her throat and her eyes ache.

"Anne—get in, will you! Damn, do you have to make a public spectacle of yourself? And a fool of me? I don't know what's been going on, but you'd better have a bloody good explanation. Your father and I have been waiting for you since last night."

She slammed the car door behind her, watching, without wanting to, Webb walking away from her, wondering, without wanting to, what might have happened between them if Craig hadn't chosen the wrong moment to appear.

His fury fed hers. Hypocrite!

"I don't know what in hell you've been trying to prove, Anne! But I tell you . . ."

She had some satisfactions at least, in turning to look at him; blanking out his angry face with the newly learned hardness of her eyes as she said, coldly and distinctly, "Don't, Craig! I don't want to hear, and I don't owe you or my father any explanations. Anything."

Chapter Eight

WEBB PASSED THE MAN in the snowplow again on his way downhill; but this time there was no friendly wave, just a glance
from under the visor of the cap that shadowed most of the
man's face. Well, that made sense. He was an outsider, an in-
truder. This was Anne Reardon Hyatt's hometown, and she
was back where she belonged, behind those electronically operated gates and the high walls. A good place for her. It was surprising that Reardon and her straitlaced husband let her run
loose at all.

Well, she was Hyatt's problem, and her father's—not his,
thank God! Not likely that they'd run into each other again,
ever; and it was just as well. Because if he'd known from the beginning who she was he might have been tempted . . . *forget
it! Forget Anne, forget Reardon—forget even the bittersweet
memory of Ria.* He had things to do and places to go, and he
didn't need anything or anybody to hold him back.

Long, angry strides took him to the bottom of the hill and
the hotel loomed up in front of him; and there, surprisingly,
Harris waited—all muffled up in his expensive ski clothes. Harris
was with Mike and a couple of the other guys in the company,
and they were all watching him. Talk stopped, a certain stiffness
grew in all of them as they waited for him.

A sense of premonition plucked at the suddenly tautened
strings of his nerves. What the hell was going on?

Harris spoke first, his voice unusually tense.

"Webb—for Christ's sake! We were almost ready to send out a search party! I tried your room, and when you weren't there I began to wonder if . . ." Voice dropping, but with a certain urgency underlying it, Harris demanded, "Where's Anne?"

"I saw her safely to her door. What the hell's going on?"

None of the others answered. They continued to look at him woodenly. Harris Phelps sighed impatiently, his pale-gray eyes swiveling from face to face as if in warning before they rested on Webb.

"There's been trouble. That damn fool Grady tried to kill Carol; thank God she had the wits and the strength to fight him off! And then we found Tanya . . ."

Shit! Why in hell didn't Harris come to the point, instead of standing there staring at him accusingly? Accusing him of what, for Christ's sake? All of his barely tamped-down anger and frustration looked for a focal point, and Webb's voice showed it, as he said with dangerous, deceptive softness, "Suppose you get to the point, Phelps?"

"For God's sake—let's go inside!" Harris Phelps said abruptly. "This is no place for explanations. Carol's been in hysterics, she's been asking for you. I think I've got Tanya under control—the girl's got a practical streak, for all her belligerence, and she's been remarkably silent—almost as if she was afraid . . ."

"Telephone, Miss Anne."

Anne snatched at the instrument as if it had been a lifeline, ignoring the faintly disapproving tone in Mrs. Preakness's formal, New England voice.

She'd avoided a confrontation with Craig by remaining stonily silent when he tried to question her and jumping out of the car almost as soon as he'd parked it, to walk stiffly to her room like a recalcitrant child. There was still her father to face, but she would get through that too. Wait for the royal summons. But all she was really doing was waiting for the telephone to ring, waiting for some contact with the reality of the outside world to remind her she was still alive and living in the twentieth century.

"Hello?" Why did her heart plummet, after soaring and pounding only instants before, when she heard Harris Phelps's worried voice?

"Anne? I had quite a time getting through to you." His voice sounded cautious. And then, falsely cheerful. "But I didn't want to leave without saying good-bye."

"Leave?" She hoped her voice didn't sound too shocked. "But I thought you had another performance . . ."

"Had. Yes . . . But unfortunately—listen, Anne, I don't see why you shouldn't know! There's been a great deal of unpleasantness, and Carol's in no state to go on. Webb's with her, soothing her, right now. It's funny, but no matter how hard those two pretend to hate each other, when it comes to a crisis, well . . ."

She listened, feeling herself turning slowly to ice while he told her.

Ted Grady had burst into Carol's bedroom with a gun, threatening to kill her. But he had turned it on himself and managed to shoot away half his jaw and still live when Carol had wrestled with him. And Tanya, found beaten up and close to unconsciousness in her room—not saying what had happened or who was responsible. *Webb? Not Webb*—Enough reason for the cast of *Bad Blood* to get out of town fast, with the surprising cooperation of the local chief of police, who had whisked the unfortunate Grady off to the hospital.

"Anne? Are you still there? I hope I haven't upset you, but I felt that you had a right to know. I had hoped I could see you again . . ." Harris sounded almost diffident.

Webb was with Carol. "Comforting" her. *What happened between Webb and Tanya?* Anne wondered. Had he merely needed Anne as an alibi, when he'd come looking for her . . . after Tanya . . . *Stop it! Don't think that way! Don't give way!*

77

There was more to be faced before she could escape—as she would, and must.

First the light, polite words to Harris Phelps. She sent her love to Carol, no message for Webb, who neither deserved nor needed any. And reassured Harris that they might just run into each other in Europe sometime. Hadn't she mentioned that she planned to be leaving for France next week?

Words. Smoke screen to hide emotions. Harris couldn't see the paleness of her face nor sense the churning mixture of rage and humiliation that made her pulse pound in her temples.

But when she put down the telephone, Anne felt strangely calm. "Empty" was a word she might think, but wouldn't let herself feel. When the phone rang again almost immediately, she could feel detachedly proud of herself because there wasn't a tremor in her voice when she answered it.

"Your father will be in his study, Miss Anne, when it's convenient for you to see him." Mrs. Preakness had a cool, aseptic voice that matched the appearance of the woman herself. She never seemed to grow any older—and yet, as far back as Anne could remember, she had always been there, part of the rigidly controlled order of life at Deepwood. Deep freeze. Her mother, so long ago, whispering "How I dislike that—that creature! She's a robot."

Well, I'm not! I'll make him understand that. Deliberately, Anne gave herself time to comb her hair and put on some makeup. She was better off now that she had some specific goal to battle for, something tangible to face. And no, she wouldn't think about Webb now. Maybe later, as a learning experience. And Webb and Carol could play their cheating, teasing games with each other, tearing each other apart, for all she cared. She wasn't playing any longer.

"That bastard! He's dangerous—he was going to kill me, the sick, rotten . . . does either of you understand that? Do you

78

know what I've been through? I want him put away, I tell you—how can I feel safe again after this?"

Carol Cochran's emerald-green eyes were bright with fury and incipient hysteria, and her face was taut white except for the crimson lower lip she kept biting.

She looked from Harris Phelps to Webb, who lit a cigarette and handed it to her silently. *Damn Webb!* It had always infuriated her that she could never really tell what Webb was thinking. She was used to being sure of her men, but she never had been of Webb.

Harris said smoothly, "You don't have to worry about Grady; haven't I already assured you of that? He'll be in the hospital for a long time, and we'll get an injunction against him to see he doesn't try to come near you again. And don't forget, *Bad Blood* opens on Broadway in two weeks. It's going to establish you as a dramatic actress, Carol. You mustn't let yourself look back. And I promise you, there'll be no publicity arising out of this nasty incident. The chief of police has been remarkably understanding and cooperative, and we're all free to go as soon as we can be ready to leave."

He saw the way Carol was watching Webb, and rose to leave them together with a mental shrug as his mind prepared the press releases he would put out. He'd already talked to Webb, who had as much at stake in the success of the play as anyone else. An engagement, "leaked" to the press, was in order. It would put a stop to a lot of things, and explain Ted Grady's jealousy if the story of his attempt on Carol's life did get out.

If there were certain fleeting regrets in the back of his mind, Harris Phelps put them away for the moment. When he left the room, neither Carol nor Webb noticed that he had gone.

"Webb . . ." Carol was suddenly a child needing comfort; she put her hand out, her ringed fingers clutching at his. "I really was scared, you know! It didn't seem real at first . . . no one believed me when I said how insanely jealous he was! He wanted to lock me up and keep me to himself. And then, when

79

he burst into my room waving that gun in my face, I suddenly thought, 'He's going to kill me; the bastard really means it. I'm going to die.' Oh damn! Why can't I stop thinking about it?"

It wasn't theatrics now; she had been genuinely terrified and was still shaking, in spite of the tranquilizers.

"You're going to stop thinking about it, though. You've always had guts, Caro. And you'll always fight back, even when you're cornered. You fought him off, didn't you?"

"You're damn right I did!" Carol tossed back her mane of hair, her voice suddenly strengthening. "And I always will fight back, too."

Folds of her negligee fell back, revealing full white breasts. Familiar. Safe ground. They knew each other so well, Caro and he. Almost as well as if they'd been married for years. There was no need for questions or answers between them, only need itself and an assuagement of thought for the moment.

Much later, with Carol sleeping off the belated effects of the pills she had taken, Webb went back to his own room to finish packing. He felt suddenly tired. *Drained is more like it*, he reflected caustically as he began to jam clothes into a suitcase, deliberately closing his thoughts to traces of Anne, scattered all over the room the maid hadn't cleaned yet—long blonde hair on the pillow, still-damp towels on the bathroom floor. Forget her! Anne Reardon Hyatt was a complication he didn't need in his life. It was a damn good thing her old man had turned up when he did. Everything was back in perspective again, and all he had to worry about now was waiting for the Broadway opening of *Bad Blood*—and his "engagement" to Carol.

"Just in case the incident with Grady leaks out," Harris had said. "You understand, I'm sure. You and Carol—the public will love it. And it'll explain Grady's jealous rage. Naturally"—Harris had paused delicately, fingers brushing his mustache—"Anne mustn't be involved in any way. I'm sure I don't need to explain why . . ."

Reardon. What had brought Reardon home to Deepwood? Harris Phelps mulled over the question. In some ways it was too bad Reardon had turned up—and that Webb Carnahan should have been the one to meet Anne first. Anne was out of his class; she was the kind of woman who didn't indulge in affairs and one-night stands. Harris wondered if she'd go back to her husband now. A rather sarcastic smile curled one corner of his mouth. Hyatt had been a fool to let her go, he mused, and he'd be more of a fool if he didn't take her back. Pity or not, there was the inescapable fact that she was Dick Reardon's daughter, and perhaps the man's only weak spot.

Anne knew better herself. Her father, a shadowy figure who passed briefly in and out of her life at long intervals, had no weaknesses that could make her see him as human. There were times, she remembered, when she had wondered if he was indeed her father. How could such a cold, passionless man have actually made love to her mother and begotten a child? Perhaps he had sent a surrogate in his place. Perhaps (and this was one of her favorite fantasies) she had been adopted.

"Father," she had been taught to call him dutifully; but she could not recall one occasion when he had shown any real emotion towards her, nor touched her, nor even smiled at her. He was a face she remembered more from rare photographs than from life, a voice she heard most often over the telephone, unreadable eyes that always seemed to be weighing or judging her in some way, so that when they met she was invariably tongue-tied and stuttered her replies to his polite inquiries.

Before she could bring herself to knock at the study door, Anne had to take a deep breath, deliberately willing herself to be calm, to remember not to start twisting her fingers together once she was in his presence. *All this formality—God, it's ridiculous! I wonder what he'd do if I burst into the room and flung my arms around his neck and kissed him?* The thought was so outrageous it almost made her giggle.

He was alone. She had half-expected Craig to be there too, facing her with his accusing eyes. But it seemed she was to be granted a private audience.

"Anne, you're looking well. Will you have a glass of sherry?" He stood up courteously as she walked into the room, digging her hands into the pockets of her faded jeans.

"I'd rather have a martini, if I may."

He didn't raise an eyebrow; merely inclined his head. "Of course you may. I hope I remember the right mixture."

She perched on the arm of a wing chair, watching him; tension coiled inside her like a spring. She was determined not to let him notice.

He handed her the glass and waited for her to taste her drink before he said, without inflection, "Are you ready to talk about it now? I understand there's been some misunderstanding with Craig . . ."

She seized on his statement thankfully. "I'm afraid it's more than just a misunderstanding. And I wish you hadn't brought Craig here with you. I wanted to tell you that I can't live with him any longer. I intend to divorce him. And—and I wanted to say that I'm going to travel abroad for a while. I have mother's money from the trust, you know, and I think I'd like to be on my own for a while. That's all. That's why I wanted to talk to you."

"I see." There was only a slight lift of an eyebrow in response, and his lack of reaction infuriated her, making her next words sound flip and almost defiant.

"I hope so . . . father. Because I didn't want there to be any misunderstandings between us. I intend starting to live my own life for a change, and Europe seems like a safe enough distance away."

"Anne . . ." His voice sounded exaggeratedly patient, as if she were still a child. "You're of age, and I've never used coer-

cion on you. Naturally I'm sorry to hear that you can't settle
your differences with Craig—or is it 'won't'? All *I* must ask of
you is that you be discreet—a little more discreet than you have
been during the past few days. You've led a sheltered life, and
I don't think you realize just how vulnerable you are. Because"—his voice hardened almost imperceptibly—"like it or
not, you are my daughter. And there are people who wouldn't
hesitate to try to capitalize on that fact. I'm sorry if the subject
is unpleasant, but you have to face it. I must protect myself
too, you see."

With neither recrimination nor accusation he had managed
to diminish her in some indefinable way. His words were pin-
pricks in the balloon of her newfound self-confidence, reducing
everything into tawdry perspective.

She had been indiscreet and incautious. He let her know he
knew and left the subject alone, leaving her unable to defend
herself.

Anne couldn't remember afterwards how the meeting ended,
except for little details.

She finished her martini and left the olive in the bottom of
her glass. He held the door open politely when she left, with
nothing more to say. And she was free—if freedom meant calling a travel agency and packing two suitcases. An empty victory,
because after all she hadn't had to fight for it.

It seemed, all of a sudden, that she wasn't escaping, but
rather running away. And she didn't want to think yet: from
what, to what?

PART TWO

THE ACTOR

Chapter Nine

ANNE MALLORY spent twelve months traveling around Europe. With enough money to make her independent, moving in the right circles, she was determined to make a new life for herself. "Escaping to find herself" was the way she had thought about it in the beginning. She even decided to use her mother's maiden name, Mallory. Paris first, where she splurged on a designer wardrobe and was offered a modeling job by the father of one of the few friends she had made at finishing school. And then Spain, enjoying the hotly purging sun, then skiing in Switzerland before she traveled to the Italian Riviera, to Venice, and to Rome. Not too long in Rome. One evening with the American ambassador, his wife, and some English friends, she sat through an Italian Western starring Webb Carnahan. She learned that he had made two movies in Italy and Spain during the previous year and quickly became a box-office name in Europe. The girl who played his romantic interest reminded her of Tanya—what had really happened to Tanya? Had Webb . . . but Webb was part of the reason why she had wanted to get away. Webb and Carol, smiling at each other in all the newspapers, with coy headlines: THEY'RE ENGAGED AGAIN! Damn Webb!

There had been one long, nerve-wracking session with Dr. Haldane before she left America—the doctor listening, and nodding his head sometimes, commenting only at the end. "So you had an adventure, eh? Very good. And Europe, I think, is a good idea too. To cut all the old cords. Have fun, Anne. Enjoy yourself and be yourself. Perhaps your new self?"

Well, no one could say she wasn't trying. Along with her new clothes and makeup, she acquired a surface polish and sophistication. And discovered that because it really wasn't too important to her, everything came her way. Like the modeling stint, which proved fun after all, and quite an experience. A four-page layout for *Elle*, only she didn't stay in Paris long enough to find out how the pictures turned out. The months passed quickly while Anne traveled. Watching Webb on the screen in Rome gave her a jolt (dammit, why did she have to remember so much about him?). But she went on from there to London with the Honorable Violet Somers and her parents, the decision already made that she and Violet would share a flat, and Violet would introduce her to "everybody who's exciting, love!"

Violet had found her the "play-at-work" job with Majco Oil, an American company with a luxurious suite of offices in a West End high-rise. Duncan Frazier, head of the London branch, and Violet's boss, was American in spite of his Scottish name; he had, it turned out, attended Harvard with Craig. It just happened that he needed a personal assistant—a young woman who was both intelligent and attractive, to accompany him to the invariable diplomatic cocktail parties and act as hostess for the ones he gave. Duncan swore that Anne's arrival in London was a godsend. She wasn't to know that Duncan was not the only person to feel relieved she had put down some tentative roots at last.

After eight months in London Anne had begun to feel like a Londoner, like she belonged there, the inevitable feeling that seemed to overtake every foreigner who lived in London for any length of time. In spite of the weather, in spite of the traffic snarls each morning, the inadequate heating, the strikes, London, with its ancient and modern rubbing comfortably along together, cast its spell on her as Paris never had.

Feeling free . . . was it a remembered song title, or just an emotion that continued to grow inside her until it became almost a conviction? Anne didn't want to stop to define it, especially after the pictures in *Elle* made her suddenly well-known and sought after as a model. She couldn't believe it at first, until the telephone calls and offers became almost a nuisance.

Duncan Frazier, upset and worried, begged her not to desert him completely. "Christ's sake, Anne! You quit and they'll probably send me some horseface from the head office! Listen— you know there's not that much to do. If you want to go ahead with the damned modeling, can't you at least work for me part time? You don't need the money, do you? And it's good psychology, to make them chase you harder. Damn it—you don't really want to be a bloody model, do you?"

"I don't know . . ." She was honestly confused. Here was the chance to do something on her own—to be someone special. Did she want to turn it down?

Violet, much more excited than Anne was, told her frankly that she'd be worse than a fool if she did. "Are you crazy? Anne—you could be famous! Have your picture in all the magazines . . . oh, what wouldn't I give to be as slim as you are, and as tall!" She added shrewdly, "Are you worried about what your father might think? Modeling's quite respectable now, you know! Look at Marisa Berenson—and a half-dozen others I could name! The kind of modeling they want you to do is respectable, anyhow!" Violet chuckled wickedly, and Anne couldn't help smiling back at her. Violet's short, curly hair and big brown eyes made her look like an amoral child, an impression that her full breasts and perfectly formed figure belied. And Violet, much to the horror of Mummy and Daddy, had once actually modeled in the nude for *Penthouse*, making it very obvious that she was perfectly formed everywhere. She had more men chasing her than she knew what to do with, and she was always complaining that she was bored, bored, bored!

"But, love, do it! Think of all the exciting people you'll meet!" Anne found herself wavering. "Think!" Violet went on urgently. "What a chance! And if you're feeling guilty about Dunc, he won't mind if you only model part time. You could pick your assignments—be choosy. All the better, because it'll make you a bigger star. Come on, Anne! And leave it to me— I'll talk Dunc into being reasonable."

Why not? Hadn't Harris Phelps said it to her once? "You have good bone structure, Anne." High cheekbones, very dark blue eyes, a naturally cool and reserved expression that, along with her cloud of fine, silky blonde hair, became her trademark.

Anne Mallory, overnight sensation and the face of the year, appeared on covers and in center spreads, making the Edwardian look popular all over again. No nudes or semi-nudes. Flowery pastel chiffons, clinging and flowing. Parasols and misty photography set against the green English countryside—usually with a lake or the river in the background. And before the camera, Anne followed directions easily and calmly, as though she had been posing all her life. Even Duncan stopped being sulky and actually seemed proud to be seen with her at dinner and cocktail parties.

"See—I told you!" Violet crowed triumphantly, genuinely, generously happy for Anne. They got on well together, perhaps because they were such opposites. And they continued to share the same comfortable flat on Cheyne Row, an arrangement that was convenient for both of them. It had two bedrooms, so Violet could invite her boyfriends into hers without disturbing Anne, and Anne could use Violet as an excuse not to invite her escorts in. She was sick of groping hands and hungry, searching mouths followed by the inevitable question most of them asked afterwards.

"What's the matter, love? Don't like men?"

She learned to come back with answers. "I like to choose my own men, thank you!" Or, depending on the man, "I was raped once, when I was very young. It's turned me off."

It really didn't matter what she told them. They didn't matter, and that was it. Maybe it had something to do with Violet's attitude towards sex. Violet admitted frankly that she liked to screw, and always had. And after all, what was wrong with that? "It'd probably do you good, love. I mean—haven't you had any affairs since you were married?"

"Of course I have!" But since Webb, Webb who had taught her too much in too short a time, leaving her craving more, there had been only one other man. Sophie's father, the elegant Frenchman who had teased and cajoled her into modeling some of his latest creations for *Elle*, had wined her and dined her and taken her to bed—all with great charm and finesse and without pressure. He'd been a gentle and considerate lover, but . . . nothing! What had she expected? Fireworks? The kind of cruel, careless chemistry that Webb had? Antoine had been very understanding, very French.

"So? Sometimes it happens, sometimes it doesn't. I am sorry for you that you could not find the same pleasure you have given me, petite Anne. You have such a lovely body, with so much passion locked in!" They had parted friends, and seeing her off on her flight to Spain, he had handed her a flat gold-wrapped box, waving aside her confused thanks as he kissed her on the cheek.

"It's you, petite Anne. I designed it for the woman who lives locked inside you, waiting to be set free." The gown hung in her closet, carefully swathed in tissue paper and thin plastic—flame-colored chiffon, daringly low-cut, made to cling from the high waist to the hips without seeming to, before the layers that formed the skirt flowed down to her ankles.

She hadn't worn it yet.

Moving into autumn, the weather turned unseasonably chill in the fog-shrouded evenings. The calendar on Duncan's office wall had been turned to a sunlit picture of the ocean, framed by twisted cypress trees. Monterey cypress! Anne thought, staring at the picture. California. She felt the familiar tug of homesickness, mixed with something else. So long ago—she had been a child, spending summers in Carmel and later on in the big stone house her artist great-grandfather had built on the lonely, majestic Big Sur coast. She had loved it. The screeching of gulls, the incessant crashing of waves against the rocks below the cliffs—soughing up the white sands of the small private beach where her mother had loved to lie, reading or sunbathing.

Dark, morbid thoughts she wanted to forget. Why remember now that her mother had drowned in that same ocean, when Anne was only seven? Very long ago . . .

Dunc wasn't in yet, and the ringing of the telephone on his desk startled Anne. She picked it up, purposefully averting her eyes from the picture that had brought up the almost-buried memories.

"Mr. Frazier's office." Funny how even here at Majco Oil they'd picked up the British formality. Where was Violet? Why hadn't she picked it up in the outer office? A slight crackling on the line, and then Marlene Cranshaw's affected English voice.

"It's really for you, Anne. I saw you walk into Mr. Frazier's sanctum, and so I had the call switched over. Hold on a moment."

For me? Anne thought, frowning; hearing the slight click in her ear and then the shock of an unexpectedly familiar voice. "Craig? What on earth are you doing in London?"

"I'm at the airport right now—and this connection is terrible, so I won't talk long. I wanted to ask you if you'd be free for dinner this evening. I'm staying at the Inn on the Park." More crackles, and then, hesitantly for Craig, "I'd like to see you, Anne."

After she hung up, she noticed the hastily scrawled note on Duncan's appointment book, lying open on the desk. "C. H.—Heathrow, 11 A.M." So Dunc had known. Why hadn't he told her? She had almost thought "warned her," which was ridiculous, of course. The divorce was final; Craig and Duncan were old friends, for heaven's sake! And they were all civilized people. No reason why she shouldn't have dinner with her ex-husband . . .

She's changed, Craig Hyatt thought. He had seen the pictures of her that had begun to appear in *Harper's Bazaar*, *Vogue*, *Elle*, and all the latest fashion journals, but he could hardly believe this was the same girl-woman who had been his wife. The photographs had not prepared him for the reality of seeing her again. Anne Mallory, top model. Wearing a deceptively simple linen jumpsuit, her face made more beautiful by her model's makeup. He remembered that she'd hated to wear any, and now here she was, with her eyes accentuated by smoky-gray eyeshadow that made them seem bigger, their blue darker. Faint sheen of blusher on her cheekbones, and the shiny moistness of her lips was obviously by courtesy of Lancôme or Quant.

Her smile was a trifle reserved, questioning him. "Craig, how nice to see you!" Formal. More than just a surface change, then. She had acquired poise, a sureness of herself. No longer defiant, the way he remembered her last.

Over their candlelit table at the Coq d'Or, Craig found himself watching her almost surreptitiously, while he wondered what accounted for the difference in her.

Duncan Frazier hadn't been too helpful. "I really don't know, and that's a fact. She keeps pretty much to herself, no girlish confidences, even to Violet. Violet's her roommate, a pretty little English dolly I was telling you about. All I know is that Anne doesn't sleep around, although not for lack of offers, I understand. She's intelligent and has a knack for getting people to open up, even while she doesn't say much herself. I had a hell of a time persuading her to stay on part time with us, by the way!"

Craig had given Frazier the approving nod he expected. Frazier was a reliable man. He had grown into his oil-company-executive role, filling it out with his basic, efficient charm.

But nothing—not the magazine pictures nor Duncan's report

—could really have prepared him for the stranger his ex-wife had become. With an assurance he was unfamiliar with, Anne had picked the Coq d'Or for their *diner à deux*. The maître d' knew her, people recognized her, even if they were too well-bred to stare openly.

"So this is what it feels like to go out to dinner with a celebrity!" Craig tried to keep his voice light, but it didn't work, Well, damn it! How could he not help remembering? She had been his wife, and he had never understood her. Marrying her young and still naïve, he had hoped to find her malleable and easy to teach; but she had begun in too a short a time to resist his patient attempts to mold her into the kind of wife he needed. And now she had suddenly been transformed into exactly the kind of woman he had wanted her to be, the ideal politician's wife, attractive, poised, and sophisticated, but still a lady.

She had even learned the art of making a polite disclaimer. "Oh, but I will never be a real celebrity, Craig! I mean—I know I'm lucky enough to photograph well, but I'm not skinny enough for high fashion, and definitely not voluptuous enough for the other kind of modeling!" She gave him a slightly mischievous smile that shocked him. "When people get tired of seeing my face and the kind of clothes I can model well . . . I'll just disappear into obscurity again, that's all!"

Looking back at her candle-shadowed face across the small table, Craig could not help his reactions. "How can you accept that now? Anne—I think we've both changed during the last year—matured, if you will. Why look forward to disappearing into obscurity? I think you've learned to look at things practically and objectively now. You realize that the modeling thing won't last forever, of course—but *obscurity*? I don't think so. You're—you've come into your potential, Anne, and there could be more; much, much more! Ambition—have you felt that yet, Anne?" Unwisely, he had let himself be carried away. Her eyes were wide and a trifle questioning—the eyes of an attractive and strangely knowing woman; leading him on to say more, promising understanding.

She hadn't said anything yet, and Craig leaned forward urgently. "Think about what I've been saying, will you? I'm going back to the States next month, and I'd like you to come with me. I'd like us to try again, Anne—only this time on an equal footing. I'm planning to go into politics—I'll be running for Congress next fall, and I'd like to have you at my side as my wife again."

Chapter Ten

"IT ALL SOUNDS SO ROMANTIC. Dinner by candlelight at a divine restaurant, and your handsome ex-husband is bowled over by the new you. He'll probably end up president someday and you'll be his first lady—smashing! What did you tell him?" Violet, curled up on the rug before the fire in her bathrobe, gazed up at Anne with frank curiosity. "Well?" she repeated impatiently with a shake of her still-damp curls. "You didn't put him off completely, did you? I know Aries tends to be dominating, but now he's discovered the change in you . . ."

"Oh damn—that's what *he* kept saying too!" With an uncharacteristic gesture, Anne hurled her jacket onto the couch. "I've just started to discover how much I enjoy being me, and doing just as I please, Violet." She kicked off her shoes, and came to sit cross-legged in front of the fire, shrugging when she encountered Violet's laughing, faintly mocking look. "What do you think I told him? He took me by surprise—it isn't like Craig to be so direct! I said I had to think about it—all the stupid, corny, evasive things I could think of."

"And?"

"And he was very understanding. Just as I remember. Being logical and reasonable for me." Anne grimaced slightly. "He said things like, 'Of course you don't want to give up your career just yet,' and 'I suppose you need time; I shouldn't have come on so strong.' He wants to see me again, and he promises not to rush me. It sounds like something from an old movie! I

96

don't really want to think about Craig any more tonight. What about you? What have you been up to?"

"Oh, well . . ." Violet stretched, and in the firelight her brown eyes suddenly flashed excited devilment. "I've been washing my hair—and plotting! Speaking of movies, and I don't mean the old ones, and the devil—do you know who's going to be in town to publicize his latest? Not that he needs to, of course, because he's already number one box-office draw in Europe. Guess?" Violet sat up suddenly, yanking newspapers off the coffee table. She held up the *Daily Mirror*'s two page picture spread. "None other than Wicked Webb himself. Isn't he just gorgeous? And I'm going to meet him—trust little Vi to find a way!"

Caught unprepared, Anne could feel the muscles in her face freeze into stony immobility, but her eyes could not tear themselves away from the pictures. Webb—with Carol, their heads close together, smiling as if they shared some private joke. Webb alone, wearing a heavy polo-necked sweater, grinning his lazy, mocking grin. And Webb again, squinting into the camera—standing with his feet planted apart, thumbs hooked insolently and suggestively into the waistband of tight, faded levis, shirt open to the waist.

Violet was peering over Anne's shoulder, sighing exaggeratedly. "That one is blown up ten times larger than life, and in color yet . . . wow! I drove past the cinema today just to see. What do you think? Want me to fix it up so you get to meet him too? With him I'd settle for a one-night stand—I'll bet he's just fabulous in bed!" Violet giggled. "Maybe I'll give him one of my famous blow-jobs, just to show him what he's been missing. And then he'll have to reciprocate, won't he? I mean . . ."

"Violet, stop it!" She'd spoken too sharply, Anne realized, catching Violet's puzzled look. Oh damn! She was used to Violet's way of going on and on about things, being deliberately outrageous. Why should she mind now? Webb Carnahan was part of the past she'd come to Europe to forget. Old affair. A learning experience.

No regrets—why should there be? It was just that seeing those pictures and listening to Violet's excited chatter had brought too many memories flooding back.

"Anne, whatever is the matter? I'm sorry, love; did meeting your ex upset you that much?" And then in spite of her real concern, Violet's face brightened again with anticipation. "Why don't you forget about him and help me plan how we're going to arrange an introduction to Webb? It says here he's going to fly here from Italy for the premiere of *Bad Blood*. Come on, cheer up, do! And rack your brains—you've met so many interesting people recently, like Venetia Tressider and her crowd. Venetia's bound to know someone who knows him; I mean, she seems to know everyone, doesn't she? Maybe . . . but then, Venetia might not want to share. I mean, she's such a bloody bitch when it comes to the really gorgeous men, isn't she? If she gets her claws in him first, then . . ."

Anne stood up abruptly, feeling stifled by the fire's heat and her own scattered, confused thoughts. First Craig, and now Webb. Could there be a connection? Was that why Craig had suddenly turned up in London—to "rescue" her from Webb? Again? Stupid . . . what did it matter? She must cling to her own newfound independence. Think of herself first, for a change, her feelings. And damn Craig and damn Webb! She'd show them both exactly how much she'd changed in eighteen months.

She crossed the room to pour herself a drink. Scotch and soda, no ice. Why wouldn't Violet stop talking?

Oblivious to her roommate's silence, Violet was reading aloud from the newspaper. " 'Carol Cochran, whose name has been linked to Carnahan's in the past . . .' Just fancy, she'll be here too! And Harris Phelps, with all those lovely millions . . . I wouldn't mind meeting him, either—he's not half bad-looking, from the pictures I've seen. Wonder why he's never been married? It says here he'll be giving a big bash at the Dorchester the night the movie opens. Do you think Dunc might have met him? Or maybe your husband—oops, sorry, darling. Ex-husband!" Violet's voice turned wheedling. "You could just ask him, couldn't you? Come on, Anne, do stop looking like a sleep-walker! Don't you have any ideas at all? I suppose Webb's hardly your type, but he *is* mine—the earthy, dominant male animal, with just a touch of cruelty . . ."

Anne made herself turn around to face Violet, the glass in her hand already half-empty, and she heard herself saying in a cool, disembodied voice, "Do stop going on about it, Violet. Carol Cochran and I went to school together, for a year, and I've met Harris Phelps. If you'll remind me to call the Dorchester when they arrive in London, I'm sure we'll get invitations to Harris's party."

Later she was to think, *It's funny, how everything seemed to happen by itself*. Scattered pieces falling conveniently into place, forming a strange and almost bizarre pattern which was to change everything—her whole secure, comfortable life-style. If she could have guessed, would she not have called Harris?

He came to London ahead of the others. There was a short piece in the papers, HARRIS PHELPS BACHELOR MULTIMILLIONAIRE ARRIVES TO PUBLICIZE FIRST PRODUCTION VENTURE, and Violet wouldn't stop nagging until Anne had made her promised phone call.

Trapped, Anne made the call under Violet's watchful expectant eyes; she hoped Harris wouldn't be available, but he was.

"Anne? I can't believe it! How are you, love? And do you practice telepathy? I've seen all the marvelous pictures, of course, and I was just having my secretary hunt through the phone book, trying to find you."

"Well . . . I'm not listed. And in any case, with all the publicity *Bad Blood*'s been getting, how could I resist calling? It's nice to hear your voice again, Harris. How's Carol?"

Oh God, how stilted she sounded! Now that she had Harris on the line and was talking to him, Violet's idea seemed ridiculous. What could she tell him, without letting him think that it was really Webb she wanted to hear about? Just hearing Harris's voice took her back much further than she wanted to remember.

Harris made it easy for her, with his usual easy flow of chatter, sounding genuinely glad to hear from her.

"Carol's just great! You know she and Webb are both up for Academy Award nominations? And Carol's just signed a contract to do a movie based on the life of Lady Jane Digby—just her cup of tea, and she's all excited about it. She's looking forward to seeing you again, Anne, and so am I. Listen—what are you doing for dinner tonight? I know it's short notice, but if you're free I'd very much like to take you out and talk to you, so we can catch up with everything that's happened to us both since the last time we met." There was a slight, almost indiscernible pause, and then Harris said softly: "I've thought about you a lot, Anne. And I've felt guilty about letting you in for something . . . well, that's all behind us now. I just want you to know I did try to get in touch afterwards, but they told me you'd left Deepwood, and wouldn't be available . . ."

Anne bit her lip with exasperation. Mrs. Preakness, no doubt! And her father, arranging everything. Shutting her off from "undesirable associations." It was past, and far behind her, but the thought still rankled. Harris had called her, and she hadn't been told. Suppose Webb had tried to call too? Oh—not possible! *Stop thinking along those lines!* She'd had time enough and experience enough to realize exactly what she had meant to Webb Carnahan. A puzzle, for a short time. A convenient, easy lay to pass away the time; maybe a means to make Carol jealous. *Don't think about it, Anne! Learn from experience . . .*

She found herself agreeing to have dinner with Harris; giving him directions to her flat. Turning away from the phone, she met Violet's accusing, yet excitedly sparkling eyes.

"If you don't take the cake, Anne! You've 'met' Harris Phelps—and he invites you out to dinner right away, he's actually coming *here* to pick you up? Oh my God—look at the mess! Do I get to meet him? Do you think . . ."

"Turn your little-girl charm on him and I'm sure you'll get that invitation you've been angling for," Anne retorted. "And don't, please, try to make more out of a casual dinner invitation than meets the eye, Violet. Harris is—well, we've never been more than friends, honestly. I met him through Carol, and—and that's all there is to it!"

Violet, lighting a cigarette, winked broadly. "Of course, darling! And when your ex calls up, you can trust little Vi to make all the proper, plausible excuses. I'll even persuade him that it mightn't be such a bad idea to take me out to dinner instead—local color and all, and I could take him to some really wicked little places in Soho that would blow his mind . . . you did say he was kind of straight, didn't you? Unless you mind, of course!" Violet blew a smoke ring, grinning impishly. "I think I can guarantee to keep him out of your hair for as long as you want, as long as I get to meet you-know-who! And once that's arranged, you can leave the rest up to me . . . that is, unless you're a teensy bit curious about him yourself. Are you?"

"I'm not curious at all! And as for Craig . . . oh damn!" That part of her speech at least was natural and quite unfeigned. She'd forgotten about Craig, who had developed the disconcerting habit of dropping in of an evening—surprisingly hitting it off with Violet when she was in. And sometimes he would take her out to lunch, never pushing again, never pressing, but just being there, so that she had almost got used to seeing him, having him around, even talking to him as if they'd never been married before and were strangers getting to know each other. Clever Craig. Persistent Craig! But why?

Anne looked directly at Violet, shrugging her shoulders

slightly. "Why don't you try your wiles on him? I think Craig probably needs to be seduced. And"—she could not resist flinging a last comment over her shoulder as she walked into her bedroom—"maybe you just might need someone to fall back on after wicked Webb is done with you!"

Bitchy—very bitchy, Anne! And of course the worst thing to say . . . Had all the warnings done her any good? Let Violet find out about Webb—let Webb find out about Violet, who was in many ways his female counterpart. Why should she mind? She was over it.

Dressing for dinner, Anne spent more time than usual in front of her mirror. She had made the Edwardian look popular all over again, and tonight, with subdued, pastel makeup, her hair up, with soft tendrils escaping artfully to cling at the nape of her neck and her temples, she looked the part of her make-believe self. Wide-eyed and innocent—until the beholder's eye caught her nearly-transparent beige chiffon jumpsuit, tied demurely at the neck, but open to the waist from there, clinging about her slim hips. And had she dressed for Harris or herself? No answers—she'd find them later.

Violet said, "Wow!" Very simply and with feeling, brown eyes widening, and then the doorbell rang, and Anne could not help sighing inwardly because she'd timed it just right, for a change, counting on Harris to be precisely on time.

This Harris Phelps was different from the one she remembered. Not Harris Phelps, the producer, but Harris Phelps, multimillionaire—charming and very sure of himself. He kissed Anne warmly on the cheek, hugging her briefly before he turned to be introduced to Violet, still keeping an arm about Anne's waist. How easily he seemed to manage things! Violet had her invitation to his party at the Dorchester five days from now, without her having to angle for it. And of course she could bring an escort—any lucky man she chose.

Harris had driven himself, in a rented silver-gray Rolls-Royce.

Behind the wheel, with the motor purring smoothly, he glanced sideways at Anne. "You've become more beautiful than ever, Anne. Although of course you know that. Europe has fulfilled the promise that was always there in you." Changing the subject abruptly, as if he sensed her sudden embarrassment, Harris added, "Are you in the mood for a surprise before dinner, or are you very hungry? There's something I'd like you to see."

She wasn't hungry, and the surprise turned out to be a private showing of *Bad Blood*. So different, and even more powerful as a movie. The stage was too real. The screen was a different, escapist dimension with its closeups and fast-moving action —speeding, crashing automobiles; writhing, bleeding bodies caught in death-throes; carefully planned, beautifully shot exteriors. And above all the sex, played up in the movie where it had been implicit in the play. Everything seemed larger on the screen. More color, more violence, more action. From distant, perspective shots, as Harris called them, to enormous closeups of faces and eyes and mouths. All this with a pounding, dramatic jazz score by Isaac Jones in the background.

Anne felt her senses assaulted and then taken over against her will. The movie was better than the play, which had been a hit. She watched "her" scene with her teeth caught in her lower lip, remembering it all too well; and they'd changed it for the movie into something much more purely visual, the suspense building up without words as the camera switched from one angle to another—curtains moving in the night breeze, closeups of Toni's face, and then more misty, shadowed shots of her almost-naked, sweat-sheened body twitching with a nervous reaction she tried to quell in a beautiful, sensitively underplayed masturbation scene. And then, starkly, suddenly, the cut from her writhing body to his; jerking in shock and agony as the bullets ripped into him.

They had cut all the dialogue out of this last scene and the camera, cutting from one face, one body, to another, said everything. And the guilt, the recognition and accusation, the belated regrets, were all there in the faces as each character found a different kind of climax.

The music screamed and then softened to a sob at the end, dying into a silence where only the camera moved, swooping backward into a misty long shot that faded very slowly as the credits began to flash onto the screen. Anne's caught breath, held for too many seconds, sighed, breaking the stillness.

"What do you think, Anne? What's your opinion, your gut feeling, if you'll forgive the vulgarity? You're in a unique position to judge, you know. You were a part of the play when it was still being formed, and now you've seen the end product. How do you feel about it?"

"It—it's good!" Anne knew that her words sounded almost mechanical, and she added, quickly and sincerely, "Harris, it was great, and I think you know it already. I'm still trying to come back to reality right now, because I was so—caught up. I knew how it was going to end, and yet I found myself wishing it wouldn't . . . my stomach's still churning! Is that a good enough answer? I hate unhappy endings, and I wanted to cry!"

"I hope everyone thinks the same way you do, Anne." Harris squeezed her cold hand. She felt that he was pleased by her completely spontaneous reaction. "I have the feeling that *Bad Blood* is going to do even better than *The Godfather*. And I plan to produce more movies." He turned to look at her, his face unexpectedly serious. "I think you of all people would understand, Anne. I want to become a name in my own right, not just the heir to my old man's millions. I think I've found my milieu at last, and I know where I'm going from here. I'm going to make going to the movies a popular American pastime again. And the hell with budgets! I can throw in a few millions of my own and be sure of more from friends who trust in my judgment. Do you know what that could mean? We'd revolutionize the dying movie industry, inject it with new blood, new ideas! Bring back the romance and the blood and thunder, the sweeping historical epics that are becoming the most popular literary genre just now. Most movie producers are too afraid of costs and failure to take a chance, but I'll give you your happy endings yet, Anne. And throw in action and sex and color too. Remember *Gone with the Wind*? I want to go back to making movies like that. I want to sign up some of the biggest stars in the business, and make new ones. And I intend to break new ground too. Do you realize just how the visual medium affects thousands, millions of people? Look at soap operas—the popular TV series where the characters become more real and important to the viewers than the actors who play them. My God! We've all been reading how TV commercials can influence millions. Movies have so much more potential! Dammit, Anne—" Suddenly, breaking what seemed like a spell, Harris gave a short, apologetic laugh; his fingers first squeezing hers and then stroking lightly. "You're a good listener, you know. I suppose I got carried away on my favorite topic. But I've always felt I could share things with you—thoughts, ideas . . ."

"Harris . . ." At first, she had been thinking about Webb— Webb making love to Carol on the screen; Webb making love to her; but suddenly Harris had trapped her, catching at her mind with the hooks of his enthusiastic, impassioned words, forcing her to listen. And Harris at least had never lied to her, never pretended. He was tactful, too.

"Forget the speech, Anne. Let's go have dinner, shall we? You must be starved. And we can talk more later, if you'll let me."

Having dinner with Harris Phelps was quite an experience, Anne found out, with attentive waiters jumping to attention when he so much as lifted an eyebrow. Fascinated in spite of herself, she found her earlier image of Harris—the fussy, talkative, touching man she remembered—changing, to be replaced by a charming, dynamic stranger who was quite fun to be with. Most of all, he wasn't pushing. Neither her nor himself. It made it easy for her to relax, to let the good French wine go to her head just a little, while she enjoyed the feeling of being subtly pampered and drawn out by a sophisticated and intelligent man. Antoine had been like that; making her feel very feminine and desirable. It had been her fault that . . . *But why am I thinking this way?* Anne thought confusedly. *My God, Harris hasn't even made a pass yet. Do I want him to? Anyway, he's being nice, and I like that. Why didn't I really notice before how nice Harris is?*

She didn't mind when he leaned across the table to imprison her hand, stroking her fingers lightly. Harris liked to touch. Once, when she had drunk far too many martinis—no, dammit! Webb Carnahan was out of her life and out of her mind. If she met him again, she would be aloof and unmoved. She'd let him see that he'd been just an experiment. That was it—end of early chapter. Now she was poised, sophisticated, and much more sure of herself than she had ever been.

Harris, as if he'd been able to touch her mind as well, seemed to reiterate her thoughts. "I like the changes I've noticed in you, Anne. And I admire the way you've managed to stay you in spite of them. You photograph sensationally, you know, and there's something about you that makes people notice you, not just the beautiful clothes you happen to be modeling. It's a rare quality you have, Anne. Star quality. Would you like me to make you a star?"

He sensed the sudden stiffening in her, the way her eyes widened and seemed to come back into focus, meeting his. Harris laughed, not releasing her hand.

"Does that sound like a very corny line? I hope you know me better than to think that. But I mean it, Anne. It's a part of what I've been talking to you about all evening. Will you think about it? I want to put you in my next movie—it'll be a period piece, a big historical that will start a whole new trend. Unlimited budget—color, splendor, everything— And you'll have one of the best directors in the world to help you—Yves Pleydel.

Did you see *La Nuit de la Rose?*" He wasn't giving her a chance to speak, to try to refute what he was saying. But then, he couldn't be serious! *What will Violet say?* Anne thought, still staring at Harris and realizing uneasily that he was serious.

"Anne, you must promise me you'll think about this. Listen, I'm not given to making snap decisions, but in this case . . . you're perfect for the role I have in mind! More than perfect. It might have been written for you. And you're not exactly an unknown; your face is known and recognized on both continents already. You won't be the first top model to turn movie actress, you know—I don't need to name them all! But you'll be better, and bigger than any of them, I promise you that. And believe me, I understand the feeling, the urge that I know is in you too, to achieve, to be, on your own. It'll set you finally and irrevocably free, love. And you'll be at the top—I can guarantee you that."

"I—Harris, I can hardly think straight anymore! Either you're crazy or I am. I mean—how do you know I can even act? Doing that scene in *Bad Blood* was bad enough—you know how I got the shakes! But really having to act, knowing it's a kind of test, that if I fail—"

"But you can't fail, Anne. Trust me. I've developed a kind of sixth sense about things like this, and I know it. I'm not trying to bribe you, Anne. I'm offering you a chance I think you ought to take. No—" Harris frowned impatiently, his fingers closing tightly over hers. "It's not a chance, I'm sure in my own mind. Damn, when I read the book, I kept thinking of you. And now that I've met you again, talked to you, I'm more certain than ever. And I'm not often wrong. Anne"—leaning forward now, his eyes boring into hers—"this is going to be the most talked-about movie since *Gone with the Wind*. A record-maker. And it's very important to me. Because, do you see, it's my chance too, to be known and recognized in my own right. *Bad Blood* was only a beginning, the groundbreaker, so to speak, but this one—do you see now how serious I am? If I didn't think you had the potential, that old-fashioned star quality, I wouldn't have broached the subject. Don't turn me down, Anne!"

He sounds as if he's proposing to me! Anne's free hand shook as she lifted the tiny liqueur glass to her lips and drained it without thinking. It sounded improbable—impossible! A dream-sequence. And yet . . .

She said the first thing that came into her mind, her voice sounding breathless. "Why me, Harris? If it's so important to you, why an unknown quantity, why not someone like Carol? Just her name would practically guarantee a big box-office hit, wouldn't it? Why would you want to take a chance?"

His lips smiled under his thin, carefully trimmed mustache. Without her realizing it, by some invisible means of communication, he had signaled one of the ever-present obsequious waiters, who silently refilled her glass, her coffee cup.

"I don't feel I'd be taking a chance, you see," he said softly. "Shall we just say I have a hunch about these things? And Carol—no, she's almost too big. She's not the type for the part I want you to play. You have a pure quality about you, Anne, that Carol can't even pretend to duplicate. When you read the book I'll have sent around to you tomorrow, I think you'll understand what I mean." He dropped his bombshell then, without a pause or a change in the tone of his voice. "Don't worry about that end of it, Anne. If you're thinking about box-office draw, you'll have one of the hottest male stars of today playing the lead opposite you. Just before *Bad Blood* was finished, I signed Webb Carnahan up for the role of Jason Ryder."

Chapter Eleven

ANNE FELT HERSELF CAUGHT between opposite moods. Trapped. Harris hadn't been quite fair, he hadn't told her about Webb until the very last minute, when it would seem, if she backed off then, as if she was still carrying a torch, and was therefore afraid. And exultant—because Harris really seemed to mean everything he'd said, because by his very casualness he'd seemed to take it for granted that Webb hadn't meant anything to her; just a desultory fling. Webb. How would he react? He'd probably be expecting a name as big as his—Carol, maybe— and he'd be furious . . . But what did she care what Webb thought?

Harris had at least promised secrecy, for the time being. To give her time to get used to the idea, he said soothingly. And to give Webb time to blow his top and then cool off? She must stop thinking about Webb like a naïve schoolgirl remembering her first, most painful crush, stop thinking about him until she was forced to face him again, and consider herself instead. She had time to think it over, calmly and clearly. And to read *Greed for Glory*, still on the best-seller lists. The title was a play on the name of the heroine, Gloriana. The part she was supposed to do, if she agreed . . . if, if! And she couldn't even talk to Violet about it; she didn't dare.

"I must say you're awfully absent-minded these days! What's the matter, mooning about your millionaire boyfriend?" Violet had been envious, at first, and avidly curious, then shruggingly resigned when Anne continued dating Harris Phelps. But her volatile, childlike personality enabled her to adjust quickly, so that she was back to teasing Anne—not only about Harris, but slyly bringing up the fact that she, Violet, was dating Craig these days.

"D'you think I've managed to catch your ex on the rebound, love? He's actually kind of neat!" Violet's use of current American phrases, delivered in her very English accent, usually made Anne laugh. This time, she could only manage a half-hearted smile.

"What a horrible expression! Does Craig know you think he's 'neat'?"

Actually, she was relieved that Craig appeared to have taken it all so well, and seemed to have found consolation in Violet. But she hadn't missed the flash of . . . what had it been? Anger—frustration—something else as well, the first time she'd told him defiantly that she was sorry, she couldn't go out to dinner; she was seeing Harris Phelps.

"I'm sorry, Anne. I'd really hoped . . ." He'd been very civilized about it all. Even to adding that there was no reason they couldn't remain friends. And then he'd taken Violet out, so that quite often when she returned from a date with Harris, she'd find Craig and Violet sitting before the fire, sipping coffee and talking. Violet at least didn't seem to think there was anything odd about the situation. She said frankly that she liked Craig. He was—neat!

"I picked that word up from a marine lieutenant I went out with—he was in charge of the guard detail at your embassy." Unabashed, Violet giggled. "He'd been in Vietnam, and he used to make love to me as if each time was the last time! But he got boring when he became too serious; and he didn't have much to talk about, in any case—he was one of those silent doers, as I always call them!"

Thank God Harris wasn't like that. Tense and very much on guard at the beginning, Anne had gradually found herself able to relax and enjoy going out with Harris when he didn't try to push her or make physical demands on her. He seemed to like being with her, and being seen with her; and she found Harris was an interesting and amusing companion.

And as long as Harris stuck to his role and she continued to live hers, it was easy enough to sail through the days and nights without making any real decision. Time enough for that . . .

Or was there? The notoriety she gained by being seen so constantly with Harris Phelps got her picture in the newspapers much more often than usual; it also got her bigger and better modeling offers.

"Take them, love! The more publicity you get during the next few weeks, the better. And listen—tomorrow night you'll be meeting Yves Pleydel. We'll have a private dinner in my suite, if that's all right with you. I want him to meet you for the first time without a crowd of other people along . . . No," Harris continued, shaking his head at the almost scared expression that sprang into her eyes, "I haven't told him anything yet. I'm sure, you see, that he'll discover for himself the same quality I've always seen in you, Anne. It's not just the fact that you photograph beautifully—you have something else, an innocent sensuality, the hint of depths that haven't been plumbed yet. Pleydel's made his three ex-wives famous; and yet you, Anne, have more star quality than any of them ever had."

"You don't even know if I can act! Harris, modeling is one thing. It's really a matter of following directions and standing here, pretending to do that, or smiling or looking pensive. I've been lucky, getting all the right breaks and becoming, well, successful before I had time to realize how impossible it really was! But speaking lines, showing emotions that I might not feel inside—how do you know, how I know that I won't make an awful fool of myself?"

"You won't. Don't worry about it, Anne. You can do anything you really want to do."

She managed a small, rather ragged laugh. "You sound like my analyst. He almost had me convinced, too. But now I— I'm just not sure I can handle this! Talk about too much, too soon . . . why me, Harris?"

"Because you've got something, Anne. Because I think I recognize something in you that reminds me of myself. We've both been trying to break out of the molds that were set for us a long time ago, don't you understand that?"

Sometimes Harris made her feel like a rather obtuse child who had to be coaxed and cajoled for her own good. If only she had someone else to talk to, but Dr. Haldane was an ocean away, and he'd told her sternly that she was quite capable of making her own decisions. Umbilical cord severed. She put in a transatlantic call to him, but an answering service answered. The doctor was on vacation. Was there any message? If it was really urgent . . .

"No—no, it isn't. I—never mind. No message."

In any case, Yves Pleydel would probably discover her for a fake. She'd heard that he insisted on sleeping with all the women he directed, to find out what made them tick. Then he undressed them for the screen and directed some of the hottest, most intimate love scenes in film history . . . He wouldn't find her his type at all! She couldn't . . .

Anne poured herself a drink, defiantly—stretching, kicking her shoes off; reveling in being all alone in the flat for a change. Violet wouldn't be back "until the wee hours," her note had said.

She couldn't . . . why in hell couldn't she? *I should have asked Harris in for a night-cap. Why not? And let the chips fall where they may.* Harris was being very sweet, being patient. What kind of corny little-girl-twenty-years-ago game was she playing, anyway? One marriage, mediocre. Two affairs, one of them bad for her ego (Anne grimaced into her scotch

112

at the memory) and one of them good. And if anyone else knew that was the extent of her experience, she'd be looked on as some kind of a freak. She should have stayed at one of Venetia Tressider's orgies and learned a lot. But then of course, that was during the period when she'd had the paranoid feeling that she was being followed. Not too way out, after all. She ought to be used to being shadowed—it used to be a fact of life she tried to blank out of her mind—but here in England? He was a young, good-looking young man with a mustache, and he'd been at that one party of Venetia's when they were all smoking hash through a water pipe . . . he hadn't! She'd noticed that, and soon afterwards she'd invented a headache.

Duncan Frazier had laughed uproariously when she'd told him. "Followed? But, honey, that's not too surprising, is it? I mean—a pretty girl like you—and there are some red-blooded Englishmen left, I understand. Maybe he was a Scot, though; they're more determined . . ."

Well, Dunc was upset at her right now—had been ever since she'd told him she couldn't keep the job at Majco and do modeling at the same time. It was becoming too much of a strain. He'd acted as if she was betraying him and it had taken Craig, of all people, to soothe him.

"Is it really modeling, or is it marrying a millionaire you're after, Anne?" Duncan asked dourly just before she left his office. "Whatever you do, for Christ's sake be careful. You're too damned vulnerable, kid—I don't think you've developed a proper sense of self-preservation yet!" A sense of protectiveness gone sour, or something else? He thought, like everyone else did, that she was already Harris Phelps's mistress—Harris did have that reputation, but Harris had shown her another side of himself. Still, it was nothing she had to explain to anyone, not even to Dunc, who'd been her friend.

Frowning, Anne walked over to the fireplace, poking crossly at red-hot embers until the fire flared into life again.

Now she was getting paranoid! Duncan had had his feathers ruffled, but there was no reason they couldn't remain friends, was there? She wondered suddenly, for the first time, if Dunc had had something to do with the fact that she'd never seen her blond-mustached "follower" again. Yes, Dunc was protective about "his girls"—even Violet went to him if she had a problem, which was almost always, and Dunc always took care of it.

Thinking about Violet made Anne smile as she sat down on the hearthrug. Violet would probably think she was crazy—and say so! "You need to sleep around a lot more than you do, love; and talk about it sometimes, it really helps." Violet really thought Anne did, sometimes. And Anne let her think so out of self-defense, just so Violet wouldn't start arranging dates or asking prying, pitying questions.

She didn't need pity—just self-confidence! Anne switched on the tape-player, fiddling with knobs until the sounds of *Misty* came softly from all four speakers, enmeshing her in sound and feeling. And then, to escape feeling, she picked up the copy of *Greed for Glory* that Harris had given her. She flicked past the first two pages—it was dedicated by the authoress "To Webb, with love and admiration"—then stared at the picture on the back cover of Roberta "Robbie" Savage, remembering having seen her on a TV talk show recently—and turned back again to the first chapter. Prologue. My God, how long since she'd read a seven-hundred-page historical romance like this one? *I'll never get through it,* Anne thought despairingly, and began to read anyway.

She'd meant just to skim, so that she could talk intelligently about the book when she met Harris and Yves Pleydel. But somewhere along the line she got hooked, following Gloriana —Glory—from her sheltered girlhood in a Spanish convent to the violent, untamed frontiers of the American Southwest and revolutionary Mexico. Glory fought her powerful diplomat father for recognition as a person, just as she fought her feelings for the violent rakehell who took her first with tenderness and afterwards as a hostage, using her with calculated brutality. But in spite of everything, Glory learned by living, by surviving, turning her weakness into strength. And before she ended up with her man, Jason Ryder had learned to admire her as well as love her . . .

Halfway through the book, without her quite realizing it, Anne had started to picture the action. She was Glory, and she alternately hated and loved Jason. Jason was Webb—she couldn't help it; she couldn't see him as anyone else. Oh damn! She felt all of her carefully erected defenses against his memory crumble when she read those beautifully explicit sex scenes that could have been—*were*—her and Webb. No wonder Robbie Savage had sold over two million copies of her first book, and it was still selling like crazy. It was the kind of book you lost yourself in, hating to come back to dull twentieth-century reality afterwards.

Anne finished reading at five in the morning, and she had a modeling date at ten. She slept uneasily, dreaming long dreams in which she was being carried off on horseback, raped and made love to—until right at the end when Jason came back to her, telling her at last that he loved her and needed her . . . turning into Webb, saying half-teasingly, half in earnest, "Don't pretend it's not there for you too, Annie-love!" And just as she reached her arms up to him, she turned into Carol —laughing, sexy, and she was watching them, trying to scream out loud that it was all wrong, this wasn't the way it was supposed to be . . .

Her alarm clock woke her at eight-thirty, when she could have slept for hours more. Violet's room was quiet, the door half-open; and she could see where Violet had dropped her clothes in an untidy heap by the bed. Violet had drawn the covers up over her head as she usually did when she was very tired and meant to sleep right through the day, which meant that Violet wasn't going to work that morning.

There was a scrawled note in the kitchen. "Do be a dear and call Dunc—tell him I'm sick or something" Typical!

Glory never seemed to feel like this after a long night! Anne avoided her own reflection in the mirror while she took a shower, trying to keep her mind a tired blank. Imagination . . . what made Harris think, what made her think she could actually play such an uninhibited role? She wasn't feisty enough, and she certainly wasn't resilient enough to roll with the punches as Glory did. But damn, she couldn't stop thinking about the book, the story. And she looked a wreck, in spite of careful application of brightener under her eyes to hide the half-moon smudges of tiredness.

Philip Cavendish, her photographer, looked disgusted. "What were you doing instead of sleeping? Fucking the night away? Jesus—it's a good thing we're shooting summer. Hide the goddamn eyes behind the biggest glasses you can find, will you dear? And to make up for the lack of face, how about giving me some really good body shots? The breasts, dear. That see-through chiffon number. There's a breeze, thank God—we get some feeling of body, with the wind laying back the skirts, right? Don't you dare complain about the cold—the long skirts will hide the goosepimples."

He cocked his eyebrows at her, waiting for her to protest, knowing she didn't normally go for the kind of shot he was suggesting. But this morning Anne was too tired and too wound up to care. Or was it because she was still being, feeling, Glory? She changed obediently in the small trailer they'd brought along, fortifying herself with a cup of steaming hot tea and felt curiously free with just a pair of sheer pantyhose under the dress.

Emboldened by her unusual apathy, Philip had her model several other creations from the designer collection he'd been lucky enough to nab. It would save him the trouble of paying another model for the sexier outfits—and Anne Mallory was "hot" just now. His earlier irritation subsided as he got some really dramatic shots—stark black and white, these; interiors, against rough stone walls, with a fireplace keeping things warm enough for the skimpy harem-type clothes she had to pose in. When the shooting was almost done, he really began to notice her, for almost the first time. She'd always shielded herself with a cool, aloof, touch-me-not air; very definite about what she would or wouldn't model. And as a matter of fact it was only because the designer himself had insisted on Anne Mallory that he'd called her up. Now, maybe she wasn't as coolly detached as she'd always seemed to be. Nice breasts—definitely nice breasts! Small, but well defined. Not just nipples and two fried eggs—the kind that never hesitated to pose for topless shots. And nice everywhere else. Long, streamlined legs, which seemed to be the trademark of most American girls he had met. Must be something to do with the diet, and playing tennis—didn't they all?

Philip Cavendish had made most of the models he photographed, but he'd given up on this one, until now. She had the look of a woman sated by love—Harris Phelps? He'd like to take some real pictures of her, to add to his private collection. What the hell—she'd been to a couple of Venetia Tressider's parties, hadn't she?

Violet was just waking up when Anne came storming back into the flat. She grimaced, clutching at her head dramatically. "Darling—did you *have* to slam the door? Ooh, I've never had a headache like this; and I'll never mix my drinks again! It's the one thing Daddy was right about; I remember when he told me . . . what on earth is the matter, Anne? You look like a thundercloud! Did you have a fight with Harris?"

"Philip Cavendish! And I don't care if he never photographs me again! That—Stop giggling, Violet! Think of your head . . . Anyway, it doesn't matter. I—I slapped his face. Really hard; I think he's going to carry the marks for ages, because I forgot I was wearing those heavy rings he made me put on."

"But what on earth did he do? Try to do?"

"There's nothing—well—more ridiculous than a man with his pants unzipped, expecting me to be bowled over by the *size* —he walked in on me while I was changing, that's what he did. Closed the door behind him, and suggested that I—that I should—oh damn, Violet, don't you dare start laughing; it wasn't funny! I couldn't move at first—I hadn't a stitch on, and he—when I just stood there, stunned, he kind of waved it at me, you know, and he was all over me. Pawing, making a dive for my—Oh all right! If it hadn't been so horrendous at the moment it was happening it would have been funny, I guess! Only I didn't feel like laughing."

Violet's voice was choked. "So you slapped him. Slapped him? That's all?"

"No—I pushed him away first, and then I—he was kind of shoving it at me, so I brushed it away—and—you should have seen his face! He was furious, he made a grab for me and then I sl—slapped him . . ."

Anne dissolved into helpless, hysterical laughter herself, feeling the tight knot in her stomach melt away, to be replaced by an honest ache. Seen in retrospect, it had been funny. And poor Philip—he'd probably never forgive her, but it might have taught him a lesson, too. Thank God for Violet, who had a way of putting things in perspective! And so much for Anne pretending to be Glory!

Anne soaked in a tub perfumed with Joy, then sprayed some more behind her ears and between her breasts before she dressed for the evening, wondering why she took the trouble. Yves Pleydel would take one look at her and . . .

But as it turned out, Harris was right and she was wrong.

Pleydel was medium tall, thin, intense, vital. A lock of dark hair dropped over his brow, to be impatiently brushed back

every now and then. The pictures Anne had seen of him
didn't really do the man justice—he was better looking in the
flesh, and had a charming smile, a quick and sincere way of
talking. He spoke in French, thankfully, after he discovered
that Anne knew the language and spoke it fluently herself.

"Such a relief! My English is not very good, not able to
express how I feel. You know we have already had a French
edition of *Greed for Glory*? It has done very well, too. Everybody is mad about Jason and Glory. And I will be honest—
I had been thinking about my first wife as Glory—she's the
type, yes? The long blonde hair, the pouting mouth—the little-
girl sexy look. But now I have seen you—ah, mademoiselle!
I may call you Anne? My old friend Harris—he has not exaggerated. You are just right, you know? The look of innocence,
yes, combined with something else, something hidden inside,
that is yet to be brought out—and once I have seen *you* I
know immediately that Marie-Christine is not right for the
part. She lacks something—the untouched look, perhaps?" As
if Harris hadn't been present, Pleydel leaned forward, his
fingers cupping Anne's face for an instant until she instinctively pulled back.

Unperturbed, he gave a soft, sly chuckle. "So you are really
like that? Such a challenge—what man can resist it? And I am
looking at you both as a man and as a director. Believe me,
I have an instinct for these things. If you had been wrong
for the part I would have said so, no matter what inducement
my friend here offered me. So—open your eyes at me, quickly.
Very wide, very innocent . , ."

Confused, puzzled by his quick, staccato speech, Anne did
as he had suddenly ordered—almost without volition. This
she was used to.

"Look thoughtful, Anne. Okay—smile now. You're happy,
the sun is shining, you're running to meet a lover. Watch your
feet, darling, it wouldn't do if you slipped on that wet
grass . . ."

119

Yves Pleydel grinned, bringing out lines in his young-old face. "So you can follow direction, too. Very good. Now you are the innocent young woman, confused by the change in her circumstances and trying not to show it. Questioning and curious, especially when you meet the man who is to change your whole life. And after you have met him—you are not a virgin, I hope?" Anne didn't know if she had given a silent nod or not, but he went on excitedly, using his hands now to express what he was saying. "Good. The rest, the gradual changing, the maturing, and the learning will come to you. I will help you. The flowering of your sexuality—that too. You have a wonderful mouth—it speaks of passion, even while your hands cross themselves over your breasts as if you wish to hide them. That's good—that's natural. I will remember that instinctive movement of yours and have you use it . . ."

Smoke from Harris's cigar drifted to her nostrils. He was leaning back in his chair, watching them both with a half-smile on his face. Harris Phelps the producer—not procurer, surely? Harris had seemed serious; Yves Pleydel, in spite of his bedroom eyes, appeared just as serious. Would he want to take her to bed? Would Harris let him? *Too many after-dinner drinks, Anne!* she thought. *And too much Philip Cavendish!*

She felt as if she was being bartered and bargained for—and at the same time she wanted this chance they were both talking about. Why not? An extension of that short, now-nebulous time when she had almost been part of the make-believe world of acting. Carol's world. Webb's world. Why not? No crowd out there, watching and weighing every movement. All the mistakes, the wrong moves, the wrong nuances in her speech could be erased on film. Practiced over and over until everything came out just right, just perfect—and voilà, she'd be a star. Just like the rest of them. Harris would see to that. Yves Pleydel would help her too. And Webb couldn't put her off. Not *this* time!

Not that simple any longer, Webb. Wicked Webb—every woman's crotch-throb. Yves and Harris were talking together now, low-voiced, and Anne took another sip of her Drambuie and let her mind run free, fantasizing. No more Annie Oakley, Little Orphan Annie. Webb would have to see her as she was now, part of his world, just as Carol was. Oh, but she'd enjoy slapping his face in that one scene she remembered. With Philip Cavendish it had been instinctive, but with Webb— maybe she could do it sloppily enough so they'd have to do the scene over and over . . . She enjoyed thinking about it!

"Anne—you've had a tiring day, haven't you, love? Listen, I'm going to put you to bed right here. I'll call your friend for you."

"I haven't learned to take my liquor yet," she whispered, feeling herself floating, but thank God, not sick! She didn't remember when Yves had left—only that he had rolled several cigarettes, passing them to her with a questioning look, and she had showed him she wasn't that straight—she'd smoked grass before!

"Come along, love . . ." Harris. She'd already made up her mind that she was going to sleep with Harris, so why not now? Violet thought she already had, so did Dunc. And probably everyone else who read the newspapers. Why the hell not? She wasn't a bloody virgin; she was a woman.

Half-asleep, half-awake, Anne felt Harris undress her. He was very gentle, very patient. The sheets on his big bed were very soft too. He pulled them up over her and then he left her for long enough so that she fell asleep; deeply enough not to have any disturbing dreams. If he did make love to her, she didn't remember it the next morning.

She half-awoke once, and he was sitting on the edge of the bed in his dressing gown, talking on the telephone. She didn't want to wake up, especially when he slid his hand under the covers, stroking her body lightly and possessively.

"Go on back to sleep, love." He had showered and shaved—his breath smelled of mint. "What . . . ? Goddammit, that was the number I gave you. Will you please try it again? *Grazie*."

What am I doing here? Thank God Harris seemed preoccupied. Her eyelids felt as if they were stuck together. And she had the faint beginnings of a headache that would probably grow worse if she came all the way back to the surface of reality. Better be a good girl and do as she was told. Go back to sleep, while Harris was still arguing with an Italian operator.

"I must say—when you get around to doing it, you do it in style! I was beginning to wonder if I should start shopping around for a new roommate. How did it feel, to be sleeping at the Dorchester?"

"Oh Violet, for heaven's sake! Am I supposed to be impressed? Alright, it was great. And I particularly enjoyed my breakfast in bed. Crêpes Suzette."

"Honestly?" Violet looked impressed. "That's what I call style—good for you, darling. Listen—Dunc called, and I put him off. And Craig was worried, until I persuaded him not to be. So everything's nifty. Cool—that's the right word, isn't it? I just hope you haven't forgotten the party tomorrow night. And is it okay if I bring Craig? I know it sounds odd, but I didn't think you'd mind . . . Anne?"

"No . . ." she said, bemused. "No, I don't mind at all, why should I? I'm sure Harris wouldn't." Funny that Harris had already suggested casually to her that she might extend an invitation to Craig as well. Particularly since he was escorting her friend around these days.

Well—so Harris was a civilized man too. No reason why they shouldn't all be friends, was there? But was Violet's offhand suggestion that Craig be her escort really her idea or his? Violet had been so crazy-keen to meet Webb, to . . .

As usual, Anne found her mind veering away from that particular thought. Think about it later. Webb would be flying in from Rome, just in time to put in an appearance at the party. Harris had mentioned that in passing this morning, sounding annoyed (was that what his call to Italy had been about?) at what he termed "Webb's usual careless attitude," ending up with, "I suppose it's got something to do with his latest girlfriend, Claudia del Antonini—she was Pleydel's last wife, did you know that?" No, she hadn't known, didn't care. Sitting beside Harris in his Rolls, she had merely shrugged her shoulders with seeming indifference, and Harris had gone on to tell her that Carol would be arriving tonight and would call her. Nice to hear from Carol again—but what had happened to her much-publicized engagement to Webb? And were they still on-again-off-again lovers?

The telephone rang, and Violet rushed to get it. Shrugging her shoulders elaborately at Anne, she embarked on a long conversation—mostly giggles and whispers at her end. Anne tactfully left the room; then Violet's usually vivacious face seemed to change, subtly, becoming more serious, rounded contours hardening.

"It's okay. Didn't I tell you it would be? Listen—I don't know! Anne's very private, for all that we're such good chums. But she doesn't seem exactly bowled over, if you know what I mean . . ." The man at the other end said something that made her frown, and then grimace into the receiver. Then: "Oh—all right! I'll try, anyhow. Just don't blame me if . . . I said I'd try, didn't I?" Violet heard the door to Anne's room open and she said quickly, "Look, sweetie, I really have to run now! Got to wash my hair, and do a million other things. We'll be talking again later, hmm?" Hanging up, she brushed unruly curls off her forehead and turned to smile at Anne.

"You booked up for this evening, too, or shall I pop out and get us a couple of steaks? I think it's time I spent a really relaxing evening at home, just doing nothing!"

Chapter Twelve

HARRIS SENT HIS CHAUFFEURED ROLLS to pick them up—Anne and Violet and Craig. Soft music played from two concealed speakers, and only Violet chattered compulsively and interminably. Craig, his hands in his pockets, face shadowed, stared ahead, and Anne too was silent, feeling every one of her nerves strung tight. Ridiculous! How many parties had she been to before? Some larger than this—and she was bound to recognize quite a few of the people there. What was Craig thinking? Did he feel ill at ease because of the circumstances? Funny, in a way, to think of Craig as Violet's date—especially with Violet riding the crest of excitement, her eyes sparkling as brightly as her burnished curls.

Once we get there, I'll be all right, Anne told herself firmly, wishing her hands weren't so cold. A few more streets, a few more minutes—and Harris would be there, of course, to take charge. Harris made her feel safe and special, and he didn't make demands! In a way, Harris reminded her a little bit of Antoine—and maybe this whole train of thought had started because she was wearing the very special original created just for her by Antoine himself—his farewell present to her.

"Darling!" Carol had said when she telephoned last night. "I'm so looking forward to meeting you again—you can't imagine! Wear something stunning—I'm going to." Then came a burst of the husky laughter Anne remembered all too well. "We'll compare notes, after we knock them all dead!"

Remember to introduce Violet to Carol . . . and Craig, of course. Making mental notes helped keep her mind occupied. *I feel like a debutante!* Anne thought ruefully, and then the Rolls, miraculously finding a space, drew to a smooth halt before the steps; a uniformed doorman opened the door almost immediately.

Harris's suite, seeming to have grown since she saw it last, was crowded with people. But there was no need to hesitate at the door—the chauffeur—or the doorman?—must have called upstairs, for Harris was waiting.

"Anne—you look stunning! No need to ask who designed that lovely gown, is there?" He hugged her lightly, turning to Violet, clad in an outrageously slit-skirted dress of bronze silk, bending down to kiss her cheek. Trust Harris to do and say exactly the right things! Even to putting Craig at ease.

"Hello, Hyatt! We've met before, haven't we? In Washington—Senator Markham's. And speaking of the senator—he's actually here tonight. Flew up from St. Tropez, where Mrs. Markham and the children are enjoying the sun."

"The senator's here?" Anne could have sworn she noticed a slight stiffening of Craig's shoulders. And then she forgot about Craig as Carol swooped down on her, hands outstretched, flaming hair worn long and curly, green eyes just as brilliant as she remembered. Carol looked lovelier and more flamboyant than ever; and as usual when she was around Carol, Anne felt herself eclipsed into mediocrity.

"Anne—sweetie!" Carol's perfumed cheek pressed against hers for a moment before she drew back, studying Anne with the unabashed freedom of old friendship. "My God—but you have changed! You're lovely, love, and I'm jealous already of that gown! Antoine, of course? The bastard, he might have let me see it first!" Carol's eyes narrowed teasingly as she drawled, dropping her voice, "Unless, of course, some of those rumors I picked up in Paris were true?"

"Carol dear—" Harris interposed smoothly, performing introductions to which Carol responded with her flashing, brilliant smile.

"How lovely to meet you . . ." How did Carol do it?

Anne straightened her spine, catching a glimpse of herself in the mirrored walls of the small foyer. She'd do fine, just fine. She mustn't let Carol give her a complex.

Her pale-flame colored gown bared her shoulders and most of her back—one of Antoine's masterpieces (she remembered how he had modelled it on her, sticking her with pins and swearing under his breath in French while she tried to stand very still), it was cut with deceptive simplicity to emphasize the slight swell of her breasts; falling away from a scarcely defined empire waist in a cascade of sheer chiffon that nevertheless clung to her slim body in all the right places.

She did look good. She looked like a stranger to herself, captured for an instant in the mirror. The Lady of Shallot. Don't turn around to look for Sir Lancelot, though! That would shatter both the mirror and the magic spell . . .

More people were coming in as Carol turned to Anne, whispering over her shoulder, "Don't wander too far away, sweets. We have a lot of catching up to do!" And then there was the usual mingling, Harris leading them at first, leaving Craig talking earnestly to an expansive, surprisingly young-looking and handsome Senator Markham, reintroducing Anne to Tony Petrillo, who played the second lead in *Bad Blood*, and leaving him mesmerized by Violet.

Harris held her elbow lightly but possessively, making sure she met almost everyone before he relinquished her to Yves Pleydel. Switching effortlessly to French, Harris said with a smile, "Use all your powers of persuasion, my friend. I want to make a formal announcement soon, and I don't want Anne to start having second thoughts."

Yves kissed her hand, looking genuinely happy to see her, and Harris was about to move away when a bespectacled woman, her press badge prominently displayed, came belligerently up.

"Mr. Phelps—where's Webb Carnahan? I was told he'd be here—and he's the one my readers want to hear about."

He wasn't here then . . . Anne felt an uncontrollable rush of relief as she listened to Harris placating the woman. "Webb's always late! But I promise you he'll be here, Miss—Ms. Warren. He's flying in from Italy, you know, and the traffic from Heathrow is pretty bad this time of the evening."

Slightly mollified, the woman moved away with a sniff, and Harris shrugged his shoulders. "The local *paparazzi*, I'm afraid! The genuine article can be found hovering by the doors. I noticed how they brightened up when you walked in, Anne!" Harris said in an undertone before he moved off. "I hope to hell Webb does show up, or we're liable to have a minor riot on our hands, not to mention a lot of very unfavorable publicity!"

Yves spread his hands, his eyes bright on Anne. "Ah—that Webb Carnahan! He has something for all the women, eh? I think I will enjoy directing him—but such a harsh, barbaric name!" His voice dropped as he took Anne's hand again, holding it tightly. "Now you, you are all music. Your name and everything about you. Anne Mal-lo-ry. Yes, I like it. I like you —but perhaps you have observed that already? Mind you, I am not easy to please. I am—how you say—finicky? Yes. But in your case, Harris was so right. You have not only classic beauty, but something else as well—inside—driving a man mad to explore, to find out . . . did I tell you all this last night? I mean it more each time I see you . . ."

Pleydel fascinated her, in a way. He was a very intense man, and his concentration on her was slightly unnerving. She felt relief when he broke off in the middle of his impassioned speech; she turned her head to follow the direction of his eyes.

His—and everyone else's, it seemed. Caught unprepared, Anne looked across the room, and there he stood, with Claudia del Antonini hanging onto his arm as if she was afraid to let go. Pleydel's beautiful, blonde ex-wife—hadn't she made a movie with Webb not too many months ago? Or was it only that they were supposed to do one together? Meaningless thoughts whirled round in her head, while she could not stop watching them. No, not them—the deliberately sensuous, passionately pouting Claudia didn't seem important at all. It was Webb she watched. Webb, with more lines than she remembered at the corners of his eyes when he squinted them at the electronic flashes. The press crowded around, and when he smiled, more lines indented themselves in his face. But they only made him seem more wickedly attractive, damn him!

Beside Anne, Yves Pleydel sighed with Gallic resignation. "Ah—I suppose it happens to everyone at some time or other, eh? Claudia was the first one of my wives to leave me. I nicknamed her my golden bitch—and believe me, she is one! I think, though, that in this instance she has met her match. He is not kind to his women, I have heard, although he loves them hard for a time. It will do Claudia good to learn a little lesson!"

Oh yes—Webb was so good at teaching lessons! Close to Anne a woman sighed audibly and whispered to her wooden-faced escort, "Oh Jesus! What I wouldn't give to be *her!*"

And in spite of everything, all her stout resolutions, Anne felt her nerve-ends tingle, sending a quiver down the length of her spine. She didn't want to see him again—God, Harris was crazy, and she was crazier yet. She didn't want to meet his eyes, flickering and burning on her like tongues of fire sometimes . . . like . . . why did she have to remember? Why now?

She wasn't far enough away to avoid watching him. Hypnotized, Anne couldn't move her eyes away. The sure way he moved, the sound of his laughter when one of the clustering reporters asked a low-voiced question with a sly look at Claudia.

"I think you should ask Signorina del Antonini that yourself. Excuse me . . ."

"Webb darling!" That was Carol; and how heartlessly he left Claudia pouting while he kissed Carol.

"I think we should go up and say hello," Yves said suddenly. He flashed Anne a gamin grin. "You don't mind if I want to make that bitch Claudia a little bit jealous? Wait till she finds out her boyfriend will be making his next picture with you! Oh—she will be like a spitting cat—ha!"

"But I don't think Harris wants anyone to know yet!" Anne whispered desperately. "And besides I—I haven't really made up my mind yet, you know!"

Yves shot her a disbelieving look. "No? But of course you have. Do you realize how many women would give all they have just for the chance to try out for the part you have been offered? You would be stupid not to accept, and I do not think you are stupid, Anne. Besides—with me directing you, you have nothing to worry about! Claudia couldn't act when I first picked her up. Yes, right out of the chorus line in some sleazy little place that called itself a theater. All she knew about was showing her body. I taught her everything else!"

Fortunately, Harris came up just then, sliding his arm through hers, whispering confidentially to Yves that perhaps he'd better go rescue poor Claudia from those nasty reporters, especially as she seemed to have been deserted by her escort.

"I suppose I should take pity on the poor creature," Yves said magnanimously. He kissed Anne's hand again, turning her palm up this time, pressing his lips passionately against it.

Oh, thank goodness for Harris! She wasn't ready yet . . . As if he'd sensed her sudden panic, Harris said briskly: "You might as well meet our celebrity and get it over with, Anne. That is," he added dryly, "if we can manage to tear him away from present company."

The affected, public embrace of Claudia and Yves Pleydel was being photographed now—the cameras, with true British discretion, ignoring the quiet corner where Webb was engaged in a low-voiced conversation with a pretty if rather plump royal princess. He concentrated on her, acting as if there was no other woman in the room. Good publicity for Webb, of course—if he lived up to his reputation and the princess to hers. She was reputed to be something of a swinger, and, it was rumored, often used her royal prerogative to be the one to take the initiative.

A big, jovial-looking Englishman with glittering decorations on his chest greeted Harris with boisterous enthusiasm, even while his small blue eyes raked Anne over from head to foot.

"Harris, old boy! You've been hiding yourself ever since that weekend in Monte Carlo—ha ha!—and I understand you were one of the few to walk off Petrakis's yacht under his own steam! Making movies now, eh? Well . . ." His eyes wandered to Webb and the princess, who had put her small, heavily beringed hand on his sleeve as if to emphasize something she was saying; and he chuckled. "Leading up to a cordial little entente between our countries, wouldn't you say? Well, I'm Labor Party myself, and liberal-minded—ha!—and I don't mind. But the young woman's mum is going to have a queenly fit—after the fact, most likely, though. Little Mary Victoria's got a mind of her own, we hear."

Anne didn't like him—even when she recognized his name when Harris introduced them. A former field marshal, he was rumored to be one of her father's counterparts in England. Rumored—but surely not? Such a loud, obviously vulgar kind of man—so very different from her father, who would never make an appearance at a party like this . . . Colonel Blimp! Anne wanted to giggle hysterically, wondering why she felt slightly unhinged.

And then Webb looked up, glancing across the room at them as if he had sensed their eyes on him. It happened too suddenly for Anne to drop her eyes away; and she hadn't, she honestly hadn't been consciously staring at him. But strangely, it seemed suddenly as if a space had been cleared between them, and his eyes, narrowing slightly, came arrow-straight to her face.

And he didn't recognize her! He looked her over appraisingly as a stranger might, taking in her wand-slim body in the flame-colored dress; and then when she looked defiantly back at him as if compelled, unable to stop the humiliating rush of blood to her face, his eyes, about to move away casually, were suddenly arrested. She saw the spark of recognition leap into them for a split second, only to be carefully extinguished by his actor's mask. Unbelievingly, anger uppermost now, Anne saw him give an insolent nod of acknowledgment in her direction.

His attention went back to the princess, where it stayed until Claudia grew tired of smiling for the press and exchanging sweetened barbs with her ex-husband. By the time Harris introduced Anne to Claudia, she felt sure she'd been presented to just about everyone else in the crowded suite. Claudia, after a lightning second of sizing Anne up, was quite charming. Poor girl! Anne couldn't like her, exactly, but she had almost a fellow-feeling for her. Anne wondered fleetingly what had become of Tanya, as they watched Webb kiss the princess lightly on the ear, and less lightly on the pink lips that parted avidly for him.

Armored by her scorn, Anne was able to extend her hand quite coolly when Carol of all people finally reintroduced them to each other, making a big production out of it.

"Webb—you remember Anne, of course? And what a sweetheart she was about helping me out with that bet we had?"

"Hello, Webb." No tremor in her voice—hardly any expression at all; but she had no control over the icy coldness of her fingers. And then, lightly, "Where's Violet? She's been dying to meet you; you must be nice . . ." Was that really her voice, sounding as tinklingly brittle as Violet's? Thank God for all the people standing around them and for her newly acquired poise . . .

"You've changed, Annie," he said shortly, cutting across the rest of her meaningless, inconsequential speech. Where was Violet? Even Craig . . .

And then his hands closed over hers, and it was as if a high-voltage switch had suddenly been turned on, jolting them both.

Webb had meant to kiss her lightly on the cheek as he had done all the other women he'd met this evening, settling whatever had once been there for both of them once and for all. She had changed into one of those coldly brittle, pseudo-sophisticated bitches—all looking and acting as if they'd been cast from the same mold; and it hadn't taken her too long to learn all their shallow tricks, had it? It had been enough of a shock to recognize her; and then to find out she was Harris Phelps's latest "discovery." Meaning, since he knew Harris, his current mistress. Or maybe Harris and Yves Pleydel shared her —shit, what did it matter to him? But now he was startled, from the moment he felt the coldness of her hands and their slight tremor, by the force of his own angry emotions. Goddamn her!

So he kissed her after all—deliberately and very perfunctorily. Mostly for the benefit of the others who stood around watching as if they were the sideshow of the evening. He and Anne, having their grand reunion. But only Anne could know how brutally his hands had tightened over her fingers, so hard he could almost feel them snap.

He turned away from her angry stiffness, laughing. "Okay—where's this Violet wench I must meet? I hope she's pretty, at least!"

They were all laughing now, joining in the game. Webb's eyes crinkled at the corners, but only Anne noticed that they remained as hard as yellow glass. She kept rubbing at her fingers surreptitiously for a long time afterwards, torn between hating him and wanting, unreasonably, to indulge in a fit of weeping.

Chapter Thirteen

WAKING UP WAS LIKE SWIMMING to the surface of a marsh, fighting the leaden fatigue that threatened to drag her back to sleep again. Violet. For some reason, she was mad at Violet. Why couldn't she let her be?

"Anne! Anne, will you wake up? You're supposed to be on location in Surrey in two hours, and I'm supposed to be at work right now. Your alarm woke me, and when I didn't hear you in the shower . . ."

Anne's eyes opened lethargically to focus on Violet's tousled head and concerned face bending over her. Violet's worried voice became sharper.

"Are you okay? I didn't hear you come in . . ."

"Of course I'm fine! I took a Valium to help me sleep, that's all. I suppose I shouldn't have, after those drinks." She sat up, feeling slightly dizzy, letting her unaccountable anger at Violet push the dizziness away. "And you didn't hear me come in because I was home and in bed already. I had a headache—Harris brought me back early."

"Oh!" She didn't miss the flush on Violet's face. Then a defiant toss of her curly head. "Well—I got in rather late. Or very early, if you want to look at it that way!"

"Oh?" Anne hoped she sounded uninterested enough as she forced herself to climb out of bed. She flexed her fingers unconsciously—they were bruised where her rings had cut into them. Webb! Memories of the previous evening came back to

assault her senses. That's why she had taken that Valium.
Dumb thing to do; she still felt half-doped. "I'd better go take
my shower now. Thanks for waking me."

Violet followed her, looking for all the world like a guilty
child. Only Violet wasn't a child, was she? For all her little-
girl act, she was a very sexy young woman. Men discovered that
quickly. Webb had. It hadn't taken either one of them long,
once the princess had been whisked away by her Secret Service
escorts. Poor Claudia had been left to quarrel furiously with
Yves, her sensuous pout becoming more and more sullen with
every moment that passed. Webb and Violet had disappeared
—Harris's bedroom door stayed closed—and Anne had felt as if
her smile was a clown-mask painted onto a face. Until Harris,
tactful as ever, had remembered she had a modeling engagement in the early afternoon and offered to take her home.

"Can I talk while you're showering?"

She didn't want to be Violet's confidante. Not about Webb.
But Violet was already following her into the bathroom. "Boy
—what an evening! And you should have heard all the gossip
I picked up! Did you know that Senator Markham has the
hots for Carol Cochran? That's why he left his wife behind in
France. Craig got mad when I told him that! He's so American
sometimes, isn't he? All senators and congressmen are sacro-
sanct! And I really think"—Violet cocked her head, considering—"that he—Craig, I mean—still feels the same old way
about you!"

"That's nonsense!" Anne said shortly, turning the shower on
with unnecessary force.

"Well—I can always sense it when a man I date is still
carrying a torch for another woman. I really think he'd take
you back, if you let him. Not that I blame you for latching
onto Harris Phelps, of course! Has he invited you to cruise
on his yacht yet? I hear it's even bigger than Onassis's!" Anne
didn't answer, and Violet changed the subject abruptly. "What
did you think of Webb? He's even more gorgeous in real life

than he is on the screen, isn't he? But"—her voice turning reproachful—"you never told me you knew him!"

Anne's voice came faintly to her over the sound of running water. "I don't. I'd met him, that's all! And I'm sure he meets thousands of women all the time. He didn't even remember me." Not exactly a lie. He hadn't. Why didn't Violet stop?

"Well—I bet he'll remember me! He even took my phone number . . ."

Anne remembered that much at least of Violet's incessant, breathless flow of chatter. She had tried to tune Violet out— not quite ready yet for whatever revelations her friend was leading up to. And in the end, disappointed, Violet had taken herself off to work in her baby-blue Porsche. Damn! Now she'd probably be late for the outdoor shooting anyway, and—

She knocked a Dresden china figurine off an end table with the sleeve of her carelessly carried jacket, swore again (she must really watch that!), and had finally reached the door when the telephone rang. Anne hesitated. It was probably for Violet, maybe Dunc demanding to know why she wasn't in the office yet. On the other hand, it might be that the weather was bad in Surrey and they'd canceled the session. She should have listened to the weather report on the radio; would have, if Violet hadn't insisted on gossiping. The phone kept ringing insistently, willing her to pick it up. Harris? It would probably stop ringing as soon as she reached it.

"Hello?" She was out of breath and mad at herself for giving in.

"Annie?" Her breath caught in her throat, and Anne felt paralyzed. *He even took my phone number!* Violet had sounded pleased and triumphant. But Violet's phone number was also hers.

"Annie?" he repeated again, impatiently this time.

She gathered enough presence of mind to say coldly, "I'm sure you want to speak to Violet, but she isn't here just now."

His voice became charged with suppressed emotion. Fury?

"Damn you, Annie—will you stop playing games? We've got to talk—don't you see that? Last night . . ."

Last night! Anne closed her eyes, feeling pure rage rush through her. She wanted to grit her teeth, stamp her foot. "I'm late for work, Webb. And I've got a two-hour drive ahead of me. Why don't you call back later when Violet will be in? You just missed her, as a matter of fact."

Click. She replaced the receiver, almost dropping it. Grabbed up her jacket and almost ran outside, not wanting to hear the rings when they started up again.

"I know I missed Violet. I waited to call until she had left. What are you running from this time, Annie?" Webb sounded conversational, but his eyes pinioned her against the door, staring at him as if he'd been an apparition.

He'd said that to her the first time they met . . . where had he come from?

He looked disheveled and disreputable in tight, faded blue levis and a shabby, equally faded denim jacket. Unshaven . . . He nodded carelessly towards the phone booth at the other end of the mews. Funny that she had hardly noticed it before!

"A good observation point, baby. I watched little Vi leave in her cute little car, and then I called you." His eyes narrowed dangerously, and if not for the door at her back she would have retreated before the look in them.

Desperation made Anne cry out wildly, "Let me be, Webb! Why must you stalk me when—when there are so many other women you don't even have to chase? We have nothing to say to each other in any case, so—"

Afterwards, Anne could never be quite sure how it happened. She'd raised her fists instinctively, as if to fight him off; and his mouth, covering hers savagely, cut her off in midsentence. And after that, it was too late. All the days and weeks and months of conditioning her mind and her thoughts . . . But her will dropped away and became lost somewhere under the force of his kisses. Her body, stiff at first, felt like parched, dried-up earth growing moist and malleable again under the first rains. And none of her doubts and questions, even her anger at him, counted any longer—swept away in the first flood of feeling.

Like a renewed drought after a deluge, reality came back after Webb had released her.

Anne could feel herself shaking. Even her voice.

"That—wasn't fair! Webb . . ."

"Do I have to remind you of the old saying? 'All's fair . . .' "

"Webb—let me alone! You know I don't mean anything to you. Old affair. Just another conquest . . ."

"But are you a conquest, Annie? What are you asking me for now, reassurance? Why in hell do you think I stayed out here in the goddamned cold, waiting for you?" He gave an angry shrug. "Stalking you, I guess you'd call it, huh? Well I'll tell you—I'm damned if I really know. You've been like a splinter under my skin, ever since you put me off that time, Mrs. Hyatt. Little mystery Annie—and I still find myself wanting to fling questions at you I know I have no damned right to ask. The kind of questions I'd resent your asking me—although you wouldn't, would you? There's a stubborn, prideful streak somewhere deep inside you, isn't there, love?—although in a man they'd call it arrogance. I know, because I have it too . . . except when it comes to you, strangely enough. Jesus —when I saw you last night . . ."

"You didn't recognize me!" she whispered accusingly. That still rankled.

"No, I didn't. I saw a damned good-looking woman—like all the others around. And then I saw your eyes, Annie. And your mouth." His fingers, rough and cold from the wind that bit into them both, traced the contours of her lips, making her quiver. "And later I found myself wondering why I was so angry. I wanted to wipe all the goddamn makeup off your face and pull your hair loose and rip that dress all the other women were envying off your back."

"So instead, you carried Violet off into Harris's bedroom."

Mistake. She shouldn't have said that, sounding like a jealous shrew. Admitting she'd noticed.

He dropped his hand, his face changing—hardening.

"So I did. But then friend Harris might not have liked it if I'd taken you in there instead, would he, baby? Your friend Violet is quite a talker."

The pride he'd called arrogance made Anne snap her head back.

"Yes, she is, isn't she? But I really do have to go now, Webb. I'm late as it is, and—and I'm sure you have other things to do too."

She could not understand either him or herself. They were like two enemy vessels on a collision course—veering away at the last minute, only to turn and head back at each other again. But why—why? She had thought herself armored against him, and she wasn't . . . damn Webb, he would sense that, of course! But what did he want with her this time?

"Touché, Annie." His golden eyes glinted at her wickedly. "But I don't have anything in particular I must do. I'll drive you wherever you have to go."

And what about Claudia? Anne wanted to ask. *What about Violet?* But she was too drained to resist any longer. Whatever his reasons, he wanted to be with her. He'd come looking for her. And the cynical part of her mind reminded her that half the women in the world would give anything to have Webb Carnahan pursue them in just this way, even while she let him take her arm and lead her past her own small car to the sleek white Mercedes he had driven here.

Webb didn't talk when he drove. Leaning back in the seat beside him, closing her eyes, Anne felt the time that separated them drop away with the miles they covered once the tangled London traffic gave way to the motorway. Too close . . . each time his arm brushed hers she felt one more particle of her built-up resistance crumble. She was far too aware of him, of the male smell of him, the feel of him, the almost animally exciting presence of him beside her in the small space that enclosed them both. She had stopped asking herself questions; it was easier, right now, simply to let go, let Webb take over . . . take her . . . Never mind if it was the beginning of a dream or just another nightmare.

The old Portsmouth Road took them into Guildford. "Where now, baby?"

Anne was able to blink herself back to reality, giving directions. She glanced at her watch. She was actually fifteen minutes early! And the weather was beautiful. Never mind explaining to Neil Richardson why she wasn't here under her own steam. She was here and Webb was with her because he wanted to be, and why not admit to herself that she was happy? Exhilarated would be a better word—but to hell with words!

"You're glowing, love!" She liked Neil. He was gay, one of the best photographers in the business, and her friend. He quirked an eyebrow at Webb, grinning at her when Sandra and Felicity, the two other models who would be working with her, recognized him, their air of cool disdain falling away. "So that's it? I've never seen those cold little bitches acting so human before! Maybe it'll put some life in their faces for a change."

Neil knew his job, and he recognized an unusual opportunity when he found one.

"Since you're here, old chum—would you mind . . . ?"

The setting was medieval; beautiful color stills shot against the background of an ancient keep of a Norman castle that dated back to 1150 A.D. The dresses they wore were starkly modern. Silken tunics over pants or gypsy-style skirts. Linen jumpsuits, blue denim skirts with buttons undone to the thigh. Webb was a shadowy male figure in the background, except for one closeup which had Anne leaning back against his arm, laughing up at him, her hair whipped free by the breeze.

She'd either smile or cry over that shot later; but what did it matter now? They picnicked on bread and cheese and drank wine, then trooped in together to the nearest inn and sat by a roaring wood fire warming themselves afterwards.

Poor Sandra and Felicity. They went back to London with Neil, and she stayed over with Webb. Plagued only slightly by her conscience.

"I have to call Violet, or she'd be frantic. I've never . . ."

"So call her. Just don't take too long, Annie. I'm hungry for you."

There was a fire in their bedroom, and Anne felt it inside herself too; watching Webb, stripped down to his pants, standing in front of the fire watching her. Wanting. Oh God, how long since she had felt this kind of fierce, physical need? Liquid fire pulsing through her—longing to be touched and taken. Why didn't the operator hurry?

And then Violet—her voice coming through the crackling on the line, sharp with anxiety.

"Anne? What on earth happened to you? When I saw your car was still here I started to get panicky! Where are you?"

She tried to make her voice sound casual. Hard, with Webb's eyes on her.

"I'm in Guildford. I—got a ride up here. And I'm calling to tell you there's really no need to worry. I just decided to stay over for the night, that's all." She let unjust irritation creep into her voice, sharpening it. "Honestly, Violet, I'm not an infant! This was just a spur-of-the-moment thing."

"Was it?" Violet sounded disbelieving. "Well, you might have called earlier! All I've been doing is answering the blasted telephone. Your friend Carol called. And Harris Phelps called three times. He wanted you to have dinner with him. So did some Frenchman. Yves somebody. Not Saint Laurent? Darling —this isn't like you at all! Are you positive there's nothing wrong? How will you get back to London?"

"The same way I got up here. I'll talk to you tomorrow,

Violet. No . . . I don't know exactly when. Why does it matter? I'm sorry you're being bothered by the telephone, but . . ."

Webb lifted one eyebrow and applauded her silently. Oh damn Webb! He wasn't making it easier for her at all! Anne tried to concentrate on Violet's slightly offended voice; giving up finally when she said with a sigh of finality, "I *will* be back tomorrow. And I'm fine. Very sleepy right now, though."

"Well, tell him good-night for me!" Violet said with an unusual note of waspishness in her voice.

And then she put down the telephone, and Webb came to her; blotting out the firelight—blotting out everything but the need in her and in him until it was met and answered when their bodies came together.

So this is how it is and this is all there is! Anne reminded herself afterwards, while they still lay tangled together in the after-mesh of lovemaking, tasting the taste of him on her lips. *I want him, God how I want him, his body and what it can do for mine. And he wants me—that part at least isn't pretense or acting. Accept that much and let it be. Never mind why!*

"You're beautiful, Annie-love. Even more beautiful than I remembered you." Webb's voice was lazy, husky; his eyes yellow-gold, reflecting the firelight. The lean hardness of his body pressed further into hers as he used one hand to brush damp strands of hair from Anne's face. Almost as if he had been able to read her mind, he murmured against her ear, "But what in hell am I going to do about you? I look at you, and all these crazy, old-fashioned thoughts come into my head. Like—I'd like to hang onto you, baby. Keep you around awhile . . ."

"Why?" His mouth had moved down to her breast; it was difficult to put her half-formed questions into words.

"Damned if I know!" He sounded almost angry, as if he didn't understand himself. "Maybe just until I discover what it is about you that keeps me asking questions of myself. What am I doing here with you? What are you doing here with me? Ah, hell—what am I doing, wasting time talking?"

Words became lost and meaningless, with the only questions and answers given by their bodies. Anne felt herself turned inside out as he took her again and again, every way there was—mixing pain with pleasure and savagery with tenderness until the thin dividing lines vanished and she could only yield and yield and let him do whatever he wanted, which became what she wanted too—and this was what it meant to be taken out of herself, pure mindless fucking: wanting needing giving getting joining.

Driving back to London in the early afternoon, it hardly seemed possible that they were the same two people . . . Webb kept the radio on, and he kept glancing in the rear-view mirror, bringing his attention back to the radio when they played the theme music from *Bad Blood*, listening to it with frowning concentration before he punched the button that got the news.

Was he angry because of that photographer, standing grinning at the foot of the stairs when they came down? She ought to be the one to worry, Anne thought resentfully, stealing a glance at Webb's frowning profile, his eyes hidden by sunglasses.

News traveled fast in small towns. All those adoring, sighing women—their attention on Webb Carnahan, curious, envying glances directed at her before they forgot her, pressing forward to touch him. Naked, sun-bronzed savage of the night before, possessing her with fierce concentration . . . how could she blame these other females for wanting him too?

"Webb—I thought *Macho* was the best movie ever! You were fabulous in it!"

"I've seen every one of your movies at least four times. And I can't wait for *Bad Blood!*"

They didn't care if he had a woman with him. It was almost

as if they expected it. Wicked Webb, living up to his on-screen, off-screen image.

I don't care—I mustn't care, Anne told herself. *It was me he came here to be with! Get used to it, Anne, if you want to keep up . . . if you can . . . ?* Could she?

A slow-moving lorry blocked their passage on a narrow stretch of road, and Webb swore under his breath, down-gearing, so that the Mercedes, like a sleek white cat, slowed its headlong pace, motor barely purring.

"Goddamn! And that ass-hole Johnnie Bardini is probably right on our tail, with a telephoto lens. Not to mention your followers, Annie." She couldn't see the shuttered, sideways look he gave her, torn between irrational anger at her and himself. Anne had been almost too quiet since he had bundled her into the car, getting out fast. Now, at least, he had a reaction from her.

"My—what? I don't know what you're talking about, Webb!"

"Don't you?" Christ, maybe she didn't. Reardon's men were hand-picked, the best in the business, as he ought to know. Was she genuinely unaware that she was kept under surveillance? Webb thought grimly that Reardon wouldn't like to see those pictures of his daughter published, especially under Bardini's byline. Johnnie specialized in taking pictures of celebrities and near-celebrities caught off-guard. He seemed to be everywhere at exactly the wrong time. And it was well known that he used an extra-strong telephoto lens on his camera. "Johnnie the voyeur"—but he was popular with the gutter press and the sensation magazines. He'd gotten pictures of Webb and Claudia, sunning themselves in the nude in the garden of her seaside villa in Italy—using one set to help expedite her divorce from Pleydel. No doubt the other set would appear shortly in one or another of the magazines that used that kind of thing—and now he'd have more pictures. No more nudies, at least, but trust Johnnie to bribe his way upstairs to get shots of the room he and Annie had occupied. Crumpled sheets and all.

"Doing a story on me, Johnnie?" he had asked at the inn.

"Well, you know, I might, now you mention it! Depends on the money, of course!" But Johnnie had kept his distance, sounding wary, and Webb thought he knew why. Johnnie wasn't quite certain yet just how far he could go with impunity, knowing what he did . . . So how was it he'd turned up, as if on cue, standing at the foot of the stairs when he and Anne walked down?

"Webb—I want to know what you meant just now! You said . . ."

He gave an explosive, impatient sigh, seeing his chance to overtake the damned truck, feeling the car respond sweetly and swiftly as he stepped on the gas, swinging around and past with the wheels skimming the grassy verge left before they straightened out.

Flung against him, Anne gasped out loud. Some other women might have screamed, or clutched at his arm. She only sat straighter—stiff against his arm now instead of yielding.

"That was taking a chance, wasn't it? Who are we running from?"

"You're persistent, aren't you, Annie?" She ignored the deliberate mockery in his voice.

"So are you. Why won't you answer me?"

"You haven't noticed brown-coat before? Maybe they change shifts." Maybe they did. But the face of the man walking his dog on the opposite side of the street when he was using the phone booth to call Anne had seemed vaguely familiar at the time—brushed out of his mind when he saw Anne—to come sharply back into focus this afternoon when he saw the same face with a tankard of beer half concealing it, brown eyes dropping from his to stare abstractedly at the bar counter. And now a name leaped into his mind, matching the face. Donahue! But Donahue had retired to go private, almost the same time he had. A cover, obviously.

"Who change shifts? Webb . . ."

Anne felt cold first, and then angry when he explained, offhandedly. Webb thought she was being followed and watched. She remembered the young man with the mustache, Duncan making a joke of it. Her father? She didn't need to ask why, of course, remembering their last awkward conversation. For his own protection . . . Ah, God, how degrading! Did they send him reports? Whom she saw, whom she slept with—what difference did it make? Would she ever get away from being Richard Reardon's daughter? She had begun to feel free, and now she wasn't. Followed . . . watched . . . Did they report directly to him or through other people in his department? *Well, I hope they get their kicks! You too, Daddy-dear!*

Webb could sense her hardening, freezing up inside. And now he almost regretted his own impatient tongue. If she didn't know, what was the point in telling her? Except maybe a perverse desire to test the unfamiliar air of self-sufficiency he'd discovered in her?

Chapter Fourteen

THE FLAT WAS DESERTED when Anne let herself in, the memory of Webb's kiss still warming her lips. Their journey to London had been accomplished mostly in silence, with Webb driving like a well-coordinated maniac—obviously in a tearing hurry to get back. To Claudia, who would be wondering where he had disappeared to? But then Webb seldom bothered with explanations; he was selfish and arrogant and . . . hadn't he accused *her* of the same sin?

After his carelessly flung-out hints he'd clammed up, and so Anne had kept her thoughts to herself too. And then he'd kissed her, after letting her out of the car. Not offering to come in with her—leaving the motor still running. Just the kiss—hard and urgent, bruising her lips, before he released her almost as abruptly as he had taken her into his arms.

"I'll call you, Annie." He'd sounded distracted already. A promise—or Webb's casual way of saying good-bye?

Violet had left a careful list of telephone messages for her—placed with reproachful neatness on the desk by the phone. Why had everybody chosen last night of all nights to call? There was a scrawled message from Violet herself.

"Call me when you get back . . ."

Suddenly tired, Annie shrugged out of her jacket and let herself sink into the comforting softness of the nearest chair. Her life had been well ordered and quite satisfying until now.

Webb, entering it like an angry wind, had blown its carefully planned pattern into shreds. Why? What did he want with her?

Choosing not to think any further at the moment, Anne picked up the telephone.

It was not Violet who answered the phone when she was put through to her office by the operator, but Duncan Frazier himself, his slightly impatient voice sharpening into a mixture of exasperation and relief when he recognized who it was.

"Anne! Christ's sake—where have you been? Vi's not been any good to any of us the past couple of days—she's been worrying her head off about you! No, she's not in right now; I sent her out for a coffee break. We've all been working our asses off since you decided to desert. Damn, I'm sorry. I didn't mean it quite like that, but we've missed you. Why haven't you returned my calls?"

When Dunc talked in short, staccato sentences it meant either that he was mad or worried about something. Closing her eyes, Anne could imagine how he'd be puffing at a half-lit pipe—shoving the papers on his desk around to look for his tobacco pouch as his face grew redder and redder.

"I haven't had time, Dunc. I've . . ."

A slightly withdrawn note in his voice now as he murmured, "Hmm, yes. So we've been hearing. Lots of pictures in the papers, you know. But are you really happy with what you're doing, Anne? None of my business, of course, but you know I've grown fond of you. It's a fast life when you get as close to the top as you are."

More discreet manipulation? Anne sat up straight, drawing in a deep breath. "So is politics. I don't see much difference!"

He sounded genuinely confused. "What in hell does politics have to do with this?"

"I'm just drawing parallels, Dunc. After all, my father's a kind of politician, isn't he? Although he stays behind the scenes pulling strings. I don't enjoy feeling like a puppet. Or being followed, as if I were—were under suspicion or some-thing!"

There was a pause, and then Duncan said slowly, "I don't think I know what you're talking about, Anne. But you sound rattled—and angry. And believe me, that makes me feel con-cerned. What makes you think you're being followed? By whom? This is serious, Anne, if you really believe that . . ."

"Dunc, stop sounding like a psychiatrist! I'm neither neurotic nor stupid; you don't have to baby me along." She added reck-lessly, having come this far and not caring any longer, "You laughed it off the first time I talked about it, but I've worked for Majco long enough to learn a few things, you know. I just don't like the idea—"

"Be careful what you say on the telephone, Anne!" Dunc's voice sounded angrier, sharper than she had ever heard it, cut-ting her off in midsentence. With an effort, he added more quietly: "Have you had time to read the newspapers recently? Read them. Particularly the left-wing rags. And I think we ought to have a long, serious talk. It's one of the reasons I kept trying to get in touch with you. If you're positive some-one is following you, I don't like the idea of your being at the flat by yourself. You *are* by yourself?" He must have taken her stunned silence for consent, for he added quickly: "You don't mind if I send someone over? Craig, if I can get in touch with him. And listen—no more talk right now. Keep the doors locked, and hang tight. Okay?"

He hung up before she could ask any more questions, leav-ing her staring at the dead receiver. Not quite understanding anything, but starting to listen to the silence in the empty flat.

All of a sudden, the startling transition from normalcy to fantasy made Anne feel as if she had stepped into a part in a spy melodrama. Oh no! Duncan was merely trying to frighten her—bring her back to heel. Maybe he wanted to find out just how neurotic she was, in spite of her vehement denials. So cling to reality, Anne! Why hadn't Webb given her a number where she could call him? Because Claudia might answer? *Don't call me, I'll call you* . . . Now she was really becoming paranoid! Cling to that thought. There was no one in the flat with her, waiting behind the closed bedroom doors. The usual mess that Violet invariably left—nothing different. And the telephone was working.

It rang then, making her jump, and she grabbed for it with a feeling of self-disgust.

Carol, taking her back in time.

"Darling, where on earth have you been? You promised to call, you know!"

Good—talk to Carol. Keep her on the line. "I'm sorry, Carol! I know I did, but I've been out of town, on a modeling assignment . . ." Carol never gave her a chance to finish her sentences, thank God!

"Well, at least you're back! Have you talked to Harris yet? Or Yves? Your roommate is terribly close-mouthed, isn't she? I couldn't stand to live with another woman. Don't you get on each other's nerves sometimes?" With her usual magnificent disregard for continuity, Carol went on, "Listen, sweetie, I have something planned for this evening, and I'll never speak to you again if you back out! I'm giving a small dinner, very intimate; and you've got to come. Did I tell you that Venetia Tressider was sweet enough to lend me her Mayfair flat? She's coming too—she knows some divine men, and she's bringing one of them. He's a real Arab, of all things! Some fiercely romantic name—can you imagine Abdul-Karim Hakem? But Venetia says everyone calls him Karim, and he's an actor. Very big in Egypt." Carol gave her husky, wicked laugh. "Very big, period, Venetia gave me to understand!"

Anne sat there holding the telephone to her ear, with nothing to say.

"Harris will be there, of course; he said he'd pick you up. And Jimmy Markham—he's dying to meet you again since the other night, so wear something stunning again, will you, love?

Let's see"—Anne heard the crackling of paper before Carol
went on—"Oh yes, Yves, of course. And Claudia—I *had* to
include her; the poor girl's been giving us all fits since Webb
brought her here and just dumped her. She says he promised
her a part in his next movie, although of course Harris has the
final say-so!"

"It sounds like an interesting, if not too intimate, gathering,"
Anne heard herself say dryly, surprised that her voice sounded
steady.

"Then you will come?" Carol hadn't mentioned Webb—not
yet.

"Of course I will, how could I possibly resist such a mixed
bag?"

Carol sounded amazed—and then amused. "Darling, I can
hardly get over the change in you! You see? I haven't tried to
warn you even once this time, have I?"

"Warn me about what?" She should have said "whom,"
sensing what Carol's answer would be.

"About Webb, of course! But you've seen through him,
haven't you? I did ask him, because of Claudia. I don't think
she understands what's happened yet. Curtain time. Of course
he might turn up with another chick in tow; it's the kind of
thing Webb does. But I believe he's going to be dancing all
night at Princess Mary Victoria's favorite discothèque, which
would hardly give him time, thank heaven! Webb has a way
of—of disrupting things."

Anne let some of her angry frustration come to the surface,
surprising both Carol and herself. "Perhaps, of us all, I've
been the only one to take Webb in perspective! You've been
engaged to him a couple of times, haven't you, Caro? And I
haven't noticed that you give him the cold shoulder, exactly,
even now. So why don't we admit among ourselves that Webb
has a—a certain something for all of us females that we find
difficult to resist, even when we know better . . . and leave it at
that? I mean, I don't feel protective towards Claudia del An-

tonini; why should you? Let her learn for herself, like the rest of us! And—and I don't really have much more to say. Are you sure you still want me for dinner?"

Anne heard Carol's exaggeratedly expelled breath in her ear. "Whew! You *have* learned jungle tactics, haven't you? And do you know what, darling? I'm glad! I've always liked you, Anne, although sometimes I haven't understood why. Now I think I really look forward to our being friends. Of course I'm still expecting you! In fact I'm really starting to get excited about the evening. You and I against Claudia! Won't it be fun?"

Fun! After Carol hung up, Anne didn't know what to do with herself. Her conversation with Duncan seemed unreal. People following her . . . Webb had put that idea into her head . . . and Duncan's sudden switch to seriousness after he'd tried to put her off before. Danger—she'd lived all these months in London, just being herself, without having to worry. Why did she suddenly have to start being afraid?

Duncan had said something about reading the newspapers. Violet usually left them scattered on the floor by her favorite fireside perch. To give herself something to do, Anne sat back on her heels, finding the front pages at least of the *Times*, the *Telegraph*, and the *Mirror*.

Headlines leaped out at her. No wonder poor Duncan had sounded so harried! MORE CIA EXPOSURES! US HQ OF MAJCO OIL IN LONDON REVEALED AS COVER. WHAT'S THE CIA DOING IN LONDON? ANONYMOUS TIP-OFF REVEALS TRUTH AT LAST!

Oh, God—how nasty! And especially now with all those delicate oil negotiations going on. Or was that exactly why? She'd heard that the British press was left-wing these days, but she shrugged off all the political gossip she heard at Venetia's parties without paying too much attention to it. Craig had been very much into it all, and it was another subject on which they'd had no common ground. Now, suddenly . . . what did it all mean? The CIA, in disrepute these days. Under fire for meddling where they had no right. But Majco Oil? A well-known firm all over the world. And Duncan himself— surely not Duncan; he didn't fit the role of secret agent some-how. Although she'd wondered . . .

Frowning, Anne remembered those messages she had spent so much time decoding, which ended up sounding like gibber-ish even afterwards. She'd had suspicions that Majco was wheeling and dealing on the sly, getting the oil that was so badly needed. All those embassy parties: the contacts. After Craig had arrived in London she'd begun to ask herself secretly if perhaps her father had something to do with Majco's deals. But her father wasn't connected with the CIA. In all the re-cent scandals and revelations his name apparently hadn't been mentioned. *Reardon the King-Maker.* Who knew exactly what he did, what his connections were? And as usual, when she thought about her father, she might have been thinking about a stranger . . .

All this is a snowball that has grown into an avalanche! Anne thought wildly. *And so fast!* Why wasn't Craig here yet? And then the short, authoritative knock on the door brought her with relief to her feet, her earlier fearful uneasiness for-gotten. It was broad daylight outside; she lived in an exclusive and very well-patrolled part of town. And she wasn't involved in some ridiculous spy drama!

Anne fumbled with the lock, and the chain she'd slipped into place earlier.

"Craig?" She threw the door open wide. But it wasn't Craig who stood there. Two dark-suited men, wearing hats of all things, and behind them another man, vaguely familiar, wear-ing a dark brown overcoat.

They were overly polite, edging her backwards all the same. "Miss Mallory? Sorry, miss. We have a search warrant, if you want to see it." One of them (or all of them? She couldn't remember afterwards) flashed a badge or some kind of ID at her. Nothing seemed to register in those first few moments.

The taller one took charge. "My name is Barnes. Like to ask you a few questions, if you don't mind. Grimsby, Leach— why don't you look around?" In spite of his surface courtesy he was tough. His eyes, under the hatbrim, were a pale, hard gray that pinned her back, fluttering as ineffectually as a butterfly caught on a pin.

"Now, suppose you tell me what kind of work you did for Majco Oil? Whom did you work for directly?" His lips, as colorless as his eyes, stretched over his teeth in a mirthless smile. Anne could hear the others in the bedrooms—the sounds of drawers being pulled open, a thud as something fell to the floor.

She found her tongue with a rush of pure rage. "Look—what is all this? How dare you force your way in here and—"

He didn't seem to hear her. She started to move past him, and he reached out, giving her a very light, almost casual shove that stopped her dead. "No games, please. It would be easier all around if you'll just cooperate, Miss Mallory. Easier for you in particular, because we don't believe in wasting time playing. Now suppose you be a sensible girl and tell me all you know?"

She stared back at the blandly impersonal face that seemed to have turned into a shadowed, menacing mask. Fear was a cold fist knotted in the pit of her stomach.

"How did you get the job with Majco? What is your real relationship with Duncan Frazier? What kind of training were you given in decoding before you were sent here?" His voice lowered, but was just as impersonally harsh. "Why did you decide to sell out? You have a great deal of money in your bank account, Miss Mallory. And considerable sums transferred here on a regular basis from the States. You should really have stuck to the modeling, you know! And we'd like to find out a little more about your friendship with Venetia Tressider. Do you subscribe to her ideas?"

Anne put one hand up as if to ward off his questions. He

caught her wrist, exerting just enough pressure, without seeming to, to make her cry out with pain. "Oh, stop! You're crazy —all these questions . . ."

"Ah, but you'll save a great deal of unpleasantness if you'll answer them like a good girl. Answer them truthfully, if you know what's good for you. Do I have to repeat that we're not playing patty-cake?" His thumb pressed down and her whole arm felt paralyzed.

"You're hurting me! I can't even think!"

"Oh? Sorry." He released her then, and she felt sick with pain and humiliation and sheer, unreasoning terror. They weren't playing, and this was real, actually happening to her! And oh, God, she was a coward, she couldn't stand physical pain. She'd probably end up telling this cold-voiced man anything he wanted to hear.

Back to politeness, he said, "Why don't you sit down? And then we'll take the questions one by one, shall we? Let's start with your friends—and your contacts. I'll need a list of names, of course." He picked up the penciled note that Violet had left her, digesting it without his pale eyes seeming to leave her.

"Popular, aren't you? Let's start with these. And go on to where you were yesterday, last night, and most of this morning. Your version."

There were sounds outside the door just then, saving her for the moment. Raised voices, then the door flew inward and Craig strode in, followed by yet another man in a dark suit. *Maybe it's a kind of uniform,* Anne thought crazily, watching Craig through wide, wet eyes as if this was the first time she was seeing him. His face was pale—set and angry.

"May I ask what is going on? Dammit, if you've—Anne, are you okay?"

The man who had let Craig in shrugged apologetically. "He said she was expecting him. And I checked his identification. He—"

"I hope you men have the correct kind of identification

too!" Anne had never seen Craig so openly enraged. "Because believe me, there's going to be a formal complaint to the highest authorities about this high-handed piece of work!"

Barnes, impassive, flipped open his wallet. "You would be Mr. Hyatt, I take it? Sorry we have to meet under these circumstances. But you ought to be the first to understand that we're only doing our job. Merely asking a few questions." His voice became heavy with significance. "And you should know why. This young woman here—"

"If you people had done your homework properly, you'd know who this young woman is—and why she couldn't possibly be mixed up in that mess!" Craig's voice was rasping as he jerked his head towards the crumpled heap of newspapers.

There was a flash of some emotion on Barnes's saturnine face for the first time—quickly hidden as he drawled, "Ah? You sound very sure of your facts, Mr. Hyatt, but our facts, coupled with the people she's been mixing with of late, add up to something different. Now, if you have any information that we don't have . . . ?"

"She's Richard Reardon's daughter. And if you don't recognize the name, I'm sure your superiors will. Duncan Frazier was on the phone to Sir Andrew when I left him. And I'm sure," Craig ended grimly, "that he'll agree with us that you've been a trifle precipitate, to say the least!"

Barnes's mask slipped slightly again. His voice deceptively soft, he said: "This is our bailiwick, Hyatt. And we have our job to do, just as you have back in the States, I'm sure. We have a search warrant, all quite legal, and I was merely asking a few questions. Questions to which I'd still like answers." He added tightly, "There was a leak, you know. And it doesn't look good for us, any more than it does for you. I shouldn't have to remind you either that the younger generation has a way of . . . rebelling against the system; isn't that how your press would put it? We merely started with the most obvious source with the most outside connections. A few straight answers could have cleared everything up. Now isn't that right, Miss Mallory?"

Suddenly they were all looking at her, Leach and Grimsby had emerged from the bedrooms to lounge casually nearby. All waited for her reply, even Craig, his face worried. He moved forward, putting his hand on her arm, giving it a comforting squeeze.

"Well, Miss Mallory? You have your protection now, if you need it. If you've got nothing to hide you surely wouldn't mind if I repeated my questions?"

They were playing a game after all. Question and answer. Truth or consequences! Hard to believe that this same bland-faced man with the polite voice had actually threatened her a few moments before. If she told Craig, it would sound as if she was being evasive. He might even think she was exaggerating it all.

Anne licked her dry lips, looking from one face to the other, finding no help in any of them.

Craig sat on the arm of her chair, touching her shoulder, leaving his hand there. "Anne? It might help. Something you know—maybe without knowing its significance. Anybody you can think of who might have seemed curious about your job. And I'll be right here to make sure Mr. Barnes doesn't get out of line."

They were all part of a conspiracy against her—Barnes and his cohorts with their threats; and now Craig with his kindness. No help—she had to muddle her way through somehow.

Anne swallowed dryly, almost gagging. "I—how can I remember? No one seemed especially interested in my job. Not the one at Majco. They—the people I met—seemed to want to know more about how it felt to be a model!" She looked up at Craig, and his eyes were hooded, thoughtful. "I honestly don't know what this is all about! I hadn't even read the newspapers until after I called Duncan. I still don't understand . . ."

Barnes took charge again.

"You don't? What about your friends, Miss Mallory? You've heard them express their views, surely? Didn't you join in? Did you argue with them or disagree?"

Stung, she sat up straighter. "The people you call my friends were social acquaintances! We met at the same places and partied together, but I can't recall that anyone discussed politics seriously. What are you accusing me of?"

"We're making an investigation, Miss Mallory." Craig's fingers pressed warningly into her shoulder as Barnes continued, "There's been a serious breach of security, and it's my job to get to the bottom of it—I think you understand that? Now if you weren't responsible, and I'm willing to listen to Mr. Hyatt's assurance that you aren't, you should be anxious to help us find who is. We're asking for your cooperation . . ." Then, as if his speech had been designed to lull her into security, he suddenly snapped out, "Where were you yesterday? And all of last night? With whom?" His pale eyes shuttled to Craig, and back to her. She could sense Craig's slight stiffening as she hesitated for a moment before staring defiantly back at her inquisitor.

"I had a modeling assignment. I'm sure you can check that up easily enough. And I spent the night in Guildford, with—with an old friend. He drove me up there and brought me back this afternoon. I think you know that already, don't you?" She gave a jerk of her head at Grimsby. "Your man here followed us up there and back! Or is it that you are particularly interested in the details of my private life, Mr. Barnes?"

Barnes let that slip by, his eyes opaque, unmoving from her white face. "Sorry, Miss Mallory. All the details are important. And women—men too, for that matter—have been known to be more than usually talkative when they're between the sheets, to put it bluntly. Now if you'll tell us . . ."

Anne tried to pretend that Craig wasn't there beside her. But she couldn't prevent the shaking of her voice as she said: "All right. I was with Webb Carnahan. Craig can tell you we've known each other before. And, in case you're taking a prurient interest in all this, no—we didn't spend much time talking—about anything!"

She didn't dare wonder what Craig was thinking. She felt his unmoving hand still on her shoulder, and she almost felt guilty, which was ridiculous! Her fingers tightened against each other on her lap as she watched their faces—carved, contemptuous masks, all of them. Watching her, waiting until they could trap her into some admission of guilt. But she wasn't guilty of anything—this was all a nightmare, unbelievable!

There were a few more questions—obviously, the search of her room and Violet's (had poor Violet had to go through this too?) had yielded nothing important. Anne repeated what she had said before. She hadn't committed any breach of security ("Sorry, but you're the only one without an official security clearance, Miss Mallory"), and she hadn't discussed her job at Majco with anyone. No one had questioned her about it either. And no, she was not in the habit of getting drunk when she partied! Brown-coat, whose name was Grimsby, had discovered a stash of grass in one of Violet's dresser drawers. No, it wasn't hers. Yes, she had smoked the stuff occasionally, socially, but that was all. What did that have to do with anything?

Finally, when Craig protested, Barnes told her he'd probably be getting in touch later.

The other men who had followed him in followed him out. So did Craig, with a hastily muttered, "I'll be back in a moment, Anne. I've got to find out what brought this on."

Oh God! Silence. Like an automaton, Anne stood up and fixed herself a drink. Then one for Craig—he fancied vodka and tonic, as she remembered. She handed it to him without a word when he came back in, his face tightly controlled.

"You see—I do have a good memory, don't I? And now you

can tell me if all this was real or not. I must thank you too, mustn't I? For rescuing me in the nick of time."

"Anne, I can't really blame you for being upset. Thank God you called Duncan when you did! Those men who were here today have no scruples. My God! If—"

"You seemed to recognize each other. What about you, Craig? You know—that's something I never thought to ask you. Are you part of the Organization too?" Not waiting for his reply, Anne turned away from him blindly; holding her glass with both hands, she stared into the empty fireplace.

"I said I didn't blame you for being upset. But, Anne—it's time you faced facts. Above all, the fact that you are your father's daughter, like it or not, and because of it you have to be careful! Careful of your friends, your associations. I don't for a moment think that you were responsible, even inadvertently, for the leak the British are investigating with such heavy-handed zeal. And neither does Dunc. You've refused me any rights over you, Anne, as your husband. But as a friend, at least, you've got to listen to me! Don't trust everyone you meet. And remember that the fact that you've changed your name and embarked on a career of your own doesn't mean a damn thing; you can't change who you are, Anne! For God's sake, exercise some caution!"

She had a feeling of claustrophobia, of velvet walls pressing in on her. "What are you trying to tell me, Craig? That I'll never be entirely free? That I must always watch everything I say, doubt everyone I meet?"

His head jerked in a parody of a nod. "Yes. I'm sorry, Anne, but you might as well realize that you aren't the average girl who's made good. It's high time you faced reality. Anne . . ." He touched her arm, held it, turning her towards him. Remembering how his touch had upheld and comforted her earlier, she could not bring herself to wrench away.

"Why don't you come back, Anne? You've proved something—whatever you were trying to prove to yourself and to

159

everyone else in the first place. Why don't you come home now? You'll be safe there—you'll be able to really be yourself. Jesus, Anne! You and I together, we could—" He must have sensed the instinctive withdrawal in her. "But you aren't ready to listen yet, are you? You think you've found something that I couldn't give you—something you wouldn't let me give you, Anne! Have you found it in Harris Phelps's bed? Or Webb Carnahan's? Is that all you're looking for, my dear—purely physical sensation that lasts for a moment, no longer?" Craig's mouth twisted in fury. "I wonder how much you really know about your actor friend. The big movie star, the international stud. Have you wondered why he decided to pay you so much attention? How much has he told you of his background? Oh Christ, Anne! How naïve you really are. If you'd only listened to me in the first place . . ."

But she had had enough for one afternoon. Goaded, she sprang to her feet, with tear-bright eyes and clenched fists.

"I won't listen to any more! Do you hear? I've had enough —heard enough. Stop preaching at me, Craig!"

Chapter Fifteen

THE FEW WORDS CRAIG had forced her to listen to colored Anne's evening; even after Craig had left, hurt and huffy. She double-locked the door after him, but what good was *that*? Those men could get back in anytime they wanted to—and there was no way she could put a padlock on her thoughts.

"You're looking lovely, Anne," Harris said. He, at least, seemed the same as usual . . . no hint in his voice or manner that anything was different. No questions. "Are you looking forward to the evening?"

Ready for Carol's intimate dinner and Carol's searching, all-too-knowing eyes. But facing Carol would be comparatively easy after everything she'd been through this afternoon.

She wore a long black chiffon tunic over black pants woven with silver thread. The tunic was see-through—nothing underneath it but Anne herself, and a silver chain that hung between her breasts as if calling attention to them.

Yves Pleydel looked at her hungrily through heavy-lidded eyes, Claudia sulked, and Senator Markham was charming. His perfectly even teeth flashed in an attractive grin when he held both her hands, kissing her on the cheek.

"Anne Mallory—Harris has confided that he has great plans for you. I can only hope that you're a Democrat!"

They all laughed and Anne joined in politely. "Of course I am—how could I help it?"

"So you're going to go 'on' for real, are you, love?" Carol whispered, hugging her. "Lots of luck—and I mean it!"

Yves Pleydel impatiently demanded what the delay was. "So this movie *Bad Blood* is a big success, *non?* What are we waiting for? I think that *now* is a good time to announce your next production, Harris, *mon ami.*" He glanced over his shoulder at Claudia, who was staring moodily into her drink. Dropping his voice, Yves muttered, "Are you going to give her a part? She keeps telling me that Carnahan promised her the lead. But of course I reminded her that without *me,* she would soon go back to the obscurity from which I plucked her. She is a stupid bitch! Not quite as dumb as Françoise—you will recall she was my last wife before Claudia? Françoise Marly—pah!" His lips twitched with disdain as his hands moved expressively. Anne found his eyes fixed piercingly on her, particularly on her breasts. "You, *ma chère,* are *not* stupid! I can tell that already. I think you will follow direction well, and if you do, you will be a bigger star than any of them. I will make you so; I guarantee it—*moi,* Yves Pleydel!"

"And of course Yves is right." Harris, standing beside Anne, slipped his hand up from her waist, to momentarily caress her breast very lightly. "It's about time to start our publicity campaign." He smiled at her slightly bewildered face. "Don't look so apprehensive, love! We're going to pull a switch on the public this time. By the time our campaign gets into full swing, you'll be under wraps, shooting *Greed for Glory* in California. We'll give them just enough information to intrigue them. The big-talent-hunt story. And we'll release a few—a very few— stills from time to time. While you'll still be appearing in the fashion magazines as a model, of course. That kind of publicity we won't have to pay for."

She remembered the last batch of pictures—with Webb— and winced.

"Harris, you don't . . ."

"Of course I know what I'm doing, love." Why did his eyes

suddenly look so shiny that she couldn't see into their depths to know what he was thinking? He leaned forward suddenly, his lips brushing her earlobe. "You're cleverer than even I gave you credit for, Anne. I talked with Johnnie Bardini earlier on this evening, and I'm buying all his pictures. You and Webb— a secret romance that would lend enormous credibility to your roles on the screen. Magnificent!"

Struck dumb, she stared up at his smiling face. Harris continued to smile. "And I have a surprise for you when we go to California, sweetheart. A present I think you'll like. Which reminds me—do you think you'll be ready to leave by the week after next?"

Carol, in a slinky green velvet gown cut very low in the back, came up just then, with an incredibly handsome dark-haired man in tow.

"Here's Karim at last. He's always late—aren't you, darling? And I had to snatch him from Venetia—she's over there, Harris, casting darkling looks at us—do you want to go over and say nice soothing things while I make sure Anne and Karim get aquainted?"

Karim had a cleft in his chin, a sensuous mouth, and smoldering dark brown eyes that gazed at Anne intently. He held both her hands; kissing them French-fashion.

"You are beautiful! I had seen your pictures, of course, but they did not do you justice. So blonde, so white-skinned— if you had been a tourist, walking down a street in Cairo, I think I would have had you kidnapped. You do not mind if I am direct? And if you did mind, I would not care. I speak as I feel. Now that I have seen you, I look forward to playing your lover in this motion picture we are to make together." His teeth, when he smiled, were a white flash in his dark tanned face. "I like it that you look amazed—and a trifle frightened. It shows how feminine you are—a quality that most Western women are sadly lacking in." He spoke fluent English, with only the slightest accent.

Carol, standing by Anne, came to her rescue with a burst of throaty laughter.

"I *do* think that was a dig at me—or was it Venetia? The trouble *is*, baby," stroking his arm soothingly, "that we seldom meet any really masterful men anymore. Men with balls like this Jason character in Robbie Savage's book." She slanted a look at Karim's frowning, considering face and added diplomatically, " . . . Or like the character that you're going to play. The handsome Mexican General. When you have to rape Anne, do you think you're both going to enjoy it?"

"Really, Carol!" Anne said crossly, and Karim's cloudy look cleared as he smiled, his heavy lidded eyes seeming to caress her slim body. As if Carol had not spoken, he said slowly, "Ah yes! I think I am going to enjoy all of the love scenes I play with you. You have sensitivity, and I think under your cold blondness, the capacity for much feeling. And in this book—does not the rape turn into a passion of the bodies? I think I understand very well this Mexican General that I am to play. I am a cynic—as he is—and I, too, in my time have made a trembling woman think she is being raped, only to force response from her. It adds excitement—what you would call spice—does it not?"

"Were we talking of excitement? Anne, I must warn you that Karim is dangerous. I mean, he really *believes* all he says about women needing to be dominated in order to find themselves as women! We're still arguing about it, although I must admit it's been fun!" Diamonds against black lace. Venetia Tressider had a sparkling, diamond-bright personality that Anne had always secretly admired.

"You've been neglecting me, pet, and I don't take that lightly. You're supposed to play my protective escort, and Yves has been whispering obscene suggestions into my ear for what seems like ages. Since I didn't really feel like going down on him with Claudia looking on I thought I should drift this way where the conversation seems to be more stimulating."

With Venetia's coming they relapsed into the usual gossip that the beautiful in-people seemed to enjoy so much.

Karim had actually started to make her feel uncomfortable, and Anne was relieved to be able to relapse into the part of listener. She watched as Venetia and Carol exchanged smiling barbs and was even able to admire objectively the way Karim toyed with them both—subtly encouraging each of them in turn. She was able to drift away after a while when all three declared a truce long enough to discuss avidly the love life of a certain multi-millionaire's widow who was an international personality in her own right.

She joined Harris and Jim Markham—the latter turning all of his much-vaunted public charm on her, while Harris went off to avert a scene that seemed to be brewing between Claudia and Yves. Jim showed her pictures of his wife and children and told her he'd like to get to know her better. Perhaps when she came to California? He was a young-looking, virile man, and rumor had it that he was almost a certainty to win the Democratic presidential nomination. There were also those other rumors that Jim Markham had a weakness for beautiful women. And everyone Anne knew shrugged and said, "So what if he does? Shows he's a normal man. Besides, that wife of his is frigid . . . she'll make a great President's lady, but Jamie-boy needs a warm cunt between his sheets—several times a day, darling, if what we hear is true!"

Gossip, intrigue—rumor! Everyone trying to find his own means of escape from the strain of living in the public eye. The moralistic, quick-to-accuse public—avid for detail, especially of the famous or well-known. "Stop it, Anne—you're sounding like a cynic. Stop and think why you're here to-night . . ."

Why was she here? Escape—that was why. When reality turned too scary, it was time to escape into make-believe. She didn't want to think about this afternoon nor its implications.

Dinner was served late, in continental fashion, and seemed

unending. Anne vaguely remembered being faced with one course after another—and tasted nothing except the wine, which was excellent. Harris and Yves and Karim talked about movies while Carol and Jamie Markham carried on their own low-voiced conversation that seemed to exclude everyone else.

Between the third and the fourth course, Claudia, who had been ominously silent, had a crying jag; and, in response to Harris' urgent hand signals, Karim turned shruggingly to comfort her. Venetia Tressider chose that moment to push back her chair, casting a telling look at Anne as she did. "I think I need to visit the loo. Anne, dear—keep me company?"

Feeling like a puppet, Anne followed her warily. What did Venetia have up her sleeve this time? Venetia was almost too outspoken in her views; she had actually hidden out an IRA agent, one of her many lovers, for two weeks.

"Darling! I'm so proud of you!" Taken aback by Venetia's impulsive embrace, Anne could not find a word of rebuttal at first. "You really are a dark horse, do you know that? All the newspapers had to story—even the *Times* rumbled a bit. It was awfully brave of you—and if you weren't so bent on going back to California to make this movie they're all talking about I'd ask you to come to Ireland with me when I go there on a visit next month. Are you sure you can't fly out for a few days at least? Every little outcry helps, you know!" Venetia had done some acting herself—with her low, dramatic voice and equally dramatic looks she usually played the part of a sexy female spy/aristocrat, with little or no scruples, who always succumbed to a more unscrupulous hero. No—correction. Hero was passé. It was male protagonist. Webb's role in *Greed for Glory*, while she, unbelievably, was to be the female protagonist.

Venetia was staring at her in a puzzled fashion. "Anne? I think I've lost you somewhere along the line. Did you hear what I just said?"

"Oh yes . . ." Anne said vaguely. "But I really don't think

I'll be able to." Suddenly, stupidly, she had an impulse to giggle. Especially since Venetia was looking so *intense*, and she remembered the same look on Venetia's face at one of her parties, when she was being screwed by two of her guests. At the time Anne had found the whole scene morbidly fascinating—and a little frightening as well. She felt the same way about her predicament right now. Those men hadn't been playing. And even Venetia actually believed that she . . . She ought really to tell Venetia that she had nothing to do with the leak to the press, but what good would that do? They could all believe what they bloody well wanted to—even Craig, her gallant rescuer. For the second time in her life she was going to run away from all the unpleasantness that threatened her.

But it was impossible to run away when they went back to the table and Anne saw Webb sitting in the empty chair to Claudia's right, his arm draped carelessly around her shoulder.

He looked up, taking her in. And how could he make his eyes change from cat-yellow to warm gold that way? He must have just come in—Claudia was still arguing with him—a stream of vituperative Italian spilling from between her full red lips even as she leaned against him, making sure he was aware of her breasts pressed against his side.

"Here comes Annie, the love of my life. I've missed you, Annie."

Anne felt herself pinioned to the spot by their concerted looks—all showing varying degrees of emotion. Even Venetia.

Oh damn him! Why did Webb always create such scenes? And yet she couldn't seem to stir when, leaving Claudia open-mouthed, he walked deliberately over to Anne. He looked at Venetia first.

"You must be Venetia Tressider. Hello, Venetia." He was drunk, he had to be. He kissed Venetia's half-open mouth very lightly and turned to Anne, "Hi, baby."

Belatedly she tried to struggle when he put his arms around her. What did he think he was doing? Too late then. His tender-hard mouth already claimed hers, rendered her helpless. Possession. Hadn't she thought that the first time Webb took her hand in his? It was diabolical, this power he had over her senses. But only her mind screamed out in protest as she found herself kissing him back; her body responding to the pressure of his. Damn them all—let them watch!

Easy to think that while Webb was kissing her. But afterwards there were the other eyes to be met—Yves Pleydel's cynical "Bravo, *mon chèr!*" Karmin's scowl and Carol's elevated eyebrows. Jim Markham looked stunned, Claudia on the verge of erupting. Only Harris, a slight smile on his lips, was his usual urbane, diplomatic self.

"As Yves just pronounced—bravo, Webb! But why don't you let Anne sit down and finish her dinner? Venetia love . . ."

Thank God for Harris! He handled Claudia as well as he had handled the girl called Tanya a long time ago. She had started to say something, her voice high, when Harris nodded at Yves, and her long-suffering ex-husband whispered something sharply in her ear.

"They're old friends? And that is how old friends greet each other in America?" Yves said something else that made her subside—turning her shoulder deliberately to Webb. "Karim— what a very masculine name! Is it true what I have heard about you?"

He laughed, after a long, smoldering glance in Anne's direction. "That depends. What have you heard? Shall you find out?"

Harris leaned across the table to engage Venetia in conversation. One of her causes that he just might back. Anne was only aware of Webb, holding her hand—holding her eyes with his.

"I called you this evening. No answer. Not even your obliging roommate!"

"Did you?" She tried to keep her voice from shaking. "But

I heard that you were busy somewhere else this evening. Violet . . ."

"Damn you, Annie. Why do you make me so mad? I had a date I couldn't break, short of causing an unpleasant diplomatic incident. But I got away as soon as I could."

She swallowed her wine too fast, almost choking; hating him when his eyes started to crinkle with amusement.

"Stop it! Why did you have to make a—a public exhibition of me? What do you think you're doing now? You . . ."

"I want you, Annie-love. And I guess this is my crude way of showing it." His eyes narrowed at her. "When I want something I usually go after it. A hangover from my street-fighting days, I guess. I'm snake-bit. I don't want to play the usual stupid games with you, baby." He talked to her quietly, as if they were alone, and Anne felt her heart pounding heavily as she tried to fight this new, strange mood of his, knowing that it was just an impulse—Webb never meant anything he said to a woman—not for too long anyway!

She shook her head, trying to refute her own crazy feelings; she felt herself stretched taut between letting go and resisting.

"Webb—then don't! Because I'm not very good at playing the kind of games you're used to." Seeing the look in his face, she whispered despairingly, "It won't work, Webb! We're too different. There's a physical thing between us, I can't deny that, can I? But it isn't going to last and I—I'm not prepared for being torn apart. Another Claudia, another one of a string. I've got to belong to myself, don't you understand that?"

"Hey, you two! We're all going to Annabell's to dance. Coming along?" Carol's green eyes were unusually dark; her ringed fingers rested lightly on Jamie Markham's sleeve.

It was like that other time in Carol's hotel suite when Webb had walked in and carried her off. Harris! Harris had brought her here. What would he think? His face was inscrutable.

"You must do what you feel like, Anne. If you're tired, Webb can take you home." He was giving her an out, which surprised her slightly. And everyone but Carol and Jim seemed to have changed partners. It was Claudia and Karim; Yves and Venetia. It didn't matter. Right from the beginning, when Webb had walked over and kissed her, she had known how the evening would end, hadn't she?

"Call me tomorrow, will you, Anne?" Harris made it easy. He kissed Anne lightly, squeezing her cold hand. "Anne— you're going to be a great actress. Keep that in mind, will you? And call me whenever you can. I'd like to have your attorney look over the contract I've drawn up for you."

Webb turned back from making his casual farewells to the others, taking her arm, and Anne could finally let the tension drain from her body, giving way to what was inevitable.

Chapter Sixteen

SHE SURFACED SLOWLY to morning with the sound of a telephone shrilling in her ears and the feel of Webb's arm reaching over her body.

"Shit! What time is it anyhow? I thought I told them noon!"

Anne's eyes felt gritty when she tried to blink them into focus. The telephone wire stretched tautly across her breasts where Webb's arm had been a moment before as he turned over onto his back, still swearing.

"Yeah?" And then his face changed, muscles tightening as he seemed to come wide awake. "What? Look, Caro, if this is one of your cute little tricks, I'll . . ." And suddenly Anne was wide-awake too, all the way, watching Webb's face. "Tell me again—slowly this time, huh?" And suddenly, explosively, "Sure Anne's here with me! And I'll tell her. Will you try to calm down, dammit? Look—call Harris. Take a couple of tranquilizers—I'll call you back as soon as I can."

He slammed the receiver back into its cradle, his body leaning over Anne's, staying there unmoving for a while, until her uneasy stirring seemed to snap him back to reality.

"Webb . . . ?" She could hardly pronounce his name, knowing suddenly, instinctively that something had happened. Something bad, that Webb didn't want to tell her about. His arms cradled her. No passion in his embrace this time, no fierce need or wanting, although he held her closely and tightly for all that.

171

"Annie—oh Christ, love! I think I'm going to make a habit of kidnapping you from now on! Hold tight, will you?"

"What happened? What is it?" She felt as if she screamed the words, her mind already starting to go numb in preparation for the shock he was about to deal her.

"Violet. I'm sorry, baby. She's dead." And now the numbness spread from her brain, all over her body, as she listened to words without wanting to understand them. "They—someone broke into your apartment last night. I guess she was alone or else she surprised them. The police patrol saw the lights blazing and a broken window so they checked. They found everything torn apart, and—her."

Mercifully, he didn't give her details. Driven by morbid urge, Anne was to read those later in the newspapers. The words that Webb had left unsaid repeating themselves over and over in her head like hammerblows. "It might have been you, Anne!" Should have been—would have been perhaps if Webb hadn't . . . Why—why, dear God? Questions screamed across her mind, over and over without the release of knowing the answers.

Violet was dead in her place. Bright so-alive Violet who had always loved life so and laughed a lot and talked too much. Violet sitting by the fire drying her hair, shaking her burnished curls loose. Don't think about it!

The doctor who gave her sedatives and shook his head over her told her that. So did Craig, pale-faced and shaken. There was an inquest—the verdict "Death by person or persons unknown." Something out of an Agatha Christie novel.

Burglars, everyone said. There had been a rash of them recently. Keep your doors and windows locked; call the police immediately if you hear any unusual sounds. What good did all the warnings do Violet?

The funeral was quiet—very private. Violet's parents wept, and even Duncan was suspiciously red-eyed. Webb didn't go —he hadn't really known Violet. It was Craig who went with

Anne, holding her arm tightly, protectively. Just as if he expected she might blurt out all her suspicions right there.

"Those men! Craig, you weren't there at first. You don't know how horrible it was!"

Craig, acting in part as her attorney, had warned her not to talk. Not to *anyone*. Emphasis on that last word. And since that terrible morning, when the ringing of the telephone had brought shock and terror into her life, she had stayed with Webb; so she knew what Craig meant. It made her angry, and brought on a scene she wished afterwards hadn't happened.

"That wasn't what you told me when that horrible man Barnes was questioning me—*interrogating* would be a better word for it! Nor when that Scotland Yard man—"

"Anne, you're being deliberately obtuse! Those men were merely performing their duty. But anyone else . . ."

"You mean Webb, don't you? Oh, let's be honest, Craig! You didn't mind my seeing Harris Phelps, but from the beginning you've been against my seeing Webb. *Right* from the beginning. And every time we're together, something comes up —first it was Tanya and Carol's ex-husband, so the company had to leave town. And now . . ."

She heard Craig's voice sharpen and could have bitten her tongue out the next minute.

"*Tanya?* Ted Grady? All right, Anne. Don't back off now. And if you don't want to explain, I can easily find out, you know!" It was the nearest Craig had ever come to threatening her. His face wore the appraising, slightly suspicious look of a stranger. Of course, Craig *had* to be working for or with her father—his friendship with Duncan (and Duncan worked for the CIA, as hard as that was to imagine) and the way Barnes and his cohorts had grudgingly accepted him as a colleague, knowing who he was . . . All the little implications had escaped her when she was still so upset, or she hadn't wanted to see, perhaps. Everything came rushing at her at once, almost stunning her. She must have been blind!

"Anne, don't you realize you're playing with fire? I'm trying to protect you, whether you want to believe that or not. And everything—every little detail—you can tell me can help. For Christ's sake!"—he looked as if he wanted to shake her— "Will you stop hiding your head in the sand? It's been difficult—you've *made* it difficult from the beginning—for me to discuss Webb Carnahan with you. Anything I said could be twisted around, you see. Jealousy, hurt pride—and yes, damn you, I felt all those things! So I tried to keep out of it, keep away from you. But now, whether you hate me for it or not, I've got to speak out. He's dangerous for you, Anne. And not just for the obvious reasons. You've got to explain what you meant by that last statement you made—or I'm going to have to find out myself. I think it would be easier all around if you told me."

There was something stern and unusually decisive about Craig now. An inquisitor, trapping her into a corner she'd backed into all by herself.

Taking a deep breath, Anne tried to explain. Sullenly and almost mutinously, letting her resentment come through clearly. "It was nothing! Just a—a bad scene! You knew about Carol, I know you did. And Tanya—it *wasn't* Webb, if that's what you're thinking. He'd finished with Tanya, he had no reason to . . . anyway, he was with *me* that night! And I thought—I thought it was something that maybe my—my father had arranged! It's just the kind of thing he'd do, isn't it? A subtle way of—of making sure we were broken up. Seeing that the undesirables left town under their *own* steam, so to speak! It *is* the kind of thing he'd do, isn't it? I mean, violence wouldn't matter—what difference do a few little pawns make? It happens all the time, everywhere in the world! Assassinations, violent death, carefully incited riots—violence, violence! It's all you read in the newspapers these days, isn't it?

And it all comes under the name of international politics. It makes me sick, Craig! I suppose just saying that makes me a subversive! Will you add me to your list of undesirables?"

"What a lot of slogans you've learned, Anne! And how little you really know. It's people like your father who are attempting to preserve some semblance of democracy and order in this chaotic world!" Bitterly Craig added, "And just so that people like you and your friends can be free to express themselves. But I'm not on a political platform, Anne. I don't think I need to defend either your father or myself. And I refuse to be sidetracked, if that's what you intended with that dramatic little speech." His eyes narrowed at her, and he was a cold, accusing stranger.

"Let's go back to Webb Carnahan. And—who was she again? Ah yes, Tanya."

"I don't want to discuss it any further, Craig. I've told you what you wanted to know, and now I . . ."

He didn't appear to have heard her half-angry, half-frightened protests.

"Sit down, Anne, and hear me out. I've kept Barnes from questioning you again in his own inimitable way. And I don't believe you had anything to do with that leak—not on purpose, that is. But there are a few facts—"

Goaded, Anne cried out wildly, "Don't be condescending, for God's sake! You don't believe . . . because I'm Richard Reardon's daughter? Caesar's daughter, and therefore above reproach? You kept Barnes off my back, but you put me on trial yourself, is that it? Well, I didn't do it. I'm innocent—isn't that the classic phrase? Because whatever I might have suspected, I didn't *know*. I just happened to be too wrapped up in my own life and my own affairs and the feeling that I was free to handle them—I thought!—to pay too much attention. But I was never really free, was I? Just let out on a long enough leash to give me that illusion. And when someone Big Daddy doesn't approve of came back into my life, then it was time to pull it in, wasn't it? Was that why you came to London, Craig? Because you knew Webb would be here and you were afraid we'd meet again?"

"I won't dignify that with an answer, Anne. And you're not on a leash, as you put it. But you are your father's daughter, and that's an inescapable fact you have to learn to live with. It makes you vulnerable, whether you like *that* idea or not! Dammit!" Craig paced angrily from one end of the room to the other, coming back to stand directly in front of her, looking down into her tear-stained, raging face. "Do you think I enjoy having to be the one to tell you this? Especially knowing what you will think of me afterwards? But it has to be done, and especially *now*, Anne. When far too many unpleasant things have begun to happen." He put his hand up as if to ward off the angry questions he saw in her eyes.

"No. Please hear me out this once without interruption. And then I'll leave you to draw your own conclusions. And forgive me if I'm brutally blunt—I have to be. Have you ever wondered what a man like Webb Carnahan saw in you? Beyond a quite natural sexual attraction, that is? Did you notice his reaction when he found out, as he must have, that you were Richard Reardon's daughter? God, Anne! Your face gives you away, you know that? And I have to give you certain information that's very confidential, information I should not be divulging at all. Carnahan has reasons—*he* thinks—to hate your father. It's a long story, and I can't go into it all, but before he got into acting, he used to work for us. And so did his wife."

Anne felt her throat go dry; she could not have spoken, even if she had wanted to. She listened to Craig, hearing his unemotional voice go on and on. And yet only part of it registered—while another part of her mind kept repeating over and over, a metronome beating time with her pulses, "Have you ever wondered what a man like Webb Carnahan saw in you?"

Craig went on inexorably: "And then his wife died. On a mission she volunteered for. He blamed your father for letting her take it, and he got out of the Service. Went into acting—something he was always good at!"

There were gaps in her consciousness, it seemed; she didn't want to hear, but an awful fascination made her listen all the same.

"How do you think he made it to the top? True, he has talent, a certain charisma—isn't that what the fan magazines call it? A reputation with women. But he also has influential connections behind the scenes. Did he ever speak to you about his sister? I don't suppose he did. She's married to Vittorio Gentile. And he happens to be a very powerful member of that organization that is loosely and collectively called the Mafia."

They were in Duncan's office, Craig having borrowed it for what he termed a serious and very important discussion with Anne. And now the once familiar surroundings—the carpet that was worn in spots, the usual untidy clutter on Dunc's desk surmounted by his overflowing ashtray, pipe still sitting in it—seemed alien and uncomfortable.

Several long moments passed, punctuated only by the distant sound of the traffic outside, while Anne stared disbelievingly at Craig.

"No, no, *no*, Craig! This time you've really gone too far!" She gave a hysterical giggle, almost choking on it. "Do you really expect me to believe that Webb—that Webb is a member of the Mafia? Just because his *sister* happens to be married to an Italian? I mean, Webb is half Italian *himself*! He told me."

"How much did he tell you, Anne? Damn, do you think I didn't realize how melodramatic all I've said might sound to you? And yet, it *had* to be said. It's a responsibility I took upon myself, Anne, in spite of—well, never mind. The important thing is that you must be very careful. I'm not accusing

Webb Carnahan of any overt involvement in the activities of the Mafia. I'm merely warning you that he has reasons—or so he believes—to hate your father and everything he stands for. He can't hurt Richard Reardon, but he *can* involve Reardon's daughter in a lot of . . . to put it bluntly, very nasty publicity. He can involve you with people and things that could injure not only your father but also a great many other people. And you could be very badly hurt, Anne! Don't you see that? As long as you persist in this blind infatuation, that I'm sure is shared by many other women. Are you going to cling to him until he tires of you or has no more use for you? I find it hard to believe that you're the same girl I married—and cared for a great deal! And I still cannot believe that you would let your resentment of your father carry you so far that you would deliberately set out to tear down everything he's built up all these years. The image of an upright and honest man who's given his life to protecting and furthering his country's interests. And whatever you think, or your friends may try to tell you, that is what he's honestly tried to do!"

Anne tried to speak, but Craig, openly angry now, cut her off ruthlessly.

"I cannot make up my mind about you, Anne! As to whether you're merely a rebellious child or honestly deluded! At this point, I don't even know why I've bothered to try to explain matters to you—or why I should keep trying to protect you from the consequences of your own foolishness. You're in an extremely vulnerable position, you know, and men like Barnes don't give up easily." He rubbed at his jaw fiercely, gray eyes blazing. "Anne, you're in the middle of a very ugly mess that could get worse. We haven't yet got to the bottom of that information leak to the press—or what really happened to Violet, and why!"

"But you told me it was . . . *burglars!*" she said in a whisper.

"I know what I told you! And I'm telling you too much as it is. That's why I chose Dunc's office for our talk, because I'm sure it isn't bugged. Listen, I didn't want to frighten you, but if it's the only way to make you see reason . . . Do you realize that if Violet's death *was* murder, there may be certain people who might think you know more than you do? Who might think she confided in you? Or who meant to find you and found her instead? You might be the target for kidnappers or worse—you could be in real, very real, *danger,* Anne. And don't let your recent bemusement with the movie industry blind you to reality. This is no screen entertainment, with actors playing roles. This is the real thing. And the worst part is that you won't be able to tell the bad guys from the good guys, my dear." And then he repeated to her white-faced silence, his voice suddenly heavy, "Won't you please go home, Anne? Go back to the States where you belong. You're internationally established as a model now, you could get work in New York—or anywhere else, for that matter, if that is what you really want to do. But you'd be safer—and out of all this mess!"

Chapter Seventeen

It was strange how everything could seem exactly the same—the afternoon as ordinary as any other—when it wasn't. There was the usual traffic snarl: red doubledecker buses towering over the horn-tooting tangle of cars of all shapes and sizes; motorscooters and bikes threading their way nimbly and riskily through the unevenly moving stream of vehicles. The sky was grayish—"typical London weather," all the tourists would say, nodding resignedly as they brought out their umbrellas, wanting to blend in with the hurrying crowds in their light-weight raincoats. Shop windows bloomed with light. On an afternoon like this, Violet would have said, shivering exaggeratedly, "Do let's windowshop awhile, shall we? And then we can grab a bite to eat at a Lyon's Corner House before we get back. It'll save having to fix supper if no one calls!"

Don't think about Violet—not now! Think about anything else instead. Craig, sitting beside Anne, gripping the steering wheel firmly, sounded incongruously normal as he said, "Where shall I drop you off?"

And Anne spoke calmly, although her fingers were tense on the leather strap of her purse: "At Carol's, please. If it's not too much trouble."

Had it only been that morning that Carol had called? Waking her up, thankfully, from a recurrence of the Dream—the one that used to wake her up screaming as a child, but only sobbing and shaking when she was old enough to tell herself it was only a dream, she was being silly!

"Let's have tea this afternoon, darling! Proper English style —little sandwiches and cakes and all! I haven't seen you in ages, and it's really time you stopped brooding, you know!"

Sheer thankfulness at being awakened before the worst part of the Dream had made Anne accede almost too eagerly. She'd begun to hate being alone, and Webb had left early, to catch a flight for Ireland.

"Some damned publicity stuff—I have a lousy press agent. Back to my roots and all that shit." And almost offhandedly, "Want to come along, baby?"

But she'd already promised Craig she'd meet him, and catching her slight hesitation, he had shrugged, turning away from her to strip off his pants before he went into the bathroom to shower. "It was a dumb idea, and you'd be bored anyhow, just trailing along. I should be back tomorrow night in any case, but I'll call you, huh? Maybe if it's not too late you can pick me up at the airport." She heard the shower turned on, and by then it was already too late to say she'd changed her mind, that she'd much rather come with him. Pride—or the arrogance he'd accused her of creeping in? They couldn't live out of each other's pockets just because they'd sort of drifted into living together, could they? And Webb didn't like feeling tied down, she must remember that. Neither did *she*—cling to that thought for her own sake!

He hadn't brought the subject up again, and now here she was, at the door of Carol's apartment, with Craig waiting solicitously until Carol opened the door. And she was inside, safely, with her mind still numb.

"Did I break up a cosy little afternoon assignation, darling?"

With difficulty, Anne forced herself to meet Carol's mocking emerald gaze. Why was she here? She was in no mood for the usual light rapier-crossing with Carol. She needed to be alone, to think . . . but could she take that just yet?

Carol's voice sharpened with something like concern. "Anne! Is something wrong? You look like hell, sweetie. Sickening for a cold? Brr!" She shivered. "How I *hate* this lousy climate! Why do people choose to *live* here?"

In Dublin, Webb Carnahan was thinking almost the same thing. Socked in. Some goddamn freak weather, bringing with it a fog blanket that closed the airport to all traffic. Who knew when it would clear up? Shrugs, eyes rolled up expressively: "Might as well have a drink while we're waiting, what do you say?" Except for a few impatient Americans like himself, no one else seemed to give a damn.

It didn't help his mood to find out, after he'd waited ten minutes to get to a phone booth, that Anne wasn't back yet. Partying it up with good old buddy Craig? He swore under his breath as he slammed down the phone, changing his mind about waiting it out at the airport.

Little Annie had the right to do whatever the hell she pleased, and so did he. Webb's eyes, narrowed with frustration and a kind of anger he could neither understand nor explain to himself, came to rest on a porcelain oval face framed by black hair. Typically Irish; why hadn't he noticed that before? Dark-blue eyes laughed into his; the shiny red mouth smiled teasingly. She didn't pretend surprise, which was in her favor.

"Hello, Webb Carnahan!" Venetia Tressider said. "I was hoping we might run into each other here. It looks as if we're both stranded for the night, doesn't it?"

Two young women who had been whispering to each other, giggling nervously as they watched him, now stared openly and enviously as Webb took Venetia's arm, tucking it possessively under his own. They weren't to know that for a moment his fingers had gripped hard enough to make Venetia wince.

"Hi," he said pleasantly. "Are you going to give me a chance to find out what happy coincidence brought you here?"

Regaining some of her aplomb, Venetia let her breasts brush against his arm.

"Darling," she murmured, pouting slightly, "it wasn't coincidence! I followed you! After all, the newspapers did give a lot of publicity to the fact that you were going to be here. And I'm used to going after what I want. You haven't been to a single one of my parties yet—and I give the most exciting parties in town, or hadn't you heard? Hasn't Anne told you?"

Grimly, not letting his face show any reaction at all, Webb kept walking, forcing her to keep up with his long strides.

"Why don't you tell me instead?"

She sounded slightly breathless. "Ooh! Must we walk so fast? Where are we going? Listen, I have a car. And a lovely warm room at a hotel not too far from here. I always try to think ahead, you see. Lovely fog! I simply adore fog and peat fires. What do *you* like, Webb Carnahan?"

Slanting a look down at her glowing, upturned mouth, he let his questions rest. For the moment. Time enough after they got away from the querulous, jostling mob in here. But in the meantime, he held Venetia's supple, yielding body close, slipping one arm about her waist under her fur-lined leather jacket, giving her a lazy smile. "I think I like beautiful women who aren't afraid to go after what they want."

He caught the triumphant catlike curve of her lips, and let her draw her own conclusions as they walked on, fencing lightly with words that were meant to add spicy titillation to the encounter between them that would surely follow. Webb had met women like Venetia before; the scenario always followed the same pattern, leading to the same final scene—the firelight inside the room, the fog pressing against the windows outside, the hasty undressing with a certain amount of aggression on her side as if to show she meant to stay in charge. An unspoken challenge: "Are you really as good as your reputation? Show me, baby!"

But something had suddenly brought the old jungle instinct, so long dormant, to life; tiny alarm signals screamed along his quickened nerves. Something was wrong, although Venetia Tressider, on the surface, was running true to type. It was all too pat, her following him to Ireland (Where had she hidden herself earlier today? Why hadn't she brought herself to his attention earlier?) and her turning up at the airport just when, by coincidence, all flights out had been canceled. What if they *hadn't* been?

There had been a time when he had lived, and survived, on instinct alone; trusting in the same tingling, nerve-end radar he felt right now. Tense inside, his muscles well trained enough not to show any signs of it, Webb let his eyes move quickly and casually over the crowd that still hemmed them in. No familiar faces—but he hadn't really expected to see any. A few stares; but he was used to that; had learned to tune out the curious stares of the public. Nothing out of the ordinary on the surface. And yet he could not get rid of the notion that Venetia had come to Ireland for more than just a fuck. And the crazy, unexplainable feeling that all this was somehow tied up with events in London—with Anne. All the questions her evasions and his pride hadn't let him ask her.

Craig Hyatt, for instance. What the hell was Craig doing back in her life, acting as her protector? Protecting her from what? More to it than just the fact that she was Richard Reardon's daughter and he was Reardon's right-hand man. Why hadn't he come on the scene earlier if that was it? And then there was—or had been—Violet. Poor Violet, poor butterfly, who had been Anne's best friend and had also worked for Duncan Frazier. Too many things, all happening at once. The big press leak, and Violet's murder. Anne's being followed, being questioned by British Intelligence. And the gallant, ubiquitous Craig coming to her defense. *Advising* her.

"About what, Annie? Or against whom?" He'd tried to get something out of her, but she'd turned his questions away almost hysterically.

"He's only *helping* me, Webb! Please—I don't want to talk about it anymore!"

Funny how whenever he met Anne, things began to happen. And trust Caro to point that out in her sweet, unsubtle way.

Over the years he'd learned how to shut Caro up. But then, even Caro had been acting differently lately. After the flaming rows they'd had during the shooting of *Bad Blood*, ending with her screaming that she'd never make another film with him, that he was a dirty, low-down son of a bitch, and she would never speak to him again, nor pose for any damned publicity stills with him either . . . she usually took a lot of persuasion to climb down from her high horse once she'd climbed on it; but she'd surprised him for a change by being friendly. Even to the surprising point of not throwing one of her usual jealous tantrums when he and Anne had started up again. More goddamn puzzle pieces!

"Here we are at last, darling! Thank God—that crawling mass of people was starting to give me claustrophobia!"

Webb felt Venetia's exaggerated shudder against his body, and felt his nerves tauten, even while he grinnned at her mockingly.

"Was that why I didn't see you earlier today, while we were shooting all those pictures?"

She gave him a wide-eyed look through black-fringed eyes.

"But I don't like competition, love. That's why I waited to catch you alone!"

She was looking down the fog-shrouded street, frowning as if she'd lost her bearings, shivering slightly.

There was a long string of taxis, yellow headlights and dark shapes, and a general scramble as other disappointed travelers began to pour out of the air terminal, whistling and waving for attention.

"Looks like a rugby scrimmage, doesn't it? I had to park my car some streets down. Do you mind walking?"

Now? Too many people around yet. Too many lights. And he was following his instincts again, improvising.

"Listen, love, if I remember right, there's a pub across the street. And I could use a drink—maybe some *real* Irish coffee for a change. It'll make that long walk you promised me seem shorter."

Without giving her time to protest, he started her off across the street, dodging taxicabs and the buses chartered by harried airline officials.

"But—but I thought we'd have a nightcap in my room!"

"Why waste time on a nightcap when we get there? In any case, I have to make a telephone call."

"You could have made that from my room, too!" Venetia almost snapped the words out. .

"It's private, baby."

"Oh!" He heard her sucked-in breath. "You really are the bastard they say you are, aren't you?"

They had gained the opposite sidewalk by some miracle, and Webb, dropping the banter from his manner, swung her around suddenly, backing her shoulders up against the wall of the pub they'd headed for.

Not much light here—a streetlamp some yards down the street on one side, and on the other a faint glow of light from the stained-glass fanlight of the front door. There was a slight vibration through the brick wall that told of a noisy group inside, and occasionally the door swung open as someone went in or out. But no one glanced at them as Webb moved his body against hers, holding her immobile while his fingers moved caressingly up the column of her arched throat, feeling the sudden turmoil of her pulsing arteries before he cupped her face.

He said softly, "I guess they were right, sweetheart. Whoever 'they' were. So why don't you save us both time we could be spending in a better way and tell me all about it? Like how you knew just where to find me, and who sent you, and why? You see, I'm also a suspicious bastard—maybe they forgot to mention that."

"I don't know . . ."

The pressure of his fingers tightened, digging into the soft skin of her face, and Venetia gave a frightened whimper. A few moments ago she'd been very sure of herself, and now . . . With an effort, she whispered, "Have you gone crazy? I told you . . ."

"Well, why don't you tell me everything now and get it over with? Some kinds of surprises I really dig, baby, and some I don't. You didn't have to come all the way over here to get screwed, now did you? Last time we met, you already had a stud."

She tried to move her head and gasped with pain, which goaded her into retorting viciously, "And now he's screwing your little lay! Right now, probably. She wasn't home when you called her, was she? Karim's used to getting what he wants, too, and they're probably rehearsing some of the better scenes from your new picture. I simply thought we might console each other, that's all! Or do you always fall in love with your leading ladies?"

His face gave nothing away; his mind seemed to have become coldly detached. "You'll have to explain all that later, Venetia. For now, let's stick to the point, huh? Like tonight particularly, and what else you had in mind besides that peat fire."

"Let go! I could scream, and there are people around . . ."

"Sure." Surprising her, he did, moving back so abruptly that she almost fell. "I guess I'll just go have my drink and get back to the terminal. Maybe I'll see you around later."

"No—wait!" She clutched at his arm, stopping him in midstride. "Webb, you really are a bastard! But I can't let you leave me alone. I—I'm frightened! I have been ever since Violet Somers was . . . Oh God! I know I'm being watched, and I thought that if you were with me and they thought that we'd *arranged* to meet here—well, what's wrong with that?" In the face of his implacable silence her words spilled out, low and almost hysterical. "I did want to make it with you. You knew that, didn't you? And I knew you were going to be here . . . I can't be alone tonight . . . if you were with me and they thought . . . well, it would seem *natural*, wouldn't it? For both of us."

"Go on."

She shivered, moving closer to him. "Oh God! I wasn't supposed to tell you anything, unless you—turned me down, or had something else planned. Nino Gennaro. Big Nino. Does that name mean anything to you?"

It gave him a jolt. Big Nino. Zio Nino. Presents when he came to visit—his father scowling, his mother all smiles. "It's your uncle. You be respectful now, he's a powerful man!" Nino always wore expensive suits. His automobile was long and dark and sleek, like the men who always lounged beside it. Smell of cologne and hair oil and his deep voice, cautioning pedantically in the accent that Webb's mother had never quite lost herself: "You stay offa the streets, you hear? You should be thinking of a profession, getting an education. You become a smart lawyer, maybe, eh? And keep going to church."

But his education had been reform school and street fighting, and after that, his parole officer—a woman. Reaching him in a different way from the other girls and women of his experience. He remembered that she'd always worn perfume, and pretty, feminine clothes, disdaining to dress down for the kids she had to work with.

Marianne. Even her name had sounded exotic and different, like she was. She ignored his swaggering rudeness and his sullen silences. "I can't help you if you don't want to be helped, of course. But it does seem like a waste, doesn't it? You have a very impressive scowl—and an even nicer smile, when you let it show. Have you thought of enrolling in acting school? Though, of course, that might be tough—you'd have to learn to talk differently, for one thing."

He'd begun by resenting her for telling him that and ended

by listening to all the different accents around him, starting to absorb them. Not long after that, they'd pulled down the building where he'd lived, forcing them to move, and somewhere along the line he'd developed ambition. Maybe just a stubborn determination to show them all, particularly Marianne.

Jesus Christ! That had been a long time ago, and he'd almost forgotten! Traveling on the subway as far as it would take him, watching people and listening to them talk. Hitchhiking further later on—starving sometimes. But learning. Coming back home one time to find his mother crying, holding a newspaper in her hands. Zio Nino had been arrested on some made-up charge—it had to be made up, he was a good man! They were deporting him to Italy . . .

Webb said flatly, looking into Venetia's strained white face with dark smudges under her eyes, "What does the name mean to *you*, baby?"

She shook her head, fingers still clinging to his arm.

"I swear I don't know! Except that a—a man I know, this friend of mine, told me I should mention it if you got leery. That's all he said, honestly! You can call from the pub if you don't believe me—I have a number. You can ask him anything you want—whatever you need to convince you . . ."

There were two coin telephone booths inside the crowded pub, both empty. Webb ordered drinks, flirted casually with the barmaid, and looked at his watch. "Damn! Gotta make that call before it's too late. Watch our drinks, sweetheart."

He could watch Venetia from the hot glass booth. She was sipping her drink and flirting in her turn with one of the musicians. And the danger signals were still going off in his mind.

A cautious male voice answered on the first ring, speaking with a thick brogue.

"Yes?"

"This is Carnahan. I'm a friend of Venetia's."

"Ah yes." No surprise in the deep voice. "There is someone here who would like to speak to you. You're alone?"

"Yeah."

And then another voice he hadn't heard in years—the same heavy accent he remembered.

"Antonio?" No one but Nino had ever called him by the Italian version of his second name. "It's good to hear you, fine to know you've done so well, eh? Now"—briskly, giving him no time to answer "—you come to see me and we talk. But be careful, you hear?" A chuckle. "I am glad that the woman did not find you too easy to convince. It makes me proud."

Chapter Eighteen

EXHAUSTION SEEMED TO HAVE SEEPED into Anne's bones, melting them. What would happen if she fell asleep right here on Carol's couch, while everyone else was still talking? Carol and Harris and Yves and even Karim, who had suddenly turned up, smiling his white-toothed grin. Carol had invited everyone to her tea party . . . and the tea had turned into hors d'oeuvres and cocktails somewhere along the line; why try to remember when?

Publicity—the new movie. Harris and Yves were arguing about just how much publicity. She heard other names mentioned for the major roles. A South American playboy, for instance, who raced cars and loved hunting. She'd heard the name before; it brought an image of smiling magazine pictures. But just for an instant. God, she was tired! Everything was catching up with her at once.

"Drink your martini up, darling. I have another one on the way." Carol was good at playing the gracious hostess.

Harris, sitting by her, stroking her arm. "Anne, can you be ready to leave for California in three days? You're becoming a nervous wreck, love, and the change of scenery will be good for you. You can relax, laze in the sun for a week before we start shooting *Greed for Glory*. And I know you're going to be great."

She must have answered him, because he leaned forward to kiss her lightly. "I'm going to make all the arrangements. You don't have to worry about anything—will you remember that?"

Everyone was insistent that she mustn't worry. Even Craig,

who wanted her to leave London—leave England. Well, it was all working out that way, wasn't it? But where was Webb? Anne remembered, belatedly, that Webb didn't *know* yet. He'd wanted Claudia to play *her* part; or so Carol had said. But surely he wouldn't mind when he found out? Because he hadn't been seeing Claudia recently; he'd spent most of his time with *her*. And she didn't care what Craig said—she wouldn't believe any of it! Tired of people telling her about Webb, warning her . . . if Webb didn't want to be with her, he wouldn't be. Keep it simple and uncomplicated, Anne!

"Hello, lovely thing. You look very lonely, sitting here all by yourself. Just like you need company." Karim put his arm around her shoulders, easing her against him; and it would take too much effort to pull away. "Listen," he whispered, his warm breath tickling her ear, "why don't we go away from here and be together? I want you—and even more when you look like a frightened gazelle!"

Rousing herself, Anne gave him a reproachful look. "Why do you keep talking that way?" she murmured. "Venetia's probably waiting up for you!"

"Venetia? Hah! I am not her property. And in any case, she's not around. She's gone to visit some old aunt of hers in Ireland. I didn't ask her when she would be back, because I did not care. Is that clear?"

Ireland! Like a needle prick the thought stiffened her, waking her out of her torpor. Coincidence? Webb didn't need to pretend, not with her. And he'd asked her to go along with him, hadn't he?

She realized suddenly that Carol was turning away from the door, having seen Harris and Yves out. She looked at them with her eyebrows raised. "Well, you two? Made up your minds yet?"

"I have made mine up!" Karim said positively.

At about the same time, Anne shrugged away from his too-tight arm, saying, "I think I've had too much to drink. I'd really better go back."

"Back to *where*, darling?" Carol sounded impatient as she crossed the room, the skirt of her long hostess gown outlining her magnificent legs. "Look, let me call first, will you? I don't care for the idea of your being alone tonight, Anne. I'd never forgive myself if . . ." Switching to a false brightness, she picked up the telephone. "Just hold on a minute, hmm, sweetie? Webb's such an unpredictable bastard, as we both know!"

It seemed ages before Carol put down the receiver with a decided "click."

"Well! I guess he decided to stay on—or catch a later flight. Who knows, with that son of a bitch? But you can stay over here. I've got extras of everything, including bedrooms. And no, baby, I won't listen to any arguments. I mean, it would be *silly*! We'll just leave a message with the desk in case Webb does turn up tonight."

In the end Karim went away disappointed, trying to hide his scowl when he realized Anne meant it. "Well, there will be other times, yes? You may play the coquette—it intrigues me even while it makes me angry! You know that, I think, because you are very feminine. You deny me because you are fascinated, and afraid because you know when the little games we play are ended, I will have you."

"Oh shit! What a character!" Carol pulled a disgusted face. "But at least he doesn't play let's-pretend, does he? Come on to bed, love. You look about ready to pass out!"

She fell asleep almost instantly, wearing a silky nightgown borrowed from Carol. Not giving herself time to miss her own nakedness and Webb's, pressed closely against her.

Unfamiliar skirts twisted around her legs, stopping her from kicking out, from trying to swim frantically to the surface, pale-green and tantalizingly close above her. And as always in her Dream, the sea had her again.

Long streamers of kelp wrapped themselves with insinuating gentleness around her body like the arms of a false lover, holding her down when she would have struck out despairingly for the surface. She was suspended in two places at once. The sand was cold and crunchy under her bare feet, and the seawater chill against her body. She could see her own hair, silvery strands floating around her face. And she knew with a mounting terror that she had to escape, had to get free of the encircling bands of seaweed that tightened, and tightened . . . but they held her fast. She screamed, and knew despairingly that now the water would come rushing into her open mouth. She was drowning, and no one could save her. How could they, when she wasn't supposed to be here and nobody knew?

"Anne! Anne, wake up! Are you okay?"

It was Carol and not Webb bending over her. Carol's long red hair brushed her shoulders. "My God, baby! Do you often have nightmares like that? The way you screamed . . ."

She was all damp with perspiration, even her face. It took her some time to realize she was sobbing uncontrollably. Last time she had had the Dream, Webb had held her close, very tight.

"Annie! Baby, you're safe," he said, soothingly. "What was it?"

"I—I had the nightmare again. The Dream . . ."

"The same one? Hey, didn't your shrink tell you that telling your dreams scares them away? Tell me about it, baby."

"I always go back there in the Dream . . ." Shaky, half-awake whisper.

"Back to *where*? Tell me."

"To the house. Spindrift, where my grandparents lived. Only everyone else called it the Mallory place. My—my mother used to take me there when I was a little girl, and I used to love the ocean, until—until one day . . ." She stopped, swallowed, closing her eyes.

"One day *what*?"

She made herself force the words out. "One day she—drowned. My mother. And I found her first, you see. We'd gone down to the beach together—I *think* we did! But I was waiting for her, and waiting—and she didn't come. I kept waiting. I was afraid to go back up alone, so I ran up and down the beach looking for her and I—I thought it was a piece of driftwood at first, and then I saw her hair . . ."

Turning her face, she'd pressed it against his warm flesh.

"In my Dream," she whispered, her voice muffled, "it's *me* that's drowning. I—I know how it feels, Webb! It happens to *me!*"

"Hush now, that's enough. Don't talk about it anymore, don't think about it, love." Webb's hand stroked her hair gently; she felt him move closer, adjusting his body to hers. Flame through her belly then, as the Dream faded and reality came back.

But this time it wasn't Webb but Carol who hung over her, long nails digging into her shoulder. A different, colder reality. Why couldn't it have been Webb?

Carol shook her, repeating something sharply. "Are you sure you're awake now? Shall I get you some water to drink? You sure had me scared for a moment. I thought there were burglars in here! Want to come in my room with me?"

Carol was treating her like a child! Anne shook her head stubbornly.

"Oh no, I'm fine now, honestly! I'm sorry I woke you up, Carol."

"That's okay." But Carol still looked doubtful. She gave a short laugh. "For a moment there I thought you were still hallucinating off that Colombian Gold we were smoking. Shit, it even sends *me* into a spin, just a couple of drags. You should have let Karim stay, and we could have shared. I understand he's got more than enough to go around!"

Anne swallowed one of Carol's tranquilizers; and this time when sleep overtook her, it was like falling into a long black tunnel. There were no more dreams, and the darkness held her fast until late into the morning.

Webb had still not returned when she tried calling at eleven o'clock, still trying to blink the heavy dregs of sleep from her eyes. The impersonal voice at the desk told her there had been no messages.

"It's so damned typical of him!" Carol snapped, adding briskly, "Well, at least you do have a key, don't you, pet? Give the bastard a shock—get your clothes and move out, why don't you? You could stay here; I'd really love to have you. And Harris will be coming over this afternoon to talk about tickets and travel arrangements and stuff. I think they want to take some pictures tonight, when he makes the big announcement. End of talent hunt, and all that!" She laughed her famous husky laugh. "Christ, I'm starting to sound British, aren't I? I'll be glad to get back home for a nice long rest after this. In time for the Awards. And who knows, this time next year maybe *you'll* be up for an Oscar! It's a crazy upside-down life, baby, but *fun*, as you'll find."

She thrust newspapers, an untidy pile, at Anne without waiting for a reply. "Here, why don't you read these if you want to while you're having your coffee and rolls? Elsie's got your bath running—she's a treasure, and I might just steal her to go back to the States with me."

Where was Webb? Stupid of her to wonder—but if anything had happened . . .

Thank God—nothing! No headlines screaming of an airplane crash. Just more politics: the worsening situation in Belfast, hints that the Irish Republican Army was being secretly financed and supplied with arms by foreign sources.

Anne tossed the papers away, torn between relief and anger. Oh, damn Webb! And damn her weakness for him! Carol was right, she should be sensible for a change and turn the tables on him. Break it off before he did.

But she had still not been able to define her feelings when Craig picked her up, his face carefully blank. "Good old Craig!" Carol had whispered over a bubble of laughter. "He *is* faithful, isn't he? And attentive just at the right times. You're lucky, Anne!" Wasn't that what everyone kept telling her?

*   *   *

"It seems as if everything I've tried to tell you recently has been the wrong thing, Anne," Craig said when they were alone. "And I'm not happy about the role I've been cast in, any more than you are, I'm sure. I'm glad you've made *some* kind of decision, though—as little as I approve of your latest venture! Carol Cochran is honest in her own way, I suppose. Which is more than I can say about that Tressider woman."

"Venetia? Why do you *keep* on bringing her up, Craig?"

His face took on its familiar, guarded look, and he wouldn't answer her directly. "For God's sake, Anne! You're not a naïve child. Venetia Tressider is a wild, misguided woman with too much money and a penchant for causes. Usually the wrong ones. She's headed for trouble, and could drag in everyone she's been associated with. Anne"—he sounded distracted for a moment, smoothing his hair back in an uncharacteristic gesture—"I don't think I've been able to make you understand yet how damned vulnerable you are! There are people who could and would use you without scruple. And whether you like it or not, you're in the middle of a damned ugly situation. The sooner you're out of it, the better and easier for us all. And look, if I've put your back up again, I'm sorry! But it's been a strain—on me, on Duncan, especially after what's happened. On a lot of other people as well. There's almost been a damned diplomatic crisis over this!

"Craig, that's enough!" Her head had begun to ache, and almost unconsciously she began to massage her temples with her fingertips. After last night, this was too much. God, she was so mixed up! What was Craig really trying to say? What was she doing with him? No, she didn't understand.

It was even harder to walk up the familiar staircase under the blank stare of the desk clerk, than to let herself into the suite with her key. Tactfully, Craig had stayed in the lobby. But what was she supposed to do now? Suddenly it all seemed overdramatic, a decision she'd somehow been pushed into. Webb hadn't called . . . but suppose he *had*, and got no answer? Anything could have come up. The fact that Venetia just happened to be visiting relatives in Ireland at the same time was a coincidence. Why was she letting herself be influenced by everyone else?

Looking around the room, so impersonal now the maid had made the rumpled bed, Anne had to sit down, her knees suddenly weak. There was no one to turn to for advice now. Just herself.

"For a change, be the one to do it to him first, Anne. Break off with the bastard!"

Carol (hadn't she been right before?) and Craig. All the examples she'd *seen* of the contemptuous way Webb Carnahan treated women; sloughing them off without even the sop of an excuse when he was tired of them, to move onto someone new. The typical Don Juan. Readings in Abnormal Psychology.

The phone rang then, saving her. Or was it?

Craig—his voice urgent. "Anne? Look—keep the door locked and don't open it. Don't answer any knocks, do you hear?"

"But . . ."

"It's that photographer fellow. He's as slippery as an eel. I wonder how he got back down here so fast? But I'll get rid of him, and then I'll explain. Just hold on . . ."

Craig's explanations were what decided her in the end. Stubborn pride won out over anger and hurt.

Johnnie Bardini (who had knocked a long time and even tried to pick the lock on the door before the hotel detective got rid of him) had flown to Ireland, too, on a hunch. On the same flight as Venetia Tressider. And Webb had spent the night with Venetia—Johnnie had even taken pictures of them strolling hand in hand down the streets together this very morning, before he left. Naturally, after all the publicity that the hot romance between Webb Carnahan and Anne Mallory had gleaned, Johnnie wanted to be the first to photograph Anne's reactions when he told her.

That he didn't get them was thanks to Craig, of course. And thanks later to Harris, who had offered Johnnie a scoop. Pictures of Anne Mallory, who was to be the star in his latest picture, with her *other* co-star, Karim. Hints that she found the handsome Egyptian even *more* fascinating. More pictures, with Harris and Yves Pleydel, both smiling. Yves with his arm about Anne's shoulder, whispering in her ear. And a quote that he found her a fascinating enigma—with much more potential than any of his ex-wives had possessed!

And so Anne's pride was salvaged and she was grateful to Harris, who had stepped in again. But Webb? How would he react?

It was Carol who answered her unspoken questions when she said shrewdly, "I wouldn't worry about Webb, if that's what you're doing, sweetie! He *does* have a contract with Harris, and he wants to do this movie. He can't back off now without making himself look silly—or jealous! I mean, I do know our darling Webb, and he's an actor, a professional." Her eyes gleamed maliciously for a moment. "Maybe he'll take up with Claudia again—if he doesn't find someone else among the extras. Just be glad you finally learned, love!"

Stung, Anne retorted lightly, "Learned? But, Carol darling, I was just practicing, and Webb's such a good teacher, you know!"

Again she caught Carol's surprised, reappraising look, and it helped to quiet the strange mixture of emotions inside her.

She was almost ready to face Webb again. Hoping, beneath her insouciant exterior, that he would act at least halfway civilized. Knowing in her guts that he *wouldn't*, that he'd make it hard for her. But in order to act torrid love scenes with Webb, she had to get him out of her blood. Like Carol, she should cling to hate and disillusionment. Brave words she'd told herself before. But with all of her preparing, Anne was caught off guard by Webb's total nonreaction when they met again.

He walked in late as usual; into the middle of the crowd and the fuss that was going on in Harris's suite at the Dorchester.

Wearing his favorite faded-blue levis and a rough-textured shirt that had to be new—she hadn't seen it before. Alone. She had half-expected him to flaunt Venetia on his arm as he had Claudia less than two weeks ago.

"Hi, Harris. Christ, the traffic coming from the airport was fucking murder! I need a drink. A damn long one."

Anne watched, fascinated, as Johnnie Bardini edged up closer, his camera held protectively. Webb raised one eyebrow, saying without rancor, "Johnnie, you bastard, I ought to kick you right in the ass. You sure get around, don't you?"

"It's my thing, Carnahan, you know that."

"Sure. So you can take my picture now I've got my drink and tell all your avid followers I'm a drunken bum."

"I'd like to take your picture with Anne." Bardini's voice sounded bolder. "How do you feel about having her for your leading lady?"

Webb shrugged. "So how should I feel? I think it's great. Annie's going to make a great actress. She's got everything it takes."

He walked over to her then, brushing an impersonal kiss across her cold lips. "You enjoying all the publicity, baby? Having fun?"

There was no way she could tell what he was thinking or feeling. He might have been a stranger, like Karim, who stayed close to her, touching her possessively when he wasn't posing for the cameras. She had the wierdest sensation that this was part of a movie—everyone acting their parts. Dress rehearsal for the real thing.

Annie's going to make a great actress. She's got everything it takes.

Webb had been a warm stranger, using her. And now he was . . . more like a detached acquaintance. No questions, no explanations, nothing.

And that's the way it is. Who was it who always ended his newscast that way?

PART THREE
THE
PRODUCER

Chapter Nineteen

AND THIS IS THE WAY IT IS, *and is going to be for a long time to come—better get used to it, Anne.*

California. Los Angeles was hot and humid. Layers of smog made the sun seem like an angry red eye, and everyone saying, "Well, you ought to have been here last week! It was beautiful then. This fog will soon burn away."

She missed cool, green England, the unhurried pace of life. But now Anne felt as if she had been taken over, to be pulled apart and carefully put together again until she wasn't really herself but an Image.

She had seen some of the advance publicity already. "Anne Mallory—Top European Model—to Play Lead in *Greed for Glory*, the Best-seller That Has Everyone Talking." She was seen and photographed at all the in places. As she came out of the Palms on Sunset on Harris Phelps's arm, there was old friend Johnnie Bardini waiting outside with the other photographers, giving her a friendly wink before his flash went off, almost blinding her. She became used to the personal, probing questions, too.

"Miss Mallory, is it true you're engaged to Harris Phelps?"

"Your name was linked with Webb Carnahan's in England, wasn't it? How will you feel having him as your leading man?"

And she learned to parry the questions, to keep smiling, giving the appearance of being sure of herself, even when she felt herself crumbling inside.

* * *

Anne and Harris had twin suites, with a connecting door, at the Beverly Wilshire. It had become a routine for him to knock gently before he opened it, then come in to make sure she was settled in for the night and had everything she needed. Sometimes he stayed for a while. She was used to his undemanding, almost comforting lovemaking by now. And sometimes he would only kiss her and leave her alone.

The trouble was, she didn't like being alone, and had taken to swallowing a Valium to put her to sleep after Harris left. Harmless—everyone did it! At least, she wouldn't dream then; wouldn't lie awake moving uneasily, pushing the covers away and pulling them about her shoulders the next moment while myriad unwanted images crowded her mind. Webb . . . why did his name keep coming up? The female reporters studied her enviously and curiously as they asked their questions. Oh, damn him! Why did she have to arm herself against meeting him again? Webb and Venetia—and from there, inevitably, her thoughts would take her to Violet, veering away, not wanting to answer any questions, even to herself.

Two weeks in Los Angeles and then a week at a "cottage" in Malibu—loaned to them by a friend of Harris's. Lying half the day on a private sundeck overlooking the ocean, Anne got an all-over tan that turned her pale skin to gold. No reporters and no public appearances for a change; she had time to study the bulky script that Harris had handed her.

"It's only a draft. We're going to have to cut quite a bit, I'm afraid, to keep within three hours. But it'll give you some idea of how we're adapting the book for the screen. And if some scenes seem a bit . . . risqué, perhaps, you must keep in mind, love, that we'll be doing two versions. One for Europe and one for the States, where it should get an "R" rating."

Why did Harris have to shoot his movie *here*? But of course his reason was logical: realism. The final and most exciting chapters of *Greed for Glory* were set in Spanish-Mexican California. The old presidio of Monterey, a mythical rancho covering hundreds of acres along the Sur coast. And Harris was determined to have authenticity at all costs, as he had explained at a conference he'd called just before they'd left London.

"I'm not going to say that *Greed for Glory* will be another *Gone with the Wind*. I am saying that it will be a landmark motion picture with a modern message, in spite of its historical setting. And I'm going to insist on absolute realism, in every way. We're sticking to the story, too—no changes." He smiled. "I promised Ms. Savage that when I bought her book. Her readers are not going to be disappointed when they see this movie!"

There'd been more—questions and answers. Johnnie Bardini protested because most of the filming was to be closed to the press and the public.

"Is that because of those explicit fuck scenes in the book? You going to keep them all in, Mr. Phelps?"

"You'll just have to wait and see, won't you?" Harris had countered blandly.

Actually, Anne hadn't paid too much attention. She'd felt herself drawn tightly up inside a brittle shell that could break far too easily. Too conscious of Webb across the room from her, lounging in his chair with his legs stretched before him. But for all his lazy attitude, Anne could almost tangibly feel the anger inside him. For some reason, he was furious with her!

Johnnie Bardini had given her a clue when he questioned her slyly: "This big romance between you and Carnahan—was it the real thing gone sour, or just another publicity gimmick?"

Anne had looked back at him without answering before she turned on her heel and walked away, hearing his jeering laughter behind her.

"I have my ways of finding out, Miss Mallory!"

Well, let him! Let him follow her around with his tele-photo lens—for as long as he could.

"Don't worry, Anne," Harris had said soothingly. "No one knows exactly *where* we're going to start filming." He chuckled. "I've let rumors leak that it'll be Mexico—or perhaps Nevada for the desert scenes."

Oh damn, forget it, she thought. *Stop going over it!*

Harris had been busy this last week, and Anne almost enjoyed being alone and on her own with just the sun and the faint sounds of the ocean, safely far below. While she acquired her tan and let herself laze, she tried not to think too far ahead. Wasn't it enough that she was away from the unpleasantness of her last few months in England, not having to worry about being watched and followed? Let Harris take care of everything; he had a knack for it. And he was good to her—protective, taking care of all the little details, *caring.* Uncomplicated.

Anne shifted position, turning onto her stomach to feel the sun warm her back and shoulders. The letters on the page she was reading blurred as she blinked her eyes. A love scene that she would have to play with Webb. Tender, savage, explicit. Dammit, and damn her own memories of him! She must try to remember that this was only a story—a piece of make-believe. He was so good at it. She would show him that she was, too.

Why then, with the heat of the sun penetrating her very bones, did she have to keep remembering? His hands on her, his lips on her. Tawny-gold of his eyes; the way he squinted them at her. Feel of him—harshness of short, curling hair against her breasts—huskiness in his voice when he whispered, "Annie . . . God, Annie, you're so beautiful!"

He hadn't meant any of it. Why was it still so hard for her to accept this? Oh, maybe for a little while, when he'd thought her out of reach. But then there'd been Venetia, a new conquest, another "engagement." How many others had there been since Venetia?

He's consistent in that much at least; he never stays pinned down for long. Thinking that, Anne realized that she had closed her eyes, forgetting the script. Harris's voice brought her back to reality.

"Darling, you're not asleep, are you? You don't have the kind of skin that can take the sun for too long, you know. And you're a temptation, lying there like that, so unaware . . ."

Why did she have to snatch at her towel, spreading it across her thighs as she rolled over? Harris, as understanding as usual, only laughed softly.

"And you're still as modest as a kid of seventeen, aren't you? Never mind, love. I've got good news for you. Everything's set at last and we're leaving tomorrow."

Leaving for where? Harris wouldn't tell her. It was part of the "surprise" that he still hinted at. Like an obedient child, she didn't try to spoil it with too many questions.

Harris Phelps's private Lear jet took off from Los Angeles Airport the next evening; just the two of them as passengers and a uniformed, impassive young man who served drinks and hors d'oeuvres while Harris talked, keeping Anne's attention fixed politely on him so that she didn't have too much time to wonder where they were going. Harris was a dear. Why hadn't she seen that right at the beginning? Why had she wanted forbidden fruit instead? Webb . . . but she was being silly, childish, stupid. Webb had been part of a learning experience she had needed. When she saw him again, she would prove both to him and to herself that it hadn't meant anything. They'd had an affair—so what? "Thanks, Webb darling, for showing me a lot about acting."

It was dark and four martinis later when they landed at a small airport.

Monterey in the summer was colder than she remembered it. But she had been a child then, spending summers with her bored, beautiful mother. It had ended abruptly with that one particular summer from which the Dream stemmed—her mother's death and her grandfather's stroke.

"Why can't you talk about it?" Dr. Haldane had asked gently. And she had cried out wildly, "Because I don't want to —I don't want to!"

She had been happy before, spending her summers by the ocean; hearing it roar like a friendly lion when she lay in her bed at night. Getting wet and dirty and covered with sand, and nobody minding or scolding. Going into Carmel for a shopping treat and ice cream at Swenson's on weekends, with Grandmother introducing her to her friends.

"This is little Anne. My granddaughter."

"Oh my! Isn't she just the *image* of her mother?"

Sand-summers, snow-winters.

"Must we stay here? I hate Deepwood. There's nothing to do! Why can't we *live* in California?"

"Because of your father, darling! He wants us here."

"But he never comes!"

Now she remembered her mother's sharp, impatient sigh and understood it. "His work keeps him busy. Will you stop pestering me, Anne?"

After that there had been the schools. Private, impersonal. And Deepwood, which she had hated even more.

"No questions yet, love!" That was Harris, helping her off the plane and a few moments later into his private helicopter. Sitting beside her, he squeezed her hand, and kept hold of it as they took off. She was beginning to feel drowsy by then, not really caring where he was taking her. Anne leaned her head against his shoulder and smelled his expensive cologne. He put his arm around her, and she felt his fingers caress her breast very lightly.

"Only a short while now," he murmured, and soon after she saw the lights of a small landing strip below them.

"Where are we?" The helicopter was descending now, almost too quickly. Anne felt entitled to her question after all the time of holding back. But Harris, smiling, only reminded her to fasten her seatbelt.

"I'm bringing you home, Anne. Be patient just a little longer, love."

There was a comfortable covered pickup waiting there to take them even further, driven by a dark-featured, politely expressionless man. Far above, Anne could catch glimpses of stars pinpricking a dark sky, although as the narrow road wound lower, streamers of fog wreathed them. She was beginning to feel really tired, trying to bring herself back to a state of interested awareness for Harris's sake.

"Only a short while longer, Anne." His arm tightened around her shoulders, and then suddenly, as if for dramatic effect, the fog seemed to thin and open up like a cobweb curtain and she had the eeriest feeling of déjà vu as the road dipped down, widening slightly, and they drove down what appeared to be an avenue of dark, twisted trees. Monterey cypress and twisted oaks. And she was a child again, telling herself, "One more bend and we'll be there."

And there, just as it had stood so often in her dreams, the house waited for her with lighted windows, welcoming her back. And she must be dreaming—she had to be!

"Welcome home, Anne," Harris said softly at her side, his voice echoing her first jumbled thoughts. "You see, I wanted the first present I gave you to be a very special one."

The garage had been a carriage house once. The doors had hardly ever been left closed. But now the closed, thick wooden doors opened silently and automatically to let them in, and it was much larger than Anne remembered it. The only thing that was the same was the sound of the ocean in the sea caves beneath when the motor was shut off. Pulsing, pushing, rumbling with a frustrated growl of anger as the waves pulled back, only to start a fresh assault.

"But if there are caves, why can't I explore them?"

"Because it would be quite dangerous. They're almost always full of water, in any case."

"But, Grandfather, didn't *you* explore down in there when you were a boy?"

"That's neither here nor there, Anne! It's out of the question!"

She had loved the ocean then—watching fascinated from her window high up when it stormed; trying to imagine herself on a sailing ship out there. All the men on her mother's side of the family had belonged to the sea, all of them had died in it or within sight and hearing of it. And her mother, too—only this wasn't the time to remember that, when she should be trying to thank Harris for his gift to her.

Whaler's Island—and long before that, Wrecker's Island. Really an almost-island squatting hump-backed in the ocean with only a narrow spit of land connecting it with the Big Sur coast. Her great-grandfather had had the bridge built so that they could cross over safely even when the tides were at their highest.

"My grandfather used to be a naval captain. And *his* grandfather was a whaler. That's when he first saw the island. Actually, they used to shine lights off the headland, long ago, to lure in ships . . . Anyway, he was a smart man, and I think he dabbled in smuggling, although Grandfather never would admit that to me. His ship anchored off the shore one day, and eventually he married the daughter of the Spaniard whose land grant included this island—and quite a bit of the land inland, as well, stretching all the way to the mountains. I used to think that someday I would write a book about the family . . ." Anne broke off, suddenly aware that she was talking too much, probably from sheer nervousness.

Harris was watching her with an indulgent smile, his eyes unusually bright under the enormous crystal chandelier.

She could feel herself flush with embarrassment. "Harris! I can't imagine how you found out—and managed to buy it! And as for calling this a *present*, just as if it were a—a box of candy, I don't know that I can . . ."

"I can afford my whims, Anne. And it seemed right. A magnificent coincidence that this place should be on the market just when I was looking for coastal property. It's perfect —don't you see that? And by rights, it should belong to you. Do you remember when I once talked to you about families, old families, and their roots in the land? Houses like this one are part of our roots. They carry a sense of continuity from generation to generation."

She shook her head, still dazed. "Oh, Harris! This is—I still can't grasp it all. And to buy a place like this can hardly be called a 'whim,' you know! I'm still in a state of shock, but I couldn't possibly . . ."

He leaned across the table, his hand touching hers where it lay clenched on the linen tablecloth. "The deed is made out in your name, Anne. And you have to admit that this would be an ideal location for shooting most of the movie! Apart from that, there are no strings attached, my love. This is your home, as it always should have been." He smiled at her. "And now, while we're having our coffee, why don't you tell me more about your great-grandfather?"

Just when she thought she was beginning to understand Harris Phelps, she didn't understand him at all! Anne felt tangled up in the web of her own confused emotions, and it felt easier for her to talk, exorcising some of her memories that way.

"My great-grandfather was a bit of a scoundrel, I suppose. But my grandfather . . ."

He'd left a trust. She could understand, of course, why her grandmother had sold the land, not wanting to be alone with painful memories. She had turned suddenly frail and old. Why keep it? Not for Anne, who was still a child, with a father who had more than enough money of his own. She had died within a year of selling it.

And then, not too many years ago, there had been pictures in one of the glossy magazines. Yes, that was it. Anne could remember the wrench in her stomach when she saw the pictures and read the article that accompanied them. Danny Verrano, the singer, owned the island now. He was the kind of man who was always surrounded by sycophants—and a lot of women. And yet, he needed his private retreat. There had been innuendos about wild, week-long parties in the carefully guarded seclusion that this particular place provided. He'd built a drawbridge over the natural moat that the ocean provided on the land side. It was the kind of colorful, flamboyant thing Verrano would do. And no doubt he and his friends had used the private beach, too—the water was always aquamarine, studded with rocks so that it wasn't safe for boats to come in too close. But the beach was part of the past that Anne didn't want to remember.

As if he'd sensed the dark direction of her thoughts and wanted to lead them forward again, Harris began to talk casually of his plans.

"You might want to change the decor, Anne. Poor Danny had deplorable taste."

Poor Danny had also developed a drinking problem; especially after his records had stopped selling. He had been relieved to find a buyer for what had become a white elephant.

But Harris had already dismissed Danny Verrano as he went on thoughtfully: "I suppose it'll have to do for the moment, though. At least he had the forethought to build guests chalets, and he did convert one of the tower rooms into a screening room. That's going to prove very useful to us. Yves and Jerry can do all their editing right here, instead of having to fly the film to the studio in Los Angeles." He smiled at her, inviting her to share his satisfaction. "It's perfect, Anne! Plenty of room to accommodate everybody—and we can be perfectly self-contained while we're out here shooting. We can bring supplies in by helicopter, and it'll be no problem keeping out the inquisitive public—and the kind of reporters we *don't* want."

God, she felt tired! And sleepy. Tonight, for sure, she wouldn't need a Valium to put her under. But for Harris's sake, Anne tried to put on a bright-eyed front as she took very tiny sips of her after-dinner Courvoisier.

Harris was telling her of his plans for the next week—a time for relaxation and acclimatization, as he put it. And for entertaining a few very select guests. Important people—and people who had put money into the movie. James Markham, an Arab emir with an unpronounceable name who happened to be Karim's uncle, and Dr. Harold Brightman, who had written the best-selling *Relaxation and Meditation*, a book that Dr. Haldane had recommended she read.

"Oh—we're going to have our own resident guru?"

Harris laughed. "Very perceptive, Anne! Yes. Nerves tend to get frazzled in this business, you know. And especially since we'll all be more or less isolated here together for a while, we're bound to have personality clashes—all kinds of petty problems. Brightman's writing another book, and in return for his being allowed to gather material for it, he's agreed to be our company doctor—more or less!"

Harris continued to talk until his silent, well-trained servants had cleared the table; after that, he took her upstairs. To her old room—it was almost uncanny, how he had picked it out. And although his own room connected with hers, he had been considerate enough to allow her a lock on her side of the door.

"If you want to be alone tonight, love, I'll understand . . ." Sometimes a demon inside her wished that Harris wasn't quite so understanding. Why couldn't it have been Harris, instead of Webb, who made the lights come on for her and could take her, even if against her will, past the point of caring or even thinking?

"I'm so tired! And I don't think I've really taken all this in yet . . ." No sooner had the words come out than she almost

213

wished Harris would stay—his closeness keeping all the unwanted thoughts and memories away. When he left her alone, her nightly routine of brushing her teeth, creaming off her makeup, and changing into her nightgown armed her against the rest of the night.

Lying in bed at last, Anne heard the distant roaring of the waves breaking against the cliffs and sucking the sandy beach, and knew how the ocean would look through her window in the morning. Its constant, unchanged murmuring had always been a comfortable, familiar sound when she was safely shut behind thick stone walls.

This was the old part of the house—what she had always thought of as the Spanish part. Amos Mallory had added on to it later, building upwards and outwards until the original estancia was almost a castle. Too many rooms, too many layers. Like her own self—empty on the inside and veneered on the outside.

But at least Amos had left untouched, the central courtyard around which the house had been built, and she would be able to see it again tomorrow. Sunbathe there if the sun showed itself, undisturbed by the winds that usually blew whether the day was sunny or not. And she wouldn't let herself think beyond that for now. Let tomorrow look after itself.

Turning over onto her stomach, Anne pulled the covers up over her head, just as she had been used to doing long ago. Maybe it would be a nice day tomorrow . . .

Chapter Twenty

"TODAY, THERE'LL BE LOW COASTAL FOG, clearing inland, by afternoon. The temperature . . ."

With a muttered expletive, Webb Carnahan turned off the radio, switching to sweet music stored up in a tiny cassette. Nothing but music; no announcer's voice cutting into sound. Stanley Turretine's "Salt Song." And at least it was sunny and hot in San Jose. Hell with coastal fog—he wasn't there yet.

The white Ferrari, top down, cut through slowpoking traffic, drawing envious looks. Especially from women.

"I swear it *was* him! Webb Carnahan! Oh God, is he ever beautiful! Even better-looking than his pictures. And he *looked* at me!"

Following Highway 101, Webb kept his attention on the traffic, which was murder—as usual on a Friday afternoon. Two-lane stretch right here, and too many stoplights to switch her onto Cruise Control. He didn't need to be held up getting a ticket. Take it easy . . . The motor, all that wasted power under the hood, purred impatiently. And he remembered how he'd made it from Pebble Beach to San Francisco in under two hours in the old days before the fifty-five-mile speed limit. Staying with David Black and his wife until Meg, who was now David's ex-wife, had developed a crush on him, and showed it too obviously. Meg—basic bitch. One of the few women he'd been attracted to and hadn't had. Which was maybe one of the reasons why he and David were still friends. He'd been a guest on David's talk show before he'd left for Europe.

The traffic finally started to move, and Webb pushed his foot down slightly, letting her move. Her. Sweet machine—responding without asking anything of him beyond a certain amount of concentration.

Inevitably, angrily, his thoughts switched to Anne. Annie with the big blue innocent eyes. Managing to surprise him with her unexpected show of spirit and stubbornness. And her deception. Was that what really bugged him? Anne Mallory—model turned movie star with a little help from her friends in high places. Harris Phelps's latest mistress. And maybe the reason her memory continued to rankle him was that he wasn't used to being made a fool of by a woman. Which took his mind back to that night in Dublin, with all its consequences.

While his hands handled the Ferrari by instinct, Webb let his mind reach back deliberately. Like sitting in a projection room, watching the day's rushes and trying to be objective. A series of fast-motion scenes; slowing down occasionally, even freezing in mid-action to hold one frame. He had a good memory—it had been trained and developed for the kind of "work" he used to be in, and had proved useful since; especially when it came to memorizing lines. Lines . . .

Strain had begun to show in Venetia Tressider's face when he'd joined her after leaving the phone booth. Her smile was too bright and she held her purse far too tightly clutched in her hands. Her eyes looked frightened as they searched his face.

"Webb darling, can't we go now? It's so noisy and so close in here! And I do hate sitting alone in places like this, it makes me feel like a—a floozy!"

His anger at her for leading him into this unprepared made him say cruelly, "Then maybe you should stop acting like one, love—picking up strange guys at airports and inviting them back to your room for a quickie."

But he said it softly, with a smile for the benefit of curious eyes of the others, and after her first snatched-in breath of anger, she retorted sweetly, "But I'd heard so much about you it made me curious to find out. Besides, I thought we might console each other—we have both been rather played along, haven't we?"

Touché, Venetia. And it seemed they really had needed each other that night. Dual alibis. But that was to come up later.

Almost imperceptibly, coming to a straight four-lane stretch of highway, Webb's foot went down on the gas pedal, sending the speedometer needle flicking up to eighty. And then, swearing under his breath, he eased it down to sixty again. Damn speed limits. Damn any limits at all! The only ones he tolerated were those he set himself; and there had been times during the past weeks when it had been all he could do to control his rage. He didn't like the feeling of being a pawn in someone else's chess game.

"Did you know that you have a dangerous face? You really do. It fits those macho parts you always play so well, and I think that under the surface you're really like that. Are you, Webb?"

He'd listened to Venetia's nervous prattling in stony, resentful silence for the most part, letting her drive her car through the thick fog that seemed to close in on them like a billowy blanket. He was busy with his own thoughts and questions.

Nino—how in hell had Nino known he was here? Easy enough to figure out, he supposed, with all the publicity. But more important—what was Nino doing here? What did he want to talk about after all the twenty years? And where did Venetia fit in?

"Women belong between a man's thighs. There, they have their uses. Not in men's business. However, this one has proved useful, and since she brought you here to me, you might return the favor she has done us by helping her. No doubt she'll explain to you herself . . ." That was Nino—not changed very much except that his hair had silvered. His embrace was still

217

strong, and his manner had been affectionate as he stepped back, looking Webb over appraisingly.

"Ah, *bene*. You take after our side of the family, eh? It is difficult to tell too much from pictures or your movies, although I have seen all of them. I am proud. And if I have stayed out of your life all these years, it was only because you were making your own way in your own fashion. And there have been times in your life when any association with me would have been an embarrassment, *sì*? A pity—but then, family is always family, and since Lucia married Vito Gentile, the ties are even stronger. You agree?"

Webb hadn't wanted Lucia to marry Vito. She was the baby of the family, his little sister. But Lucy, for all her gentleness, had a stubborn streak in her, and she had said she loved Vito. She didn't care what they said about him or who he was—she loved him and he loved her, and that was all that mattered. And he'd thought at the time, what the hell, he was living his life; why shouldn't his sister do as she pleased with hers? At least she still seemed happy, glowing with contentment after she'd borne two children, both sons.

Women like Lucy seemed meant for marriage and motherhood; and Vito, though he was accounted ruthless in his "business" dealings, seemed to worship her. Met socially, they seemed like any other young couple who had something going for each other, and the boys were normal kids for all that they had been taught Old World manners for company.

"They're really proud of their uncle, the big movie star!" Lucy had laughed the last time Webb talked to her on the phone. "You should have seen them when they were going through their cowboy phase!"

He hadn't met her since he'd made *Bad Blood*, although he'd wondered grimly what Vito would think about that. Still he was fond of his nephews and always tried to remember to send them souvenirs from his movies. A serape from Mexico he'd worn for two in a row. A battered flat-crowned hat with a bullet hole in the brim. They were all the family he had since his mother had died, and he'd always been close to Lucy.

But—what exactly did Nino mean when he talked so significantly of family? Had Nino known or suspected something even then?

Webb swore impatiently under his breath as he accelerated to pass a slow-moving camper, then slowed down to sixty again. Careful. He needed this time to think. To go back very carefully over everything that had been said and that had happened since that foggy night in Ireland.

They had talked, he and Nino, in Venetia Tressider's comfortable, firelit room in the inn owned by a friend of hers. A man called Mike, with red hair and a mustache to go with his name. Mike had taken Venetia with him into the tiny bathroom, and from there through the connecting door to the next room, which he said with a wink was coincidentally unoccupied.

Melodrama. Webb had felt almost silly, standing there with his shoulder against the mantelpiece while he waited for Nino to tell him what he wanted.

"So!" Nino said briskly. "Time to waste we both do not have, eh? And you stand there impatiently and warily like a young mountain lion sniffing danger—or is it the woman in the next room? She will keep. I saw the way her eyes looked at you. However, after you've had what you need to take from her and the newspapers have made much of an affair between you two, I think it might be well if you drop her quickly. She is far too reckless, and too open in talking of the things she says she believes in . . ." The older man's voice took on a contemptuous, cutting edge. "That is why she is being watched, and an interest is taken in her movements. But that is for her and her friends to worry about. They will not involve you, because they need what I and my friends provide them with, and she will not dare to involve you because she knows that if she does, she will die."

Very matter-of-fact, but Webb could sense the power behind the casual words, and it kept him quiet—and watchful.

"There is no need for blood oaths between us, because we are in truth and in fact uncle and nephew." Nino's dark, strong face was seamed more than Webb remembered it, but his eyes were the same—burning darker than his brown Sicilian skin. He chuckled suddenly. "I like it that you have not yet asked questions. Questions are for fools, and those who listen learn— it is so? So now I will tell you . . ."

Webb listened in silence, feeling the tautening of his muscles. This whole situation was fucking incredible. Nino, making a "simple request" that was in reality a thinly disguised order.

On the surface, it all sounded so damned reasonable. No risks involved—no real involvement at all, for that matter. Just a matter of information that he was the one logical person to provide because he was soon to leave for California to begin the shooting of Harris Phelps's latest production.

"This film itself—it's not important. It is the people involved—behind the scenes, as you would put it perhaps—who are of interest to us—I and my associates in the United States and elsewhere. Perhaps there are others who also find it a matter of some curiosity that so many important people, people with very big money, with much power internationally, should make themselves interested in the shooting of a movie?"

He mentioned names. Just a few of them were enough to make Webb's eyebrows rise. Some he hadn't heard of, but Nino, as if he could read his mind, explained very carefully who they were and what they represented.

"They have contributed—very generously—to the almost limitless budget. Harris Phelps himself does not need the extra money. But you see, it makes them associates of a kind. A good excuse for meetings, *sì*? For social occasions when they will all come together at this secret place where you are to film the movie—merely to visit and observe, you understand? Still, I do not think that is entirely all . . ."

Webb had sat there with a drink in his hand, listening with a growing sense of incredulity he had to fight back because he knew Nino wasn't fooling. Wherever Nino had gotten his facts, Webb had to accept them as facts—men like Nino didn't fool around with suppositions. And the facts he presented added up to some very intriguing questions. Damn Nino for making them stick in his mind, too, like nagging splinters.

"You find out what you can, eh?" Nino's voice said heavily at the end. "Call your sister—ask to talk to Vito. He'll be expecting a call from you. And be careful. If you run into any trouble, then you call him, too."

There was a sense of sureness in Nino that age hadn't taken away. And his embrace at parting was still strong and affectionate.

"You take care now!" he said again.

"You, too, Zio Nino." Webb caught the pleased look his uncle gave him and grinned, in spite of the dark thoughts that still raced through his mind. "By the way," he added casually, "it's a stupid question, but—what would you have done if that plane I was supposed to be on hadn't been fogged in?"

The older man chuckled. "Ah, I had wondered if you would ask that. Well, if the fog hadn't helped us, you would have been—accidentally detained. An unfortunate accident to the taxi in which you traveled to the airport . . . ? And then there would have been this beautiful woman to offer you a ride."

After that last touch of humor, the tautness stayed in Webb, reaching to his loins when Venetia returned to the room—alone this time.

"I've been taking a bath. Wasn't that nice of me, darling?" Her hair was still damp and she was flush-faced and warm-fleshed when she dropped her towel.

"Webb darling, I want you! And I really meant what I said

221

when I told you I always go after what I want. I didn't mean our first time to be this way, but we can both unwind now, can't we?"

She had a cameo-perfect face, the type that some Irishwomen were born with, but he couldn't see it now, hidden by the swing of her damp black hair. He felt the softness of her red, avid mouth sending age-old, wordless messages to his groin and felt the wet-silk texture of her hair as he wrapped his fingers in it, yanking her up and across his body. Venetia had a smooth-muscled body developed by tennis and riding and lots of screwing. And at the moment, he needed only the answers her body gave to his.

Webb and Venetia spent most of the next day together, acting like newly met lovers for the benefit of her watchdogs and the photographers that followed him. Including Johnnie Bardini. Webb didn't try calling Anne again.

His new leading lady, Harris Phelps's latest discovery. Damn her, why hadn't she told him? It didn't surprise him to learn, when he arrived belatedly in London, that she'd moved herself out of the suite they'd shared. Annie was good at running away—and he should have kept that in mind.

When he saw her again at Harris's press conference, she'd looked white-faced and almost guilty—trying not to meet his eyes as she pressed closer to Karim, as if for protection. And he'd damned her silently again. She ought to feel guilty, the false, scheming little bitch!

It was almost a relief to find out that she would be leaving England, along with Harris. He had other things to take care of, including Venetia, who had begun to act as if their muchpublicized "romance" was the real thing.

Bardini had already sold his pictures, and the *Mirror* and *News of the World* had them captioned, "Webb's latest love is a British Beauty . . ."

One of the women's weeklies quoted Venetia as saying shyly, "This time it's different for both of us. We wanted to be

alone somewhere so we could get to know each other as people
. . . Webb's other romances have been mostly publicity things,
but I'm not interested in getting into films, and I see him as
a man and not a movie star . . ."

"Jesus Christ!" he'd sworn disgustedly, throwing the page
back at her, and she'd raised her eyebrows reproachfully.

"But, darling, I think it was very clever of me! And none of
it was really *untrue*, you know! Besides helping get us both off
the hook. When those nasty men started asking me all those
nasty questions, I simply looked indignant and told them I
didn't know what they were implying, because I'd only flown
to Ireland to be with *you*! Should we get engaged before you
leave England, do you think? Webb, I'd adore a big, really
vulgar ring—if I don't have to return it to you afterwards."

He'd been thinking of the new and obviously expensive ring
that Anne had been wearing at that press conference. Karim?
Harris? Christ, she was turning into a little whore—or maybe
she'd been that way all along and he'd been the only one too
blind to see. The thought made him grit his teeth with rage
before he answered Venetia.

"I'll think about it, if you stop pushing me, Venetia." He
was getting tired of all the publicity their "romance" was getting—the questioning from reporters whenever they were seen
together, which was too damned often. In fact, he had almost
begun to regret dumping Claudia del Antonini, who was at
least an Italian peasant at heart—direct, earthy, and naturally
passionate. Venetia was kinky—always looking for new varia-
tions, different twists, her own brand of thrills. Like the time
he walked into her bedroom to find her making it with another
girl, as blonde as Venetia was dark, in slow motion, under a
red-shaded light.

"Aren't we beautiful, darling?" she had whispered, smiling.
"This is Jill, and she'd like you to go down on her—afterwards."
Her lips had been wet and shiny . . . from Jill. Her eyes held
their usual teasing, sensual challenge. Venetia enjoyed brutal

lovemaking; she was good at exciting and provoking the male animal until it erupted in the savagery she seemed to crave.

Webb couldn't say, looking back now, that Venetia had ever bored him. She had simply begun to disgust him with her demands—her "surprises" and little tricks. Like the time she'd arranged for Johnnie Bardini to photograph them making love by her indoor pool—twin fireplaces and mirrors everywhere to reflect every flickering movement. And Johnnie standing in the dark at the top of the stairs, taking it all in.

He'd slapped her when she showed him the pictures, sending her falling backwards against her bed. And she came up crying, clinging to his thighs.

"But, darling, I thought you'd enjoy looking at them as much as I do! I wouldn't show them to anyone else, you know I wouldn't!"

"I hope the bastard had a hard-on that hurt! And if he tries publishing *those* . . ."

The next time he ran into Johnnie, the usually cocky little photographer looked strangely subdued.

"Listen, Carnahan, I swear I was only doing the little gal a favor! 'Just for kicks,' she told me. 'Souvenirs just for the two of us.' And I give you my word those pictures aren't going to get published anywhere—not if I get offered a million for each print. In fact, when she told me you'd gotten so mad, I even burned the negatives. Honest! No hard feelings, huh?" But it was the last, muttered sentence before Johnnie turned away that really gave Webb something to think about. "Uh, give my regards to Vito when you get back to the States, will you?"

So the word had been passed around that he was an adopted member of the Family. For his protection, or was he being set up? At that point, Webb hadn't been too sure of anything. His meeting with Nino seemed absurdly melodramatic in retrospect, like something dreamed up by a writer of sensational novels. Until little things kept reminding him, like the feeling he'd developed just before he left London that he was being followed—and he'd shrugged it off. So what? Maybe the word had been spread around a little too far, and although he didn't like that idea, there was nothing he could do about it. Hell, he didn't even know what he was supposed to look for —or if there was anything to find! So what if Harris Phelps's rich friends wanted to dabble in moviemaking?

He'd changed his mind since then. Had it changed for him, was more like it.

Webb's fingers tightened over the wheel as a shock wave of rage jolted through him. Careful, he warned himself grimly. Stay cool, and play it by ear. Cooler than he'd been just two days ago, when he'd found out who else was interested in Harris Phelps's latest venture.

The flashing red light that warned him he was approaching the Carmel Hill Gate to the Seventeen-Mile Drive brought Webb back to the present. Hell, he'd done enough thinking for now, and there were some things he didn't even want to think about yet—not now, when he was tired and his mind was tired, and Dave would expect him to be in a partying mood.

Dave had left word at the gate. He gave his name and the uniformed gatekeeper grinned, saying, "Hi, Mr. Carnahan, good to see you again!"

Obviously the man remembered him from the times he'd played at playing golf for one of the annual charity tournaments. Pebble Beach was one of the toughest courses there was, and he hadn't exactly done well.

Only two more miles to go now, and he'd best keep his mind in the present. Firmly.

Chapter Twenty-one

"WEBB! HEY, MAN, it's good to see you!" Dave Black, genial host. He carried his TV role into real life—hating to be alone except when he did his meditation bit twice a day.

The house hanging over the ocean was ablaze with lights, noisy with voices and loud rock music.

"Jesus, that's some machine! You gotta tell me how long it takes to ship one out here. Hear you did some racing in Italy? And how was good old London town? Listen, we've got to play some tennis together while you're here. I'm counting on you to get me a visitor's pass when you start filming *Greed for Glory* . . . What the hell is this 'closed set' bit? By the way"—voice dropping—"Robbie Savage is here tonight, and she's dying to meet you. Says she had you in mind for her Jason character right from the beginning, and couldn't be more thrilled. Maybe I'll get you two together for one of my shows, huh?"

"Sure, if she's passable." Stretching cramped muscles, Webb forced himself to grin. Thank God that Dave at least was always predictable. Old-home week—the party and the girls and the pot, and for the rest of the night he wouldn't have to think—just make the right motions at the right time.

"How's Meg?" Dave would expect the question, since they'd all been friends at one time. Webb saw his friend grimace slightly.

"Ah shit, you know Meg! She's having a ball screwing

226

around. She's here with her latest stud, checking everything out—and regretting it, I hope, the bitch! I'd better warn you, though, she still has the hots for you. She was telling me the other day that you just need the right woman to help you settle down. And then she's been seeing Dr. Brightman, which makes her a triple bitch in my book. He wrote last year's nonfiction best-seller, *Relaxation and Meditation*, and I had him on my show a couple of times, which probably helped sell a few million extra copies for him. No doubt she's having fun telling him what a bastard I was to her! He's here, too. He was telling me Harris Phelps has invited him up to Danny Verrano's old place on Big Sur, where you'll be shooting most of your movie." For a moment Dave's grin turned sour. "Christ, I can't believe all the mystery! What's the deal? Just another publicity gimmick?" And then, brightening slightly: "Hey, speaking of publicity—you going to turn me on to the straight scoop on all that stuff you had going on in England? Who's this Venetia Tressider chick? And what's Anne Mallory like?"

They climbed the steps leading up from the underground garage Dave called his parking lot into a room filled with warmth and sound and people; and all of Dave's questions would keep until tomorrow.

Except the one about Anne, because Roberta Savage repeated it later, turning in the waterbed with her arms clinging.

"Anne Mallory—I've seen her pictures, of course, and I know she's a famous model—but is she the right one to play Glory? I mean, can she act?"

It was a question he'd asked himself, too. How much of Anne had been acting and how much real? All the Annies he had known, and had even come close to loving. Annie Oakley, the mystery waif, Anne Reardon Hyatt, Anne Mallory, who had been sophisticated enough to fool him—which one of them was real? Any one of them? Or had she just been a chemical reaction, a lust-produced image on the radar screen of his loins?

Annie laughing in the snow. Annie in the firelight, not laughing at all, her face solemn and almost frightened. Cold hands, warm mouth . . . a mind as coldly calculating as her father's?

Robbie moved against him questioningly and Webb muttered, "Ah, who cares?" Consigning both Anne and her father to hell before he brought his mouth down over Robbie's—harshly and brutally—wanting to keep her from talking and himself from thinking.

She moaned softly and excitedly, spreading her thighs to receive him as he rolled on top of her.

"Mm—God, yes! Ohh . . . *Jason!*"

He fucked her into silence and oblivion, burying both her senses and his under feeling and sensation. Burying questions and regret and frustration and anger in a hot, convulsively grasping cunt. One more like all the others he'd fucked. Wipeout. Forgetfulness for the moment.

But afterwards, when Robbie had finally fallen asleep, Webb found himself too wide awake. Damn Dave's waterbeds, anyhow! And he could tell that the woman would expect him to make love again in the morning.

Ah, shit! Waiting until her breathing was even, Webb eased himself cautiously onto his back, cursing every movement of the bed. He hoped to hell she wouldn't wake up—and that she wasn't the kind of woman who had nightmares, remembering fleetingly, with an ugly frown in the darkness, Anne's favorite nightmare . . . and from there to his own.

Ria. There'd been nights, after they'd told him what had happened, that he'd waken up shaking with hatred and with nausea—escaping from mind-pictures of how she might have died, and how long it might have taken for her to die. And then he'd forced all his memories of Ria far back into the recesses of his mind until she'd become a dream-image, like a faded picture.

Until two days ago . . . then the picture had changed, coming back too sharply into focus with the black-and-white image of her face, blown up larger than life by a telephoto lens. Ria— unbelievably but unmistakably Ria. Smiling, but not the old shy smile he remembered. Confident and sexually flaunting. Smiling for the man whose face bent over hers, whispering something to her. Sideshow during a Mayday parade.

The shock had sent him all the way from white-hot rage to frozen immobility.

"Sorry, old buddy. But we didn't know ourselves until a few months ago . . ." Peter's voice had suddenly seemed to come from a long distance away. Peter the Wolf, they had nicknamed him, because of the way he grinned, and because he was just as dangerous and just as predatory. And still one of "Reardon's boys."

They had picked him up soon after he'd gone through customs at JFK. Very unobtrusively. Peter himself fronting the act.

"Webb, by gosh! Been hoping your flight wasn't delayed or anything like that. Got your baggage okay? Barry here will take care of it. I've got the limo waiting right outside for you."

Very clever, very smooth. But all the men Reardon handpicked to work for him had to be just that, as well as totally unscrupulous. He knew the rules, and the way they played their game, which was rough. And he'd gone along with them without protest, even while he was seething inside—noticing how the three men formed a kind of protective phalanx, one on either side and one behind him.

"What the fuck's with the welcome committee?" Trying to keep his voice cool, his rage tamped down.

"Hey, buddy, surely you're glad to see an old friend again? We were partners once, remember?" And then shrugging in the face of Webb's stony silence, the man had said, "Oh well . . . it's nothing to worry about, really. We're not after you, if that's what you're thinking. In fact, we could use your help in a certain little matter . . ."

"Like making me an offer I can't refuse?" Webb said evenly.

Wolf-Grin chuckled. "Glad to see you haven't lost your sense of humor since you've made the big time, feller! And we're not taking you for a ride either!" He laughed again. "Nope. This won't really take too long. And to show you that fair's fair, I think we've got some information that might interest you in trade."

The information was about Ria. And when he saw the first pictures, Webb had almost gone for Peter with his bare hands. Clever fakes—something they'd rigged up to get him off guard. And then that one, very clear shot.

"It's possible, of course, that she was one of their agents from the beginning. Or that she wasn't. There's always the survival instinct to be reckoned with, isn't there? That's Petrov with her, by the way. One of Castro's closest friends and advisers. An extremely hard man to get close to. And we know, because we've tried."

Webb found himself wondering why he didn't seem able to say anything, while Peter's dispassionate voice went on telling him things he didn't really want to know.

"She's Sal Espinoza's mistress now. You ever race against him? He's one of the money men behind this movie you're going to be doing. And rumor has it he's been offered a part—and might take it, for kicks. South American." Another picture flicked onto the screen. "Good-looking bastard, isn't he? International playboy type—plenty of money, winning smile, no visible means of support. And his latest lady—he calls her his fiancée, by the way—has ash-blonde hair and brown eyes. She's supposed to be from Nicaragua, daughter of rich parents who sent her to school in Switzerland—but nobody can find any records. This one's a very recent picture—taken when they were skiing in Gstaad . . ."

Another blown-up picture. Blonde this time, but again, unmistakably Ria.

"Not many people knew her, did they? Or would remember her. How old was she when you met her? Seventeen, eighteen?"

Eighteen. And so damned naïve and innocent, no matter what they said. A raped virgin. He could remember her sobbing wildly against his shoulder.

"I cannot! I'm not the way I should be, the way I want to be for you. Those men came out of the hills with their fierce beards and their dirty clothes and their guns. And they— they . . ."

He hadn't let her go on. Hadn't wanted her to. Christ, but she had been beautiful! So young and so soft and hurt and helpless. With a kind of purity that set her apart from all the others. Old-fashioned girl, with all the old-fashioned words applying to her. Like "lady." And she had been educated, too, speaking five languages. Her parents had been rich plantation owners before the revolution. Or so she'd told him. Everything he knew about Ria was what she had told him . . .

"Sorry we had to spring this on you without warning, old buddy. But you understand . . ."

"Sure, I understand." By then Webb had managed to regain some control over himself. He looked back at Peter, his tawny-gold eyes narrowed and filled with the rage he had been able to keep out of his voice.

Recognizing this with his own animal instinct, the other man let his teeth show. "Good. I thought you would. And now let's get down to business, shall we? I was hoping that after seeing the slides you might become as curious as we are. Maybe we can—help each other out, huh?"

"And if I tell you I'm not interested? That I don't give a damn about Ria or what she was or what she's become?"

They'd had the answer to that, too, the final, deadly piece of persuasion.

231

He'd wondered at the time why Peter hadn't been more insistent, hadn't threatened. Instead he'd only shrugged.

"Ah well . . . !" Tinge of regret creeping into his voice. "Thought you might want to do us a favor in return for doing you one. But in case you change your mind, I'll give you a call in a couple of days, shall I?"

Now, remembering, Webb could understand why Peter had been so sure of himself. Vito had given him the reason, and along with it, all the more reason to hate Richard Reardon. Cold, analytical, calculating bastard! Finding everybody's weakest points and using them. Reardon, the chess master who sacrificed pawns too easily . . .

"You understand why I cannot tell anyone? Only you know and I know—and my mother, whom Lucia is supposed to be visiting, along with our sons."

Vito was still a young man, dark-haired and handsome, in his middle thirties. That day he had looked much older as deep lines of worry etched his face.

"You know what precautions I take? As a matter of course, although the old days are past. She had gone shopping with the boys. They needed summer clothes. That was only yesterday." Vito's voice sounded jerky, and Webb could see a muscle jumping in the side of his jaw. "And then—I had this telephone call. To say that they were safe—spending a nice vacation in a sunny climate with old friends of yours." Vito added carefully, "The man who made the call said also that he hoped you considered these old friends still your friends."

They needed Webb's cooperation—and Vito's, as well. They had ensured that they would have it. And that meant that Reardon thought something big was up. But if that was so, why in hell hadn't Reardon sent in one of his own, a man he could trust, instead of an ex-operative who had plenty of reason to hate his guts?

Christ! Too many questions he couldn't answer yet. Somewhere there had to be a solution, but right now his mind was as tired as his body, and he needed to have his mind clear—to start thinking forwards instead of back.

Robbie Savage stirred and moaned, then snuggled closer to him. Under them, the bed undulated gently. Webb closed his eyes, deliberately blanking out all thought. Riding an ocean swell on a gigantic air mattress. Only the sound of breathing and the ceaseless sigh of the Pacific Ocean on the other side of heavy-glassed windows.

Chapter Twenty-two

THE OCEAN was a glassy greenish-gray when Anne looked out. From her room on the third floor of the house—"the Captain's floor," it had been called ever since she could remember—the ocean looked so close she could almost fall out into it. If she opened the windows and stepped out onto the narrow widow's walk, she would hear better the crashing roar of the waves against black rocks and yellow-white sand, the sighing rumble as the tide rushed into the honeycomb of caverns that slept under the island. Prehistoric rocks—monolithic phallic symbols encrusted with gray and green—stood out black against the lightening sky that always presaged dawn. A dying fog like wisps of transparent smoke still clung to the edges of land and sea, merging them into one.

She shouldn't be awake—she would be tired later on today; but the Dream had roused her, and watching the ocean from a safe distance was infinitely better than feeling herself drown in it. The Dream, like so many other submerged memories she still carried with her, must be exorcised by being dredged up to the surface—examined and rationalized and explained. Dr. Haldane had begun to do that, probing carefully and gently back through her life. But she hadn't had the Dream for ages. Not until London—and Webb ...

Frowning with the faint beginnings of a headache, Anne pushed strands of hair off her forehead, massaging her temples absently. *Analyze it—you can do it yourself, Anne. You've read enough books on the subject, haven't you?* Webb—the feeling of drowning, losing control, when he touched her. He made her not care about anything but the reality of his body and the heat of passion in hers. And if she had stayed with him, where would he have taken her? To what depths after the heights had all been scaled? Better this way—to see Webb again as an actor instead of a lover. Reduce everything to its proper perspective.

There was a faint sound behind her and she whirled, the thin silk of her nightgown silhouetting her against the tall glass windows.

"I'm sorry, Anne! I thought I heard a sound in here, but I didn't knock in case you were asleep. What's the matter, love? Did anything disturb you?"

There was sharp concern in Harris's voice as he came towards her. He was already dressed—in a pair of casual slacks and a yellow shirt open at the neck. Catching her look, he glanced down at himself and raised his shoulders apologetically. "I'm an inveterate early riser, I'm afraid! And there's a lot that has to be done before the horde starts arriving. But you—what is it, Anne? I've been noticing the held-back look of you lately, and your tenseness. Can't you sleep?" Coming up to her, he stroked her cold arms, his eyes, fog-gray, studying her face intently.

She managed a wavering smile and what she hoped was lightness in her voice. "I just woke up early, that's all. And I couldn't go back to sleep, so I decided to watch the dawn."

"Yes, it's beautiful, isn't it? Pale and unawake yet. Sometimes I think of you that way, Anne. You should have been born a medieval lady—protected and waited upon and cherished."

"Waiting in my tower room for my lord and master? No, thank you. I think I much prefer being a woman in this day and age!"

"Are you really as independent as you sound?" Harris said it teasingly, but his fingers tightened for just an instant about her shoulders and then he gave a disapproving click of his tongue. "You're very tense, sweetheart. Hold still, let me massage the back of your neck for you." As his strong fingers massaged her neck and shoulders she could feel the tension flow away. After a while she let him lead her back to her bed and strip off her night-gown, tossing it to the floor.

And this time she honestly tried to let go—to let Harris do whatever he wanted, willing herself to feel, to fly. As before, it didn't work.

Later, brushing her hair and braiding it against the wind, Anne stared ruefully at her reflection. So she did have a problem. Ice maiden. And Harris had been very patient, very understanding; not saying anything except, with a short sigh, "You should really learn to relax, Anne. Especially when we start shooting. I don't like the idea of your falling into the tranquilizer habit, like too many actresses I know. Have you thought about using the medi-tation technique Hal Brightman has made so popular? He's a great guy to meet—very warm and friendly. I think you'll like him."

She went downstairs in blue jeans, a blue and orange madras shirt, and a windbreaker. Breakfast smelled good in the dining room, but she decided to skip it today. The coffee and rolls Harris had ordered brought up to her room had revived her, and she wanted to explore—see how things were coming.

There were men, carpenters and painters by the look of them, wandering everywhere carrying the paraphernalia of their trade. Some of the more garish and strikingly modern examples of Danny Verrano's taste had already disappeared; and the house, especially the older section of it, was beginning to look authen-tically period, even to the massive Spanish furniture and oil paintings of Spanish dons in black velvet and steel.

"You don't mind, Anne? It'll just be this way while we're mak-ing the movie . . ."

"Harris, I love it! Everything looks—just as it should be."

She especially loved the huge central courtyard. Even when she was a child this had been one of her favorite places, where she had come to read in the sunshine or dream that she was back in the past—a Moorish princess in old Granada.

This courtyard might have come straight out of the Alhambra.

236

Very Moorish with its fountains and blue tiles, galleries looking down on three sides, and a high wall on the fourth. Even a miniature bathing pool. Anne saw how many of the courtyard scenes they needed could be shot right here. Harris had explained how the workmen could transform it with paint and plywood from grand to shabby overnight. There was even a massive wooden gate set into the wall already. Yes, Harris had been right from the beginning. The house was perfect, and so was its location.

Anne looked out, hesitating when she saw all the activity that was going on. Scaffoldings had been built against the walls, and some men were slapping on paint, while in the center three more worked on nailing together a very authentic-looking whipping post.

No use her going out there today. Turning back into the house, Anne wondered which scenes they'd shoot first. She'd learned enough about filmmaking from listening to Harris talk to know they wouldn't do anything in sequence. And that reminded her that she should be studying the script.

"We'll stick as close as possible to the book, Anne. Just remember when you're reading that this is all visual. We'll be shooting very small segments at a time, so you won't have much to memorize. And there'll be cue cards, of course, if you need them. Don't worry about anything."

But that was the least of her worries, although she couldn't say so to Harris. Perhaps talking to Dr. Brightman would help, after all. Another guru. And his book had been very intriguing— an easy way to relaxation and from there to meditation.

She saw the thick guest book that Harris, meticulous as ever, had installed on the magnificent carved sideboard. The telephone beside it struck a jarring note. She had started to flip idly through the book when the phone began to ring. There were extensions all over the house, and all those servants as well. Should she? Silly to hesitate when she was standing right here! Another insistent ring and she picked it up automatically, almost saying, "Majco Oil," and that trigger reflex was what made her pause to

237

hear a woman's voice, a slightly accented, contralto saying, "Who is this?"

Anne hated people who started off telephone conversations that way. And the woman sounded arrogant, as if she were talking to a servant. She had opened her mouth to retort, "Whom did you want to speak to?" when she heard the receiver being lifted from somewhere else in the house.

Harris's voice, sounding slightly impatient. "Hello?"

"Harris? This is Anna-Maria. Who was it who picked up the telephone just now?"

Her cheeks burning, feeling absurdly guilty like a child caught eavesdropping, Anne replaced the phone before she could catch Harris's reply.

Oh damn! That was stupid of her, too. She should have said something—explained. Too late now. Still feeling guilty, she walked quickly out of the room, threading her way through other rooms until she was safely outside, looking up at a sunlit sky, freckled with small fleecy clouds to the west.

No doubt the fog would come back later in the evening. The weather here was always surprising, never the same. Like the ocean . . . as she should remember. Funny how she could remember so many things from before. The happy things, the good things. But not much of *after*. But then, Dr. Haldane had explained that, and it was pointless going back.

Harris's chauffeur, who looked more like a bodyguard, was lounging outside, smoking a cigarette. Perhaps she should ask him to bring one of the cars around and drive herself into Carmel, spend the day wandering around the shops, looking for the familiar ones.

He stamped the cigarette out under his heel, looking at her through black incurious eyes. Maybe he was Harris's bodyguard—she should ask. She wondered if he wore a gun in a shoulder holster under his leather jacket, and realized that she didn't even know his name.

Who was Anna-Maria? One of Harris's ex–girl friends?

Angry at her own curiosity, Anne nodded at the man and started to walk briskly, as if she knew exactly where she was going. It was really none of her business. Harris had a lot of friends, most of whom she hadn't met.

"If you're going down to the beach, Miss Mallory, you'd best be careful. Those cliffs fall away real sudden."

She turned her head over her shoulder, inexplicably annoyed that this stranger should be warning her.

"Thanks, I know that. I used to live here as a child."

Almost true. Childhood summers. Happy times until the very last summer. And so much for asking for a car. Now she was committed to her walk. Digging her hands into the pockets of her windbreaker, Anne followed the faintly defined path that led to the beach, knowing that when she was out of sight of the house she would swerve off it to the north, following another path she remembered, with twisted oaks leaning their branches over it. Sherwood Forest to the child she'd been. Funny how the real thing, when she made a point of seeing it in England, hadn't seemed half so magical!

And then she heard the helicopter, and stood there shading her eyes until she had located it—hearing its peculiar whirring sound grow louder as the clumsy-looking thing came closer and lower, to disappear at last behind the treetops.

The first contingent of guests! Well, that would give her walk some direction. Feeling the wind whip color into her face, Anne took consciously long strides as she headed towards the small landing field.

She was halfway there when the chauffeur caught up with her. He walked alongside and muttered a human "Well, here we go! That'll be the first lot, and they'll have a bunch of baggage with them that needs carting back to the house."

She decided that he didn't look like a bodyguard at all, not really. Just a middle-aged Mexican or Italian with muscles under his jacket. No doubt from helping to carry Harris's guests' luggage.

Chapter Twenty-three

As it turned out, Harris had golf carts to take the guests and their baggage back to the house. Anne rode in one beside Yves Pleydel, who laughed. "American efficiency! Everything made very convenient, eh?" He was looking tanned and fit, and had kissed her soundly when he first saw her. "And you—you are looking very beautiful, just as I remembered you, *chèrie*." His quick eyes took her in, appraising her in that open way of his. "Although you could use some extra weight, you know. Has Harris not been feeding you? You must remember you are a movie actress now, and not a skinny model!"

"Oh, but the sea air is doing wonders for my appetite!" Anne countered, smiling at him. Yves at least was familiar. The others he introduced her to were strangers—mostly camera crew, headed by a taciturn New Yorker called Davis who kept squinting suspiciously at the sky, as if he expected it to be obscured by fog in minutes.

"Be extra charming to him and he will make sure you get all the best angles!" Yves whispered drolly. "I have seen some of his work, and he is very good. The best, in fact—like me!"

Angles, cuts, costumes, editing. The conversation over dinner was mostly technical, leaving Anne the silent listener, wondering if she would ever learn enough. Harris, like an orchestra conducter, guided it smoothly.

The helicopter had made two trips today. And by tomorrow, apparently, everyone else would be here.

"So what do we do about extras?" Yves asked sourly, and Harris smiled patiently. "I've arranged for that, too. We fly them in from Los Angeles—and add a few locals with previous experience for the right diplomatic touch. But they'll be mostly union people, and that should keep everyone happy."

"I'll stay happy if we shoot with the weather," Davis grumbled. "And we could use some dry runs." His glance slid over Anne, shifted away. And she told herself she mustn't blush. It was the first time in weeks she'd thought about some of those scenes she was supposed to do. Mostly with Webb—and when would *he* turn up? *Keep your mind on the conversation and learn from it,* she reprimanded herself.

A name brought her back to sharp awareness.

Harris was saying to Yves, "Espinoza is bringing Anna-Maria with him. She called me this morning." Was it really casual, the way his eyes moved to Anne's suddenly still face? "Sorry, love, I haven't had time to bring you up to date. Sal Espinoza—you must have heard of him? And Anna-Maria's his steady lady. I think you'll like her. She's beautiful, very charming—and the world's greatest masseuse. Ask Yves; he'll tell you she has a magical pair of hands."

"Truly a gift," Yves said. "She's better than any professional one could go to. Espinoza won't let anyone else close to him before or after a race."

"We'll have to get Anna-Maria to give you one of her special massages whenever you've had a really hard day, Anne. And I'd better warn you—Yves is a devilish hard taskmaster!"

Pleydel rolled his eyes. "I've been called much worse than that, *mon ami*. But before you scare off our little one here, you should also tell her that I'm very patient as well." He grinned at Anne. "Don't wear that frightened look, there's really nothing to it." A note of cynicism edged his voice: "Most women, I've found, are born actresses!"

Harris didn't come upstairs with her that night. He walked

with her to the foot of the stairs, teasing her because she wouldn't use the elevator Danny Verrano had installed.

"But I'm used to these stairs! I always did enjoy walking up to bed."

Was he coming with her? No, he looked apologetic, explaining that Yves and he were going to sit up and go over the schedule for the next few weeks. He looked down at her with something like regret in his eyes—it was there and then it was gone. And the sleepless night before, the cigarette smoke, and the after-dinner liqueurs had all combined to make her feel very tired.

Harris bent his head, his lips brushing hers in a light, affectionate kiss.

"Anne, you're very beautiful. And I wish that I—" He broke off abruptly, caught her questioning look, and gave a wry smile. "Damn! This is hardly the time or the place for a serious conversation, is it? But in my clumsy way I've been wanting to tell you that you must never feel obligated to me in any way. Do you understand? I want you to be a free soul, to feel free at all times."

Later, lying in bed, with her script on the night table beside her, Anne wondered at his almost solemnly serious speech. Underneath it all, Harris was really a very sensitive man. He couldn't fail to have noticed the lack in her. Was that why he had practically invited her to try out other lovers? And was that the answer?

So many people, all different, thrown into close proximity for several weeks. "Closed set." Did that mean that they were to be closed in as well? There were bound to be personality clashes, little feuds, shows of temperament. But perhaps, above all, that feeling of working together, being part of the exciting business of making a piece of make-believe come alive for millions of viewers. And she could recall the almost wistful feeling she'd had almost two years ago about the theater people, when she'd been the outsider looking in. It would be different this time.

Anne lay there for a long time, looking into the darkness and listening to the distant sea-murmuring outside her windows.

After a while she got up, went to the bathroom, and took a Valium. And when she came back to bed she switched on the small radio, letting the music play very softly. Harris hadn't come up to bed yet, but she didn't expect him to visit her tonight.

Just before she fell asleep, she thought she heard the sound of the helicopter again. Coming in to land or going away? It really didn't matter; she'd find out in the morning . . .

She hadn't heard the sound of opening doors and voices downstairs, nor the elevator coming and going. Waking with the daylight that suddenly filled her room as the heavy drapes were abruptly drawn open, Anne felt the aroma of steaming coffee tantalize her nostrils. Turning over onto her back, her eyes still sleep-filled, blinking into focus, Anne made a smothered sound and instinctively pulled the covers up to her neck. Karim stood there holding a tray and smiling at her.

"It is almost noon and everyone else is up enjoying this beautiful day. What did you do last night to make you so tired?" His smile widened, showing those white teeth. "And you look like a frightened virgin, all covered up against lustful eyes. I find that intriguing."

Anger sent all the lingering drowsiness from her brain. "What are you doing in here, Karim?"

"Offering myself as a substitute for that prune-faced woman who was bringing you this tray. Won't I do?"

His teasing voice carried subtle undercurrents as he stood there, looking undeniably handsome in his close-fitting silk shirt and tailored slacks, a silk scarf knotted rakishly about his brown throat. And his coal-dark eyes rested on her with a burning look that was unmistakable.

Anne felt her face begin to flame. "Thank you for your thoughtfulness. You may put the tray down and leave now."

The laughing mockery left his face as it darkened. "You make a mistake when you talk to me as if I were a servant, *ma belle*! And I think, too, that you have a lot to learn about men. I am no emasculated American or Englishman who would tolerate insolence from a woman, and I think I am going to enjoy teaching you that!"

"You're not in front of the cameras now, Karim, and I'm not in the mood for a dramatic scene. Will you please go away so I can get dressed?" Anne tried to keep her voice cool, but she was frightened, and her eyes were wary.

He slammed the tray down on the dresser so hard the coffee spilled; and turned back to stand looking down at her. "What are you so afraid of that you try to cover it with words of contempt? Just as you try to cover your body from my eyes? I think you are the kind of female who incites men to rape them because that is the only way they can enjoy sex—by being forced and mastered. And then, after that, you would fall willingly onto your knees whenever I clicked my fingers—so!—and take my cock in your mouth if I ordered it."

The deliberate crudity of his words shocked and startled her, as he had meant them to do, and he laughed with harsh satisfaction.

"What—have I made you afraid again? Of me, or of yourself and the secret desires that you try to hide under your cold airs? But then, you are far from being a trembling virgin, aren't you? And I know that there is much passion in you, for I have heard the sounds of delight that came from your throat while you were being fucked—your friend Carol played a tape for me one night." He laughed mockingly at the look on her face.

"Could it be that you did not know of the amusing game that she and your *chèr ami* Webb Carnahan had devised for their own titillation? It was like a contest between those two. Each one would keep a taped record of lovemaking with others, to be played back when they were together. A clever idea, no?"

Anne felt sick, bile almost choking her. No—not true! He was making it up to hurt her, to avenge the insult he felt she had inflicted on his pride. "No!" she said aloud. "You're lying—and I won't listen anymore. You had better—"

"Be careful what else you say to me, Anne Mallory, or I might lose my patience. I do not often waste so much time on talk, and neither do I need the sounds of other people making love to turn me on."

He stood looking down at her, his handsome face turned even darker by the flush of anger that suffused it. And involuntarily she shrank from his look, her reaction bringing a twisted smile.

"But then," he went on softly, "I am a patient man after all, and I am certain—that there will be a time for us. And I will teach you a great deal that you have not yet experienced." He made her a sarcastic bow. "So—I am sorry that I dared disturb your slumber, and I will wait—and so will you. *Bon matin.*"

Long after she had heard the door slam behind him, Anne lay huddled under the bedcovers, fighting the feeling of sickness and degradation. If only she could shut out the sound of Karim's mocking, sneering voice! Was it true? Webb and Carol, playing "an amusing little game," turning each other on? "You show me yours and I'll show you mine." She wanted to laugh hysterically. Perhaps she should have let Karim make love to her— he had been so sure of her, so sure of himself. And then he had reacted like a spoiled, sulky boy who wasn't used to being thwarted. But had he spoken the truth? And if he had, was she going to let it keep her cowering here like a frightened rabbit? The hell with Webb and his sick games. And the hell with Karim, who played a different, stalking game. She would face them both, and face them down.

The sudden anger that flowed through her was cleansing, vivifying. There were Harris's other guests to meet, and they all sounded fascinating, especially the Greek shipping millionaire, Petrakis. If she remembered right, he had just divorced his second wife. His current mistress, Sarah Vesper, would be playing her— Glory's—stepmother in the movie.

I'm free, Anne thought. *Free!* Hadn't even Harris encouraged her to think that way? *And*, she thought to herself, after she had showered and was putting on the last touches of her makeup, *I'll find a way of getting even with Webb—I'll pay him back in his own coin, the low-down bastard!*

Downstairs in the formal dining room that had been turned into a very authentic-looking Spanish *sala*, the cocktails were already flowing, even though it was still early afternoon.

Anne walked almost hesitantly downstairs, wearing a silky sundress with flounces on the skirt—very Spanish with its corselet waistline that pushed her breasts up and made more of them. Part of the last Saint Laurent collection. It helped her feel poised and ready to face anything—or anyone.

Taped music playing discreetly in the background masked the ceaseless growl of the ocean, and was in turn almost drowned out by the murmur of voices and laughter.

Today the camera crew, engineers, and technicians she had met yesterday were not in evidence. These were the elite—the fun people—Harris's guests from the highest international circles. And they were obviously starting to enjoy themselves early.

Anne allowed herself one last, wistful thought of the cool, fresh air outside, with its odor of pines and ocean, before she walked forward to join them. Almost immediately, Harris Phelps was at her side, his eyes searching her face questioningly.

"Didn't you sleep well last night, love? I was beginning to wonder if you were coming down at all. I'd have come up to find you myself, only"—he gestured apologetically at the crowd —"you can see how it's been!" Then, his hand closing gently over her arm, he drew her close to kiss her, his lips brushing the corner of her shiny, reddened mouth. "You look exceptionally lovely, darling. Now come along and meet our guests."

Our guests, he had said, reminding her gently that she was supposed to be playing hostess. His understanding made her feel guilty.

"I'm sorry I slept so late," Anne whispered, wondering if she should tell him of Karim's visit to her room. And then she had no more time to wonder, because Harris was beginning the string of introductions, propelling her from one group of people to the next.

The names seemed to blur into each other after a while; it was like reading the society pages, Anne thought dazedly. A few stood out ...

Taki Petrakis—stocky, dark-haired, and dynamic, with a sensual mouth that lingered a shade too long on the back of her hand when he kissed it. His elegant auburn-haired companion didn't seem to mind; she smiled conspiratorially at Anne. Sarah Vesper —society woman turned movie actress, throwing up her career to marry one of the few really rich English dukes left. Making her comeback in *Greed for Glory*, now that she was a widow. Sarah wore a fortune in jewels and had a small chiseled face that didn't show her age. Anne liked her instinctively—she had a charming, magnetic smile that lighted up her face, and a friendly, natural manner that showed no jealousy at all.

Rufus Randall owned a chain of newspapers, several of the leading magazines, and two publishing houses. He was also a major stockholder in one of the biggest television networks. He stayed out of the news himself, for the most part. "Randall House published *Greed for Glory*, Anne." Harris, tactfully jogging her memory in case she had forgotten.

Randall was broad-shouldered, medium-built. And he gestured constantly with a cigar—lit or unlit. His bright blue eyes regarded her piercingly from under bushy eyebrows, studying her with the unabashed openness of the very rich. "One of our favorite cover girls, eh? Sure you'll do just as well as an actress."

She felt her hand caught in his bear-paw grip and murmured something polite, wondering uncomfortably why he kept studying her face, until he said abruptly, "You take after your mother, you know. Used to know her. She was a lovely thing."

Without giving her time to absorb the shock of that statement he swiveled his gaze to Harris. "Is it okay with you if we run a story on her in *Personalities*? Cover story, of course. Get the jump on our competitors." He gave an unexpected bark of laughter. "Didn't think you'd mind, so I told Jeff—where the hell is that son of a bitch?—to try to corner her sometime this evening. That all right with you, Anne Mallory?"

He was the kind of man who would ride roughshod over anyone in any case, Anne thought resentfully, even while she gave him the answer he had already taken for granted.

All this, once she had thankfully escaped Rufus Randall, turned out to be more introductions to more people.

Claudia del Antonini, wearing a daringly backless little nothing that clung intimately to her ample curves, was definitely hostile, although she did manage a polite grimace that was supposed to pass for a smile. Yves Pleydel, standing with his ex-wife, kissed Anne full on the lips and complimented her extravagantly, which did little to improve Claudia's mood.

Karim's uncle, the emir, wore an Arabian headcloth that looked incongruous with his European dress. He was a hawk-nosed, elegant-looking man who was nevertheless polite as he, too, kissed her hand, speaking to her in French, as Karim did. She felt his eyes assessing her all the same. Standing with him, Karim did nothing more than bow politely, even while he gave her a meaningful look that reminded her uncomfortably of her awakening.

It was a relief when the emir detained Harris and Anne was free to wander off on her own, after returning the apologetic squeeze Harris gave her hand.

In her present frame of mind Anne knew exactly where she was headed. To the bar that had been set up against one wall of the room. She had done a good job of acting a part this afternoon, and she deserved her reward for being a good girl.

"Fix me a martini, would you, Dave? Beefeaters—up. And hold the olive."

Webb wasn't here yet—thank God for that. She wasn't ready to face him. Damn him—damn him! She'd been a new amusement, a new tape to add to his collection and Carol's. She didn't want to see Carol again either. Imagining them listening together, laughing, making love against a background of his making love to her. Sick—there were worse words to describe Webb and what he was, and sometime she'd take pleasure in using them all on him—after she'd used him!

"Cheers. You're the first woman I've met who knows how to order a real martini."

For the first time Anne really noticed the man who had been leaning against the bar when she'd come up. A face that was somehow familiar. Florida tan under prematurely gray hair. Sideburns, twinkling blue eyes. She took a sip of her martini, considering him, and he put out his hand rather tentatively.

"I'm Harold Brightman. Have I been too bold?"

"Oh, how nice! My new guru. I'm Anne Mallory, and I need to be taught how to relax. Hasn't Harris told you?"

He had a friendly, puckish grin. And no reaction to her too-flip speech. "How nice to meet *you*! And you seem perfectly relaxed this afternoon. Harris only told me how happy he was at having discovered you. And a few other very complimentary things."

The martini tasted cold and good. Very good. Too short, though. She pushed the glass across the bar and Dave gave her a refill without comment, while she smiled at Dr. Brightman.

"Would it be talking shop if I told you I read your book and enjoyed it? My analyst, my old guru, Dr. Haldane, used to quote from it."

He looked pleased. "Well, I'm afraid I was gathering my courage up enough to talk shop and ask you how it felt to be a movie actress. I'm a hopeless movie fan, I'm afraid."

The second martini tasted better, and this time they laughed together.

"Seriously, I can't think why a charming, self-possessed young woman like you should need a—how did you put it?—

a guru." Anne heard herself giggle. Oh dear, hadn't martinis always been her undoing? But what the hell!

She slid her glass back to Dave again, recklessly, and said lightly, "But you see, I drink too much at parties like this. And there's really a lot of tension inside me. I keep wondering if I'll ever be able to *act*. Being a model is another thing—it was almost a game, you know. I don't know anything about acting . . . oh damn! Now I am talking shop, aren't I? I'm sorry."

He was leaning toward her attentively, not seeming to mind at all. In fact, he looked flattered. He was a kind man, Anne thought, and she wanted to pat his hand.

"What you're feeling is perfectly normal, of course, but if you really want to—"

"Anne, here you are! Hi, Hal, glad to find you've met each other." Harris, sounding fussy. Preparing to drag her off to meet more people she didn't really care if she met or not, and just when she had begun to enjoy herself.

"We were talking shop," she said. "Dr. Brightman is going to teach me how to relax—aren't you?"

"Of course I am, if you really feel you need it!"

"Well, I do!"

He smiled at her, raising his glass somewhat regretfully as Harris dragged her off to introduce her to yet another group of people.

Chapter Twenty-four

IT WAS YVES PLEYDEL'S IDEA to start shooting a few scenes earlier than anticipated.

"It'll keep the crew busy," he explained apologetically, spreading his hands in an expansive gesture. "And it will perhaps provide some entertainment for our guests. And you, *ma petite* Anne—you will gain some experience, *oui*? The scenes between Glory and her stepmother, in the very beginning—they will be easy, for there is very little dialogue that you will have to learn. You are playing a naïve girl—young, shy—and it will be mainly 'Yes, madame,' and 'No, madame.' You are not on the stage, trying to project your voice, so you will keep it low and hesitant, you comprehend? *La belle* Sarah will help you. She is very kind, a great actress. We are lucky to have her."

Anne had to admit that it would give her something to do. She had hardly seen Harris for the past two days—he seemed preoccupied and back to his Harris Phelps, Producer, role. He spent most of his time closeted with Rufus Randall, Petrakis, and Karim's uncle. Business, he had explained to her soothingly. And thank goodness she wasn't supposed to entertain everyone else. They all seemed perfectly content to do their own thing—wandering around the island or driving into town. And Karim hadn't tried to force himself on her again, although whenever she saw him she could sense him watching her—and waiting, as he had promised. The only ones she had really got close to were Sarah Vesper and Dr. Brightman, and she had learned that the method of relaxation he advocated really did help, although she probably would never be as good at it as Sarah was.

In any case, when Yves made his suggestion at dinner, Anne was all for it. She had to get her feet wet sometime, hadn't she? And slashing across her mind was the thought that Webb hadn't turned up yet—she would much rather make her first mistakes without his watching eyes taking away her confidence.

More people were expected to join them. Sal Espinoza and his Anna-Maria—she of the magical hands and the arrogant voice that Anne still remembered with a sense of annoyance. And Jean Benedict, the singer, who was to play a bit part in the movie. She wondered if Jimmy Markham would really turn up—remembering the way he and Carol had looked at each other on the last occasion she'd met him.

Harris had so many friends from so many different worlds. *And I'm not cut out to be an international hostess,* Anne thought ruefully. She supposed that the business of making movies, make-believe magic, fascinated everyone, no matter what walk of life they came from or how sophisticated they professed to be. Look at *her*. She was scared, and excited at the same time. The kid who wanted to be a movie star grown up.

"This is going to be very short, very easy," Yves said soothingly. "Sarah will help you. Watch her—she will give you your cues. You have not much to say. Try to feel the part of the young woman you are portraying—so young, so reckless, and so innocent at the same time. A protected young woman who does not know much of the world, but is curious. Perhaps you understand the feeling? Forget the cameras, the lights, everyone who will be watching, including myself. You are a girl who is nicknamed Glory, and you are meeting your new stepmother for the first time. She is a stranger to you, but she is nice—quite young, too, in fact. Use whatever mannerisms you think a young girl would use under such circumstances. The downcast eyes, the nervous plucking at a fold in the skirt. Lose yourself in the person you are supposed to be, and if you feel awkward, diffident, shy—that is all right; that is how you are supposed to be!"

The set was an interior scene, for which they were using one of the spare bedrooms. Anne tried to think of it as another modeling assignment. She had been through Costume (pins, uncomfortable stays that dug into her hips and breasts) and Makeup; she had submitted to Yves's studying her through the viewfinder he wore on a strap around his neck as if she were some strange insect.

But Yves had been very kind, very patient, once the scene had been set in exactly the way he wanted it. And Sarah, too —whispering to her comfortingly, "Just remember, dear, that all of us, in the beginning, started out with no experience at all!"

All she had to do was to pretend that Yves Pleydel was just another photographer telling her how she should stand or sit, what kind of expression he wanted her to wear. "Smile, Anne! Twirl around to make that gorgeous long skirt flare out over your ankles. Come on, you can do better than that! Try dreamy —wistful . . ." And she was used to onlookers—the crowds who gathered to stare when she was modeling, say, in Trafalgar Square or balanced precariously on the edge of the fountain in Piccadilly Circus.

"Yes, madame," and "No, madame." If her voice sounded low and hesitant, the mike would pick it up anyhow.

It wasn't too hard after all; and when it was all over, Yves kissed her hand, his voice jubilant. "You see? I am never wrong in my predictions. Only two takes, and for a novice, that is exceptional! You are going to be magnificent, *ma chèrie*. And tomorrow you will watch some of the others, so that when your turn comes again, you will be much more confident."

Sarah Vesper kissed her, too. "You were wonderful, Anne. And now that we've got that behind us, I think we could both use some refreshment, don't you?"

Harris, after giving her a preoccupied hug, went off with his friends again. All those meetings—it really seemed to be business and not entirely pleasure that had brought all those friends of his here. Anne decided to go along with Sarah and Dr. Brightman, who would help them both unwind, as Sarah put it. Better than trying to evade Karim, who had come up to whisper to her significantly that he could hardly wait for *their* scenes.

What had started out as a gray morning had turned into a sun-speckled afternoon. Brightman chose a place where a large flat rock looked out over the ocean.

Anne turned her back to the ocean, watching rather enviously as Sarah Vesper, slim and straight-backed in her blue denim slack suit, was able to sit cross-legged with no apparent effort. With her head thrown back and her hair knotted at the nape of her neck, she looked like a Buddha statue—a study in concentration. And all it took for Sarah was a few whispered words, Hal Brightman's hands touching her shoulder for an instant. With her eyes closed, the lines in her face seemed to smooth out almost miraculously until she looked like a young girl.

"How long does it take? I mean, it can't be as easy as it looks, can it?"

This was the first chance Anne had had since the evening they'd met to really talk to him alone—Sarah, lost in a trance, seemed not to be there at all.

He smiled deprecatingly. "That really depends on the subject. The willingness to let go and to absorb."

"But . . ."

He said gently, "I can help you, Anne, if you'll let me try. But there's a different technique for everyone, and in your case I'd like to begin by going back."

"Back? Back where?"

"You said something about a recurrent, frightening dream yesterday. And you must know that such dreams have a great deal of significance." He shrugged. "A dream of drowning—and you're very uneasy about this place, aren't you? Yet you were brought up here. Surely all the memories could not have been unhappy?" Before she could say anything he leaned forwards, his voice earnest. "Going back, Anne, simply means to go backwards in time—perhaps under hypnosis. And then, once you understand the traumas of childhood and the leftovers from other, previous lives, then you can understand as an adult. It'll be like a slate wiped clean—and all you write on it from then on will be the real, uncluttered you. Your present and your future will be controlled by you, with your new knowledge and understanding of yourself. Meditation isn't easy. It needs strength of mind and concentration, and the strength has to come from within yourself. If there are barriers, there—"

"Is it okay if I join in? I just got in, and they told me you might be out here. Traveling always makes me so damn uptight."

The girl who sauntered up had a black mane of hair flying in the wind. Her fists were stuffed into the center pocket of a faded sweatshirt, her faded blue jeans were unhemmed and dirt-rimmed at the bottom, and they clung to her slim-hipped body.

"I'm Jean Benedict," she said simply as she dropped down easily into a lotus position, not waiting for Dr. Brightman to answer. "I've been into yoga for a long time, and I guess that's what kept me sane. But it always helps when there are other people you can touch minds with." Her shoulders lifted, unbound breasts straining against thin cotton. "They want me to do this short acting bit, you know. And suddenly I'm scared shitless. What the hell do I know about trying to be someone else, when all this time I've been trying to learn about being me? I don't know!"

She brushed flying strands of hair from her face and smiled at Anne, white teeth showing against her tan. "Hi! I caught the tail end of that scene, and I guess you're going through the same trip, huh? What sign are you—Libra?"

It made Anne blink, even though her first reaction to the woman's intrusion had been annoyance. How could she have guessed?

Jean Benedict's smile broadened into a grin. "I'm right? I usually am. I'm a Sagittarius. We should get along well together."

Sarah Vesper, who had been as motionless as an ivory statuette, suddenly seemed to blink herself back to awareness. She gave Jean Benedict one of her warm smiles. "Hello! I'm one of your greatest admirers, you know. I've been looking forward to meeting you. Are you going to be joining our little sessions?"

Jean Benedict shrugged, her brown eyes turning from Anne to the other woman. "I don't know. Like I was just telling the doctor, I'm into yoga pretty heavy. But it takes time and privacy, and privacy is what I don't have a lot of the time! I'd like to know more about your thing."

She had given a jerk of her head toward Hal Brightman, but her eyes stayed fixed on Sarah.

Later, Anne couldn't remember too much about the discussion that followed, except that Dr. Brightman had controlled its direction without seeming to. She stayed silent for the most part, thinking about what he had started to explain to her earlier, before Jean had arrived. Going back—would it help?

The tide was coming in, and the rising roar of the breakers battering against the rocks below them became suddenly oppressive. Without turning her head to look, she could imagine them rushing avidly into the sea caves, licking down their length like forked, spittle-flecked dragons' tongues, only to draw back again with a sullen sigh of regret. Cheated, because there was no victim there . . .

"I can't wait to go down to the beach," Jean Benedict said when they were all walking back to the house together. "What's the best way?"

Just in time Anne closed her lips against the words that had almost burst out. "Oh, but it's too dangerous!" she'd wanted to say. "If you try going down the cliff you could slip and break your ankle and lie there *forever*. And if you go through the caves, someone could be waiting for you out there." Why had she thought that? There was a sudden jagged tear in her memory. A long shadow—no, it was *two* shadows . . . she couldn't remember; it was all part of her Dream.

As they followed the narrow path, Sarah and Jean seemed to have got ahead, both talking animatedly. Or was it that Dr. Brightman had dropped back?

"You really *are* afraid of the ocean, aren't you?" he said in a low voice at her side.

"Yes." She answered him baldly, turning her head to look at him, meeting his thoughtful blue eyes.

"There's a reason? I couldn't help noticing how tense you suddenly became when the tide started to come in. Is it because of your dream, or does the dream stem from your fear?" He was probing now, but very lightly. And her answer seemed to slip out quite naturally.

"I don't know—but it's always the same. I'm drowning, being sucked under, just like—"

"Just like your mother was?" In some strange manner, the calmly matter-of-fact way he made the statement counteracted part of her shocked reaction.

He squeezed her hand, his voice still low-pitched. "It would seem to be a very normal reaction to what must have been a terribly traumatic experience for the child you were at the time, Anne! But don't you see, if you know the reason for your dream, then . . ."

Anne found that she had stopped dead and was staring at him. "How . . . ?"

He gave her a faint smile that was almost troubled as he studied her face. "I remember reading about it in the newspapers. The Mallory House Tragedy. Mallory House—Anne Mallory. You see, I, too, spent part of my boyhood here. In Monterey. My father was a colonel in the army, stationed at Fort Ord. I graduated from Monterey High School, and spent a year in the junior college, as they used to call it then. Spent my summers bumming around the beaches—surfing, diving for abalone. There's something about this part of the world that gets into the blood, isn't there?"

Chapter Twenty-five

THE EMIR, Karim's uncle, walked slowly through the central courtyard, looking about him with interest. His bodyguards walked a few discreet paces behind him, and he was accompanied by Rufus Randall and the Greek, Petrakis.

"Most impressive," he said in his slightly accented English. "It already looks like a film set. It was clever of our friend Phelps to discover such an ideal place. I have enjoyed his hospitality. A pity I have to leave tomorrow, but I have already been away from my country for too long." He looked questioningly at Petrakis. "You will be visiting us soon?"

The stocky, heavy-shouldered man grinned. "Soon after I have gone back home and made the arrangements. In the meantime, I'm sure that Rufus here and Harris between them will see to everything else."

Randall's inevitable cigar spilled ash over his jacket front, and he brushed it off impatiently. He was a man who didn't particularly care how he dressed, so long as his clothes were comfortable. "Everything's under control, so far. And I think we're well prepared for most eventualities. It's a pity Markham couldn't get down here as early as planned, but he's being kept busy. Says he ought to get a break during the next two weeks. To play golf at Cypress Point."

"With his bosom friend Parmenter—the CIA man?"

"Of course Parmenter will be with him. It wouldn't look genuine if he weren't. But Parmenter's no problem—he's looking to be appointed Agency chief, and as you know, there's no love lost between the CIA and—the Organization."

The emir said thoughtfully, "You do not, I hope, underestimate this man Reardon? What about this actor, the one who is to play the lead in your picture, who used to work for Reardon? If they have got to him . . ."

Again, Randall answered. "It's not likely. From what I've heard, Webb Carnahan dropped out of the Organization a long time ago, with several good reasons for hating Reardon. In any case, we're checking on that."

"And what could he find out?" Petrakis added quickly. "Nothing. Only the few of us know. The rest of the people here are merely concerned with making a film. And I've no doubt our friend Phelps will have his movements carefully monitored." He gave a sudden burst of laughter. "That video monitor! It's quite an ingenious setup, eh? Trust a man like Danny Verrano to think of such a thing."

Randall laughed, and the emir permitted himself a dry smile. "I am glad to note that our friend had the tact to leave our rooms uncovered by hidden television cameras. Naturally, I had my men check very carefully to make sure. But I must admit it might have been interesting to have a videotape of the performance that young Italian woman put on for my benefit last night. She was—quite exceptional, even for a man of my jaded appetites."

Petrakis, who was without inhibitions, grinned. "I was in Sarah's room last night. I must say that I am quite interested in watching a replay."

"I would like to see what the blonde model is like when she is really aroused. That is, if a man is capable of arousing her. She did not receive my nephew too well, although I must admit that Karim is inclined to be too impulsive." The emir looked meaningfully at Randall. "He will need to be watched —and checked, if necessary. My sister was a very flighty, silly woman. And her Egyptian husband was a wastrel. Karim needs to learn self-discipline. Even the training camp of the PLO did not teach him that."

Randall gave a short, imperceptible nod of acknowledgment; and as the three men began to retrace their steps, the conversation turned to other topics.

The courtyard was deserted at this time—hot under the afternoon sun, protected from the cool breeze that had sprung up outside. Now that the crew had been banished from the main house and the others had sought the coolness and privacy of their rooms, it was again the private place that Anne remembered as she came outside, unzipping her long terrycloth robe. She had watched impatiently from one of the galleries while the men were walking around, engaged in what was obviously a private conversation.

Now perhaps she'd be able to lie in the sun in peace for an hour or so, trying to collect her thoughts. It had been a shock to realize that Hal Brightman knew so much about her, and even remembered about her mother's death. But he had sounded kind, and understanding. Perhaps, after all, she *should* take his advice about going back in order to go forwards. Maybe that was what she needed to rid her of the Dream.

She laid the robe down by the fountain and settled herself on it facedown, unfastening the top of her bikini at the back. She missed the sunbathing she had been able to do in Malibu, and this might be her last chance for a while.

Taki Petrakis's room opened onto the gallery overlooking the courtyard. He kept the French windows half-closed as he watched her. So—she must have been waiting for her chance. He hoped their voices hadn't carried up to her, wherever she had been watching from, and then dismissed the thought with a shrug. They'd been talking softly, had deliberately chosen the courtyard for privacy, because it was one of the few places they could be sure hadn't been bugged. Business allies or not, it never paid to trust anyone else completely!

For a few moments Petrakis toyed with the thought of going out there to join her. She really had a lovely body—slim. He liked his women slim, like Sarah, who was one of his favorite mistresses. The emir wasn't alone in being curious about this woman—Richard Reardon's daughter. Idly, he wondered what color her nipples would be. Rose-tinted—she looked like a natural blonde. Yes, he'd like to try her out, but perhaps it would be wiser not to, since Harris Phelps had apparently developed a soft spot for her—or had he? He didn't underestimate Phelps, who had got the girl here in the first place, and very smoothly, too. Time would tell. In the meanwhile, there were those very explicit scenes in the movie—especially those to be shot for the European version. He grinned to himself. She shouldn't bother with that ridiculous little bikini bottom. Within the next two weeks there would be opportunities for everyone to look their fill at Anne Mallory's unclothed body. What would Reardon think of that, if he could know?

It was not the extent of Richard Reardon's knowledge, but what he intended to do with it, that occupied the two men who sat in a small cluttered office located on the fifth floor of a nondescript building in Washington, D.C. The discreet sign on the outer door read: FINANCIAL PLANNING. Few of the people who passed down the long, shabby hallway noticed the sign or paid it any attention. Only a select few entered that door. General Tarrant was one of them. He and Ted Barstow, the man who occupied this particular office, were old acquaintances, talking comparatively freely.

"Markham's been coming out with some pretty heady speeches recently, hasn't he?" the general said. "All that on-the-line stuff, and the lines are being more clearly drawn. You read the copy of the last one?"

"Who hasn't? It's in all the newspapers. Détente is old stuff, and as for armed neutrality—where have we heard that before? So the latest line is 'Keep the people informed, let them take a share.' And they're eating it up, of course. Look at the coverage he's been getting! The new Golden Boy. Young and idealistic. 'Clean-cut and clear-cut in his views.' Isn't that how that bastard Rufe Randall put it in his last special editorial? And it isn't like him to give a plug to any politician . . . which makes me wonder what's up."

"It was that bit about his having the perfect wife and the perfect family that really made me want to throw up. The Jack-and-Jackie buildup without the backstairs rumors . . . and how come? Normally, the press would be right on to the rumors, and they'd be printing them. Jimmy boy and Carol Cochran . . . we know and they know, but no one's using it. And we all know that if Markham gets in come election time, its farewell for *us*. Christ, don't we all know his much publicized feelings about 'secret organizations which are answerable to no one'? And we even let him get away with *that* quote!" The general was thinking aloud, and he knew it. Reardon was playing this one close to his chest. So close it was getting to be marginal.

"You know damn well why we did!" Ted Barstow was usually a graven image of pipe-smoking stolidity; now he sounded acerbic as he knocked the bowl of his pipe against the glass ashtray with unnecessary force. "Here it is—something big—and we have to play hands-off for the time being because a dumb, spoiled kid got in with the wrong crowd and decided to play the rebel. They all do it, don't they? They kick out at what they call our brand of propaganda and fall for another. And considering who's involved and what we think is involved, the only way we can play it is cool. We don't have any official reason to go in there, you know. And with the people involved . . . goddammit, we'd be playing into their hands! Besides, at this stage there's nothing we can pinpoint—"

"And for that we're depending on an ex-operative of doubtful loyalties? A goddamned actor? Surely . . ."

Barstow's face seemed to close for a moment; he had refilled his pipe and now he puffed at it furiously before he answered. "I think he'll come across. If there's anything, he can find out."

The buzzer on Barstow's desk sounded and he pushed a button. A bright feminine voice broke the sudden silence. "Those portfolios are ready for the general now, sir. And Mr. Reardon's in, if he has any questions."

As General Tarrant eased himself to his feet, his square, heavy-browed face still grim, Barstow permitted himself a rare flash of humor. "At least, General, you must admit you've been getting some darned good financial advice for the past few years!"

Tarrant lifted an eyebrow in acknowledgment but continued to look sour as he went through the door.

Barstow put his pipe down carefully and went back to his methodical study of the files—about four of them—that were stacked neatly on his desk. Innocuous-looking manila folders that purported to contain detailed reports on certain investments. Only he and a very few other persons knew that the tiny star on the colored identification tabs meant that these were ultraconfidential documents. Top secret. Not even the CIA or the FBI had access to these files, although they incorporated data supplied by those two agencies. Everything that filtered up to the National Security Council found its way here—plus some information that did not get that far, because it was suppressed (there was still a certain amount of jealousy among the various intelligence organizations) or discarded as not being important enough.

Barstow had a photographic memory—a natural talent later trained and developed. He had been with the OSS during World War II; stayed with Intelligence until he was hand-picked as one of "Reardon's Boys" by Reardon himself. His record showed that he had long since been retired, was now comfortably employed by a large and prosperous private corporation. But then, not many people were left alive who would remember him. The small group he'd worked with had taken a lot of risks and suffered a lot of casualties. The last and most recent one being Duncan Frazier. Officially CIA, but working for them.

Barstow's face was cold and hard as he bent over the thickest file. Dunc's. Filled with his reports, including the last. Cross-referenced, with references to the other files stacked along with it. When he'd gone through them all he might find something—some clue.

Damn those recent leaks anyhow, and goddamn the newspapers that printed them! So many agents dead because their cover had been blown. He hoped that Hyatt was okay. He was expected in today, and Security had already been alerted, just in case. Fortunate that Hyatt had been in France—digging up some background on Yves Pleydel, his ex-wives, and that Egyptian fellow who professed to be an actor—when Frazier bought it.

Bought it! Barstow grimaced. He'd picked that particular phrase up from the British. Some of their reports ended up on his desk as well, especially since they'd been working together—almost!—on the Irish matter. And then the telephone call on the hotline only this morning. Quiet, rather drawling voice that to Barstow's ears always sounded rather affected.

"Sorry to be the bearer of bad news, old chap. Afraid your man Frazier bought it. Late afternoon, our time. A bomb. There'd been threats, of course, and we'd been taking all the precautions we could, but these IRA boys have been getting cleverer at slipping past. At least that's who we think it was. You have any different ideas?"

He'd passed the call on to Reardon and sent for the files. And he hadn't said anything about it to Tarrant. Let Reardon be the one to tell him, and calm him down when the general blew up. Dammit, he didn't have any answers to the enraged questions that Tarrant would snap out. His job was to sift through the mass of detail that lay before him, memorizing and correlating, checking fact against surmise. Hoping he'd come up with *something*—some tiny coincidence or common denominator that would provide a clue. When Hyatt arrived, maybe his personal report would help.

Barstow kept reading doggedly, scanning pages with incredible swiftness. Occasionally he picked up a pen to mark a section for microfilming. Get all the salient facts together into one document.

Christ, but there were a lot of people involved! Unfortunately including Reardon's daughter. Just an unwitting pawn or a member of the other side herself? Fleetingly, while he drew on his pipe, Barstow permitted himself to wonder what she might be doing right now. How much did she know, what was she thinking?

Lying in the sun always made her feel drowsy. Her body felt sun-drenched, heavy and warm, even after she stepped out from under the shower. Quickly, without stopping to think about it, Anne shook a capsule out of the bottle in the mirrored cabinet and swallowed it. She grimaced at her flushed reflection. Not really an "upper." Just something to keep her alert and alive during the evening that loomed ahead. And she'd better hurry, or Harris would be upset.

She wore the thin choker he had given her—very tiny platinum beads, each studded with a miniature diamond. A little-nothing crepe-de-chine blouse, open almost all the way down the front, worn with a full gypsy-style skirt and high-heeled sandals. Her hair up tonight, but artfully untidy, with strands escaping down the back of her neck and framing her face. Lip gloss, a touch of mascara. That should do it. She looked very different from the Victorian miss she'd played this morning. Tonight she was ready to play the sophisticated hostess; the role was becoming easier.

"Darling, you look simply stunning this evening! Is that one of Thea's creations you're wearing?" Sarah Vesper, in floating green chiffon, pressed her cheek lightly against Anne's.

"You look great. Wish I could wear the kind of clothes you do, but I guess I'll stick to my own style." Jean Benedict's formal evening wear was a buttoned-up blue denim skirt, with a matching vest that left most of her midriff bare. She wore chunky Indian jewelry, and it suited her dark good looks. Her hair, as usual, flowed down her back.

But later on, when she sang, her guitar picking out lonely chords, the whole room was hushed. "I like to sing for the ocean, and the wind and the mountains—for everything that's free, and I hope to hell that includes me," she had said quietly. Singing, her voice was pure and true and soaring, taking the highest and lowest notes without effort; wrapping its spell around everyone there.

"She's beautiful, and she's real," Sarah whispered, watching Jean take her ovation as unself-consciously as she'd sung.

Real, Anne thought. *Are any of us real? Is any of this real?* She was remembering Jean's dedication of her first song to "everything that's free." Well, Jean was a free soul. Maybe it was her talent that had made her that way, or the yoga. *I've got to talk to Dr. Brightman*, Anne thought distractedly. She was watching Harris talk to a tall, dark-haired man who was starting to go gray at the temples—someone she hadn't seen before. And that reminded her that she had heard the helicopter fly over while she'd been sunbathing. More new arrivals? He looked vaguely familiar, but then all of Harris's friends did.

Jean Benedict had stopped singing and taped disco music took over as everyone scattered into small groups. This could have been a fashionable house party anywhere in the world. "Coming home" was not really like coming home at all. This was still Danny Verrano's house, in spite of all the changes that Harris had promised and made. Perhaps it was best this way.

"Anne, I'd like you to meet Sal Espinoza." Of course, that was why his face had seemed so familiar.

He bowed over her hand, kissing it. Flashing her his consciously attractive smile. "This is such a pleasure. I've been looking forward to meeting you."

His friend, Anna-Maria, exhausted from too much traveling, had asked to be excused. She'd retired to bed already.

Harris left them alone, and he was a charming man—an excellent dancer. Better than Taki Petrakis, who had held her close enough for her to feel his erection, while he kissed her ear. He had invited her to visit his private island, and to cruise with him on his yacht.

Dexamyl and martinis didn't exactly mix, but Anne was past caring. She liked Espinoza, who talked to her about the races he'd been in instead of whispering compliments and innuendos in her ear.

Anne danced with him a second time, because she enjoyed his company and because she wanted to avoid Karim, who had been glowering at her from across the room, where he stood dutifully by his uncle.

Danny Verrano had converted one of the seaward-looking balconies into a covered terrace, and they had just come indoors, Anne laughing at something that Sal had said, when she saw Webb. He looked as if he'd just got in—he was wearing faded blue denims and a patterned blue silk shirt, open to the waist. He had a drink in one hand, and he was kissing Claudia, holding her around the waist with his free arm.

It was like watching one of those movies where the action was frozen for a few seconds to catch everyone in midmovement. Anne felt herself frozen, too, and then Espinoza said, "Shall I get you another drink? It's beginning to get quite hot in here," and everything came back to normal again.

"I'd love one. I'll come with you and get it." She didn't look at Webb again. "Not tonight," she thought. "Tomorrow will be time enough."

Chapter Twenty-six

ALL THE WAY UP HERE he had damned the fog and Harris Phelps's halfhearted directions that had almost gotten him lost, and most of all his own mood of frustration. On this occasion, driving took all his concentration as he took curves he shouldn't have tried to take at the speed he was traveling. And his thoughts weren't worth thinking. Far better to concentrate on the sweet wonder of the Ferrari that responded better than any woman he had ever known.

Harris had wanted him to fly in by helicopter, like the rest of his "guests." But hell, this fog would have kept the chopper grounded. And he needed the time and the fresh air to clear his mind of its own fog of emotion. Ever since the telephone call from good old buddy Peter, coming just after he'd finished a particularly strenuous set of tennis with Dave, who couldn't stop chortling over the fact that he'd beaten him.

"You're getting out of condition, old man! Too much of the fleshpots of Europe?"

"I don't have my own private tennis court where I can practice every day, like you do!"

He had almost started to relax by then—almost. But then Hiro, Dave's houseboy, had come outside.

"Telephone call for Mr. Carnahan. A Mr. Markus, from New York."

Leo Markus was his agent. And he had given Leo Dave's

unlisted number, just in case. He knew that Leo wouldn't call unless it was absolutely necessary. Leo wasn't the kind to make casual telephone calls—especially when he was on the verge of starting a new picture. Leo was a soft-spoken chain smoker who preferred to have business discussions with his clients in person.

He should have known. And yet when he heard the slightly nasal voice over the line, it was all he could do to keep from slamming the receiver down.

"Hi, Webb. This is your old school buddy Peter here. You were expecting to hear from me, weren't you?"

Just like old times. And his conversation with Vito suddenly fresh in his mind, Webb forced himself to swallow his anger while he listened.

"Glad we're going to be working together again. We used to make good partners in the old days." Peter used to enjoy snapping necks. "Just like chickens . . . but then, you weren't brought up a farm boy like I was, were you, old buddy?"

When there was killing to be done, Webb had preferred using a gun or a knife. And he'd never liked Peter. It came back to him in a rush of hate and self-disgust. A feeling that stayed with him all the way down the road until, almost unbelievingly, he'd traveled through all of the elaborate security checks (electrified fences and gates with armed guards, no less) down the dirt-road turnoff he'd almost missed—to arrive at the water's edge and a goddamn drawbridge.

"What the fuck is this? A missile base?"

They had turned the lights on when the Ferrari roared up, stopping inches away from the black-painted wooden shack. *Checkpoint Charlie*, he thought, even while he tried to hang on to his temper.

"Sorry, sir. Do you have your pass?" The man who spoke had an expressionless face, and a shotgun cradled in the crook of his arm.

"It's starting to get worn out. It's already been checked three times."

Webb's voice was dangerously soft, and he had to fight the impulse to swing the wheel around and head back the way he had come.

"I'm sorry, Mr. Carnahan," the man said without inflection. "Just doing my job. You know how it is. I'm supposed to keep uninvited visitors out. Not too many of the guests chose to drive all the way down here." He gave a wave of his arm to the other man in the shack. "It won't take long now. He'll press the button, and the bridge will come down. When you drive across it, swing to the right and follow the road that takes you up towards the house. You can't miss all the lights."

A fucking island, of all things. And more security than Fox had used while they were shooting *Superman*.

The man had been right about his not being able to miss all the lights. Up here, the fog was below, and the house looked more like a castle, with lighted outbuildings sprawling on either side of it.

Webb brought the Ferrari to a savage halt before a flight of shallow stone steps, gravel spurting under the tires. A massive wooden door, relic transported from some ancient castle, like the damn drawbridge, stood open. Music and more light, and a man came down the steps.

This time, at least, he didn't have to show his pass. Maybe they'd called ahead.

"Mr. Carnahan?" He had a glimpse of a swarthy, acne-scarred face. "I'm Palumbo, Mr. Phelps's chauffeur. And I can drive her into the garage for you and see that your luggage is taken to your room if you'd like to go right in and join everyone for a drink."

Palumbo was letting his eyes run over the Ferrari's sleek lines. Admiringly, a little enviously. She sure was something! And then he watched Webb Carnahan uncoil his long frame

271

from the cramped space behind the wheel, coming easily to his feet in one lithe motion. He had an easy smile, too—a pity he couldn't tell Gina he'd actually met her idol (she watched all of his movies on TV, and bought all the fan magazines that had his picture in them). But then, he never discussed his work with Gina; it was an understanding they'd had ever since they'd gotten married five years ago. On this job he'd met a hell of a lot of people he and Gina had only read about before.

"Thanks. It seemed like a damned long drive behind about five cars piled up behind a goddamned camper. A drink sounds exactly like what I need." Webb added carefully, *"Grazie."*

And almost saw Palumbo's eyes snap into focus on him before the man said politely and carefully, "It's straight ahead, sir. Through the hall and some double doors. You'll hear the music and the voices."

Contact? Time to make sure later. Right now there was a damn party he was supposed to attend.

The bright lights and the laughing faces formed a startling contrast to the blackness of his thoughts. They were all here— the crowd pleasers. Some faces he had expected to see and some he hadn't. Nonetheless familiar. A cross section of the world of money and power: mass media, music, acting, even politics. All big, all celebrities. People who influenced people in one way or another. Right now they all seemed engaged in having fun.

Webb headed straight for the bar. "Scotch. Chivas, if you have it. Over ice." He turned back to the room with his drink, to meet Harris Phelps's tight-lipped, reproachful look.

"Webb! They called me to say you were on your way up to the house. If you'd thought to call me yourself . . ."

"Hi, Harris. Nice party." He met the cold gray eyes and shrugged. "Sorry I didn't give you any notice, but what the hell, I was in the area and decided I might as well come up a few days early. Got tired of having Dave beat me at tennis. Do you mind?"

"Mind? Of course I don't mind. I would have made arrangements to have you flown in here, as I suggested originally, had I known."

"Well, I kind of like driving myself. More freedom of movement, if I feel like riding into town some night. And what's with all the security?"

Harris began stiffly, "I'm sure the man at the gate explained to you," but another voice, sounding rather slurred, cut across his.

"So you're here? And maybe you don't remember me, it's been a long time, *sì*? But I remember you, and what a dirty bastard you are. You . . ." Claudia del Antonini was weaving very slightly, her accent more pronounced than usual.

Better Claudia, who was at least predictable, than exchanging insignificant nothings with Harris Phelps. And he knew how to handle Claudia when she was in this mood; he shut her up with a long, deliberately brutal kiss. She tried to fight him at first, but Webb put his hands on her tight, squirming ass, squeezing hard, until she relaxed against him with a moan of surrender, closing her eyes.

Webb cocked an eyebrow at Harris, who gave a shrug and what was meant to be a smile before he moved away.

Webb was making a mental catalogue of the faces he recognized. The IRS would have tabbed most of them as "self-employed." Quite a house party! Claudia, who wouldn't stop talking if she was given enough encouragement, would fill him in later. And he'd have time, during the next few weeks, to find out what was going on here.

Webb gave his full attention to Claudia, kissing her ear when the soft wetness of her lips became too cloying. She whispered soft obscenities to him, keeping her arms fastened around his neck. Dave, the usually impassive bartender, wondered if they were going to set some kind of record. Some kiss! He came to attention again when Anne came up to him with her latest escort.

She smiled at him, deliberately keeping her eyes averted from the spectacle Webb was making of himself with Claudia. "The usual, please, Dave."

"And I—I think I will switch to something very long and cooling. A frozen daiquiri, perhaps?"

Espinoza was watching Anne, noticing many things about her; she seemed too taut, for all her insouciant attitude. He had made it a point to charm her, and it hadn't been too hard. She was an exceptionally attractive girl-woman, but there was too much surface to her. He thought he could understand why Harris Phelps, whose tastes were almost as jaded as his own, might be intrigued by her. What was underneath the veneer? He promised himself to find out, sure of his own attractiveness. He treated every woman he met as a separate entity, patiently delving until he found out which button to press. He enjoyed women who presented a challenge, and this one just might be . . .

"*Salud!*" Smiling, he touched his glass to hers, noticing how hard she tried to ignore the Italian woman and—his attention sharpened without being noticeable—Webb Carnahan, at last.

So the play begins, he thought, and laughed inside. Because he was, after all, a gambler at heart; and not only that, he enjoyed intrigue and the game of playing one person against another. *Better keep Anna-Maria under wraps until just the right moment*, he cautioned himself, and all the time he was flirting with Anne Mallory, who was lovely enough but without fire, although he knew as well as any man that banked coals burned much hotter. Maybe . . . ?

"Shall we have another drink, or would you like to dance again?"

"Can we do both?"

The bastard, the bastard, she was thinking furiously, not stopping to wonder why she was so furious. He's so busy whispering in that creature's ear he hasn't even noticed me, and we're standing right next to him! She would have liked to throw her drink right at him, drenching them both.

All the same, she jumped when Espinoza, seeming to read her mind, said drolly, "I agree with you—it's too much, isn't it? Shall we break it up?"

Too late for her to protest. Sal Espinoza, showing he could act after all, made a deliberately clumsy movement that sent his glass crashing onto the floor within inches of Claudia's not-too-slender ankle.

He swore vehemently in Spanish before he apologized. "I'm so sorry! A thousand pardons . . ."

And Anne, filling in, enjoying it, said sweetly, "Oh, but it was my fault. I jogged your elbow. Why—hello, Webb! When did you turn up?"

Claudia, who had given an unladylike yelp before she realized what had happened, turned a smoldering look on Anne.

Webb merely quirked an eyebrow. "Accidents will happen, I guess. And hello yourself, love. I just got here. Can I stay?"

There was something in his tawny-gold eyes that she hadn't seen there before when he looked at her. Something ugly and indefinable and—almost measuring.

Thank God for Sal, who was being very South American polite, introducing himself, apologizing again to Claudia, who had begun to melt under his charm.

Somehow—Anne couldn't quite remember how—they seemed to have formed a foursome, leaning companionably across the bar while Dave mixed them refills. And Webb and Sal Espinoza were talking cars and racing while she and Claudia were left to stare at each other, lips curved in insincere smiles.

The effects of the Dexamyl were wearing off, and the martinis were giving her a headache. Why in hell had Webb decided to turn up early, and without notice? Where was Harris?

Claudia, her lips redder than usual and kiss-swollen, was

being sweetly bitchy, and Anne was beginning to reply in kind when she noticed that both men had broken off their conversation to watch them, exchanging looks that seemed to say, aggravatingly, "Women!"

Even in her half-drunken state, Claudia del Antonini was enough woman to interpret that look. A moment before she had been needling Anne with a patronizing comment that certain types of skin just couldn't take the sun without becoming red and ugly, and now she lifted her shoulders in an elaborate shrug.

"Sometimes men are so boring, don't you agree? All this talk of machines, machines . . . who cares? Me, I think I would like to dance a little while before I go to bed." She gave Webb a significant, darkly challenging look as she said the last, but then she turned her most provocative smile on Espinoza. "I think you owe me a dance, after that drink you spilled all over the hem of my new dress. You will wait for me, *caro?*" This, possessively, to Webb, who played her game by kissing her lightly again.

"I'll wait for you, *cara.*" He added something in Italian that made her smile and flash Anne a triumphant look over her shoulder as she bore an apologetic-looking Sal Espinoza off as if he had been a prize of war. Two up for Claudia-baby! Sure enough of herself to leave Webb alone with Anne, who didn't want to be alone with him at all . . .

His eyes looked her over, and she couldn't read anything behind them. He was like a stranger, and yet he wasn't. Her senses told her so.

Because her hand had started to shake she drained her glass and set it down too abruptly.

He smiled at her, but his eyes weren't involved. "Want to dance, Annie?"

"No!" she said sharply, tired of playing games.

He shrugged agreeably. "All right."

Sizing her up. Anne Mallory. Reardon's little girl. Deliberately blanked-out space in his mind. Use her if he had to. Just like Reardon used people. Instrument of his ultimate revenge? But it was hard to be objective about Anne, remembering what he did. Too much, maybe? But he could get over that, thinking about risks and rewards.

"Well, I'd better circulate, I suppose. Do make yourself at home, Webb."

Her voice sounded as brittle and as cold as the tinkle of ice cubes as the bartender mixed her a fresh drink—no eyes and no ears.

And suddenly, contrarily, Webb wanted to force some reaction from her. He put his hand on her arm, stopping her in mid-motion, sensing her desire to escape. "You're a lousy hostess, Annie. Aren't you supposed to make the latest arrival feel at home?" He heard her sharply drawn-in breath, and it gave him a sadistic pleasure. "I thought maybe you'd show me to my room. Make me feel welcome. Just like old times."

While he was saying it, each word a calculated cruelty, he was watching the rise and fall of her partly exposed breasts under the thin blouse. And he had already noticed the light golden tan.

If he hadn't held her wrist she would have slapped him, forgetting her control that much. Tears of rage and humiliation stung her eyelids and she forced them back. "What a bastard you are! And will you have your little tape recorder turned on so you and Carol will have another one to add to your collection?"

This time she had drawn blood, even though the look that came into his face made her wince instinctively. He said softly, between his teeth, "And what in hell did you mean by that crack?"

She forgot Dave, behind the bar, forgot the room filled with people. There were only her and Webb, battling it out, and she was fighting for her own survival.

"You ought to know—very well. Was it supposed to be a

secret, the little contest you two have going? A form of tallying scalps, I suppose. I think the first time we met it was because of a bet between you . . ." Her voice almost cracked, but she held it steady, looking contemptuously into his suddenly opaque eyes.

"Not the first time we met, baby. The first time we fucked." His voice was conversational, but he might as well have struck her a blow. "And I still want to know what you were talking about just now."

"Forget it, Webb. Just forget it, will you? And let me go—you're making a spectacle of me, and of yourself. I'm not Claudia, I'm not so easily taken in by a—a Judas kiss! So play your sick little games with her, with anyone else, because I . . ."

"I hope I am not intruding? Please excuse me." The look on Karim's face belied the overly polite tone of his voice. "But, Anne, my uncle wishes to bid you good-bye. He's leaving tomorrow, you know."

She had never thought she would be as glad to see Karim as she was now, with the rage she sensed in Webb striking at her like a live thing as he let go of her, his face smoothing out into his actor's mask.

"Sorry—have I been monopolizing our charming hostess? See you later, Annie." His words carried both a promise and a threat.

Chapter Twenty-seven

ANNE HAD WATCHED the patterns changing; small groups of people expanding into larger ones or contracting. And she had wanted nothing more than to go upstairs to bed, but she felt herself trapped.

She had watched Webb disappear with Claudia soon after she said her polite good-byes to Karim's uncle. And had been rescued from Karim by Yves, who had had too much wine to drink. From Yves, by Sal Espinoza again. She felt like a balloon being tossed from one hand to another. Even her head felt expanded and light—especially after the hash pipe had been passed around a few times, filling the small screening room with its sickly sweet odor.

"You're not used to it? It's good stuff—pure. The best. But do not overdo it the first time. Here, let me show you." Sal Espinoza was nothing like the playboy he was painted to be, Anne thought fuzzily. He was a nice man, very thoughtful; and she was being neglected by Harris, who was fussing around with cans of film while he and Yves Pleydel engaged in a low-voiced discussion.

They were here to watch the first rushes. Sarah Vesper and Anne were the only two women present. The men were all Harris's closest associates, except for the emir, who had retired early, and Karim.

Pleydel said, "I think we have it now," and the lights dimmed. Anne was faced with her own larger-than-life image on the screen. She watched herself with a sense of detachment, as if she were watching a stranger.

"You are very good. I hope that when it is my turn, I will be able to give a credible performance." Espinoza's shoulder brushed against Anne's as he leaned forward to take two glasses of wine from a tray.

"I really don't think I'd better. This is much later than I'm used to staying up."

"But the show is only just beginning. Watch . . ."

She had wondered why everyone stayed, watching the screen expectantly. And then she didn't have to wonder any longer. The screen filled with color and light. No sound. But sound wasn't necessary, with everything being said by bodies. People making love. All colors and combinations.

Anne hardly noticed that Harris had come to sit beside her, taking her hand as he leaned over to tell Espinoza, "This is for your benefit, Sal. And Anne's. She hasn't seen my private collection before."

Anne felt him take her hand, but for a time she was incapable of either motion or coherent thought.

Espinoza held the small silver-engraved pipe to her lips, chuckling softly. "Ah! I always wondered about Madame la Comtesse. So that's it!"

She felt frozen in her chair, although the heat had started to spread from her face to the rest of her body as the toke made what she was watching seem suddenly more vivid. She had begun to realize that this was not mere acted pornography but the real thing, involving real, recognizable people.

Anne could not help gasping when she suddenly recognized Venetia Tressider. One of those talked-about orgies that Venetia so enjoyed. Venetia naked, with her legs spread open. A girl going down on her before three men joined in.

"You're not shocked, are you, love?" Harris said from the darkness. His fingers moved caressingly up her arm, playing with her breast.

"What, you have not watched this kind of peepshow before? I am afraid you must think us all very decadent. But it is—interesting, no?"

Anne didn't know what she might have said. She had meant to say something, but the words got lost in her throat.

Venetia again. Venetia with—Webb, this time. Her country house—Anne recognized the indoor swimming pool, all the mirrors. Oh God, she didn't want to watch. Webb's body, dark gold in the firelight. Watching him fucking Venetia, she could almost feel him in her. Feel of his flesh under her clutching fingers. Musky whisper of his voice between kisses.

"Bardini was responsible for that one," Harris was saying across her to Espinoza. "Do you recognize his special touch? He's an expert at using the zoom lens at exactly the right time."

Was this part of Carol's collection, lent for the occasion? Did they exchange film as well as tapes?

"He's quite a stud," Espinoza drawled. "I wonder how I would measure up? Of course, she's quite a woman, too. I shall have to make her acquaintance!"

Harris's fingers gently pushed aside the silky material of Anne's blouse, finding her nipple. On the screen, Claudia was giving an off-screen performance, and Yves grunted caustically, "Huh! That was her screen test. She has a natural talent for sex, that bitch!"

"It's hard to tell where the silk leaves off and your skin begins, Anne."

She tried to empty her head of everything but the sound of Harris's voice. She was in bed, and he was undressing her. There was a light on, and it kept getting in her eyes until she closed them.

"Anne—Anne, what do you need that I'm not giving you?" Craig's words from long ago.

"If you can't make it, fake it." That had been Violet.

Kaleidoscope of colors and pictures in her mind. Coldness and heat on her body. Not ecstasy, but, at last, release.

Three men, Espinoza, Pleydel and Rufus Randall, had remained in the screening room after the others had left. Randall, grimacing distastefully, had turned on the exhaust fan to dispel the sweet-acrid odor of the hash; but now the room was filled with his cigar smoke.

Against one wall of the room, what had appeared to be a locked closet door had been slid away, disclosing an elaborate arrangement of screens, pushbuttons and tuner knobs. One of Danny Verrano's interesting "amusements," part of the reason why he had asked so much for this house and the land it stood on. Harris Phelps had been his guest on a few occasions, and Harris hadn't quibbled at Danny's price.

Espinoza, lounging back in his chair with his legs stretched before him, drawled lazily, "A most fascinating and useful little toy, eh? I must confess that this is more than I had hoped for. And you say that there are hookups in every room?" He raised an eyebrow. "That must have cost a great deal of money, besides ingenuity. The cameras are not easily noticeable then, I presume."

Pleydel, busy fiddling with dials, shrugged. "Not at all. Some of them are concealed behind speaker grills, some in elaborate light fixtures, vases—you know? They are all positioned to give maximum coverage. Especially"—he winked—"of the bed. And not all the rooms are so equipped. Some of the chalets, the rooms in the outlying buildings where the technicians and the extras are sleeping, were not worth the effort. Also our friend Phelps installed cutoff switches in the rooms that some of us will be occupying, so that if you desire, you'll have your privacy."

"Don't like the idea of a seeing eye myself," Randall growled, puffing on his cigar. "But some people seem to find it a turn-on. Taki Petrakis wants a videotape of his farewell performance with Vesper before he leaves."

"She does not know?"

"She does not. Nor does Anne Mallory. Just the few of us who might have to take turns to monitor this thing." Randall jerked his head towards the machinery. "I'm still learning—that's why I'm up so late tonight. Normally, I'm an early riser."

"Here," Pleydel said. A picture suddenly appeared on one of the monitor screens, and Espinoza leaned forward with interest.

"He gets around, doesn't he?"

Webb Carnahan and Claudia were engaged in a flaming row, and wrinkling his nose expressively, Yves turned the volume up slightly. Sitting naked in the middle of her rumpled bed, Claudia hurled a stream of vituperative Italian at Webb, who continued calmly to get dressed. It was obvious that, having fucked her, he was getting ready to go back to his own room and that she didn't like the idea.

"There are numbered buttons for each room. Of course you might have to adjust the focusing slightly, but otherwise it is just a matter of pushing a button—so!"

Fade out and fade in.

The senator slept with his head pillowed on the shoulder of a young man. One of the extras who would play a Mexican officer.

Randall grunted. "That's interesting." He glanced at Espinoza, adding without expression, "We're keeping videotapes, of course. Phelps has had an underground strongroom built, leading off that garage. And that's where we'll store the more explosive tapes—the ones that might be useful later."

"Also, once we start shooting the sex scenes, some of those as well—those that would otherwise have to end up on the cutting-room floor."

Espinoza chuckled. "I am beginning to understand better. And Markham? Is he going to be told?"

There was a slight hesitation as the other men glanced at each other. At last Randall gave a shrug of his bearlike

283

shoulders, stubbing out one cigar before he began to light another. He frowned thoughtfully.

"We're not sure yet. Depends. And Phelps doesn't think Carol Cochran ought to be told, because sometimes she talks too much."

"It's probably better not . . ."

Most of the other rooms Yves tried, casually, were dark. "Ah well, it's very late." He shrugged. And then, grinning, "But one more. You'll notice I have given our friend Harris time!"

There was a diffused light in Anne Mallory's room, and she slept on her back, naked, with one arm thrown over her eyes. Her body glistened as if it had been oiled, and her nipples were still erect. She was alone.

"Quite lovely," Espinoza mused, his eyes narrowing. "And I see Harris used some of that special ointment I brought with me. It's quite effective with a woman who has difficulty achieving a climax."

"Really? What's in it?" Pleydel sounded interested. Randall merely grunted.

"Many things. Including yohimbine—it's an extract from a plant that grows in certain African countries. When used with a very small amount of cocaine, it can—well, the effects are quite pleasurable. But the most important thing is to remove the inhibitions first. American women! They are full of these hangups, as you call them!"

Randall stretched, yawning hugely. "Well, I think I've seen enough for one night. I'm about ready to turn in myself."

Espinoza looked at his watch, a smile coming to his face. "Why don't you wait a few minutes longer? You might catch something very interesting."

Christ! After four already! Swearing under his breath, Webb Carnahan heard the door lock behind him. The cloying odor of Claudia and sex seemed to cling to him, and without bothering to turn on the light switch, he began to strip, leaving his clothes wherever he dropped them on the way to the bathroom.

He had been allotted one of the guest chalets—closer to the house than most, and conveniently close to the one Claudia occupied. He had left her, still cursing at him to relish the bite of fresh air on his face, penetrating his body. It had at least driven away the feeling of staleness, the traces of tension and tiredness that had been with him all evening. Fucking Claudia had been like making war. *C'est la guerre!* What he needed now was a shower and the comfort of sleep. Blanking out thought until much, much later.

The shower was as hot as he could stand it, ending with a very short burst of cold. The towels were large, and there were plenty of them. Harris Phelps didn't do anything by halves. All the comforts of home, including soft piped-in music that he'd turned on almost automatically.

Or had he? Suddenly he couldn't remember. When he stepped back into the bedroom, his body still damp from the steam, his mind fitted a name to the music. "Concerto de Aranjuez"—soft guitars. The kind of mood music he didn't need. He stopped still, all his senses suddenly alert. Something —a breath of perfume, a whisper of movement in the dark— warned him before the light came on, and he saw her sitting curled up in the chair beside the bed, eyes wide and questioning.

Ria. Wraith out of the blackness of the past. Dream or nightmare? Caught unprepared, he felt frozen, until her voice, soft and hesitant, came across the distance that separated them.

"Webb? I'm sorry it had to be this way . . . but I wanted— I wanted our first meeting to be private, after so long . . ."

His mind clicked back into focus, and now he was able to look at her objectively. Her hair was different—blonder. And she hadn't worn makeup before. But the eyes were the same, and the slight trembling of her mouth. Christ, all the mental preparation hadn't quite made him ready for seeing her again.

Sound surprised, the monitor in his brain warned him, even while she stood up, green and brown dress clinging.

"Webb"—voice rising slightly—"please—you will listen to me first? If I can find the words to explain what happened—how it happened . . ."

His voice came back, sounding flat. "Hello, Ria. And after all these years, why bother to explain?"

He stayed where he was, noticing how she licked her lips nervously. But if he had had any doubts, her words warned him to be cautious: "I did not know what to expect, but—you knew?"

"Excuse me." He picked up one of the towels he had discarded and knotted it around his waist, still watching her. And then he said politely, "Knew what? How did you expect me to react to something like this? Maybe I'm dreaming it all up. My long-lost wife—missing, presumed dead—turning up to surprise me. To explain—isn't that what you just said? So what the fuck am I supposed to say?"

"I don't know. Anything—how can I expect you to understand? They—the people, your friends who sent me back to Cuba—expected me to die. It was a matter of survival, you see, and I discovered that I wanted to survive. Don't blame me too much. If I could have let you know, I would have, but there was no way. And then, after a while, I was afraid to try. I didn't know if I would ever be allowed to leave, and I didn't know if you—what you . . ."

"Turn the goddamn music off, will you?" "Largo." Lone guitar hesitating in the silence, joined by violins. Great background music for whatever kind of scene she'd planned. They'd played it on the cheap record player that was all he'd been able to afford then. Ria's music. Supposed to soften him up for now.

"Webb, please . . ."

"It's just that I like jazz better these days, baby. And a lot of things have changed since way back. Including you."

He walked toward the bed, glad that she was on the other side of it.

"You have changed, too." Her fingers plucked nervously at her skirt.

"So I have." With a vicious motion, he pulled the covers off the bed. "And I don't know if I'm ready to listen to anything you have to say. The shock hasn't worn off yet."

"Do you think he's telling the truth? He seemed too calm. After all, a shock like that . . ."

"But you forget he's an actor, yes? He has had the training."

"All kinds of training. And if he knew she was going to be here, there's only one way he could have found out."

"But we have time." Espinoza's voice was soothing. "We can find out whatever we want to know. And don't underestimate Anna-Maria. She is a well-trained weapon in herself, don't you agree?"

The three men had been joined by Harris Phelps—showered and looking fresh. Now, watching the screen, he smoothed his mustache abstractedly.

"I don't think we need to worry about Webb Carnahan. In fact, he might prove useful to us in the end. And he has useful connections."

Webb and Anna-Maria faced each other across the bed—wary adversaries.

"Don't send me away. Please let me stay, and—and talk to you. Listen to me, at least."

"Listen, baby, I'm very tired. And still trying to absorb everything. Talking's the last thing on my mind right now."

"Whatever you want. You don't have to talk. Let me."

"Ah shit! Do you have anything on you? I might need it."

"I don't know what you mean . . ."

"I think you do. Didn't you come prepared?"

"Ah—now!"

"You're not jealous?"

"Why should I be? Anna-Maria has always belonged to herself, just as I belong to myself. And there's no need for concern—she can give as good as she gets, that woman!"

She had amyl nitrate—four capsules stashed away in her tiny mesh purse. Webb snapped one under her nose, and another for himself, hardly waiting to hear her gasping cry. The thin chiffon ripped under his hands, and they fell on the bed together, grappling with each other. More war games.

Randall rubbed wearily at his eyes. "Christ, I can see this going on all morning. When did you say he was supposed to film that sequence with Sarah Vesper?"

"The day after tomorrow." Pleydel's eyes were glued to the screen. "It ought to prove interesting."

"He hasn't asked her if they're still married," Harris said thoughtfully.

"I don't think he's had time to think about that yet."

"Put out the fucking light."

And now there was only sound.

PART FOUR

THE
PLAYERS

Chapter Twenty-eight

MAKE-BELIEVE WAS HARD to believe in, seen from the other side. Wires trailing everywhere, too-bright lights. And cameras. Now that she wasn't in front of them, Anne noticed more. She was starting to learn the jobs of the men who swarmed everywhere. Director, assistant directors for setting up the scene, director of photography, camera operators—and all, in turn, had their own assistants. Lighting gaffers, sound men, electricians. Too many people crowded into one small space.

Anne was watching Webb and Sarah Vesper. Their first scene together. And she was here to watch, and to learn. While they were setting up the scene, Anne tried not to think. Especially of the time when she had first watched Webb, feeling the force of his personality leap out and almost touch her as he had touched her later irrevocably.

The continuity girl, Meg, brushed past, carrying her clipboard, looking harassed, calling, "Toni—wardrobe . . ." What wardrobe? They're hardly wearing anything," came from Jean Benedict, pressed against the wall next to Anne.

Well, forget it. She hadn't seen Webb at all yesterday, and hadn't missed him at all.

Bastard! The word leaped into her mind as she watched him smiling down at Sarah Vesper, who contrived, somehow, to look incredibly young. They weren't using stand-ins, and they spent a lot of time standing around while the set was being adjusted about them—in this case, one of the bigger bedrooms in the old part of the house. Not that they were wasting their time, exactly. They seemed to have plenty to say to each other; engaging in a low-voiced, animated conversation that ignored everyone else. Sarah was obviously relating some anecdote, her hands and her mouth expressive, and Webb was smiling down at her, watching her more than listening. All his charm turned on. And then when Yves called for a run-through, it was amazing how they both changed, faces and attitudes instantly transformed into those of the characters they were playing.

"Now you both get wet. Very thoroughly. I want to see the water running down your faces."

A hose accomplished that, and there was general laughter. Sarah grimaced and wrinkled her nose. Webb grumbled, "Jesus! That was cold!"

"You are supposed to be very cold—and very wet, both of you!" Yves reminded them pointedly.

"I'm shivering already." Sarah looked slim and supple under her clinging blouse and riding skirt. Her fine-boned face looked beautiful in spite of the carefully arranged strands of hair straggling about her face and shoulders.

This one scene, four or five minutes of screen time, took almost two hours of work before Pleydel was satisfied, in spite of the fact that there were very few extra takes.

A rape-love scene, one of the many. Anne's mind carefully blanked out the thought of those that she would be expected to participate in.

Webb and Sarah seemed intent on each other. Only acting? Why should she care? The sudden contortion of Sarah's face seemed all too real, neck muscles straining as her head was flung back.

Sarah Vesper had a beautiful body—slim and firm-muscled—and she didn't seem to mind all the people watching. It was Webb's body that was too achingly familiar. Making love for the cameras—did he get turned on that way? Anne found her mind going back again to Webb's love scenes with Carol in *Bad Blood*. The play of light and shadow on sweat-glistening flesh as they came together, moved apart, and then together once more, with the wild music rising to a crescendo . . .

Here in this room there were the sounds of lovemaking, whether faked or not. Even down to the creaking of the bed springs.

Jean Benedict clutched at Anne's arm, her breath catching in her throat; expelled audibly when Yves called, "Cut!" And then Jean said softly, "Christ!" Her voice sounded almost shaken.

"It was quite a performance, wasn't it?" Anne hoped her voice sounded calm.

Jean had bitten down on her lower lip until it had turned a dark crimson, and her eyes seemed unusually bright. She shook her mane of hair back over her shoulders, saying speculatively, "I wonder if that was all acting? She likes having her breasts kissed—the nipples of women with small breasts are usually much more sensitive. Did you notice how she . . ." Suddenly shrugging as if to shake off a spell, Jean dug her hands into the pockets of her levis. "He seemed to know what he was doing, too. Webb Carnahan. Some men are almost like women that way—they seem to sense what turns each particular woman on most, and they're usually the worst sons of bitches. The calculators." Her eyes narrowed for an instant. "I haven't met him yet—officially. I never did go for those too-goddamn-macho roles he plays. But I think I'd like to, now."

Anne said carefully, "I'm sure you'll get the chance. I understand that Webb spreads himself around." *Bitchy*, she thought, and didn't care, wanting only to get out in the fresh air somewhere—away from the stifling, crowded set. To clear her lungs and her mind. She started to edge her way out, avoiding the wires that lay everywhere.

Jean Benedict had turned back, saying in an almost too-casual voice, "I guess I'll go talk to Sarah. We're getting together later to practice our hatha yoga."

In spite of all her resolutions, Anne could not help turning her head to look back, just as she reached the door.

The three were standing together. Webb, with a towel knotted carelessly about his waist, using another to dry off his face and hair. Sarah in a loosely belted terrycloth robe, smiling as she talked to Jean—turning to say something to Webb. He grinned down at the black-haired woman, dropping one arm around her shoulders to give her a squeeze. Would Jean feel the tug of that certain chemistry, too?

"He does not believe in wasting too much time, does he? Although I doubt he'll get far with Benedict—unless he catches her in a certain mood. I understand that after a performance she will screw anyone. Otherwise she likes women best. Tell me, is that the secret of your coldness? Do you like her? You two seem to have hit it off."

Anne forced herself to meet Karim's malicious black eyes. He was deliberately blocking the doorway, or she would have walked past him.

"I like her, yes. But not in the way you're implying." She looked at him coldly. "May I get through, please? I have an appointment with Dr. Brightman."

"Ah yes, the good doctor, who helps women to relax—does he also teach them to become true women? I have missed you while I was being forced to dance attendance on my venerable uncle. So you'll allow me to escort you."

It was more a statement than a question and she didn't want a public scene. Anne surprised him by saying coolly, "Why, thank you!" and let him take her arm possessively to lead her out.

He said smoothly, "And what did you think of that passionate little excerpt we just witnessed? Do you think, my little blonde *chèrie*, that you could ever give such a performance as Sarah did? I'm sure you have read the script, and your scenes are so much more fiery. Would you like me to help you rehearse?"

She stopped, trying to pull her arm free. "Really, Karim! If you can't find anything else to talk about but . . ."

He pounced on her tiny pause, lips curling mockingly under his black mustache. "Sex—are you frightened of the word, even? Why do you shrink from desire? I am a sensual man, and I am not ashamed to admit it. I desire you, and I think we both know that in the end I will have you. So why do you continue to play these childish games with me? Are you afraid of me?"

"Karim, stop it!"

His eyes glittered at her, and without warning he dropped her arm, only to pull her roughly against him, cupping her buttocks with his hands as he almost lifted her off her feet. Anne had no choice but to clutch at his shoulders or fall backwards, as he took her off balance. He ground her pelvis against his thigh, so that she could feel the hardness of him.

"When will you stop fighting me, and that which is inside yourself?"

He began to kiss her fiercely, seeming to take a perverse pleasure in her squirming movements as she tried to escape.

Anne could have wept with rage and humiliation. He was making a public display of her—it would seem to anyone who passed them that she was responding wantonly to his embrace.

"Excuse me." Webb Carnahan's voice was as icily cutting as the bite of frost. He had almost to brush past them as he walked down the narrow corridor with Yves Pleydel. Anne wanted to die in the instant when she met his eyes—their metallic-gold sheen seemed to look right through her.

He nodded curtly at Karim who, with a false laugh of apology, let her slip down the length of his body.

Pleydel shook his head playfully. "That scene must have been better than even I thought! But you two love birds should find a more private corner—they will soon be bringing the equipment through here."

He hurried then, to keep up with Webb, who hadn't paused at all—walking with his long, effortless stride, not deigning to turn his head again. But he'd been angry. There had been fury mixed with contempt in the ridging of the muscles along his jaw, the hardening of his mouth. Anne had sensed, in that split-second when they'd looked at each other, the rage in him, sensed it with the answering shiver that ran down her nerves. But why had he been so angry?

Karim was laughing softly, satisfaction tinging his voice. "Have I embarrassed you? You need to blush more often, blushes are becoming to a woman. And I think we have managed to make your ex-lover angry—do you think he is jealous?"

Webb was startled by the force of the rage that had swept through him when he'd seen her. Them. Anne and Karim. The bitch! Rubbing herself up against him, both of them lost to everything but each other. And what did Harris Phelps think about that? Maybe, like Ria, Annie had been nothing more than a plastic image—a paper doll cut out of his own imagination.

"It's the weather out here," Pleydel was saying pontifically, lacing his fingers together. "It is so uncertain, and we have all those outdoor scenes to do. So I am afraid everyone will have to work harder, and memorize more lines. If it's a fine day, we'll shoot outside. If not"—he shrugged—"we work on the interior scenes. I am sorry to be so demanding, but . . ."

"Sure. I can understand the problems." Webb kept his voice flat and expressionless. Through the window he could see the treetops bending against a sharp, fresh wind blowing in from the ocean. A door slammed somewhere, suddenly, he saw Anne and Karim again, holding hands as they ran against the wind. Going to find a more private spot for their lovemaking? Shit— why should he care? He had enough problems of his own to take care of. Including Ria.

Upstairs in the screening room, Harris Phelps was at the monitor screen when Pleydel walked in, looking pleased with himself.

"Well, it all went off very well! Wait until you see the

dailies. And I have explained to everyone why they will be extra busy. They all seemed very understanding."

"Good." Phelps seemed distraught. Did he know how furiously Karim was pursuing his little protégée? A *pity*, Yves thought, as he sank into a chair, *that a man as intelligent and farsighted as Harris Phelps should have a weakness.* Or did he? After all, he had cleverly arranged to get the girl involved, and she was one of their most useful pawns.

He heard Phelps give a chuckle. "Look at this. Do you think we ought to give Petrakis a copy of the videotape?"

In Jean Benedict's room Sarah Vesper and Jean sat together on the bed. They smiled at each other. Sarah reached out her hand, touching Jean's wild, wind-tangled hair.

"You'll be all right. You have such a beautiful voice, so pure . . . and you lose yourself when you sing, don't you? Acting is just like that. You have to forget yourself and feel only what you are supposed to be."

"Is that what you do? Do you find it easy?" As boldly as a man, Jean unbuttoned Sarah's blouse—her small breasts with their large, pointed nipples sprang into view. Sarah smiled again, and Jean, bending her head, put her mouth to one breast. Sarah bit her lip, and her body seemed to arch backwards from the waist.

"Was he good to them, too?" Jean demanded after a moment. "Could you lose yourself with him too?"

"Yes," Sarah whispered. "Is that what you wanted to find out?"

Jean laughed, throwing her head back suddenly. "That, too. But mostly about you. You have a beautiful body, you know. I like beautiful bodies." She bent forward again.

"Mm . . . so do I. And anything that gives pleasure."

"We think the same way." Jean's voice sounded muffled, and this time Sarah's hand moved under the other woman's loose sweater as they fell together on the bed.

* * *

"So that's the way it is?"

Harris said abstractedly, "It's an open secret. Sarah's always been bisexual. Taki knows it. And Jean—I'm not sure. Sometimes."

"We have an interesting mixture of people here. I wonder how they will all react to each other after they've been shut in here together for a few weeks?"

Without answering, Harris shrugged. He made a random check of some of the other rooms, pretending to be absorbed, until Pleydel left. And then he punched the button he wanted. Harold Brightman's cabin. And that was where he found Anne.

He had promised to help her learn to relax, just as Sarah Vesper seemed able to do with hardly any effort at all.

Earlier in the day, she had tried to think of excuses to give him. Now, after Karim, and after Webb, Hal Brightman's comfortable, undemanding presence seemed exactly what she needed.

"I ordered sandwiches, in case you haven't eaten, and because I'm starving myself!"

He set her at ease almost immediately, pouring out chilled wine to go with the roast beef and cheese. "How did the filming go? Did you get in to watch? They told me it was a closed set, so I stayed in here making notes." He gave her a sudden, direct look. "How do you feel?"

"Oh, I don't know!" Her laugh sounded nervous. "Sarah and Webb were both fantastic, and the way they handled it only seemed to point up my own inadequacy! I'm only a model, not an actress!"

"But you can be anything you want to be. And you must keep on believing that."

He did remind her of Dr. Haldane. Not pushing, just understanding. And receptive.

Now he added, grinning, "I'm no Svengali, and I can't exactly see you as a Trilby, but I do mean that."

"Maybe!" And then, in a burst of candor, "Or perhaps it's just that—I'm an escapist! When things get unpleasant or too tough to face, I want to run away."

"So do most of us! Escaping always seems the easiest way out. But sooner or later, there's nowhere left to escape to, and that's when we have to turn and face whatever we're running from. What are you running from, Anne."

She sighed. "I don't know. Everything? Memories—this place haunts all my dreams, but then that's natural, isn't it? I remember from when I was a child. And then there's me—and you know, I really feel I oughtn't to be taking advantage of you this way!"

"But you're not. I'm here to make myself useful. Company doctor and all that!" His deliberate parody of an English accent made her laugh, at last.

"All right, company doctor, you have a willing subject. I need to learn to act—and that's only the beginning."

His voice was gentle. "Do you mind if I try hypnosis?"

Harris Phelps watched, forefinger rubbing at his neat mustache, as Brightman put her under. He was too well disciplined to gnaw at his fingernail, but he got up to lock the door as he continued to watch the screen. How far back would he take her? Could he?

Prompted by the voice that kept urging her to go backwards, Anne was running down the corridors of sleep. Escaping again. Running away from the ocean; from an enormous tidal wave that blackened the sky at her back. Her bare feet sank into wet sand that sucked at her ankles, making every step an effort in slow motion. Run, run! You have to tell them . . . and make it not true . . .

"Tell them what, Anne?"

She looked as if she were asleep, but her head moved restlessly against the high-backed chair.

"No!" Almost in a whimper: "About her . . . floating . . ." Tears started to slip down her pale cheeks.

She was doing something she shouldn't do—something for-, bidden. She'd been warned that if she went down in the caves, the waves might catch her when the tide came in. But then it wasn't fair that on pretty days like this one she shouldn't be allowed to go down to the beach. She was scared of the cliffs, but the caves were cool and damp-smelling and a short cut. And Mommy was at the other end. She might be mad for a little while, but afterwards, maybe she would let Anne stay.

She wasn't running anymore but walking, very quietly, pretending she was an Indian princess. Pocahontas. Except that her hair was blonde, like Mommy's, instead of black. But in make-believe, things like that didn't matter. She could be whoever she wanted to be; the Voice kept telling her so. She must listen to the Voice, and try to forget that her feet were beginning to drag. She didn't really want to go any further. Because she could hear the other voices now. Angry, shouting voices cutting into the quiet sounds of the waves running up the sand all white and foamy and kind of melting back again, leaving millions of tiny holes where the sea creatures had dug themselves in.

The voices were the beginning of everything that was bad and frightening. The tidal wave turned itself into dark shadows that blanked out the sunlight coming through the mouth of the cave. This was the part she didn't want to remember—she wouldn't!

"No, no, no! I can't—please don't make me!" Her voice, turning high and shrill, almost brought her out of her trance.

Sighing, Brightman held her wrist, feeling the racing pulse; his voice soothed her quietly until her breathing had become even and steady again.

"It's all right, Anne. It's all right. Come forwards now. But remember, that next time you'll go further back. You won't be frightened any longer. Take it easy now."

Easy—each time would be easier for her. Brightman was frowning with concentration. He could have given her sodium pentothal to help her remember, but it was too risky at this point. She had just begun to trust him, and might have balked at the thought of a drug. Whatever the memories were, her mind wouldn't let them be dredged up yet, and it was too risky to try to force her. She had to be ready.

And he had to resist the temptation to play God, in spite of his curiosity. Finding her mother dead was a traumatic enough experience for any child—but had that been all? Was there something else her mind refused to accept? He wanted to unlock the secret door that her subconscious kept tightly shut. And he would; but he had to be patient.

Meanwhile, he would win her trust by helping her cope with her present problems. He, and not Yves Pleydel, or even Harris Phelps, would make her an actress. Svengali and Trilby . . . Recognizing his own vanity, Hal Brightman gave a self-deprecating grimace. But he'd achieved tremendous results with Olympic athletes—even tennis players, championship golfers.

He checked his tape recorder, even though it was always his habit to make written notes during any session with a patient. He disliked that word—he didn't treat invalidism. He tried to help people with certain mental blocks that prevented their complete functioning as individuals—the use of all their potential.

Anne Mallory had turned to him because she wanted to succeed as an actress, and she would. That part was easy. When she played Glory, she would be Glory, throwing herself into the role as easily as a child slipped into make-believe. And what simpler trigger word than the director's cry of "Action" at the moment before the cameras started rolling?

Chapter Twenty-nine

IT WAS HOT, very hot, in the huge central courtyard with the sunlight and the even fiercer heat of the artificial lights beating down on them all. Anne could feel the sweat trickling down the length of her body, soaking into her tight fitted bodice and dampening layers of petticoats that Yves's insistence on historical accuracy forced her to endure. And yet she could not stop herself from shivering.

It was no use telling herself it was only nerves—she couldn't control the pounding of her heart, nor the sick feeling of tension in her diaphragm that seemed to make breathing difficult. The letters in the section of script she held seemed to blur and run into each other, making no sense at all. Thank God she didn't have many lines to say! In any case, the lines weren't important. She should try to concentrate on what Yves had told her earlier, being very kind and patient.

"It is mostly reaction I want from you in this scene, Anne. The words, if you have memorized them, will come easily. There will be the cue cards, if you need them. For the rest—you will imagine that you are a model again, eh? The photographer told you, 'Look happy,' or 'Look pensive'—is that not how it was? Imagine that I am the photographer, and do exactly as I tell you." He had smiled, patting her apprehensive face lightly. "Don't worry, *petite*. Just react naturally to what is happening. You are a pampered little rich girl, face to face for the first time with ugliness. With pain and disillusionment and fear. Try to think yourself into the role, and let your face mirror all these emotions. The others will help you."

The trouble was, Anne thought resentfully now, that all the time Yves was talking, being sweet and soothing, she had not been able to stop herself from being too conscious of Webb's presence—the knowledge that he was there in the same room, lounging across from her in a chair with his booted legs crossed and looking bored and cynical.

Why did he have to make his resentment of her so obvious? She didn't want this any more than he did, but they were both stuck with it. And she wouldn't back off and run. Why should she?

And yet, she'd felt unaccountably annoyed by the fact that he'd acted as if he would rather have ignored her—acknowledging her presence with only the briefest of nods and not a single word. He'd smiled at Sarah, though, whispering something in her ear that made her smile and touch his arm. Why did she have to notice all over again how a smile could change the saturnine hardness of his face, bringing out the creases at the corners of his eyes and mouth? Why did she have to remember that once he'd smiled at her that way?

They were all closeted in a hot little room for a short run-through of the scene that was to follow, and it was a tense and miserable experience for Anne; showing up her inadequacy, especially since she was matched against two very experienced professionals.

Perspiring and uncomfortable even before she had to go out into the sun-baked courtyard, Anne tried to concentrate as Yves had them go through their lines. The first short preliminary scene with Sarah and Anne. And then he told Webb what he was supposed to be doing when the cameras switched to him.

She watched him—not wanting to, not being able to stop herself. He hadn't shaved since he had arrived here—his whisker stubble was growing into the beginnings of a beard. She hadn't seen too much of him since she'd watched him do that scene with Sarah Vesper, except to notice that he seemed to have dropped Claudia for Sal Espinoza's girlfriend, Anna-Maria. And it hadn't seemed to bother Espinoza, whom she rather liked. Anna-Maria of the arrogant voice. Anne hadn't met her officially yet, but she didn't think she would like her.

Webb looked every inch the renegade he was supposed to be playing—a leather vest with crossed bandoliers worn over it, a pistol and knife stuck in his belt. He had given her a cynical "I told you so" look when her dialogue came out sounding stilted and forced. Yves had been encouraging, though, and Sarah understanding and sympathetic.

"It'll be quite different and so much easier when we're actually on the set, my dear. You can't really feel the words you're saying when we're sitting across from each other in a little room like this, knowing it's only a rehearsal! You'll be just fine, just as you were the other morning."

"Of course you will be!" Pleydel's eyes had twinkled at her. "And how can you learn to swim if you don't jump in the water first?"

Again that flat, measuringly sardonic look from Webb—why did he look at her that way? She wouldn't think about him until she had to—and remember then that everything that happened between them was only acting.

It was hard to cling to that thought when outside the sun grew hotter and Anne's nerves crawled under her skin. She stood there clutching her script. There was utter confusion around them—the usual trailing wires, the testing of the camera tracks, arguments when Yves and the director of photography couldn't agree on what kind of filter to use.

She felt like a marionette, or a store-window dummy.

"Stand here . . . now try walking forwards . . . check that lighting on her face!"

Why didn't they start, and get it over with? It hadn't seemed half so bad the last time.

Someone handed her a drink—something very cold and very strong. Anne swallowed it down without thinking, noticing that Sarah did the same; and now at last she was able to relax better. She couldn't see Webb—and Sarah came to stand beside her, whispering comfortingly, "It's always like this, you know! You'll get used to it soon enough." And then, wrinkling her nose, "Isn't this heat just appalling? I didn't think it could get so hot in this part of the world!"

And then at last there was no more waiting. First take— action. Suddenly, Anne could have laughed at her earlier fears. Sitting in the carriage beside Sarah she could feel herself become Glory. . .

From behind the camera it was a long shot. Dusty carriage, escorted by armed soldiers. Zoom in to closeup as they waited for the massive wooden gates to swing open. Cut to interior of carriage . . .

Six takes before Yves grudgingly pronounced himself satisfied. Sarah Vesper glanced sideways at Anne. "You're not nervous any longer, are you? You did just fine!"

Anne laughed, surprising herself. "Thank you! And you were right earlier, you know. Now that we've started, I don't feel nearly so apprehensive!"

Sarah smiled understandingly. "I know. Before I started learning to relax, I used to get all nervous and tensed up before every single scene."

They were waiting for Yves to get the courtyard scene set up, and Karim, handsome and dapper-looking in his Mexican Army uniform, quite at ease on horseback, leaned in the carriage window, flirting with both women. He really could be quite charming at times, Anne thought—if only he wouldn't come on so strong at others!

She was still hot, perspiration dripping down her body, between her breasts, making her thighs feel sticky. But now the heat from outside seemed concentrated within herself, reaching out in waves to flush her face.

"Hot weather suits your blonde-and-white beauty. You should give yourself more often to the sun. Maybe it will melt away the shell of ice around your heart."

This time, instead of drawing away when he reached in to touch her arm caressingly, Anne surprised him by smiling up at him. "Isn't it a woman's prerogative to blow hot and cold? Think how dull too many easy conquests would be."

What he didn't know was that she was still being Glory, not Anne. Glory—heroine. Strong-willed and determined. Winning out in the end. Glory was a flirt, enjoying the kind of game that Karim played so well.

There was a flare of something—surprise? calculation?—in his eyes, and he started to say something else, only to shrug resignedly when Pleydel's voice brought them all to attention.

The carriage began to roll forward—stopped. The bright sun and artificial light blended until they were almost dazzling, making every shape of every other person clearly etched shadows against the background of blinding luminescence.

She climbed out, remembering to lift her long skirts gingerly as she did; laughing up into the face of the handsome young officer who had helped her and letting herself lean against him for an instant. Why not? He was the man her father wanted her to marry, and in addition to his charming manners, he was undeniably handsome. He wanted her. Perhaps she wanted him, too; she wasn't certain. But she had the feeling of waiting. For something else—or was it someone else?

The cameras kept rolling—Yves Pleydel hadn't yelled "Cut!" yet. Tom, the assistant director, glanced at him once, but Yves was concentrating—chewing his fingernails as he did when he was really excited.

Jesus, Tom thought, *she's good this afternoon! That little bit of flirtation as she got out of the carriage—perfect improvisation.*

It was one of those things that sometimes happened. The perfect take, when everyone became caught up in the action and it seemed as if nothing could go wrong. But how long would it last?

So far, no false moves anywhere. Pleydel was conducting now, with his eyes and his gestures, although it seemed unnecessary. Every element blended into a perfect meld; and God help the film editor afterwards!

There was a staccato explosion of shots. The action froze for an instant and then picked up. From the false-fronted adobe building the prop men had painstakingly erected, figures erupted. Sarah Vesper—Sophie—was screaming, flattened against the side of the carriage.

And make-believe turned into reality under the hot blue sky.

Anne, still being Glory, found the shock she had been waiting for almost without realizing it when she recognized the man who came to stand in front of her and heard his familiar, mocking laughter. Her disillusionment was real, feeding her fury.

"You!" she panted. "You!"

She clawed at his face, taking him by surprise; and scratched like a wildcat again, her rage perversely fed when she drew blood. She wanted to hurt him! Webb, who had lied to her and deceived her and humiliated her—she could very easily kill him at this moment!

She heard the material of her bodice rip under his hands, baring her to the waist, and didn't care, not then. She wanted to scar him, to maim him so that he'd never be able to cheat with another woman again. The script was forgotten, even the cameras and all the watching people. There was only him, and the heat of passion and anger that drove her against him, unthinking and uncaring. Over and over until she saw an answering rage in his puma-gold eyes and he struck her viciously—

the force of his open-handed blow numbing the side of her face and sending her sprawling to the ground.

"You goddamned bitch!" Webb was panting—the force and fury of her attack had taken him by surprise, bringing out an answering savagery in him. He looked down at her—loose strands of hair straggling down her neck and clinging to her sweat-damp face, the sunlight harsh as hot hands on her pale gold breasts, nipples erect now that they were freed from the confining material of her dress.

She was trying to clamber back to her feet to come at him fiercely again, but the long skirt hampered her attempts, and now, as the grinning, villainous-looking band of extras crowded closer, either jeering or applauding, Anne seemed to become aware for the first time of the torn bodice and her exposed breasts. Her eyes widened, she seemed to stay poised there on her hands and knees as if she had been frozen in place; and then, sitting back on her heels, she made instinctive, ineffectual motions to clutch the ripped bodice over her nakedness. A second ago she had been still glaring at him; now she appeared to shrink into herself as the circle of grinning men tightened. The male animal smell of lust was only too real now. Any moment one of them would reach for her, and it would be like a signal, they would all . . .

Rufus Randall and Harris Phelps were watching. Randall's eyes were slightly bloodshot. He was chewing on his cigar, hands thrust into his pockets. Harris Phelps wore a fixed, mirthless grin, and there were beads of sweat on his forehead that he did not bother to brush away. *Now,* he was thinking, *Now! I wonder if . . .*

They were all caught up in what was happening—the extras, even the crew. And Yves had wisely seen to it that there was plenty of cover—cameras following the action from all angles. Expensive, but in this instance expense didn't matter, just so long as the results were what they needed. And Anne was reacting perfectly; that surprised him. He had almost expected take after take, but as long as this one was going so right and so well, Yves wouldn't call for a cut. If Webb Carnahan didn't blow it . . . he seemed to be holding back for some reason, almost as frozen as Anne herself.

But then one of the extras, obviously a man with imagination, reached down with a laugh and fondled a breast, his fingers brown against the creamy flesh. She cried out wordlessly, striking out, and at last Webb moved, knocking the man aside as he yanked her ruthlessly to her feet.

"Seems like you keep asking for it, Glory!"

She struggled against his grip. "You—you brute, you bastard! Let me go . . ."

She noticed with satisfaction that blood oozed from the scratches she had put on his face. She hated him, hated him!

"Don't think I will. You're going to make a useful hostage once I get you tame."

"You'll never—don't you know how much I hate you and despise you? I don't want you to touch me. I'd rather die!"

"Would you rather I turned you over to them?" He grinned down at her, openly mocking, far too sure of himself. "Come on, baby. Once you let go like you did before, you might even enjoy the time we're going to spend together."

"No, damn you!"

"Stop fighting me. You know damn well you're going to give in, in the end."

Why did she continue to fight against him when she knew how useless it was? Taking her sudden stillness for surrender, he laughed again, pulling her up against his body with a sudden, savage motion, releasing her wrists to catch her hair at the nape of her neck. And if she let him kiss her she knew with a feeling of despair that she would be lost. He mustn't know that the closeness of his body and just the thought of his mouth crushing hers could reduce her to a prideless nothing.

There was no one else but the two of them and the struggle

309

between them under the hot blue sky, and some instinct as primitive as the merciless sun that beat down on her head drove her now. There was a knife in his belt, and she grabbed for it without thinking. The knife was a silver flash in the sunlight that almost blinded her as she struck out wildly with it, the bone handle feeling heavy and unfamiliar in her grasp . . .

"Cut!" Pleydel shouted, trying to make himself heard over the startled cries of some of the bystanders. "Anne! *Merde*, have you gone crazy with the sun? You were not supposed to . . ."

She didn't hear. Her arm felt shattered and nerveless from the wrist up, and she knew she'd dropped the knife only when Webb gave her wrist a second, savage twist, making her cry out with pain.

"Holy shit! She stabbed him for real!"

She heard the words from somewhere off in the distance, but they didn't register. Webb's eyes held hers—as yellow as the sunlight and just as harsh. There was the warm stickiness of blood, running down his fingers, dripping onto her skirt to mix with the sweat that still poured from her pores. Why was he standing there looking at her? And then he dropped her wrist, and she flinched instinctively when she saw his hand go up, knowing that he was going to strike her again. But he was touching his arm gingerly, still looking down at her without having said a single word. It was only then that reality came flooding back, engulfing her.

Chapter Thirty

"I DIDN'T . . . I don't know what happened! It's like a . . . some kind of dream . . ."

Hal Brightman put a soothing hand on Anne's arm.

"Listen, it was one of those things! A freak accident—you just got caught up in the role you were playing. In any case, it was only a scratch—you heard Carnahan say so himself."

"But—but I wanted to kill him! Don't you see? I kept thinking 'Webb' instead of 'Jason,' and I was trying to kill him, and I might have . . . I killed my grandfather, too, did you know that? And maybe Violet as well, because if not for me . . ."

"Anne, be calm. You haven't killed anyone. If you were the cold-blooded murderess you try to make yourself out to be, you wouldn't be so upset! Relax now, I'm going to give you a shot of something that will help you and make you see things in their proper perspective. But understand—you haven't killed anybody."

She hardly felt the needleprick—she was sobbing now, trying to get words past the constriction in her throat. "You don't know about my grandfather? He had the heart attack when I told him—because I told him. He had been asleep when I came running up from the beach, and his face . . ."

"Anne!"

"And Violet—if I hadn't been with Webb that night . . . it was me they were after, I know it! If I hadn't . . . if I hadn't . . ."

The sodium Pentothal began to take effect and her words became slurred. Her head fell back, and Brightman held her pulse, keeping his voice low and soothing.

"It's all right, Anne. Everything's going to be fine. You're going to forget about Violet and about your grandfather and go back to long before—to when you were a little girl. You're going back now, Anne. To the time before the beginning of the bad dreams. And this time you're not going to be afraid to talk about it, because when you do, the Dream will go away and you'll be free of it forever. Do you understand?"

Free. Running backwards down passages of time that turned almost imperceptibly into the caves. Forbidden. But she'd grown bored and tired of minding, and there was her curiosity as well, her resentment at being left behind on the nicest days while her mother went down to the beach alone. Well, not always . . . She wanted to giggle, but not for long. It wasn't fair, why shouldn't she go, too?

She was running towards the light now; she didn't really like the damp darkness of the caves, they were scary, even to an Indian princess. And then she saw the shadows that partly blocked out the light, and heard angry voices. Voices . . . What was he doing back? Why did he have to come? She didn't want to go away again, back to the cold and that big old house that was too quiet and dull and . . .

He didn't really love them, and that was why he stayed away so much. She'd heard Mommy saying so, crying. Mommy only laughed these days when she was down on the beach with her nice friend that Anne wasn't supposed to know about. He didn't want them to be happy, and she didn't really like him—oh, why did he have to come?

The voices beat against her ears, and even covering them didn't help. They seemed to come out of her head now, for all that she tried to shut them out.

"How long has this been going on? These clandestine meetings on the beach? Damnit, don't try to evade me—never mind how I heard! Who is he, Helen? What's his name? Do I know his face, this secret lover of yours? Tell me, damn you!"

When Mommy laughed this time it wasn't like the other times. It was a shrill, funny-sounding laugh like the sound of beating your hands on a piano without looking at the notes.

"You mean that something I do can really get under your skin?" More hurting laughter. "Well, why don't you try and find out, Richard dear? Not that it makes any difference at this point, because I'm going to divorce you. Yes, I am, and you can't stop me! My God, I've finally found a real man who wants me and treats me like a woman, instead of a—a commodity, and I just might go away with him, do you hear? I don't give a damn about your precious job or the scandal you worry about or—or you, either! Yes! At least he's helped me find out what you are. Not even a ...a ..."

"What happened then?"

"I don't want to tell!"

"You must. For your own sake. What did you see or hear after that?"

"I don't know, I'm not sure, really! They were shouting so, and I was so scared! I—I think he hit her, and she made a funny noise and I saw her fall—and then I ran! I thought he might hit me, too, I guess—only I was so scared I forgot the way back and got lost, and that was more scary even than the beach, so I—went back. And that's when I ..."

"That's what started the nightmares, isn't it? But you're not going to have them anymore. No more guilt. You're not to blame for anything, Anne, and now that you've been able to talk about it, all the fears are going to go away. You'll remember that when you wake up. You'll remember only that you're among friends who want to help you, who care about you. And you're going to be a great actress. Never mind today ..."

The voice went on and on, very gentle, very quiet, sinking

into the suddenly empty space inside her mind before she drifted into a peaceful sleep.

Dr. Harold Brightman tried to hide his elation as he stored the little cassettes away carefully. Breakthrough at last! And he'd done what other psychiatrists hadn't been able to do over years—although, of course, it had taken a traumatic shock to lower the barriers thrown up so long ago by her subconscious mind. But he'd done it, just as he'd made her an actress. Right up to the moment she'd actually stabbed Webb Carnahan on the set in front of a hundred watching eyes, it had been a perfect take—she'd reacted perfectly, without a flaw in her performance!

He frowned slightly. He'd hoped it wouldn't take the sodium pentothal to do it. However, she wouldn't remember, he'd made sure of that. And he'd got rid of her nightmares for good. She'd wake up feeling fine. His method always worked.

He allowed the feeling of satisfaction to seep through him as he stretched, looking down at the sleeping girl with traces of the tears she'd shed still etched against her cheeks. In spite of the tear stains and the ripped, blood-spotted clothes she hadn't had time to change out of, she was beautiful. There was a kind of purity about her, and yet at the same time, in costume, she was Glory—every man's fantasy woman.

With difficulty, Brightman brushed away his own forbidden thoughts, superimposing the image of his wife and children smiling back at him from the photograph he always kept on his desk.

Sighing, he sat down and began to write, forcing himself to concentrate on adding to the detailed notes he had kept making. But even while his pen moved doggedly over paper he found his mind going back. "The Mallory House Tragedy," the newspapers had labeled it. He remembered his mother reading aloud in a hushed, pitying voice. "How terrible for that poor little child! Can you imagine . . . ?"

Strange that that same child should be Anne, and that he should be the one to finally discover the secret she'd carried locked away in the deepest caves of her mind.

Thoughtfully, he tapped the end of his pen against his teeth. Of course, there were the implications. Her father—wasn't he someone very important in government circles? And how much, even with changing names and locales, could he actually incorporate in his new book? And then he went back to writing again. Harris Phelps would know, and advise him. And Harris had a special interest in Anne Mallory. As soon as he finished with his notes, he must go and talk to Harris.

Harris Phelps was still sweating, Randall noticed, in spite of the air conditioning. But Randall himself was too elated, in view of what they'd just witnessed and heard, to pay it too much attention. He expelled his breath heavily, lighting up another cigar.

"Jesus Christ! If we needed a final ace, that should be it, huh? That goddamned sanctimonious bastard . . ."

Harris shrugged, and except for the beads of sweat on his forehead, he showed no emotion as he carefully put away the videotapes.

"It won't pay to underestimate Reardon, in spite of *that*." He nodded towards the screen. "However, it should help, no doubt of that. I'll see that these are stored away in the vault at once."

"How about Brightman?"

"Hal is very sincere, of course. And very cautious. I'm sure he'll come to me with his little dilemma, and naturally, I'll give him the right advice."

Randall said abruptly, "I wonder what made her do it? Go for him like a hellcat with that knife, I mean. She didn't strike me as the type. Jealousy? Didn't I hear rumors that there used to be something between them?"

He was a man who prided himself on his observation of

315

people, and now, without seeming to do so, he watched his companion's face narrowly.

Harris Phelps's fingers went up in a characteristic gesture to touch his mustache, but apart from that he showed no real emotion. "Oh, there was something to the rumors—for a time. But I think Anne's seen through him. No woman enjoys being lied to, after all."

"Huh!" Randall sounded doubtful, although he didn't pursue the subject, switching instead to another. "What about Carnahan? You hear anything yet? Think we ought to know for sure where he stands."

This time Harris allowed himself a smile. "I don't think that really matters at this point, do you? He doesn't know about *this*"—his fingers tapped the videotapes—"and these, along with the movie when it's released, should be all we need. Webb Carnahan's an actor, no matter what his connections, past and present, might be—and a cocksman. Leave it to Anna-Maria to find out anything else there is to find out about him."

His arm had begun to hurt like hell only after Dr. Brightman's offhandedly solicitous ministrations.

"We won't need more than three or four stitches, and the scar should go away in time." Obvious that Brightman was in a hurry to get back to his *other* patient. Anne—surprising him first, and then shocking him with her reactions. She had appeared to be in some kind of trance, and for a few moments back there, so had he. Until she'd pulled that cute little ad lib with the knife. Bitch! But what the fuck had gotten into her? Some kind of brainwashing?

Webb didn't like the thought that he was actually making excuses for her. He ought to face the thought that she was, after all, Dick Reardon's daughter, a chip off the old block. And there was Ria, coming out of seclusion, to comfort *him*. His considerate little wife . . . Christ, *was* she still his wife? Did it matter? He refused to remember the image he'd carried in his mind all these years—the laughing, innocent child-bride he'd loved and even wept for. She was a familiar, dangerous stranger, and he had learned caution.

"Oh Webb! I was trying to stay out of your way, but when I heard . . ."

"Does Espinoza know you're here?"

She shook her head at him, and he could have sworn, if he hadn't know better, that the tears gathering in her eyes were real.

"I've tried to tell you—he understands! We have a—a relationship, we know each other, there is no jealousy in it. I want to be honest with you, can't you hear me?" And then, in a lower voice: "Can't you forgive me?"

His arm throbbed like hell in spite of the pain pills the good doctor had so thoughtfully provided him with; and he looked at her and saw a familiar image that he recalled pulling out of his mind a million times before—almost the same, but different in some indefinable way. Difference between real and fake. Or, hell, maybe it had all been in his own mind.

Like Annie—breath of cool fresh air. Girl-image running down a snowy hill, arms outspread for balance. Annie laughing, Annie hating. In a killing rage this afternoon—and for Christ's sake, *why*? She'd been acting, surprising him, taking him off guard. And then, the bit with the knife. Mere reaction or calculated? And that brought him full circle back to *why*. Had he been set up? Or maybe he was just becoming paranoid.

Webb felt the brush of Ria's hair against his face, and deliberately closed his eyes, wishing he could close off his mind as easily.

"Webb, why won't you talk to me? Don't you see that we have to talk? I beg of you—please . . . !"

He let his eyes open again, squinting them at her, seeing her as a blurred shape, still bending over him. Let his voice come out tired, just the way he was feeling.

"Okay, damnit, okay. But not now. Sorry, baby, but I hurt

like hell right now and those pills make me feel real sleepy. Thanks for coming, anyhow. That was real thoughtful of you."

He caught a flash of her Cuban temper then, as she sprang to her feet.

"Maybe you shouldn't fuck around so much—you wouldn't have jealous women sticking knives in you then! And just remember . . ." Through half-closed eyes he saw her pause and bite her lip. Letting the pause run into a sigh. "I'm sorry. We are both different now, aren't we? But when you are ready to listen, let me know. Because there are several reasons why we must speak with each other."

When he gave her no reaction, she left the room, showing enough control to close the door quietly behind her. Some women would have slammed it. Claudia, Carol. Anne, who had gone one step further.

In the mirror of his mind Webb saw her face, drenched with sweat and tears. Hal Brightman's arm tightening comfortingly over her shoulders as he led her away. And superimposed on that, like a transparency, Lucy's face as he had seen her last. Smiling up at him, brown eyes loving. Dammit, it was Lucy he had to think of first, and his promise—both to Vito and himself. Find Anne. Maybe she was the key and the solution. Because she was obviously part of whatever was happening behind the scenes.

She was floating back, quite comfortably, to the surface of an ocean that shone like an iridescent turquoise above her. Hadn't the Voice told her she need no longer be frightened of the ocean? She wasn't drowning any longer, she could breathe naturally, even underwater. And there was nothing more she had to worry about—nothing at all . . .

Until she felt herself shaken violently, taking her away from her pleasant dream to unpleasant reality.

For a few moments, it seemed quite natural to see Webb's dark, angry face looming over her. Webb—hadn't he been part of the dream? And then, like the click of a switch, Anne came completely back to the present, staring up at him as her eyes came back into focus. Remembrance rushed back in a series of jumbled images turned flame-hot by the sun and the lights and the surprising anger that had burned inside her, driving her to do what she had done. Had he come to take his revenge? She noticed that he wore a white bandage about his upper arm, and had his shirtsleeves tied around his neck like a cape. He looked dangerous, like a stalking tiger, with his narrowed, yellow-gold eyes fixed on hers.

Anne shrank back instinctively, her eyes darting about the room as if looking for rescue. It was unfamiliar, and yet now— and then she recalled that Hal had brought her in here. Afterwards . . . But where was Hal, and what was Webb doing here?

His look traced the outline of her face and her exposed breasts, and she couldn't know what he was thinking, or that he had waited until he saw Dr. Brightman hurrying past his window toward the main house, carrying his little briefcase. As fast asleep as she had been, she didn't know that Webb had searched the room either—reading the notes Brightman had left lying carelessly in his desk drawer.

Right now Webb didn't know why he had bothered to wake her up. He had learned plenty, and he should have left her just the way she was, lying half-naked in Dr. Brightman's bed —marks of tears still staining her face. Anne Mallory *Reardon*. That at one time Reardon had been human enough to react like an ordinary man might be useful to know—or dangerous. But Anne herself was the key, and what in hell should he do about her . . . or with her, for that matter?

"Webb . . . what are you doing here?" She didn't like the way he was staring at her as if he were almost looking through her; nor the strange, sarcastic half-smile that twisted his lips for a moment, only to be wiped away as his actor's mask came back on.

319

He sat beside her on the bed, ignoring her instinctive wincing away. There was fear mixed with righteous anger in her eyes, and he would have liked to have smacked her hard, leaving another bruise to match the one that purpled her cheekbone.

"What are *you* doing here, Annie? Where's your faithful guru?"

Angry color flamed in her face. "That's really none of your—"

He leaned towards her slightly, and her eyes were drawn unwillingly to the bandage that showed up white against the sun-darkened skin of his upper arm. "Hey . . . ! You stabbed me, baby, remember? You were really out for blood, and it's goddamned well my business to find out why. Were you set up to do it? Or did you just want another co-star?"

"You—you slapped me! You didn't have to . . ."

"And you didn't have to go for me like a damned wildcat either! We were supposed to be acting out a scene, only it got out of hand. What the fuck got into you?"

Anne drew in her breath, unnerved by his closeness; wanting to fly at him again with her nails and her teeth—not quite understanding the force of her emotions.

Be calm, her mind warned her, and she said raggedly, "I— I don't know! Perhaps it was the heat—and waiting around and trying to really get into the part. I didn't really *mean* to—to stab you. It just seemed to happen! You—those men . . ." She shuddered involuntarily, remembering belatedly that she was still half-naked.

"You'd read the script before, Annie. You were willing to go through with all those explicit scenes, weren't you? And why should you give a damn about showing your breasts? Everybody's doing it these days—on just about any occasion. You've got nice breasts, Anne. And a nice body, which you'll be showing much more of for some of those other scenes. Sure it was only *that* that set you off?" His voice sounded reasonable and quiet, but the way he looked at her was—

"Webb, please get out of here!" She hated herself for pleading, and she wouldn't give him the satisfaction of seeing her tug the rumpled bedsheets up to cover her breasts. Besides, he was sitting on the sheets, keeping her partially trapped. Why had he really come looking for her? What did he really want?

"Why do you want me to leave? Expecting good old Hal back so you two can finish your little session?"

"Damn you! You've no right to question me about anything, or to fling your ugly imputations at me. And now I'm only sorry that I didn't really hurt you where it counts with that knife! Why'd you carry a real one? For the macho image you try so hard to project? You're a cheat and a fake, and I'd like to cut out your . . ." She stopped, appalled at how far her words had carried her. Halted as much by the change in his eyes as by her own realization. Oh God! Perhaps that shot Hal Brightman had given her was still acting in her bloodstream.

He laughed—a short, ugly sound. "Jesus Christ! You sound like a jealous, slighted bitch! Is that what's been bothering you, Annie-go-lightly? You want my balls to add to your growing collection?"

His face was inches away from hers and she hated him more at this moment than she ever had before; striking back at him with the rage that kept spilling over.

"How goddamned wrong you are, you low-down bastard! Is that what you want to think? *My* collection—what about yours? Yours and Carol's. Your little fuck tapes you played back to each other when you needed a little something extra to add spice to your screwing? Where did you hide the tape recorder, Webb? Under the bed? Did any of the other women you've—you've *laid* find out? Or . . ."

"*What?*" And now she had really made him furious, for all that his voice was deceptively soft.

"Ohh—never mind! I don't care, do you hear? Just get out and leave me alone!"

"Oh no, baby. You've come too far to back off now. Just keep talking."

"No!" She tried to squirm away from him, but he pushed her back against the pillows, putting his good hand against her throat, fingers exerting just enough pressure to keep her there; looking up at him with sick terror, making a pulse flutter against his fingers.

"You ever heard about the carotid arteries, Annie? Just a little pressure here . . . and here"—she gasped while he went on inexorably—"and you're out. And if I were to keep on pressing—no more oxygen to the brain, sweetheart. I wouldn't leave any marks on that pretty throat, either. There was a time when I learned a lot of ways to kill without leaving traces."

She tried to speak—to say something to repudiate the hard-eyed, frighteningly dangerous stranger he'd turned into—and couldn't. She could only continue to watch him while he went on in the same softly uninflected voice: "So why don't you be a good girl and come with me now? Back to my room, where we'll have a little talk—catch up with what's been happening with each other since the last time, huh? When I came back from my trip to Ireland to find you moved out—no note, no call, nothing. Though I guess Harris had more to offer than I did. Does he stay up nights to keep your bad dreams away? Or is that Karim's job now?"

Her voice came back as sheer rage overcame her terror.

"You and Venetia—you damned hypocrite! Did you expect that I . . . God! I saw that very interesting little movie of you two screwing beside her swimming pool. Did you send a copy to Carol? Is that your latest . . . oh!"

She thought for a few frightening seconds that he would actually carry out his threat, and her eyes closed.

And then she heard him say in the same deadly voice, "Were you keeping tabs on me, Annie? I wonder what else you found out. All the more reason for us to have a talk. And some honesty for a change. Come along, Anne. Or do I have to knock you out and carry you with me?"

He meant it—and she knew he did. He let her up, and

almost flung her his shirt. Her arms shook, like the rest of her body as she slipped them through too-long sleeves. Why didn't Hal come back?

She made one last attempt at rebellion as he led her through the door, his arm tightly clamped around her waist.

"How can *you* talk about being honest? You've never been."

"Everyone's got to start sometime, baby." His voice sounded almost pleasant for a change, but the pressure of his arm tightened warningly, almost cutting off her breath, so that she stumbled against him on her bare feet.

Chapter Thirty-one

THEY PASSED NO ONE on the narrow path that wound among cypresses as twisted as the path itself. It gave each of the guest chalets the illusion of privacy.

Anne didn't know why she went with him, except she was sure he would do exactly as he had threatened if she didn't. A voice from long ago repeated itself in her mind. *Webb carries his bad-guy role over into real life . . .*

How far would it take him—and her? She felt dazed, removed from reality, as if this, too, were a part of the make-believe, and they were still acting out their roles. Jason and Glory. This had nothing to do with Anne and Webb, who were modern and civilized—at least on the surface.

"Make yourself comfortable, baby. Want a drink?"

She sat in the soft chair he offered her with exaggerated politeness, a childishly defensive instinct making her curl her feet under her. She watched him lock the door and walk across the room to fix himself a drink—and one for her, whether she wanted it or not. How many times had she watched the way he walked, the way he held his body—watched his body, felt its length and hardness against hers with fierce possessiveness? She wrenched her mind away from those thoughts with a conscious effort, forcing herself to see him as a stranger she must be wary of. A suddenly frightening, threatening stranger who wanted something of her. Like that cold-eyed Englishman in London in his spy raincoat, who had probably had Violet "executed" in place of *her*. Had she really turned to Webb for protection? Thought he was protection? What did he mean when he'd talked about learning to kill without leaving traces? God, she must be going crazy!

Webb set a glass down on the table beside her. He sat on the bed, the liquid in the glass he held as amber as his eyes. Only she couldn't see through his eyes into what he was thinking.

"All right, Annie." She wished he wouldn't keep calling her that! "Why don't you just start at the beginning? The story about the tapes Carol and I used to make. Who told you that? Caro baby herself, or your friend Harris?"

So he wasn't denying it! It made her feel sick all over again, arming her against him. Boldly, she took a sip of the drink he had fixed her. She looked back at him and tried to let the disgust she felt for him show in her face.

"It wasn't Carol, or Harris either. It was—it was Karim. He —was laughing at me. He said I couldn't be as cold as I pretended to be, because he'd *heard* . . . Oh God, how *could* you? Did you think it was funny, a great big joke to be shared with all your friends?" She almost choked on her drink.

Webb's face seemed to tighten, closing against her. "There never was a tape made, that *I* know of, of what happened between you and me, Annie." He shrugged, wincing as he did, keeping his voice even. "Sure, Caro and I used to play all kinds of sick games at one time. One of the stupid bets we were always making with each other. But I'd quit a long time before I met you. So if someone had my room bugged, I didn't know about it. And that makes me wonder, too . . ."

When, for Christ's sake? And why? And what if *this* room had a bug planted in it, too? He'd have to look . . . Anne was worrying her lower lip with her teeth, staring at him with contempt and mistrust. Was she being used, or was she one of the users herself?

"Do you expect me to believe you? Why should I?"

"I don't really care if you do or not, baby. All I want is the answers. The honest answers. Let's skip to that film you talked about, shall we?"

She put the glass down with unnecessary violence, and her hands clenched the arms of the chair as she answered him.

"Oh yes, of course! You and Venetia by firelight and water, with all those mirrors reflecting you—it must have been quite a kick for you both, and you gave a good performance, as usual. Are you going to deny that, too?"

"Uh-uh." He shook his head, but his eyes were thoughtful. "That happened—only I didn't learn until afterward that the whole damn thing was being filmed. Johnnie Bardini. The bastard promised me he'd destroyed the negative. So how in hell did someone get hold of a copy, and how did you happen to see it?"

"Oh, but you're disgusting, do you know that? Tapes, cameras, action. The kind you're so good at! You do it for the movies, too, so why should you care?"

"I was asking you for some answers, Annie." His voice had turned dangerous again.

She frowned rebelliously, but answered him all the same—throwing words at him with all the scorn she could muster. "I'm sure I don't know how anyone got hold of a copy, and I didn't care to ask! Why don't you ask Harris to show you his private collection of real-life porn sometime? Your little episode was only one of the many—it was really quite amusing, after a while, to see so many real, recognizable people doing so many—ugly, unspeakable things!"

"Didn't it turn you on, love?" He squinted his eyes hatefully at her. "Didn't you feel like volunteering? Or maybe Harris has already put you in one of his party movies. Did he give you a screen test before he offered you the part of Glory? Don't worry—lots of the biggest female stars got started that way, with very special screen tests, shot in private. Haven't you and Karim started rehearsing yet?"

"You bastard! Don't try to turn your own perverted ideas of

—of *fun* onto me! Oh, I could almost feel sorry for you, because you're so sick in the head! And I'm disgusted with myself because I actually let you touch me!" She went on recklessly: "And thank God I was never quite fool enough to take you seriously. Although you were a good teacher, Webb, I'll grant you that much. You—"

"Annie, why did you walk out on me that time?" His words took her by surprise, cutting her angry tirade off short. "Cut the crap—it wasn't because I happened to run into Venetia—you couldn't have known then. Because I called you when the damned airplane was fogged in, and you weren't there. And why hadn't you told me you'd accepted the role of Glory?" His voice hardened again. "You were playing your own little games, baby, and you can't deny it. So who's the hypocrite?"

"You are—you are!" She pounded a fist on the arm of the chair, wishing it could have been his lying face instead. "You lied and pretended with me from the beginning—and I was stupid enough, at first, not to believe anything they told me."

"*They?*"

She was too far gone to care now, even if he did kill her. "Craig warned me. Oh, I thought at first he was just jealous, but later I began to wonder. There were too many things—and when I was away from you, I could see them more clearly. He said—he said you were only playing around with me because you had reason to hate my father—and that's true, isn't it? That time in Deepwood, when you asked me about my father . . . and Craig said you're connected with—with the Mafia!" The sound she made was half hysterical giggle and half sob. "Well, are you, Webb? Is that why you're so good at killing? Is that why you knew we were being followed when we drove back from Guildford? Are you used to being followed? Is that why you're always so suspicious? God, I feel as if we're all playing in some melodrama! Why are you asking me all these questions? What does it matter to you?" She brought her hands up, pushing them against her temples as if to ward off the ugly thoughts that whirled in her brain, emerging from her mouth almost without volition. Why did he just sit there staring at her? Why didn't he say something? Wasn't he going to deny anything? Or was he only planning how he would get rid of her? She could have, and should have, killed him earlier this afternoon—but . . . could she have lived with the thought?

Webb's thoughts had taken another, darker direction. Craig Hyatt had "warned" her. Hyatt and Reardon—there was a connection there, and not just through marriage. Why had they let her come here? They could have stopped her; he knew Reardon's methods as well as anyone else did—better than most. That cold-blooded, aseptic bastard with the computer brain. Would he use his own daughter, and discard her as easily as he had his other pawns? And if he suspected what Anne knew . . . all the more reason, wasn't it? Use her by letting the others think they were using her, to smoke them out of cover. And then . . . get rid of her? A picture flashed across his brain of Peter smiling. The killer who enjoyed killing. What would they do about Anne?

Suddenly, he was tired of questions and answers. Even the questions he asked himself and the answers he came up with. He was tired, period, and only one question remained: How much did she really hate him?

He drained his glass and put it down, crossing the room to where she sat huddled in the chair and pulled her savagely to her feet.

"No—don't!"

"You cut that scene short with your knife trick, Annie love. Now we're through with talking, why don't we finish it, just for the record?"

His mouth cut off the rest of her protests, along with her breath, and even her will. He was exacting his final revenge, and she knew it with her mind, before the treachery of her own senses and his body subjugated everything to the flood of passion that took over like an uncontrolled demon.

The battlefield was a different one now as they fell across the bed, still kissing. Why Webb? Why always Webb and only Webb who could take her, without any effort or preliminaries, up to the heights and send her over the edge of desire and beyond, only to take her up with him again—and again—and again? In Anne's mind, in the pulsing in her ears, it was like the sea-breakers pounding, drawing back, rearing up to come crashing down again. Never-ending, everlasting. Her body was the earth with all its curves and hollows, and his was ocean—endlessly, insinuatingly taking more and more until she was shredded from rocks to sand. Giving herself up to destruction, wanting it.

Bodies—feeling. His hands and mouth tracing continents. Exploring inside her to ignite ancient volcanos that had lain dormant since he had found them last.

She was lost—wanting to be lost, needing to be lost. Like this. Crying without knowing she was crying, until at last she felt his fingers wipe the tears from her face with surprising tenderness.

Sal Espinoza turned away from his intent scrutiny of the video monitor when Harris Phelps came into the air-conditioned room, shutting the door behind him with a snap. Harris wore a frown, and he was stroking his mustache as he usually did when he was upset—or extraordinarily pleased.

"Is something wrong?"

"Yes." Harris was unusually blunt. "Anne's disappeared. Brightman came up to have a talk with me—he said he'd left her sleeping off the effects of the afternoon in his room. He just called me in a panic—says she apparently woke up while he was gone and just walked out. She's not in her room—I just checked. And Karim hasn't seen her either . . ."

"You need not worry. She's with Webb Carnahan." Catching Harris's momentarily unguarded expression, Espinoza gave a lazy chuckle.

"Ah, come, my friend! You ought to be glad that our two

stars seem to have made up their differences. That was quite a performance this afternoon, wasn't it? She surprised me with her—fire. But then, you know what they say about love and hate. Such a thin dividing line, eh?" He nodded towards the screen, and Harris, his face muscles drawn tight, saw the miniature picture of the bed, covers trailing onto the floor—Webb Carnahan's body still partially covering Anne's. He watched, and saw them kiss, heard her sigh on the turned-up soundtrack.

"You've been taping all this . . . ?"

"Of course. I found it most fascinating. Especially her very uninhibited reactions to his rather rough approach. For a short time I thought it would be a rape, and then . . ." He shrugged, taking pleasure through hooded eyes in Harris's stiffness. "I wonder what Anna-Maria will think of all this? He sent her away from him, you know. And she wasn't too happy about it."

"What the hell kind of game is Carnahan playing?" Harris said with suppressed fury. "How did he get her back to his room? Why?" He tried to control himself, realizing that Espinoza was observing him quizzically.

The other man's shoulders lifted again. "Our friend the doctor was careless enough to leave his door unlocked, I suppose. And I can only suppose, also, that Carnahan was curious—or maybe he was angry. After all, she did try to kill him! So I can only surmise that he saw Dr. Brightman walk by, intent on finding *you*, and Carnahan wanted to find out what had happened to make her so angry with him. I did not get much of what went on in Brightman's room, but when he took her back to his, he asked a lot of questions. Some of them may interest you."

"Oh?" Harris Phelps was frowning again. After an infinitesimal pause he went on in a smoother voice: "I'm sure that *would* prove interesting. I had several telephone calls, in between seeing Brightman and looking for Anne. One from Carol —Markham's flying down here next weekend with his CIA friend, Parmenter, and she'll be down the day before. And the other from our useful friend in high places, who had some extremely interesting information to pass on—about Webb Carnahan." His voice sharpened. "What kind of questions did he ask Anne? What did she tell him?"

"She does not know very much, does she? Only little things she has picked up—and our friend Karim has a big mouth, as his uncle warned us. You'll learn for yourself when you play back the tape. But what did Brightman have for you? Did he make any headway?" Espinoza's voice was noncommittal, but his eyes were as watchful as ever, and he saw Harris's tiny hesitation before he answered.

"He made quite a lot of headway, as a matter of fact. He came to me for advice, and gave me the tapes he'd made—for safekeeping in the vault. In fact"—and he smiled at last, lips thinning—"I think we have enough on Reardon now to make sure he's rendered useless. We'll have a private meeting tonight, of course."

"Sure!" Espinoza nodded, his face a politely smiling blank. He wondered what Harris Phelps was keeping back, and was glad that he, in his turn, had had the opportunity while he was up here alone to secrete a small segment of video tape that might or might not come in useful sometime. Harris need not know just yet that Carnahan had made a search of Brightman's room before he woke Anne up. Or that he had read Brightman's notes. It was Webb Carnahan's connections, if what the girl had said was true, that interested him most. And he had learned, through experience, that one should never completely trust any other person, partner or not. It was always useful to keep a hidden ace somewhere, just in case . . .

Anne wanted to keep floating forever, dreamlike, on the edge of sleep, not waking up to thought or reality. It was as if all the ugliness—question and answer and defiance and hate and fear—had never happened. For the moment, at least, there was only this present. She and Webb, skin to skin, mouth to mouth, isolated on an island in the sea of time. She didn't want to think any further, and neither did he. Slip into sleep —don't think . . . At her halfhearted movement to pull her body from under his he had murmured against her mouth, "Stay with me, Annie-love. Don't go." And after that the only motion she was capable of making was to adjust her body more closely to his. The room grew cold after the heat of their passion, and he pulled the covers up over them both. They both slept and the late-afternoon sun moved its sullen spears of light through cracks in the blinds, across the bed and up across the opposite wall, until they faded into nothingness, swallowed up between the twisted cypresses and the ocean in the end.

Darkness was a cool-warm blanket. Safe, enveloping membrane within the womb of early night until jagged-shape splinters of light ripped it open. A woman's voice, slightly accented, said, "Webb? I could not stop worrying about you. I know I am a fool, but . .. *oh!*"

Ria stood there with her hand on the light switch—face and hair blending into different shades of gold under the light she'd turned on. No makeup except for lip gloss. A thin slip of a dress—pale beige accented by gold satin ribbon with spaghetti straps barely caressing her shoulders. She was dressed for dinner, and her surprise and embarrassment seemed genuine.

"I'm *sorry!* Truly I am. I didn't realize . . ."

Only Webb caught the quickly veiled flicker in her eyes that might have been anger—or spite. To Anne, the voice was familiar—warm honey overlaying arrogance and an obvious assumption of familiarity.

So this was Anna-Maria—letting herself into Webb's room with easy assurance because she was "worried" about him. Oh God, how humiliating! How many times did she have to be taught how casually Webb used women?

And now, while he kept her body pinned unwillingly under his in spite of her attempts to extricate herself, he was looking straight at the other woman, with the strangest smile—not showing any signs of perturbation.

"Hi, Ria. You do turn up at the most unexpected times, don't you? What time is it?"

Just like that. Easy conversation with a drop-in guest. They knew each other very well, too, from the wary way they eyed each other.

"It is almost dinnertime. And when I left you this afternoon, you said you were feeling very sleepy. I didn't know you had company."

"Well, Annie and I decided to talk things over, didn't we, love? Have you two met yet?"

Giving up the silent physical struggle against his strength Anne said, trying to emulate his careless attitude, "I don't think so. But you must be Señor Espinoza's friend."

"I am Anna-Maria de Leone. You're Anne Mallory? I apologize for intruding, but I did not know . . ." She cast a flickering glance at Webb and went on smoothly: "Webb and I are very old friends, you see, or I would not have come in without knocking first. Perhaps I should go now."

Anne surprised herself by saying sweetly, "Oh, please don't! Since it's so late, I must be going myself. I hope Harris hasn't been sending out search parties for me. It was very thoughtless of me not to have left a note or something."

"Oh shit!" Webb said with unexpected violence. Just as unexpectedly he set her free—yanking the covers back up to her neck as he swung his feet off the side of the bed, standing up like a naked satyr—just as uncaring. "If I guess right, you're a search party of one, aren't you, Ria sweet? So now you've been properly introduced, why don't you be a good little girl scout and call up to the house for something Anne can wear?" He picked his pants up off the floor where he had dropped them, smiling wickedly into Anne's startled, angry face.

"You weren't wearing much when you came in here, Annie love. I could lend you something of mine to wear, but it might cause a lot of speculation if you walked into the house like that. So why don't you two girls decide on something while I go take a shower . . . unless you'd care to join me?"

Chapter Thirty-two

SHE HAD ONLY HERSELF to blame, Anne told herself stonily afterwards. She had let him drug her senses, just as she had so many times before. Even after he had threatened her and insulted her. Oh, but Webb was consummate at the kind of cruel games he played! Perhaps he'd planned to make the woman he called "Ria" so familiarly jealous. Perhaps—but why torture herself with suppositions? She hated herself even more than she despised him. Especially when she remembered how he'd extricated himself from an awkward situation—just by walking away from it, and leaving her and Anna-Maria staring at each other, sizing each other up for the first few seconds, before Anna-Maria shrugged expressively.

"I am sorry. He can be very cruel, can't he? Me, I should know. When we met again I had thought myself armed against him, and then . . . but it doesn't matter. He is only cruel when he is angry, and it was me he was angry with just now."

"Why?" Anne asked bluntly. She felt ridiculous, lying naked in the bed she'd shared with Webb all afternoon and talking calmly with one of his other lovers, who obviously understood him much better than she did.

"Why? It is a very long story. Forgive me, but I don't know if I am ready to speak of it yet—or if I should." And then her voice turning brisk. "But if you don't mind, I think perhaps I should call Harris? He has been worried about you, it's true."

Harris sent one of his discreet servants down with a pair of jeans and a shirt for her, while Webb took his time in the shower. And Anna-Maria stayed, while Anne, feeling ridiculously guilty, had to face Harris himself soon afterwards.

She felt even more guilty when he didn't reproach her—merely looked at her searchingly. "Are you all right, Anne?"

Color suffused her anger-pale cheeks, and she dropped her eyes. "Yes. And I'm sorry—I didn't mean to . . ."

"Anne, remember when I told you you were free? I meant that, love." He sighed then. "I just don't want you hurt. Webb Carnahan—but you know what he's like, don't you? I suppose you felt guilty, although you shouldn't have." He was making excuses for her, and his understanding made her squirm inside.

"I suppose I had to get him out of my system!" she said lightly. "And besides, that shot Dr. Brightman gave me must have been stronger than I thought—I hardly knew what I was doing for a while, and then I fell asleep . . ." She wanted to ask him about Anna-Maria, but didn't dare.

He left her in her room after asking her solicitously if she felt up to joining them for dinner—or after dinner, if she preferred. He could have a tray sent up to her room. Pride and stubbornness made Anne insist that, though she was not particularly hungry, she would enjoy joining everyone soon after dinner, which mustn't be held up on her account.

In the end, it all went off much more easily than she could have imagined. Anne went downstairs and mingled. And no one asked questions—no one mentioned the stabbing. They were all relaxed—laughing, gossiping, planning to make an early night before tomorrow's shooting. There was no sign of either Webb or Anna-Maria (and Anne had to catch back the thought —*Is she still with him? Didn't she mind?*), but Karim kept casting her dark looks, which she tried to ignore. Yves was smiling, obviously pleased with himself. He was being patronizingly nice to Claudia, who was pouting as usual. Sarah wore jewels again—diamonds; and she sparkled just like the jewels. Jean Benedict was back to wearing levis again, this time with a red silk shirt that made her look like a gypsy. And Sal Espinoza was as charmingly urbane as usual, seemingly unconcerned that his mistress was nowhere in evidence. Hadn't he said they had an "understanding"? And if he didn't care, why should she? Let Webb play his games. The next time they met, Anne thought fiercely, she would be completely indifferent. She wouldn't let him use her again, or ask her pointless questions, or listen to his bland, lying explanations. She took the drink Espinoza handed her and smiled up at him.

Ria had stayed in Webb's room, listening to the sounds of him taking a shower, and wondering how much she could make him tell her. He had changed from the ardent, tenderly protective lover she remembered—but hadn't she been prepared for that? She had changed, too, but found that the new Webb excited and challenged her much more. She had learned to enjoy playing with danger, and her senses told her he could be a dangerous adversary—which made this game much more exciting.

And as for Anne Mallory, who had shared his bed . . . she had seen the videotape, before they sent her down here to find out what she could. Anne Mallory was stupid, even if she was Reardon's daughter. And she was easily manipulated. Perhaps Webb, too, was out for revenge—wouldn't that be ironic? Also, he made love beautifully, especially when he let the savage in him escape. Like the other night . . .

Webb came out of the bathroom, slinging the towel he'd been using carelessly over his shoulder. He looked at her without expression.

"Aren't you going to be late for dinner?"

"I am persistent, you see. And a little jealous. Why did you send me away this afternoon, and then go to her?"

"How do you know I went to her? She might have come here on her own, you know." He thought her face changed slightly, but the next moment whatever expression he'd surprised was wiped out as she shook her head doubtfully.

336

"Oh no—she stabbed you, didn't she? I was watching, there was hate, and the real urge to kill. That's why it surprised me to find her here—and it's not like you to make yourself foolish over a woman, unless she made herself a challenge to you. Be careful, *querido*. If she's jealous, she might try again; you two have many scenes to play together, have you not?"

Suddenly, as if he were tired of the subject, he shrugged. "And you're trying to make me believe you're jealous? Isn't it a little late for that, Ria? Suppose you come to the point and tell me what brought you back, and what you want from me."

She changed tactics as easily as the wind changes direction, he thought cynically, watching the way her hands clasped each other in her lap as her eyes widened at him. "Would you believe anything I told you? You wouldn't listen before."

"Maybe I'm ready now." He sounded reasonable, but his eyes were unreadable. She did not know quite how to handle him, or what to say. And when he stood there naked, looking at her, there were other things to be contended with. Like desire. She would like for him to make love to her for a long, long time, without the aid of pills or coke or any of the other aids that even she, on occasion, had enjoyed.

"Webb," she said softly, "do you remember when we met? How it was then?" Of all the things she might have said it was the one thing he hadn't expected. Caught off guard, Webb felt the hammer blow of memory break open the tight lock he'd kept on those particular memories.

He first noticed Maria de Leone because she alone of all the girls on the beach wore a severely cut one-piece bathing suit. She seemed to stay by herself, discouraging all attempts at conversation—or to be content in the company of a black-clad older woman. And he thought at first, so what? The Florida beaches swarmed with brightly bikinied butterflies—long-legged, tanned beauties who used makeup cleverly and knew how to handle themselves.

"She's one of them refugees. Shit—she ain't that much when

you get up close, and she acts scared if anyone as much as says 'hi' to her. Like it's some kind of sin to talk to a guy. Why waste your time, buddy? There's enough action to be had here so we don't have to spend any night alone!" Mel Gillis was a tall, handsome Louisianan who happened to be black—not that that ever stopped Mel from getting more than his share of the action he talked about, even in Florida. He ended up being their best man a month later—but that was after Webb had met Maria de Leone, discovering to his jubilant surprise that she was supposed to tutor him in Cuban Spanish.

It was part of a special training program. Although as it happened in the end, *he* wasn't the one to be sent to Cuba, but Ria herself. . .

Maria de Leone. He used to tease her about her name, which meant "lionlike." "You're not a lioness—more like a baby lion cub or a golden kitten." Her skin was light gold all over, and all the time he knew her she never used any makeup. Her hair was long, with enough natural curl in it to make it unruly. Light brown, streaked gold from the sun. Enormous hazel eyes.

And innocence—oh Christ, wasn't that what had intrigued him so in the first place? Webb Carnahan, cynic. It had shaken him, and bound him more closely to her to discover how untutored and shy she was. That and her shame at not being a virgin, because she'd been raped. Ria never did see the suspicious, skeptical side of him; nor the hardness and harshness that had been part of his nature until then. She was too easily hurt—too naïve, too vulnerable.

Her parents had been killed in the revolution while she was away at school. And after the revolutionaries from the hills had come and gone, she had been one of the lucky ones to be smuggled out of Cuba by the nuns. The old woman who kept her so strictly at her side was a distant relative, a courtesy "aunt" who looked on the girl as an unwelcome duty, and kept reminding her dolefully that she must work hard; no man would want to marry a girl who wasn't a virgin. The woman was relieved to have the girl taken off her hands; and Webb, knowing only that he wanted her, didn't bother to ask permission of anyone when they got married.

If it came down to facts, he married her because she wouldn't sleep with him otherwise. He had no illusions about the kind of work he was engaged in at the time, and he might be dead in a month. But then he ended up loving Ria, and with the loving he developed a sense of responsibility for her—worrying about her, taking precautions he hadn't bothered with before because he didn't know what might happen to Ria, who was too honest and too trusting.

When he lost her as suddenly as she'd entered his life, there was nothing he cared about after that—least of all himself. That was when his crazy plan to kill Reardon was born, and he would have carried it out if they hadn't been one step ahead of him all the way. They should have had him killed—there was a time when he'd wished that. But instead they sent him, forcibly, to one of their experimental think tanks. For debriefing, they said. For weeks psychiatrists played games with his mind and his reflexes. Later, because he'd made it tough for them, the CIA offered him a job, playing up the revenge motive. They could get him into Cuba, with the perfect cover. His purpose—assassination. And they even promised him the name and whereabouts of the man who had been directly responsible for killing his wife.

But by then he'd had enough. He turned them down—played it cool and close to the cuff. No more threats against Reardon. And no more patriotic crap, no more risking his life for shit. He "retired" with an excellent service record—they did him that much of a favor—and when he got tired of digging ditches and supervising recreation activities at a Los Angeles park, he'd drifted into acting, and his affair with Carol.

The past was a write-off. Each year that passed was busier and more successful than the last, and dammit, he *had* managed to forget, until his bad-chance meeting with Reardon's daughter had got him entangled in all this—and Ria.

Webb had turned deliberately away from her question to rummage for a pair of clean pants in a bureau drawer. Not Ria any longer. Anna-Maria de Leone. A very persistent young woman . . . hadn't she said so earlier?

When he straightened up, she had crossed the room to stand close to him, expensively perfumed with Joy. "Webb, you *do* remember, don't you? Even if you do not want to. And so do I. I've never forgotten, believe that, even if you won't believe anything else."

"Why should it matter now what I believe or don't believe? There's one thing we both know, Ria, and that's that the past is dead—long live the present!"

He kissed her lightly on the cheek, and patted her bottom, almost surprising her into swearing. "Be a good kid and fix us each a drink, will you? And then, we'll talk—if that's all you really came here to do."

The light in the room had been turned down, its illumination just enough to outline the two figures who lay on the bed. But the voices carried clearly over the audio monitor. Anna-Maria was clearly on the defensive, her voice beginning to sound strained.

"But I have told you and told you! I had no choice! I only thought I was doing something brave and good, and then I found I could not stand torture. And when they laughed at me and told me how I had been fooled . . . what would you have done? I used my body—yes, I did that! After a while, it ceased to matter what I did, as long as I stayed alive."

"What I can't understand is why you came here."

"Sal was coming. Since—since we have been together I usually go where he goes. And then I heard that you were to be in this picture. So . . ." She shrugged faintly. "Do you know that there were times when I thought—I actually wondered if you had known all along what was to happen to me? They let me think that, too. Even now I'm not sure. You were not very surprised when you saw me, and some of the things you said . . ."

"I don't recall saying much of anything, Ria. And I don't know why we're bothering with this question-and-answer routine—except it was your idea. To explain, I think you said? Well, okay, if it makes you feel any better, I accept all your explanations. And I've only one more question to ask before it's Lights Out." His cigarette made a small arc in the semi-darkness before he stubbed it out viciously. "Did you ever get around to getting a divorce? Because I sure as hell didn't."

"He is full of energy, that one!" Espinoza chuckled lazily. "He fucks one woman for most of the afternoon, and now he'll probably stay up half the night with Anna-Maria—she's quite insatiable herself."

"He's a clever son of a bitch!" Randall chewed on the end of his cigar. "Didn't give anything away, did he? And didn't ask *her* any too-obvious questions either. I wonder . . ."

Harris Phelps said with uncharacteristic violence. "The bastard smells of Reardon! I know they got to him somehow, and we'll find out . . ."

"Maybe after sex, he'll make a slip. It's the time, unfortunately, when men are weakest." Espinoza sounded urbane, but Harris glanced at him sharply. He shrugged. "After all, what does he know? And if he tries to contact anyone, we'll find out. So what is there to worry about? In any case, we all know that what we have on Reardon now can smoke him out of cover." Deliberately changing the subject, he added, "Any news from our friend Taki since he left?"

They had been watching a videotape play-back, and it was very late. Pleydel had already retired to get some sleep before the shooting in the morning. Anne had declined to watch the day's rushes and had gone up to her room before the others had come up here.

Mixing pills with alcohol wasn't good, she knew, but she didn't care, and she needed sleep and oblivion. So heavily did she sleep that she didn't quite wake up when someone slid into bed beside her.

A little later she stirred and moaned. Why had she begun to dream? She didn't know if the dreams were pleasant or not. She was somewhere else, someone else—Glory. Was she Glory? There were hands on her body, a weight between her thighs. She gasped, and felt her nostrils sting and then just as suddenly she was floating somewhere, uncaring. *Don't wake up, and then the dream will go away.*

"You are too dry—come, I'll help you." The voice was a different voice, one she knew and didn't want to remember. There was a soreness and then a numbness between her thighs as her body began to arch and convulse on its own while her mind stayed detached and free-floating, still hovering between sleep and dream.

"Have you forgotten how to fuck? I watched you in action this afternoon, and now it's my turn. You'll fuck me now, you blonde-and-white bitch! Put your arms around me and beg for it. Beg, I tell you—you want to be fucked, don't you? You enjoy it, for all your cold pretense."

"Please . . ." Was that her voice, sounding disembodied, or Glory's?

"That's better. Spread your legs wide and beg me again. For this—and for *this.*" A shaft of pain that drove her body upwards with a cry that almost woke her completely—*was* she awake or asleep? Why did her nostrils seem so numb while her brain and her body exploded with the longing for a release she had to have? Even the pain was pleasurable, because she had to . . . she had to . . . and against that longing she couldn't control, the words he was making her say didn't seem important at all.

Chapter Thirty-three

ANNE WOKE TO THE SOUND of the helicopter; she opened her eyes with an effort to find Harris looking down at her. Her mind felt fuzzy . . . why was his look so strange, and why did she feel so—so—

"I think I'm coming down with a cold." Her nose was running; she felt embarrassed as she reached for a tissue, only to find that her whole body ached abominably.

He handed her the box, his face set and almost grim-looking. He looked as if he hadn't slept very well. "Cocaine has that aftereffect, especially if you—overindulge."

She tried to sit up, and fell back against the pillows again with an exclamation of pain. "*Cocaine?* But I didn't—I've never tried it!" Why was he accusing her? She must be getting the flu, or she wouldn't hurt so whenever she tried to move.

"Oh, for Christ's sake, Anne!" His control slipped for a moment before he regained it again. "There's no need to lie to me, although I must confess I don't understand last night. But I'm neither blind nor deaf."

She blew her nose helplessly, staring at him. "But I don't understand! I honestly don't. What are you trying to say?"

"I'm trying to keep things in perspective, Anne. And, I must admit, to hold on to my temper. When I told you you were free—don't you realize that there's a difference between freedom and licence? With some of the other women here—yes, I

343

suppose I could understand. But you . . . what has happened to you since Webb Carnahan got here? It was him yesterday afternoon—you explained that, didn't you?" For a moment a mirthless smile twisted his lips under his mustache. "But Karim last night—I thought you didn't even like him."

"*Karim?*" It came out as a whisper—she felt sure she must still be dreaming. Oh God, it *had* to be a dream, no more than that!

"Karim," Harris repeated heavily. "I suppose he left early this morning. I didn't sleep too well myself. I let you sleep— Yves is shooting around you for today. I told him that you were—unwell."

Even her arms ached when she put her hands up to her head. And now the rest of the pains were becoming localized. Her legs—especially between her thighs. Her bed was all mussed up and damp—she could feel a stickiness under her, along with the smarting, the throbbing.

"But I—I don't *remember*! I took a Valium, and then . . . if Karim was here last night, then I didn't know it! But I couldn't have slept through . . . oh God!" She felt sick, those half-dreams coming back into her mind.

Harris said stiffly, "I've run your bath for you. I didn't want the maid coming up to find you like this."

He was denying her a hearing, and her head had begun to hurt, too, along with the rest of her body. She cried at him wildly, "How can you be so sure it happened if I'm not? Or that it was Karim? If he did come in here while I was asleep, then it was . . ."

"It wasn't rape, Anne. My God, I could even cope with *that* better! He's not the most tender lover in the world—I'm sorry, but when I walked in, you weren't covered, and I could not help seeing the bruises he left on you. But you seemed to be enjoying his lovemaking."

"*What?*"

He said with deliberate lack of expression, "I could not help

hearing you. He kept laughing and urging you on, and you . . .
I'm sorry, Anne, if you don't want to remember this. You were
crying out—you kept begging him to fuck you, to fuck you
please. Do you think I wanted to hear that from *you*? Or that
I enjoyed listening?"

After Ria left his room, Webb had barely had two hours'
sleep before they woke him up. Brightman, looking stiff and
reproachful, had come in to dress and bandage his arm and
pronounce that it was doing fine, healing well. And then getting to the set—another courtyard scene, since the sun continued to shine. It didn't help his temper to find out that
everything had been switched around. He was to go through his
first short scene with Claudia (who didn't seem in too good a
mood herself) and a scene with Karim, playing the dapper
Mexican general. So where the hell was Anne?

"We are shooting around our big star this morning!" Claudia
whispered to him maliciously. "They say she is not feeling well,
but do you observe how Karim struts? Hah!"

Karim's eyes were slightly bloodshot, but he did seem extraordinarily pleased with himself at that.

Yves Pleydel's apologies were perfunctory as he confirmed at
least part of Claudia's gossip. "I'm sorry—but we all know that
these things can happen, yes? Tomorrow we will do what we
were supposed to do today." He sighed expressively. "Today—
well, we will all do the best we can, eh? The cantina scene.
I am sure you can memorize your lines—there are not too
many—while we are setting up." He looked at Webb, who
merely grunted, his thoughts dark. "Miss Benedict will do her
song, and we will have reaction. And the little scene between
you and Claudia"—he gave a sly chuckle, ignoring Claudia's
smoldering glare—"that will go well, I'm sure, for it is mostly
action—not many words!"

Webb let his thoughts wander, and they weren't pleasant.
Anne was throwing a temperament fit—or was she? Karim

continued to look pleased with himself, throwing apparently triumphant looks Webb's way.

Why the fuck should he care if Claudia's insinuations were true? He had other things to think about. Ria, for instance. Brightman's notes, and what he ought to do about what they'd told him. And about what was really going on around here—behind the scenes—while he and the rest of the dupes were making a movie. Christ, he was in no mood to think this morning. Just do what had to be done and get it over with.

The filming went off comparatively well, to begin with. Jean Benedict looked nervous and uncertain at first ("Christ! This costume—why didn't they let women wear pants in those days?") but she had Sarah Vesper to coach her with her lines, and once she began to sing, the nervousness disappeared and she gave a creditable performance for a beginner.

Webb, his dark mood persisting, was suitably morose and monosyllabic during that particular scene, although Yves told him sharply that he obviously wasn't at his best today, and a few early nights might help—in fact, that would help everybody!

"But some nights spent making love are worth everything—even an early morning," Karim commented, and again his dark eyes rested maliciously on Webb's impassive face.

They had a short run-through of his scene with Claudia, playing the tempestuous gypsy dancer who was his girl friend; the role suited Claudia's sultry beauty. But she threw a fit of temperament about camera angles, complaining that Yves was picking on her, and she knew why . . . until the harried director threw up his hands in frustration.

"*Merde!* Women! So—until she cools down—and she will, if she does not want to be replaced . . . !"

Claudia turned her back on him after muttering, "Good—so you realize that *I* am a woman, too!"

Pleydel continued, ignoring her: "Perhaps we should continue with the scene in the cantina—it is set up already, and if you two gentlemen know your lines . . . ?"

The "gentlemen" were Webb and Karim, and Pleydel's suggestion, although he couldn't know it, came at the wrong time.

This was one of the fight scenes—pointing up the rivalry between the two men in Glory's life. A barroom quarrel between the arrogant Mexican officer and the American renegade. The scene itself was almost stereotyped. First the insulting words being traded, with fisticuffs following.

Karim made his first mistake when he asked Pleydel, grinning, "You did say realism? And no holding back? In Egypt we did not use doubles or stand-ins, but perhaps in this country . . ." He looked at Webb, shrugging with overdone politeness. "I'm sorry, but I must warn you that when I get in a fight, I tend to forget that I am acting. I have been trained to fight—perhaps you might care to use a double for this scene?"

"Oh, that's okay. I guess I can take care of myself," Webb drawled, but his eyes had turned leopard-yellow.

Karim shrugged. "Ah well . . ." He turned back to Pleydel, still grinning. "I guess we are ready."

It was back to the makeshift cantina, and the laborious business of adjusting the cameras and checking the lighting.

"Do I have to do my thing all over again?" Jean Benedict inquired, and Yves shook his head impatiently. "No, no. We will intercut. When you watch the dailies, you will see how it is done. For the moment, all you need to do is stand up there the way you were when you were singing. Pretend you are singing, if it will help."

"Everybody in their places." Tom, the assistant director, took over when it came to setting up a scene. Meg, the continuity girl, scurried around, checking on every little detail, showing everyone their positions, if they had forgotten. When she was through, she looked longingly at Webb Carnahan from behind the shelter of her clipboard. Maybe one day he'd actually notice her. He'd smiled at her this morning, but she had sensed that he did it absent-mindedly. Perhaps if she put blonde streaks in her hair, like her friend Toni had suggested . . .

"Okay, we're ready." Tom looked at Yves, who nodded. Meg kept watching Webb, although she knew she was supposed to keep her eye on *everything*. She couldn't help it. How easily he seemed to shrug himself into the role he was playing, unlike some other actors she had watched. And from the backstairs gossip, he obviously fitted the part he was playing. God, what wouldn't she give for just one night with him!

The "quarrel" was in progress—weighted sarcasm turning into open insults and from there to blows after the jeering young officer had slapped the American with his glove.

As he had threatened, Karim didn't hold back, and there was a red streak down the side of the beard-stubbled face that turned slowly to face him.

"Would you like to settle this matter between us here and now, or would you prefer to go outside?"

"Nothin' wrong with now, is there?"

And then it erupted. The fight. With the extras yelling encouragement that was real, once they understood that this was for *real*, just like the courtyard scene yesterday.

"Christ, one or the other is going to get marked up good," Tom whispered to Pleydel, who only shook his head, a twisted smile pasted on his face.

"It is good because it is real, *mon chèr*. It is always very good when two men fight over a woman. We will let the cameras roll until it is over."

Meg held the clipboard tight against her lips to stop from screaming. God—fantastic, she thought dazedly. The furniture was meant to splinter, and it did, with satisfying crashes, intermingled with the sound of breaking bottles and glasses. This was *cinéma vérité*—she must remember to write back to Marcella, and tell her all about it. Marcella loved watching the fights on TV; she would have adored this.

The two antagonists were intent on each other. Karim had been smiling at first, but now his smile had disappeared. And the way they fought was a mixture of karate and kick-boxing and plain slugging. Until it was over—and it was over very suddenly. Meg couldn't quite remember exactly how it happened afterwards. They had been grappling with each other, up close at one moment, and the next Karim went crashing backward across a table to land on his back on the floor. He made an attempt to get up and fell back again, just like a KO'd boxer. Meg almost expected to hear a countdown. Instead Yves called, "Cut!"

"You did say realism, didn't you?" Webb snarled. And then he turned from Pleydel to Claudia, who was staring at him, her eyes very bright. "What say we go get ourselves a real drink, *bambina*?"

"It was another one-take scene—I really do not think they could have gone through that fight again—not our friend Karim, especially! The so-useful doctor had to put two stitches in his chin, you know, and he is not in a very good frame of mind. But cinematically, it was great. We can use most of the footage, with just a very few intercuts. So—what do you think?"

Yves Pleydel sounded jubilant—but then, he was mainly concerned with the movie itself. Harris and Rufus Randall exchanged looks, and Sal Espinoza was his usual relaxed self.

"One wonders why those two should hate each other so," he drawled, hooded eyes resting for just an instant on Harris.

This time Phelps didn't rise to the bait. He was being very guarded ever since that little episode between Karim and Anne. But he did say slowly, "Maybe the rivalry between them might prove quite useful to us. I've been thinking. . ."

* * *

349

Anne had been thinking, too. Her earlier feelings of shock and degradation and horror had given way to pure, cleansing anger, once she had got through soaking in the hot bath that Harris had so thoughtfully run for her. Harris! She was mad at him, too, for accusing her, brushing aside her explanations as if they didn't exist. Most of all, she was filled with rage towards Karim.

Parts of what she had believed were bad dreams came back to her while she lay in the sunken tub that was one of Danny Verrano's "improvements." Her grandparents' house wasn't the refuge it had been once, before the day she'd found her mother dead. She should never have come back here—Harris shouldn't have found it and bought it for a movie. The film was catching everybody up in make-believe, making it difficult to distinguish it from reality. She should just walk out—go back to being a model, which didn't call for too much acting. She had signed a contract, but Harris wouldn't hold her to it. He couldn't, if she really fought it. And he was disgusted with her, he thought she had really . . .

Even now she couldn't face the thought squarely. Karim. What had he said, besides the ugly, obscene things?

"I watched you in action this afternoon, and now it's my turn." Strange how some of what she hadn't at first chosen to believe came back to her now that she deliberately tried to recall it.

What had he *meant* by that? Had Webb . . . she didn't understand why even now, after all she had learned about him, her mind shied away from that particular thought.

After her bath Sarah Vesper came up to see her, to ask sympathetically if she was feeling better—the flu was miserable, wasn't it? And Sarah told her about the filming this morning —the fight between Webb and Karim that had turned into a real battle. Perhaps Sarah was trying to console her for the previous day, with its own share of realism. "Things like that sometimes happen—one gets caught up in the feeling of a part

—acting, real acting, is like that. You *become* a character you're playing, both on screen and off."

Anne forced herself to ask, "And how's Karim?"

"Oh, resting, I understand. Very angry. I think it's more his pride that's been hurt than anything else! It *was* exciting to watch, though. You ought to see the rushes, if you feel up to it." And then, commiserating, "Shall I ask Hal to come up and see you? The poor man's been kept busier than he anticipated, I'm afraid, but I'm surprised that Harris hasn't told him you don't feel good."

"Oh, that's all right," Anne said quickly. "There's nothing much one can do about the flu except get lots of rest, is there? And I feel better already."

She didn't—but no one needed to know that but herself. Dressing, she ignored the tray that had been sent up for her. Everyone would be dressing for dinner, and there was no better time to pay Karim a visit in his guest chalet.

There was a mixture of rage and passion and malignance in his usually handsome features as he whirled about to face her.

Anne stood just inside the door, with her back to it, taking in the surface cuts and bruises on his face—the stripe of white bandage on his chin. She tried not to let emotion show on her face as she said quietly, "Hello, Karim."

He didn't want her pity—he had thought they were making a movie, which was why he had been unprepared. But there would be another time, a time for revenge. . . The things that poured out of him in his rage were both ugly and puzzling. Anne would have liked to avoid this confrontation, but she had been pushed to the point when she was tired of cowering away like a—a—what had Webb called her before? A frightened rabbit. . .

So she endured Karim's sneering at her. "What is this? You were sleeping very deeply, it's true, but you wanted it! Everything I did to you and for you—you are no virgin, as I very well know! I had your cooperation. Would you like to repeat what you experienced last night? I am surprised, I must admit, that you are here, and not with the victor—the temporary victor!"

He came to her, brushing his hands over her breasts; and she felt like a whore as she shrugged away with a brittle laugh.

"You move too fast, Karim. And I don't like the idea of being—taken, while I was asleep. Why did you do that?"

He was so close that she could feel the heat of his breath on her face.

"Why? Because you were playing the usual silly games. You would not give yourself to me, and yet you would to Harris Phelps—and Webb Carnahan!" He said the last name like a curse.

"But I'm very fond of Harris!" she said reasonably, while she silently prayed he wouldn't try to touch her again. "Don't you have anything to drink in here?" Anything to distract him for a while. "And as for *Webb*—I've never tried to hide the fact that we were lovers once."

"Once? Only once?" His voice was a snarl. "You lie! You lie! You were so cold to me, and all the while you would let him do whatever he wanted to with you—yes, and enjoy it, too! When you stabbed him—that, too, was a form of love, of passion, wasn't it? You put a knife in him one moment, and the next you are lying with him, wrapping your arms and legs about him."

"You sound as if you were right there, watching!"

"I might as well have been!" He gave a sneering spurt of laughter that jarred her nerves. "Do you mean to tell me that you are not in on the secrets? The convenient, clever little machine that watches everything—just like Big Brother? I am sure Harris has shown it to you. And should you wish to go over *our* little scene last night, I am positive there was a videotape to register it. Perhaps we should let Carnahan see that, eh? Do you think it would make him jealous, or only turn him on?"

Anne felt frozen from the toes up. She could only look back at Karim, trying to take in the enormity of what he was telling her. What *was* he telling her?

She heard her voice emerge from her throat, sounding lightly flirtatious—but not knowing how she managed it. "Well, I just wanted to look in on you. But you don't seem in a very good mood, and since I don't remember anything about last night, I think I'd like to watch a replay before I decide whether I should repeat the experience. Harris was very angry with me, you know!"

She didn't remember how she got away from him. She had the vague impression that he had regretted his impulsive, malicious speech already—perhaps the mention of Harris's name had done it.

In any case, he had made no attempt to touch her again during the short time they talked. And his words couldn't hurt her— or could they? It all depended on whether he had been telling the truth or not. She would face one thing at a time.

Self-disgust, revulsion, the feeling of being used—the time she had had to herself seemed to have drained her for the moment of all feeling except anger. And the anger was good because it was cleansing.

Good—be angry—stay angry. She left Karim to his ugly mood and his thoughts of vengeance, and she could feel her mind moving coldly and quite rationally above the level of her anger.

Everyone would be at dinner right now. If there was anything to find, now was the time to find it, and she wasn't even thinking of afterwards as her feet, in flat-heeled sandals, took her back to the main house and up the narrow servants' staircase to the tower.

Chapter Thirty-four

THEY WERE UNUSUALLY QUIET at dinner, with only Dr. Bright-man and Yves Pleydel carrying on an animated conversation about the psychology of actors, and those in films in particular.

Sarah Vesper and Jean Benedict smiled at each other often, but said little. Harris Phelps and Rufus Randall conversed in undertones, while Sal Espinoza stroked a sulky Claudia's hand under the table.

"So where is Webb?" Claudia asked abruptly. "And your girl friend, this Anna-Maria?"

Espinoza shrugged. "They planned to have dinner in Carmel —it's a quaint little town, you know, quite European in a way. She hadn't been there before, and I think he has friends who live close by. It's a pleasant drive on a clear night like this." He smiled at her lazily, toasting her with his glass of wine. "Don't you think it's too nice a night to be wasted on thinking what other people are doing?"

Snatches of the conversation between Brightman and Pley-del drifted to them. "Now, what happened today—and˙ the day before, too—I have observed the same thing before. It's interesting, yes? Everyone is thrown together in this gigantic make-believe, playing parts—and suddenly all that is hidden inside themselves is out in the open. The jealousy and the hate, the rivalry and the anger . . ."

"Yes, I must admit it is quite fascinating to observe. It happens, I think, because the barriers are down. As you said, they are consciously playing roles, and that releases everything that

354

the veneer of what we call civilization would normally keep in check. When called upon to act out certain emotions and make them appear real, it becomes all right to let go . . ."

"*Et voilà!* We have *réalité*—with the real feelings laid bare, and an excuse as well. Am I right?"

The servants had already cleared the table—only the bottles of wine and the glasses remained. And before Brightman could answer, there was almost a concerted movement as chairs were pushed back—everyone making their polite excuses.

Randall was going up to his room to write an editorial, and Harris Phelps said he thought he'd look in on Anne.

Jean Benedict announced that she was going to take a walk outside, to watch the ocean and sing. "I think I'll come with you—it's *such* a nice night!" Sarah said in her soft voice. "Hal, do you want to come, too?"

"I suppose I had better go upstairs and watch some of the scenes we have done," Pleydel said. He shook Dr. Brightman's hand. "I would like to continue our conversation later. Ah, I could relate such incidents to you!"

Espinoza whispered to Claudia, "Will you wait for me? I have to speak to Harris for a little while, but afterwards I would like to visit you—for an after-dinner drink, perhaps?"

He noticed cynically that there was no hesitation in her manner now as she looked up at him and smiled. Well, so much for that—he had done his part so far. Harris, in more of a hurry than usual, had already left the room, and it was barely nine o'clock. Dinner was over at least an hour earlier than was customary. For a fleeting moment he allowed himself to wonder how Anna-Maria was doing with Carnahan.

They had had several drinks apiece at one of the oddly named bars in Carmel that was frequented mostly by locals. Then they decided to have dinner at a restaurant in Monterey that boasted excellent food and a VIP room where celebrities and near-celebrities could dine in private without being bothered by autograph hunters.

The drive up the coast in Webb's new Ferrari had been wild and exhilarating. And the wildness in her appreciated the wildness she had discovered in him. This game they were playing, this contest of wills, was turning out to be an excitement in itself. He had accepted without comment, the fact that they might still be married, and she felt confident enough to believe that after the drinks and after dinner—and more drinks— they would make love somewhere. And eventually, he would begin to trust her again, and talk to her. . .

It was a good thing that she had been watching the monitor screen when he came back to his room after the filming that morning, had seen him get dressed and drop his car keys into his pocket. She'd telephoned Harris and gone down to the garage; she was already there, talking to Harris's chauffeur, when Webb had arrived.

"Hi, Ria." His voice had been uncompromisingly offhand at first.

"Webb? How strange—are you going into town by any chance? I have never been to Carmel, or Monterey either, and I was just trying to borrow one of the cars. . ."

He seemed to accept her story, and took her with him. And it had been an easy, pleasant evening with no more serious discussion, no questions. Until, to her annoyance, he'd called his friend Dave Black, asking him to join them for dinner. And this man Black had turned up with the woman who had written the book *Greed for Glory*—Robbie someone. Webb, casual as always, introduced everyone by first names.

But although she didn't show it, Ria was furious. Why? Why had he asked these people who were strangers to her along to share what should have been an intimate dinner for two? And the Robbie woman was jealous of her being with Webb—not hiding it too well. A typical, forward American woman. While she swore at him in her mind, Ria kept her smile and her manner light. She excused herself to go to the ladies' room, and noticed that the other woman stayed. Well, at least she would have him to herself on the ride back to the island.

It didn't help her mood to find, when she got back to the table, that Webb wasn't there any longer. Where the hell was he? While the other woman sat glowering at her, playing with the catch of her too-elaborate purse, Ria was forced to endure Dave Black's curious questions; followed, when she evaded them with shrugs and short answers, by a lot of pointless information she didn't care to hear about the history of the Monterey peninsula.

And when Webb came back—it must have been at least fifteen minutes later—he typically didn't offer any explanation. Just slipped into his seat and ordered more cognac and coffee.

"Why did you stay away so long? What were you doing?" She asked him more sharply than she had intended, after they had started back. "I was bored, bored almost to tears with those stupid people!"

His sideways look warned her to silence as he drawled, "We're not *that* married any longer, Ria. You going to ask Espinoza what *he* was doing to console himself this evening?"

She subsided into sullen silence while she thought about her next move; and Webb, letting the Ferrari go once he had taken the exit back onto Highway 1, let himself think about the telephone call he'd made to Vito.

He'd picked Vito over old buddy Peter, and they'd both been slightly guarded, not knowing if the telephone was tapped. Vito had answered the phone himself, which was unusual, his voice sounding faint as they went through the preliminaries.

"How's Lucy? And the boys?"

"I had a postcard. They're still on vacation. And you?"

"They keep me busy. I'm having dinner in Monterey right now, with Dave Black and Robbie Savage. And Ria. Anna-Maria. Remember her?"

"I think so." Vito's voice had been careful. "Has it been

interesting? The newspapers have had a few stories. How is the filming going?"

Lapsing into rapid Italian, Webb told him as much as he'd learned, which wasn't much—except for Brightman's notes. And there, not quite knowing why he did, he held back a little. Ace in the hole? Security? Let Reardon sweat this one out for a while. Anne was going back in time, remembering quite a bit. Figures outlined against the sunlight—angry voices. There had been a tape made, but Brightman didn't keep it in his room. He might have handed it over to Harris Phelps.

"Also, my room is bugged. They probably know I know, and wonder why I looked. The microphone is behind the speaker grille—camera hidden behind a wall light fixture. Takes in the bed, mostly. I don't know if they've got all the other rooms set up the same way, or if they just picked on me." He heard Vito swear softly and added grimly, "You got any messages for me? Because I don't know when I'll have a chance to call in again. They try to keep us busy."

There had been only one message. From a man who gave his last name as Wolfe. Peter's macabre sense of humor, if you could call it that.

Webb heard Ria's gasp of fear, and the car swerved—barely avoiding the cliff's edge that would have taken them hurtling down to the ocean like a wrinkled skin far below, missing by a hair's breadth the startled deer that bounded across the road. Damn! He'd better keep his mind on his driving. He slowed down slightly, almost grudgingly, noticing as he did that the dashboard clock showed it was after one.

"Webb, why do you drive like a madman?" A strand of Ria's hair blew against his face, faintly perfumed. Ria—his dream phantom. Succubus turned skeleton in the closet. He'd taken her with him today because he'd had no other choice. But it had been Anne that Peter's message concerned.

Why had she been so persistent, so determined to find out? Like the young wife walking into Bluebeard's locked chamber and being trapped inside, Anne found herself caught—and now she was sorry. There were some things she would have been better off not knowing—or seeing.

Why try to retrace her footsteps, or wish that she had turned back and gone to her own room after she'd left Karim? Why waste time on "should-haves"?

She had knocked softly on the door to the screening room, not expecting anyone to be there, turning the knob almost at the same time. If there had been a bat-wing brush of presentiment across her mind in that instant, it was too late to go back. They had finished dinner much earlier than usual; faces showing various degrees of surprise (and anger, too?) were turned to her, and beyond them she saw the open closet door and what it revealed.

Sheer force of will carried her inside the room, made her voice sound confused and puzzled.

"Oh—but I'm sorry! I didn't want to miss watching the rushes—oh, is *that* what Karim was talking about this evening? How fascinating. Harris, you should have *told* me." Her words carried her further into the room and the blurred mold of faces resolved itself into separate, recognizable entities.

It was Sal Espinoza, and not Harris, who laughed, lightening the tension.

"So! I am afraid you have caught us men at our little amusement. We are all voyeurs, I am afraid, and this Danny Verrano was inventive, no?"

"He was inventive—yes." It was a relief to let her righteous anger creep into her voice. "I think you are all disgusting. Is this the only way you can get your kicks?"

Rufus Randall looked at her through a swirl of cigar smoke that obscured his cold blue eyes before he said dryly, "I wouldn't say that. It's merely a form of entertainment, like those films you watched with us the other night. Why don't you join us again? I'm sure you can keep a secret better than our Egyptian friend can."

What had she let herself in for? And yet, she *was* curious. Anne looked directly at Harris, who wore a curiously taut smile as he belatedly came forward to take her arm.

"I'm sorry I didn't tell you about Danny's little toy before, Anne. I wasn't certain how you would react. But since you're here—would you like to see how this little gadget works?"

She wasn't shocked—after a while her feeling of stunned disbelief wore off, to be replaced by a mixture of emotions Anne couldn't name to herself. Anger—disgust—a feeling of queasiness to know that everything that had happened between her and Webb had been *watched*. And did Webb know, too? Had he deliberately led her on so that she'd give a better performance? Had *he* seen what had happened last night, when Karim came to her room?

And yet, in spite of everything, she discovered that there was a certain sick fascination about watching other people who didn't know they were being observed. Sarah and Jean . . . no, it wasn't possible! Claudia, with different men—one of them Webb. Webb and Anna-Maria . . .

Harris, standing by her side with his shoulder brushing hers, said softly, "They've gone into town tonight. They should be back soon. Perhaps there'll be another entertaining scene between them."

"They're well matched, don't you think?" Espinoza murmured on her other side. He gave a soft laugh. "No, I'm not jealous—far from it. Jealousy is for fools, and children. Anna-Maria does not belong to me, nor I to her. We merely—enjoy each other's company. Don't you believe in the freedom of the individual?"

Why did she suddenly feel trapped—caught up in a scene and circumstance she didn't quite understand? Her own fault for being so impetuous . . .

Anne forced herself to shrug lightly under the weight of Harris's arm about her shoulders.

"Of course. But isn't this—what you have been doing—an invasion of the privacy of individuals?"

Speaking for the first time, Yves Pleydel said, "But, *petite*, we are not your FBI! This equipment was already here, and has proved an amusing *divertissement*—a way to pass the time. These people are all actors, after all, and they would do the same thing for the cameras they are aware of. Besides, as a director, I find it brings me a better understanding of character, and natural reactions. Come, confess you are as intrigued as the rest of us!"

There was a slightly mocking tinge to his voice, as if he were subtly accusing her of being a hypocrite. And maybe she was, Anne thought miserably. Because she couldn't stop watching. There was no sound—there had been earlier, when she first walked in, she was almost certain of that—but now there was only the movement of lips, and bodies . . . Randall cleared his throat, she could hear the sound of her own breathing, sounding far too fast, the slight creaking of Harris's chair as he leaned closer to her.

"Of course she's intrigued. And you'll keep our secret, won't you, love?"

"So—do you think she will be silent?" Pleydel, Espinoza, and Randall walked down the passageway to the elevator at its end.

"Don't see why not!" Randall grunted. "She'll be less anxious to talk about it once she's seen a rerun of that little scene with Karim, I should think." He slanted a look from under his bushy eyebrows at Espinoza. "And speaking of Karim, that young man's tongue wags when he loses his temper, doesn't it?"

"Our friend the emir warned us, didn't he?" Espinoza murmured, adding with a cynical smile, "As for Anne Mallory— I don't think she will tell anyone else. What woman can resist being part of a conspiracy? I think we can safely leave her to become convinced by Harris." He gave an exaggerated sigh.

"A pity we have to miss what takes place between Anna-Maria and Carnahan when they get back—but I have an appointment to keep tonight, for which I am already late."

"Ah, that woman!" Yves Pleydel rolled his eyes. "Do I need to warn you that she is a bitch? But she comes to heel once she is shown who is master. And then—she can be most obliging." But Yves was more interested in the outcome of the little tête-à-tête between Harris and Anne. A puzzle—a mass of contradictions, that one. Cold and hot. Quite amazing how she had developed into an actress. But had she been acting or reacting? She had a very sexy, very passionate love scene coming up with Webb Carnahan tomorrow, and he wondered how it would turn out.

"Do your cameras watch me, too?" *Big Brother*—she remembered Karim drawing that comparison, and couldn't help shuddering at the other thoughts that immediately flooded her mind.

Harris's face was a blur, the room was lighted only by the flickering black-and-white pictures on the video screen. She didn't know Harris any longer. She didn't even know herself, nor understand the *thing* inside her that made her keep watching what other people, people she knew, were doing, thinking themselves safe and unobserved.

Almost compulsively, Anne heard herself adding, "Does Webb know?" Giving herself away. Why should she care? It was enough that she knew Webb, and what he was like. Why then did she wait for Harris's answer with a thickly pounding heart?

"Anne." She heard the impatient sigh that escaped him; felt that he had started to say something different and changed his mind before he said carefully, "Which of your questions shall I answer first? No, he doesn't know—and yes, when I knew that Karim had come to you, I was jealous enough and curious enough to want to find out . . ."

She licked dry lips, but had to ask anyway. "To find out—what?"

His voice dropped. "To find out how you would respond to him, Anne. All right, it was inexcusable. Perhaps I should have come into your room and ordered him out. But you have to understand, Anne, that I wanted to know. To know *you*. The fire under the ice. Passion hidden behind your look of untouched purity. We're the same kind, my dear; we hide our feelings."

His fingers brushed her face, tracing the outline of her jaw and cheekbones before he turned it up to meet his kiss—its sudden violence a contrast to the quiet, controlled way in which he had spoken to her just before. And Anne could neither respond nor resist; her mind felt battered and numb; her eyes stayed open.

Over Harris's shoulder she saw the screen become bright as a light was turned on. Anna-Maria was smiling as she kicked off her shoes. She flung herself across the bed, turning on her back with a graceful, catlike movement. It was Webb's room, his bed, and suddenly he was in the picture, too, standing looking down at the woman who lay there offering herself to him so confidently. Waiting for him to take her.

Chapter Thirty-five

"ANNE," YVES PLEYDEL SAID PATIENTLY. His face wore a long-suffering expression. "My dearest—you are not paying attention again. And this scene is very, very important. It must be done just right, and I am trying to explain how I want it played. It is the kind of scene where much of the spontaneity would be lost if I had to call for too many takes. You understand that, surely?" He shook his head reproachfully at her. "You should have gone to bed early last night. All of you!" He let his eyes move around the small room, resting on Webb Carnahan, who had just smothered a yawn; on Sarah Vesper, who gave him a bright smile belying the faint smudges under her eyes. Yves sighed. Christ, actors! All temperamental children—even Anne Mallory, who seemed to be learning fast. He hoped she would do as well today as she had done before, but there was an unusual tenseness in her, a faintly abstracted air. A pity he could not have stayed longer in the screening room last night. He wondered what had finally transpired between her and Harris Phelps. A strange relationship, that one. Phelps was not the kind of man one expected to have a weakness. It was to be hoped . . .

Yves snapped his mind back to attention. He'd find out the details later. For the moment he must concentrate, if he was to force concentration from all these blank faces.

Why the fucking run-through? It wasn't really necessary any longer, with even little Annie turning out to be quite an actress.

On screen and off. Webb let his eyes flick over her where she sat across the room from him, noticing sardonically how she deliberately looked away, fastening her gaze on Yves.

Big seduction scene coming up—he supposed he ought to be relieved he wouldn't be wearing a knife this time. Anne was all contradiction. How much of her father was in her, hidden under the silver-cool front? His mind went back to the first time he'd seen her, skimming downhill with her arms outstretched. Little girl lost, looking to find herself. And since then he'd found it difficult to keep up with the changes in her.

He stretched his legs out in front of him, keeping the frown in his mind from showing on his face. Tension. Too many questions still unanswered, and time was running out. Reardon's Boys didn't play patty-cake, and he had to keep thinking of his sister and his nephews—he could only imagine what Vito must be going through. This was a job like any other, except that he had a personal stake in it. And Anne, for all the sweet chemistry between them, was Other Side. Use her. And he would, because he had to.

Harris and Rufus Randall weren't watching the filming that morning. They played back videotapes from the previous night, and Phelps's eyes were red-rimmed. He'd been up very late. First with Anne, and then with the machine—that was what Sal Espinoza called it, laughing.

"This Danny Verrano—he must have been an imaginative man. Apart from the fact that this machine has its uses, it also makes voyeurs of us all, eh?"

Espinoza had come back upstairs after leaving Claudia. Of them all, perhaps Espinoza was the most detached and relaxed. Everything was a game to him—a contest. Perhaps that was why he still risked his life racing cars all over the world. Outwardly a playboy, he had money and connections and power. He traveled everywhere and had entree everywhere as an international sportsman. He was the perfect liaison man—the objective looker-on, in spite of his own stake in this particular venture.

No, no longer a venture or a carefully planned project, Harris corrected himself mentally. A long-term goal that had finally been reached. The rule of the elite. Generations of money and power that would reach beyond national boundaries. He remembered talks with his father, long before he had quite been able to comprehend. The responsibility of money, and the power it wielded. The challenge of manipulation. And now all the waiting, the careful planning; going slow, one step at a time—all of the time and thinking he'd spent had finally paid off. Only a few weeks more. Carol would be down here by the weekend, and Jimmy Markham—traveling separately, of course. Markham still had some freedom of movement, with the elections some time off. He was supposed to spend the weekend golfing at Cypress Point, accompanied by his closest friend and companion, Bob Parmenter. Parmenter, like Sal Espinoza, was an international sportsman. Head of a multimillion-dollar corporation, he raced yachts, played golf and tennis, and traveled all around the world to do these things. He was an excellent marksman, too, and practiced target shooting with the Shah of Iran and King Hussein of Jordan; was chairman of the board of directors of an international company that owned cattle ranches in Texas, Argentina, and Australia. Only a very few people knew that Parmenter had originally been financed by and still worked for the CIA. And the CIA, for their own reasons, were just as anxious to be shut of Reardon and his bunch.

Reardon—Anne. Harris frowned slightly, finger going up to brush at his mustache. The only piece of the puzzle he couldn't fit in. He knew that both Randall and Espinoza wondered how important she was to him. Well, let them wonder! He wasn't sure himself. She was complex, more depths than he'd thought at first. For all that he'd succeeded in making her his mistress, he hadn't yet been able to possess her or to understand her completely—perhaps because he was too used to women who came to his hand too easily, dazzled by his name and wealth and position. How would she react when she finally understood everything? He wanted her admiring, appreciating, finally impressed—giving without reservation. Not only physically, but mentally.

Last night she'd been cold and more than usually inhibited. "Are we on camera?" she'd asked him, putting off all the lights in her room before she began to undress. He'd admired her resilience and the stubborn courage that had kept her sitting there with him, watching the monitor screen. He'd kissed her gently and left her. One day, after all the explanations had been made, she'd understand why he'd left her free, to find her own way back to him. She'd realize how much alike they were, and that Karim had been an example of her body's weakness under physical stimulation. Like her weakness for Webb Carnahan, which meant nothing more than just that. When she finally realized that Carnahan had only been using her . . .

They were shooting outdoors, and today, although the sun still shone, the face of the sky was flecked with fluffy white clouds, and a cold wind blew in from the ocean, making everyone shiver. Even the cameramen wore heavy jackets.

But *she* didn't have the recourse of being muffled up, Anne thought resentfully. It was just as if she were modeling again, wearing cool and frothy summer dresses in the chilly English spring. If she could just think that way—keep her mind blank to everything else, forget that day in Surrey with Webb being so obliging—running towards him, laughing, with her hair blowing in the wind and her skirt flying out behind her. She'd seen those pictures since, and had torn them up, wishing soon afterwards that she hadn't. Pay attention!

Yves was being extra meticulous with the short early scenes. She and Sarah stood huddled in the shelter of some twisted cypress trees while he got long shots of wagons—Spanish-

Mexican *carretas*—moving slowly forward in silhouette against the sky. Glory coming home to California from the Southwest, escorted by her father's *vaqueros* and an American renegade. That's right—think Glory. She sipped her steaming coffee-and-cognac, willing the warmth of it to penetrate to her bones.

"Brr!" Sarah shuddered. "I hadn't realized how cold it could get here, even with the sun shining."

Sarah was being as nice as usual, and she must try to forget Sarah and Jean, turning together in bed. It didn't matter, it wasn't any of her business. Had Jean braved the biting wind to watch?

The scene was finally set up to Yves's satisfaction. A small stream, thickly shadowed by trees, where Glory was to escape to take a forbidden bath in privacy at noon, the hour of siesta.

"Do try to take a nap, dear. I'll leave you alone for a while." Sarah, bending over her, brushing a light kiss on her forehead.

The wagon bed was shielded by canvas—and it was strange, Anne thought, how easy it was, now that she was *acting* consciously, for her to slip into the role she was playing.

Pause, several beats. She must remember to count in her mind, as Yves had instructed her. And then, peering cautiously around her, she must push aside the canvas and clamber out— willfully determined to have her own way.

Remember the script! Don't think forward. Her mind kept sending messages to her body, and she must have done all right. As critical as he was being today, Yves let it go after only three takes. "Very good. And now . . ."

His mood must have improved since the morning, for he actually smiled.

And now, Anne thought furiously as she stood shivering in a thin silk chemise, standing waist-deep in icy water and having to pretend she was enjoying it, *now I have to wait for him!*

She was so cold that her whole body felt numb, rendering her incapable of caring that the wet silk against her body hid nothing. All she wanted was for this to be over.

. . . JASON'S POINT OF VIEW. HE'S WATCHING GLORY SPLASHING IN THE STREAM, ENJOYING HERSELF. CLOSE-UP—JASON'S FACE. HE'S FURIOUS . . .

The script told her when to turn around, becoming aware of his intrusive presence. The script told him to take hold of her shoulders and shake her violently. The rest seemed to happen and become real, just as it had that last hot afternoon in the courtyard.

If there'd been a knife handy, she'd have stabbed him, aiming better this time. She tried to pull away from him and fell, quite naturally. He yanked her up by her long, dripping hair. And then—and then when he kissed her the cold gave way to heat. Fire inside her, ignited by his touch, turning her will to ashes, gray powder falling away to keep only the flame alive. And it was the same for both of them; she knew, or rather sensed, that much, as he pushed her backwards on damp green earth, wet silk tearing under his hands.

They were alone, playing different roles, and there were no longer the cameras or all the other watching eyes. It didn't matter that he muttered, "Oh, Christ, Annie!" instead of the lines he was supposed to say. That could be dubbed in later, Yves thought, his grin almost a grimace. These two—there was something there between them. Let Harris draw his own conclusions. They weren't acting, they were reacting to each other now, oblivious of anything else.

"Please don't . . ." She managed that much of a protest before his mouth cut it off ruthlessly and his body moved over hers.

They were through for the day. The beige four-wheel drive Chevies marked H.P. PRODUCTIONS, INC. were taking them all

back to the warmth and comfort of buildings again, with hot
food for the belly and liquor to dull the edges of thought.

Anne rode in one with Yves and Sarah, a blanket wrapped
around her. Webb had snatched it from someone and draped
it about her shoulders—just as he had done so many months
ago in the musty old theater in Deepwood. He had started to
say something to her but she had turned away, sickened at
what had happened, sickened by him and most of all by herself and what she had let happen—right there, for the cameras.
She was as bad as *he* was—she should see Dr. Brightman again,
ask him to exorcise the eyeless demon of desire inside her. Oh
God, how *could* she have let it happen? Her mind refused to
say "again." It was something she would have to take out and
examine later, when she was alone.

"What a good actor you are! Both of you, I should say."
Ria's voice was as silky as the dress she was wearing.

"I can return the compliment, so cut it out, will you, baby?"

He wasn't in the mood for coping with Ria's belated fit of
jealousy; not now, when he had to do some thinking and soul-
searching of his own.

She had come to watch, had ridden back with him, every
jounce of the pickup pressing her body closer to his. Now she
sat in a chair with her feet curled up under her, watching him
through slightly malicious eyes as he stripped, getting ready to
take a shower.

Shit, he didn't owe Ria any explanations, not any longer;
what he had to explain to himself was himself and his half-
crazy reaction to Anne—soaking wet and shivering with nothing
between her and him but that ridiculous excuse for an under-
garment she had been wearing. And he'd responded like the
animal he was supposed to be, forgetting caution and everything else but the feel of her body and the taste of her lips.
Crazy! Damn right—he had to be insane!

"Do you want me to scrub your back, darling?"

He wondered if the hidden TV camera was taking all this in, and remembered that he needed Ria—not in the old way, that was dead; but differently now.

"Sure," he said, his shrug making it sound indifferent. "That would be great. And I could use a massage afterwards."

The lines had been drawn. Play the game now. He was an actor, wasn't he? And Ria was a very desirable woman. Like so many others he'd taken and used before, making love to them without love. Never bothering to lie to them, because it wasn't worth the effort. One-night stands, two- or three-month affairs. There had been no difference, because he'd always known there would be an ending.

He walked into the bathroom, turned on the shower, knowing without looking that Ria had followed him, her dress falling away from her body. *Ria.* Reality negating all the years he'd tried to will her back from the dead.

She didn't mind getting her hair wet. Her every move was calculatedly "natural" as she turned her wet face up to his, laughing.

"Shall I do your back now—or did you have anything else in mind?"

"She really gets carried away, our little one, doesn't she?" Yves Pleydel pitched his voice low enough to be heard only by Harris—his look in the other man's direction was sly. "You should have been there today, it was really interesting. The contrast—all hate on the surface, and she seemed to mean it at first. Until he put his hands on her . . . I wonder what the good Dr. Brightman will make of it? She seemed in a hurry to go to him."

Harris wasn't rising to the bait, although his face looked set and strained. He shrugged indifferently, intently watching the day's rushes. "Anne's very high-strung, and Brightman seems to be able to get her calmed down. And that's what he's here for—to help smooth out frazzled nerves."

In the concealed closet, the videotape was running, automatically recording whatever was happening in Webb Carnahan's room. Whatever happened between Anne and Hal Brightman, Harris would be informed of. Tactfully, Harris had made sure of that, by offering to store Brightman's taped sessions with his "patients" in their vault for safekeeping.

Although his eyes appeared to be fixed on the brightly lit screen, Harris Phelps wasn't really concentrating. His mind was rapidly sorting through various solutions to the problems he and Rufe Randall had been discussing earlier. Anne he could and would take care of when the time was right. And before then, she'd be shown how deluded she had been. Her ambivalent love-hate relationship with Webb Carnahan would turn into pure hate. Perhaps Brightman could help . . .

That left Carnahan—and Karim, who talked too much and had proved himself unreliable. There was already bad blood between the two. Thoughtfully, Harris had begun to stroke at his mustache. A tiny smile touched his lips, hidden in the dark room. The script—almost abstractedly he watched the sudden eruption of violent passion between the two on the screen, angry rebellion ending in surrender. Yes, the script itself would provide the perfect solution, although timing was important, especially with Markham and Carol expected at any time.

The lights came on; everyone began to stretch and talk among themselves.

Yves started talking technicalities with the film editor and the dour-looking director of photography. Karim, sitting off by himself, wore an ugly expression. Webb Carnahan wasn't present, and neither was Anne. Sal Espinoza sauntered up, raising an eyebrow.

"Well, what do you think? Such fire, such passion!" His smile was as enigmatic as usual. "I wonder why those two did not want to watch how their scene turned out?" He studied Harris with hooded eyes, noting the total lack of expression in the other man's face that was belied by the sudden gleam of something—was it triumph or malice—in the opaque gray eyes.

"Anne's probably waiting for us downstairs—she's with Hal Brightman and Jean. As for Carnahan . . ."

"Anna-Maria tells me he was not in a very good mood. She, by the way, also decided to join the good doctor's meditation classes, although I understand he does not want them referred to as such. What do they call it now? Encounter groups, rap sessions?" Espinoza shrugged. "Shall we be joining them for dinner soon?"

Making up his mind, Harris said quietly, "I think we ought to talk for a few minutes first. I've had an idea of how we might settle a few of our little problems."

Determined not to take a Valium tonight after all the wine she'd drunk at dinner, Anne found herself unable to sleep. She'd locked her door. Both doors, in fact, so that Harris, if he tried the one that connected their rooms, would know she wanted to be left alone. Harris never pressured her. He was patient, always understanding. She was comfortable with him, he made her feel protected while he showed how he loved her without being obtrusive about it. Why couldn't she love him back and uncomplicate everything?

"I'm human, too, Anne," he had said during that morning-after discussion. He'd been honest with her—up to a point. Was he back upstairs watching everyone else on that video monitor? Never mind. Push back the inclination to get dressed and go upstairs to join them herself. Now she understood the sick fascination of the voyeur, watching other people in their most intimate moments, revealing themselves without realizing they were being observed.

Just as she had revealed her own sickness earlier today, with everyone watching. Don't think about it! That's what Hal Brightman had told her before all those others came in. Jean Benedict, black hair flying. And later, surprisingly, Anna-Maria, smiling. Her hair was damp—she had knotted it at the back of her head.

"I've been under the shower for *hours*. I'm glad there's no water shortage this far down the coast, or I would have felt guilty." Was there something to be read in the look she flashed at Anne?

But Anna-Maria had a way with everyone, just as if she sensed all their weaknesses. She flattered Dr. Brightman; she smiled at Jean as she sat down next to her, letting their shoulders brush. "I hope I am not intruding, or interrupting anything? But this evening I, too, need to—how do you say it here? To unwind. I do not like the feeling of tension inside me."

They had all been tense, for different reasons. After a while, Jean, without any apology, produced a joint from the pocket of her sweatshirt, lit it and pulled on it deeply, then passed it around.

"Carmel Valley Gold—the best!" she said. And it had been strong. Anne could feel her head become light after just one drag.

After that they had sat around talking, the discussion getting franker as the effects of the grass became felt.

Jean had been married for a while, to a fellow political activist. She had a daughter, four years old now, whom she adored. "But she lives with my folks—hell, what kind of a life could I give her? I found out I have to do my own thing, or go bananas. And *he* didn't do anything for me. It was a symbolic kind of thing, us getting married—you dig? We were trying a different trip, and after a while we found out for sure where we both were at. Now I'm really free, in my head."

"And you?" Like an orchestra conductor, Brightman had looked at Anna-Maria.

"Me? Oh, I suppose I will sound like something from a book you might pick up to read. I am Cuban, you know. I escaped to this country during the revolution. I was very young then, but I had seen much—too many bad, frightening things. I tried to put the memories out of my mind. They gave me a job, teaching Spanish, and it filled my time until I met someone. He worked for your government—you understand? We fell in love, and we got married. But I guess they didn't like that too much—his bosses. So"—she had been looking down, Anne remembered, her fingers playing with the edge of her silk skirt; Jean had produced another fat joint, and Anna-Maria had sucked in the smoke deeply before she continued speaking—"one day, when my husband was away, on a mission for them, they sent someone to see me. They told me that I could share in what he was doing, that I could help them, if I would. It meant going back to Cuba. But at the time, do you know, I was actually proud that they had asked me to do this thing? They warned me of the risks that might be involved, but I did not think of them. So, I went, and they caught me. I think I was meant to be caught." How matter-of-fact her voice had sounded! Even when she said in the same quiet voice, "They tortured me—I found I could not stand pain and I told them everything I knew, which was not much. One of the Russian advisers they had then gave me this truth serum, and when they knew I had really spoken the truth, they set me free. By then, I was a different person. They had made me believe that my husband had known, and let me go—oh, I didn't know what to believe, but it was easier to believe what they told me, you understand? The Russian was kind—he loved me in his way and protected me until he had to go back home. And by then I had been accepted, and there were other protectors. One day I found myself set free to travel if I wished— and I met Espinoza. We get on well together without too many demands. And that is all . . ."

"The bastards! Jesus Christ, most men are bastards!" Jean Benedict had been vehement, Dr. Brightman quietly soothing.

Anne had stayed silent, feeling removed and out of it. Because the other woman had experienced almost everything, and she had not—spending most of her life protected from reality.

There was nothing she could contribute—everything she had been through was nothing in comparison. Jean had been in jail for voicing her indignation at the Vietnam War. Anna-Maria had been duped and tortured. She hadn't been set free in the jungle of life to survive—or perish.

She had been relieved—and guilty because she felt relieved—when the call came to say that dinner was being served.

Webb had been there. Even now, Anne's mind shied away at the recollection. Her head had still been buzzing from the effects of the dope, but she'd noticed, resentfully, that he ignored the carefully lettered place cards and chose to sit next to her, where Harris should have been.

"Hi, Annie. How's it going?"

"Fine! Why do you ask?" Her attempt at lightness a miserable failure. *His* hair was still damp, too. How long had that shower lasted? She'd seen him ride off with Anna-Maria, pretending not to notice, and the thoughts were beginning to crowd themselves in her mind. It wasn't fair—he wasn't giving her a chance.

"Why? Because I want to know, I guess." His eyes were yellow-gold: stalking eyes, like those of a Bengal tiger she'd watched in a zoo—pretending to be asleep, but watching and wary, all coiled-spring muscles under smooth skin.

Her eyes dropped away from his as she made a production of buttering a roll.

"I wish you'd stop playing games with me, Webb. Why not spend the effort somewhere else?"

He had surprised her by laughing. Taking the knife from her shamefully shaking fingers to finish the job she'd started efficiently.

"Why don't *you* stop playing?" His fingers, brushing hers, sent shock waves jolting through her body. His voice was soft, meant to disarm her. Soft, and curiously caressing. "You're a coward, Annie-love. Always running away. Is it only me you run from?"

She hated him at that moment. He was so sure of himself, words like tiger claws striking in beneath her guard to the softest, most secret parts of her. And it shamed her that he *knew* and had the power to play on her weakness. Damn him!

She forced herself to say coldly, "What do you want with me, Webb?"

Anna-Maria was watching them. So was Claudia, from the other end of the table. And Dr. Brightman, looking worried.

"I'm not sure, Annie. I can think of a lot of reasons, but I haven't come up with the right one yet. You don't stay around long enough for me to find out."

"That's not an answer!" She had been playing with the knife, and his fingers closed over hers, stilling their compulsive motion.

"I know it isn't. And don't go for me with that thing. Do you have an answer? I'd like to walk with you in the moonlight and talk to you, baby. Away from all the watching cameras. Will you come?"

She gave him a sharp, startled look, and saw his eyes narrow speculatively. There was no time for her to reply—and later, yes even now, she didn't know if she was glad or sorry that Karim, arriving late, had chosen to plant himself in the seat to her right.

With his coming the moment—whatever had been there for a short time between her and Webb—had disintegrated.

"We have been watching the dailies. What an actress you are! You should have been there, Anne. Surely you're not embarrassed at seeing yourself on the screen? I am looking forward to *our* scenes together, especially since I have seen how well you throw yourself into the role you are playing."

Karim had smiled at her, but his black eyes were malicious. Anne had smiled back deliberately, her mind and her senses at

377

war with each other. She didn't dare look at Webb, but she was all too much aware of him; of the fact that he had let his hand drop away from hers and had turned away to talk to Sarah, who had come down from the screening room with Karim.

His question and the question inside herself had gone unanswered—so much the better! With Karim, whose motives were all too obvious, it was easy to stay cool and uninvolved.

Uninvolved . . . if only she could have stayed that way! She should have listened to Craig when he tried to warn her in London of what she might be getting into. And Webb was right in a way; she'd made a habit of running away, camouflaging it by pretending she was searching, seeking her own identity —but did she have one?

The distant thunder of the surf outside her windows drew Anne from bed. With a quick, almost vicious movement she tugged the heavy draperies apart and undid the catch on the French windows that led out onto the narrow window's walk. Cold, salt-spiced air iced her face and her body.

"Walk with me in the moonlight," Webb had asked her before Karim came. The three-quarter moon was broken quicksilver running between black rocks—riding on swells, contrasting with the darker shapes of kelp beds. The pewter ocean seemed to breathe with the rise and fall of waves that would break, lace-fringed, on the beach and against the cliffs the house stood on.

When she was a child she had crouched clutching at the wrought-iron railing of the balcony, watching the ocean and willing tall-masted ships to sail out of the horizon. Sometimes, when it was foggy, she could almost see the wind-filled sails, the skull-and-crossbones flag breaking out at the last moment. Pirates. And because she was a princess and not at all afraid of them, they would accept her as one of their own—their chief would adopt her and she would have a ship of her own, like Anne Bonney . . .

A light blinked far away on the horizon, and the grown-up Anne thought, *A fishing boat, out late.*

What if she *had* gone walking in the moonlight with him? What then?

Chapter Thirty-six

ANNE'S VOICE CAME OVER CLEARLY on the tape—courtesy of Brightman, who was conscientious and obedient, but fortunately a fool.

"I hate him—I really do! And I despise him. I don't want him to touch me, but when he does . . . I don't understand what happens to me then. Like today—with all those people watching. I forgot there was anyone watching, do you understand? I forgot . . . oh God! What does that make me? I used to think I wasn't normal, there was always something inside me that held back. I can't respond, I can't feel as a woman should—except with *him*. And I don't know why. He's a womanizer, I don't mean anything to him. He's a—what do you call the male equivalent of a nymphomaniac? A satyr—oh, good! That's Webb. He just likes fucking—any woman that's available. I *know* all this. I know what he is. But when he puts his hands on me, I'm lost. It's like I become another person. It happened the first time we met, and by then I'd accepted the fact that I was—frigid. I still am—with everyone else. People I really care for, who care for me. But not with Webb. He turns me into a hungry bitch . . . Did I tell you I despise him? Well, I despise myself more!"

Brightman's voice was soothing. "He was the first man who gave you an orgasm? That's normal, Anne. All your feelings are completely normal. Stop telling yourself anything different. You've been hemmed in and controlled all your life; you associate your first time of breaking out of your cage with your

380

first time of sexual satisfaction. Stop feeling ashamed of your feelings. Accept them—we're all sexual beings, and have been from childhood, whether we realize that or not."

"But it doesn't explain the way I react to—to the bastard!"

Harris turned the volume down. At that point, unfortunately, Jean Benedict had decided to intrude. Keeping his face expressionless, he turned to Espinoza.

Typically, the man stretched and yawned before he made his comment. "She sounds very vehement, does she not? And confused as well. Typical of most American women, don't you think? After centuries of repression they find everything handed to them on a silver platter, and they don't know how to react! They must equate sexual satisfaction with love. When the two don't go together, they don't know how to take it. It makes her intriguing, somehow. I myself would like to find out if I could make her feel—without this thing called love coming in the way."

Harris merely shrugged irritably. "That would be up to you— and Anne, naturally. Right now I'm more concerned with Webb Carnahan, and what he's up to. Anna-Maria hasn't been able to find out much, has she?"

"Not more than that he is being extremely cautious. But that may be for several reasons. What have you heard from our contact?"

Harris did not answer directly. Fingers went up to smooth his mustache before he said tightly, "Tomorrow's filming should tell us a great deal, don't you think? And when Markham and Carol get here, we'll know more. In the meantime, Rufe's having little hints planted in the political columns—in preparation for the big revelations, when the time is right."

Espinoza was a patient man—he waited.

Almost unwillingly Harris said, "Carnahan's working for them all right. More or less. They snatched his sister—she's married to Vito Gentile—and the two children. I suppose that didn't give him much of a choice. But all the same . . ."

"Yes." Espinoza smiled, revealing white teeth. "But all the same, that means he has more reason to hate Reardon, doesn't it?"

A hint that Webb Carnahan, because of his connections and his past, might be useful to them in the end. Harris registered it, remembering that Espinoza had Mafia connections because of his role in the drug traffic business. But at least he hadn't objected to the clever plan Harris had come up with while he was watching the last set of dailies. Very clever—even Rufus Randall had admitted as much. Pleydel had been enthusiastic. The next few days would tell.

Anne had locked the door to her room. Harris could understand that. Brightman's latest tape had been very revealing— he was glad she had gone to see Brightman soon after the filming. She was fighting her own sensuality—that was normal. By the time this was all over and behind them, she would be different. She might even be grateful to him for rescuing her.

Harris looked at his watch. Today was tomorrow already— four o'clock in the morning. The moon had set a long time ago and everyone should be asleep.

He'd been a long time falling asleep, and now, suddenly, he was awake. He was alone tonight, thank God. No heady, overpowering scent of woman and sex. Webb pressed the button on the watch which was all he was wearing, and the dial glowed red. Four-twenty-five, and his wakeup was for five-thirty. Christ, what was he doing awake at this ungodly hour? Automatically, he reached for a cigarette. Might as well. He'd turned out all the lights when he'd gone to bed, and left the heavy drapes open to the soft darkness that was broken now only by the distant glow of the lights they left on all night. Not many in the big house. A very pale, diffused glow in the cabin next to his—occupied by Jean Benedict. Maybe she was afraid of the dark.

Just a short scene to get over with this morning. With Anne. He frowned into the blackness. Annie baby. Was she safely snuggled in Harris's arms or Karim's?

Why had he bothered, last night at dinner? Seeing her there, without her usual escort, looking lost, had proved irresistible, but he didn't know, even now, what he had been trying to prove.

The cigarette tasted lousy. All filter and no flavor. He ought to quit altogether or take up cigars, like Rufus Randall.

Tomorrow, after he'd done his stint, he'd drive into town again—without company, this time. Call old buddy Peter and get his orders. Think about Lucy—he hoped she wasn't too scared. Big Daddy Reardon would look out for Anne.

Suddenly, a shadow moved against the dark outline of the patio doors. Becoming twin shadows. He stubbed out the cigarette, suddenly alert.

Jean Benedict's husky whisper was song and lyric merged into one.

"I can tell you're not asleep. Did you know I was one-fourth Cherokee? It's too late to sleep and too early to be awake alone. We decided, Sarah and I, that we could maybe keep each other company, the three of us—like warm against the cold outside. Like finding out and learning . . . and early morning's no time to be alone . . ."

Half-chant and half-music, pulling his mind out of the dark places where it had been wandering.

Anne's eyes felt gritty from too little sleep and the fine sand thrown up by the tires of the pickup driving them to the location of the morning's filming.

She was too tired to feel keyed up as she usually did—or to care that Karim, sitting beside her, kept his arm about her shoulders, pulling her more closely against him each time they bounced over a rut in the road.

The sand dunes were on the far side of the island, slipping

down into the ocean. Occasionally they had picnics there during her childhood summers. Today, they would be a part of the desert. Special Effects would take care of all the little details, and no one watching *Greed for Glory* would ever realize they hadn't traveled to the Mojave Desert for this particular segment.

Yves was anxious about the light—he had come out here very early, with the camera crew, to make sure everything was set up just right.

"I wonder what he would have done if it had turned out to be a foggy morning?"

"Probably stood there like Moses ordering it to roll back!"

The girls from Makeup and Costume talked over Anne's head as if she weren't there—or was merely a window mannequin. So much the better—she herself didn't feel quite real. And she was glad that Yves had skipped his usual little pep talk this morning.

The sunlight looked pale in comparison to the van with its bright artificial lights. Anne sat in a canvas chair and looked down at the script. No more nerves—just another stint to be got over with. And then, if the day stayed fine, maybe she would go into town and see if Carmel had changed very much. Perhaps she'd have lunch there, go shopping in the plaza like any tourist. Wear her oldest, most faded pair of levis—she needed to get away from this closed-in artificial atmosphere.

A shadow fell across her shoulder. She looked up quickly, and into Karim's smiling face. Without a word of apology he lowered himself into the chair next to hers.

"Are you studying the script only now? I think I know this part by heart." He was wearing sunglasses and she couldn't see his eyes. She only knew she disliked and mistrusted him, and yet circumstances forced her to act civilized towards him. "Civilized"! It was an overdone word—meaning something before, but not now, not recently, when she'd watched the layers of so-called civilization peeling off almost everybody around her, to show their real selves.

"Has Pleydel told you of this insistence of his on realism? We are to fall into our parts and become what we are supposed to be. You did very well yesterday."

She was in costume, a peasant-type blouse that left her arms bare, and he stroked the length of one arm before she pulled it away from him instinctively.

"Please, Karim! I really am trying to concentrate."

"Are you? Very good." He laughed—she had the impression that he was about to say more, but just then Yves walked over to them, looking impatient, a frown of concentration between his brows.

"Anne, here you are! Come along, my dear, we have to set up the first scene."

No stand-ins today. And the standing around was kept to a minimum as both Yves and the camera operators kept an eye on the sun. She and Webb. He did nothing more than raise one eyebrow at her—his idea of a greeting, she supposed wrathfully, wondering why he always had the power to put her into a temper. And where was Anna-Maria this morning? Standing on the sidelines watching?

No more moonlight, sending her mind spinning and dancing on the silver edges of swells; breaking like splintered glass against rocks and beaches. This was the morning after, and she was sane again, able to take Webb as he was.

But what was he? She once knew what she had been looking for—herself, maybe, freedom, whatever that meant. She was no longer certain. But Webb—the image, the women—

"Very well, we are ready at last." Anne heard Yves' voice with relief. She was ready to get this over and done with, so she could have the rest of the day to herself, to be herself.

"Good morning. Christ, is it afternoon already? They still filming?"

Harris had stayed up later than any of them last night, and had risen early. He'd been on the telephone all morning; and mixed with a sense of satisfaction at having accomplished so much was a feeling of resentment at the others. Espinoza and Randall had taken off at dawn to play golf; and Randall still wore his golfing clothes, his cigar stuck at a jaunty angle in his mouth.

"They're still out there, as far as I know." Harris made his voice sound noncommittal. "You know what a stickler Pleydel can be. Where's Sal?"

"Downstairs having a shower and changing, I guess. His girl friend came with us, to caddy." Randall gave a bark of laughter. "You should have seen those guys' faces! Hear anything new?"

"Carol's arriving this afternoon. Parmenter and his *friend*" —Phelps's look was significant—"ought to be here sometime tomorrow. It's the weekend, so everyone else will probably go into town or fly down to the city. We ought to have time to talk and plan the last-minute details."

"Uh-huh!" Randall grunted around the cigar that was already filling the room with foul-smelling smoke. "And Carnahan? We have his angle figured out yet? Can't underestimate his connections, you know. When this thing breaks . . ."

Randall watched as Harris Phelps tried to keep the annoyance from his face.

"Nobody's underestimating anyone. And we do have the advantage of knowing what he's up to, don't we? And why. As I've said, we could turn that to our advantage. Right now our contact in Washington is working on finding out where they're holding his sister and the children."

"And in the meantime, what's Reardon up to?"

Harris permitted himself a tight smile. "He's playing it slow and cautious. Remember that he has only suspicions to go on, the bastard. And he daren't pull anything too obvious. Not now, with the press"—he nodded at Randall—"screaming at his heels. Parmenter doesn't like all those CIA exposures Norm's been printing in his column, by the way, but he understands what we're doing and why—we'll have to do a certain amount of explaining when he gets here, you know."

"Oh sure." Randall had a way of dismissing unimportant details with a wave of his cigar. Now he actually grinned. He was a man of action, and the weekend promised plenty. The first big move forward. A few more weeks, and . . .

He snapped back to attention when Harris Phelps said carefully, "I had a call from Petrakis, too. Everything's going well at his end. I talked to him about our—slight problem with Karim, and he felt sure the emir would understand whatever measures we have to take. Although they do not have to be too extreme—on our part, that is."

The two men exchanged a look. They had talked until late the previous night.

"Which scene were they shooting today?"

There was a flickering change in Harris Phelps's cold gray eyes—there for an instant, then gone, as they turned opaque.

"A very short sequence between Anne and Webb Carnahan. The scene—if you remember the book—where Glory steals Jason's horse when he's asleep and takes off, planning to turn him over to the soldiers who are looking for him."

She was riding bareback—remembering how to ride, although the horse, well trained, made it easy for her. Glory, running away from the man she alternately loved and hated. Looking for the soldiers who would rescue her . . . although the small patrol into whose midst her bolting horse took her was more interested in Glory herself.

A series of short scenes. She had to say few words, only to register various emotions. With her hair hanging loose and tangled and her face deliberately dirt-smeared by the makeup girl, it wasn't too difficult.

At least there was no Webb to cope with. This was really acting. Easy to show fear and revulsion when the grinning soldiers began to paw at her body.

She was being dragged along with them, screaming—and then they let her fall, moving away from her as their commander rode up, barking out an order in Spanish. Boots polished to a meticulous shine. Whip tapping against them. Fearfully, she looked up, to encounter malicious black eyes, nasty-smiling face.

"So! I find you again, eh? Or you have found me." She was pulled to her feet. "Which is it? You look a trifle the worse for wear since I saw you last, señorita. Did your Americano tire of you so quickly?"

"Please—please! I ran away from him . . ."

"Did you? Were you looking for me? You must tell me all about it."

Dream—or new nightmare? Yves had only to call, "Action!" and she moved and reacted like an automated doll.

They had erected a makeshift tent, and he threw her down on the ground just inside it, thrusting her ragged skirts up as he threw himself over her. Her blouse ripped under his hands.

"You must show me what he has taught you since he made you his whore. And I think my men are anxious to find out, too."

Not real, not true. This was Karim, not Webb, and his face looked just as it had that night when she had been asleep and not quite asleep. Her struggles to escape him were in earnest now, but he kept laughing. Putting his hand over her mouth, half-smothering her when she would have screamed. Putting his other hand, hidden from the cameras, between their bodies, and between her thrashing legs. Hurting her so much that her arching convulsions looked as if she were responding to him.

"You will like this, and this—and anything else I choose to do with you. I am making you mine, do you understand that? Just as you were the other night. And when this is over, you will come away with me—I will have you begging for my favors, blonde bitch, just as you beg for his with your eyes that follow him everywhere!"

Karim's voice was only a whisper, but through the nightmare of pain and degradation she heard every word he said.

Rape. "Don't fight it, or they might kill you." "Lie still and enjoy it." Other words she had heard or read jostled themselves in her mind. Don't worry, this wasn't real—it wasn't happening to her, to Anne, any of it. Only to Glory, a make-believe woman who didn't know her own mind—in a make-believe book written by a woman called Roberta Savage. She'd read it in London. She'd read the script, which was all words and camera angles on different-colored pages. Let her mind cling to that and forget everything else. In the end she'd wake up and find she had been dreaming again.

In the end she stopped resisting. Even when one body followed another. She let her mind detach itself from her body, which was aching and bruised and being used.

Webb didn't know why he had stayed to watch. He had intended to take off soon after he'd done his bit. With the weekend coming up and his head still not where it should be, he'd planned on going up to visit Dave. Make the phone calls he had to make, and get his priorities straightened out.

He'd headed for the transportation—but everyone was busy watching the filming. No drivers, no ignition keys. When he headed back, in a frustrated, ugly mood, he'd run into the ubiquitous Joe Palumbo in his black leather jacket, smoking a cigarette. Palumbo's eyes, too, had been glued to the action.

"I need a ride back . . ." And then he had seen what was going on and a sheerly primitive instinct had made him start forward, to be stopped by a hand on his arm.

"Better not. She ain't fighting, is she?"

She hadn't fought too hard against him either, but what he was seeing made him sick. If he'd had a gun that worked, he'd have sighted it on Karim's back and squeezed the trigger.

As if he'd read his mind, Palumbo handed him a smoke. "Sorry. I'm supposed to stay here until they're all finished.

Gotta haul a lot of equipment back in the truck. But there's room in the front with me if you'll still be needing a ride then, Mr. Carnahan."

For Christ's sake, he'd better bring himself back under control. It might be all faked, or she might actually be enjoying it. In any case, he'd only make himself look like all kinds of a fool if he strode out there. And he'd been wanting to talk with Palumbo in private in any case.

Webb turned his back—wondering why he felt like Judas, wondering why a muscle he had no control over jumped in his temple. She'd turned him down last night for Karim, hadn't she? She damn well knew what was going on.

Even after Yves had called, "Cut!" she kept lying there, feeling herself broken in a million places.

"Anne, you were *magnifique!* What an actress you have turned out to be!" Yves himself handed her her robe, and helped her up off the ground.

Didn't he *know?* Didn't he realize? There were some things the camera couldn't record, and her thighs still felt wet and sticky. She *hurt*, all the way inside her, but everyone kept rushing around just as usual, as if nothing had really happened. *Had* it? She mustn't let herself become hysterical, Anne thought. She'd fall to pieces if she let herself go. Better to pretend, like everyone else, that it had all been a piece of pretense.

"Are you all right? You look pale, *chèrie*. Perhaps you should go into the dressing room and rest—take a pill, eh? We will be ready to go in a short while."

Yves looked searchingly at her. She couldn't force a smile to her face but she managed to shake her head. The robe was soft and warm about her body, protecting it. More than anything she needed a bath. Hot water to soak away the bruises, the traces, the indignity.

Now, standing on her feet again, with Yves leading her

solicitously to the van that served as her dressing room, it was hard to believe.

Heading toward the van, Webb passed two women, earnestly discussing the scene they had just witnessed.

"Come to think of it, all of Pleydel's films contain a certain amount of sadism, which must appeal . . ."

"Don't you mean sado-masochism? He puts down women, and makes it seem as if they enjoy it!"

"Well, Bergman . . ."

He almost ran full tilt into Karim, headed the same way, and they faced each other like wary, antagonistic dogs, ready to fight each other over the same bitch. Until Pleydel's voice called Karim sharply back to heel.

Very interesting—but this was no time for a confrontation between these two. That could come later. He was wondering what Harris Phelps's reaction would be, even as he walked up easily, clapping his arm about Karim's tensed shoulders.

"You were very good, *mon ami*. But there are a few things I would like to discuss with you. If you'll excuse us?" This to Webb Carnahan, who didn't even have the courtesy to nod, or to knock at the door to the van before he opened it and walked in.

Chapter Thirty-seven

ANNE DIDN'T KNOW how Webb had found her—or why. She had taken another tranquilizer, but there had been no time for it to take effect yet. Still in her robe, she found herself bundled unceremoniously into the front of a pickup truck—the taciturn Palumbo, driving, pretending not to notice anything but the rough, rutted track ahead.

Sand flew up from the wheels. There was sand in her hair, between her skin and the robe, chafing her. Anne found her mind shying away from any further thought. Think only as far ahead as a bath, a change of clothes. Carmel seemed far away, and a part of her past. She wanted to go *home*, to hide. But where was home?

She had been trying not to think about Webb. Practically dragging her away with him. His arm holding her tightly against him now. Why?

He had hardly spoken to her, except to say tightly, "Okay, prima donna, you're going back now. With me." And she hadn't had the strength to argue against the dangerous look on his face. What could Webb do to her that he hadn't done before?

A sharp curve in the road threw them even closer together. She stiffened, feeling the tenseness of his muscles, and readied herself for the attack she sensed was coming.

"Christ, Anne! Have you begun to enjoy being raped? Or was it rape? Did you frequent the partouze circuit when you were spending time in France? Variety and watchers turn you on, baby?"

He was being deliberately cruel and she would have shrunk away from him if she could have. He didn't let her. She was lying half across his lap, his arm both a barrier and a trap.

She said faintly, "Oh, Webb, please! Why did you have to . . . why won't you leave me be?"

Cruelly, he mimicked her. "Please—please! In your language, that's an invitation, isn't it? You said that to me, and I heard you say it to Karim. And you're damn right, I should leave you be, only I keep remembering the way you used to be. What happened to you, Annie? What are you doing here?"

Welcome rage flooded through her. Hypocrite! She didn't quite understand why he had kidnapped her this way, but she sure as hell wasn't going to lie back and take his calculatedly patronizing barbs. And if *he* didn't care about Palumbo's presence, then neither would she!

"What are *you* doing here? Money, publicity, lots of new women? Or just plain kicks?"

"And what do you mean by that?"

She had gone too far to turn back now. She had to twist her neck around to look into his dark, angry face, but she did, wanting to watch his expression. "Why do you keep pretending? Do you ever stop playing a role? You *like* watching yourself on film, don't you? Cameras, videotape—does Claudia know? Does your latest female friend, Anna-Maria? I've watched . . ." She could have bitten off her tongue the next moment, feeling his arm almost choke the breath out of her lungs.

"Videotape, huh? Who's the hypocrite now, baby? You enjoy being a voyeur? Guess that gives us one more thing in common, doesn't it? Except you have the advantage over me in this case. You're going to have to tell me more about it. Seems like you sure get to watch an awful lot."

"I don't—I didn't . . ." She was digging herself in deeper with every gasped-out word.

And now his voice had become dangerously soft. "Why don't you tell me all about it, Annie? Why don't we stop playing roles around each other?"

Anne had no time to feel relieved, because the truck stopped just then. Palumbo, as imperturbable as ever, said stolidly, "I got to get this stuff unloaded and get back."

And Webb half-carried, half-dragged her out.

The pickup sprayed gravel and sand over them from a tight U-turn. Webb was still holding her, looking down at her with a smile that wasn't really a smile. He said mockingly, "My place or yours, baby? Mine's closer."

"No!" She tried to pull back from him, feeling all the aches in her body start up again. "Stop it, Webb! I won't talk to you—you can't force me . . ."

"Can't I? Hell, you seem to enjoy being forced. Or is it really that? Has your guru explained yourself to you?" His face was far too close to hers, and sheer instinct made her close her eyes against the look on it.

He had her by the shoulders now, holding her stiff, unyielding body against his while his words cut into her like knives.

"Maybe you just enjoy being fucked, Anne. Especially when it's like rape on the surface. You resist for a while, and then you give in—no guilt feelings, huh?"

She shook her head violently, hair flying against his face, stinging it.

"No . . . no! It's not like that at all—you know it. You just want to hurt me." The tears came unbidden, making tiny channels down her dust-smeared cheeks.

And in spite of the rage inside him, Webb could not help gathering her close, holding her against him and feeling her ragged breathing. The need to comfort her overrode everything else as she sagged against him, no longer fighting. He didn't understand himself, didn't try to.

"Annie! Goddamn your crying eyes. Listen—I'm not trying to hurt you. Christ, I don't understand myself what I'm doing with you!"

She kept shaking her head, as if to negate every word he was saying, and there was only one thing left to do, and that was to kiss her. So he did, tasting the salt of her tears and the grittiness of the sand, and blood from her cut lip where Karim had put his hand too hard over her mouth. To stop her crying out . . .

She couldn't cry out now, either. Here they were, in full view of anybody who might be watching, and neither of them cared.

He kissed all of the pain out of her body and the hate out of her heart. Her arms went up of their own accord, holding him. She didn't care—she didn't care! So she was weak, but he was wiping out everything and everyone else—Karim, the others who had come after him, all she didn't want to think about or remember.

"Annie," he spoke against her ear, still holding her closely. "Annie love, will you come with me now? Let's get the hell out of here—we'll drive into town and find a place to stay for the weekend. We'll walk on the wharf and on the beach like tourists. And make love and drink wine and talk to each other."

Talk! God, how insidious his words, whispered against her ear. His lips against hers. He knew she had no defenses left. Her angry, hastily spoken words had intrigued him, and like before, the lovemaking would only be a preliminary or an aftermath to the talking.

"I'm not stupid!" she wanted to scream at him, and yet all that came out of her tightening throat was: "But I don't have any clothes . . . I can't go anywhere like this!"

"So who gives a fuck?" His voice was husky, his arms wouldn't let her go—back to sanity. "I'll buy you clothes, love. Whatever you think you need."

She had to try and fight back. "You're crazy! We'd never get a place to stay in Carmel—it's the tourist season . . ."

"Who cares? There's always Dave's place in Pebble Beach. Stop making excuses."

Her legs ached, her thighs ached. She had just been raped by five men, and he was making her forget it. All her excuses and her rationalizing wouldn't wash, and didn't seem to matter any longer.

They had been standing in the driveway, and just like Jason would have done to Glory, Webb picked her up off her feet, carrying her in his arms, down to the garage.

She made one last try, saying feebly, "But—we can't just— I ought to *tell* somebody . . ."

His voice turned harsh. "Who? Harris Phelps? Karim? Let's just leave it to the guards at the goddamned drawbridge, shall we? And stop crying, Annie."

It was only then that she realized the tears were still streaming down her face.

"So he puts her in his Ferrari and takes off with her—just like Sir Lancelot, eh? You should find this paradox just as interesting as I do, my friend." Espinoza sounded amused; he knew that Harris Phelps, sitting across from him, was furious —barely able to hide his fury, which was unusual for Phelps. "However," he continued, "I do not think that there is any reason for us to panic—it's the weekend, is it not? And we're expecting company. They'll be back before Monday."

"Reardon's capable of having her snatched before then!" Phelps's voice was too tightly controlled.

"But how would he know? And what difference would it make *now*? In any case"—Espinoza stretched lazily—"Anna-Maria has gone after them. Randall has given her press credentials—she called up the woman who wrote the book, and had herself invited down for an interview. So, we can surmise that they have probably gone to the house of this David Black, who is a friend. Roberta Savage has entree there. And an enormous crush on Webb Carnahan. She goes there, with

Anna-Maria. And we have agreed, have we not, that it is time for Anne to be enlightened? The groundwork has already been laid. When she finds out that her lover is married . . . what do *you* think she will do?"

Randall had been silent so far, but now he laughed harshly. "And we show *him* that tape of the time Karim got into bed with her, without her fighting him off. What the hell—Sal's right, you know."

"And I am looking forward to—how would you say it?— doing my thing on Monday," Espinoza said softly. "It should prove most interesting. I hope Pleydel will not be too critical of my acting abilities."

She had to be absolutely crazy, Anne told herself. What had happened to her backbone? Why did Webb have to be the one to turn all her bones to water? She didn't understand what he wanted from her, or why he had brought her here with him.

"Here" was David Black's house. Another house by the ocean. One of the showplaces that tourists pointed out to each other when they took the famous Seventeen-Mile-Drive.

Webb had called from Carmel, while she sat huddled in his car, trying to look inconspicuous under the curious gaze of passers-by. She'd thought hysterically, *They probably think I'm some hitchhiker he picked up along the way*. Her face had still been dirty, in spite of the wad of tissues he'd handed her grimly once they were on their way. She supposed now that she *had* been in a kind of stupor all the while she'd sat beside him after he'd practically dumped her into the car.

"Being raped is no fun at all, you know!" she'd wanted to scream at him, but his tense, angry silence had kept her quiet. They hadn't exchanged a word after he'd turned onto the highway. The weekend traffic—campers and vans and slow-moving VW's—was already clogging up the two-lane highway, and apart from swearing under his breath a few times, Webb had concentrated grimly on driving—passing sometimes when he had no right to try. But she wouldn't give him the satisfaction of hearing her cry out or show any signs of apprehension. In any case, she was still numb, and beginning to shake from delayed shock. She hadn't thought he'd noticed, until after he'd found a parking space for the car at the side of a tree-shaded and comparatively deserted side street.

"Keep the doors locked, huh? I've got to call Dave. I'll be back as soon as I can." Throwing the words like a sop to a child, his voice curt and detached. But then he'd come back from making the telephone call with a large box bearing a Magnin's label.

"Just had time to get you a couple of things—they ought to fit. The saleslady informed me that everyone's wearing dresses that are loose and blouson . . . whatever the hell that means! Go ahead, slip into something, I'll keep an eye down the road. You'd better be wearing something a little more formal than that scruffy robe when we get to Dave's place."

As it was, he'd had to help her, because even her fingers were shaking now. A silk two-piece by Calvin Klein. Wrap-around skirt, dark brown, with a tiny flower design on it that matched the pale-wheat blouse. Typically, he had forgotten about getting her any underwear, although to keep herself sane she'd tried to imagine the saleslady's face if he'd asked . . .

He'd been helping her button up the blouse when she'd looked up to encounter the shocked and disapproving eyes of a middle-aged lady walking her dog. The woman had averted her eyes, and Webb had started to laugh.

"Do you think she thought I was trying to *un*dress you, Annie love?"

And the next minute, the laughter wiped away as if it hadn't been there at all, he'd turned away from her, twisting the key in the ignition with unnecessary force. His voice had become curt and hard again. "Fasten your seatbelt. Once we get to Dave's, you'll be meeting another old friend of mine. He's a doctor. Lucky they happened to be playing tennis together when I called."

One wall of the huge bedroom was all plate-glass window. She had a view of the ocean, the moon cutting a silver swath through it. Silver separation of black and black. She was alone, having been left to "rest" on the king-sized waterbed after Dr. Bernstein, tactful and very professional in spite of his tennis clothes, had checked her over. He hadn't asked questions and she hadn't felt up to volunteering any explanations.

"You'll be okay. You're on the Pill? I'll leave a prescription. The cream will take care of any soreness, and the penicillin of —any aftereffects."

"Can you give me a tranquilizer? I've been taking Valium lately, but I forgot to bring any with me."

"Sure." He'd said, sounding matter-of-fact, and left after patting her on the arm. "Try to relax now."

She wondered at the time what he had really been thinking, and pushed the thought away. She lay on the waterbed that moved constantly like the ocean and tried to shut out all thought. Like why Webb had brought her here—and left her. Shut out the first embarrassing moments when she'd been introduced to Dave Black, a smiling, friendly man, just as he appeared on his talk show. There were other people staying over—Webb had warned her that Dave loved company—but he'd promised her privacy and, like Dr. Bernstein, had asked no questions. She couldn't help wondering what, exactly, Webb had told him.

"So part of the gossip from London wasn't all that off-center, was it?"

Dave's serve, and Webb, returning it, planted the ball in the net. He swore and Dave laughed. "Your tennis game hasn't improved any. Somehow, I don't think you're mind's on tennis right now. Let's can it."

He guessed he owed Dave some kind of explanation, but all this time he'd been trying to find his own explanations. He couldn't blame Dave for being curious, especially after he'd had Ben Bernstein go up and see Anne.

"Is it serious between you two?" Dave persisted. They were walking together towards the cabanas.

"Look, Dave, we're both kind of thinking this thing out right now. Shit, I don't know! But Anne's been having a rough time with the filming, and we decided we both needed a break."

"She get hurt?"

He should have expected that question, it was a natural reaction. But all the same, he could feel himself getting tense, remembering.

"Pleydel believes in *cinéma vérité*," Webb said noncommittally. He saw Dave's eyes narrow.

"Yeah? I actually read Robbie's damn book. Must admit it had me hooked." And then, smiling again, he thumped Webb between the shoulder blades. "Okay, buddy, okay! I won't ask any more questions! But you will get me a pass sometime, won't you? And"—brightening at the thought—"maybe you and Anne can be on my show together. It'd be good publicity. Especially if you two *do* decide to get serious." He laughed. "How's Carol Cochran doing, by the way?"

When he went upstairs, Anne was standing by the window, looking out. Hiro, Dave's houseboy, had gone into town to get Bernstein's prescriptions filled, and Webb put the package on the dresser. She didn't turn around, and he felt the same unreasonable anger rise up in him. She was wearing her robe again—he knew she wouldn't have anything on underneath it, and he had to fight the blind impulse to tear it off her body, discovering all over again how easily she gave in.

Now that he had her, what he really should do was to find out exactly how much he could use her. He was in an ugly, frustrated mood. He'd made telephone calls, but Vito hadn't been available, and the other call had brought one of Peter's associates on the line. "Call back tomorrow, won't you?" Christ, what the hell was going on? If it had been an emergency . . .

Anne kept looking out the window, diffused moonlight turning her hair to silver. She hadn't moved; she was standing there like a marble statue.

He said harshly from behind her, "Have you had anything to eat? Do you want anything?"

"No. I'm not hungry. Just . . ." She swung around to face him at last, not finishing what she had started to say. The space between them was as wide as the universe before he cleared it with three strides. Her body, once the robe had disappeared, was as silky-textured and soft as he remembered it. Yielding. Yielding too easily, as he'd accused her of earlier, but this was not the time to think about it. Later he would ask her the questions he had to ask. Later—not now.

She had been hungry, but not for food. She realized that when he took her with the bed moving under them, knowing that he knew that having her was hurting her. But he was exorcising those others, and she knew it and he knew it.

It—whatever there was between them—had taken hold, and there was no retreating, only a going forward and meeting. A war that was not really a war. A contest that was equal on both sides. And now wasn't the time to think about all the women he'd had. He wasn't fucking her, he was making love to her, and she was here because he'd brought her here, because he wanted her. If there was a question in the back of Anne's mind, she pushed it away until tomorrow.

Chapter Thirty-eight

"I AM SORRY TO INTRUDE on your privacy at such short notice. You have been very gracious and kind—you make me feel as if I've known you for a long time!"

Anna-Maria lit a cigarette. She wasn't addicted to the habit, but she'd noticed right away that Roberta Savage smoked, and so she had done the same.

"Oh, I've enjoyed every minute! Do you know, you're the first person to interview me who hasn't asked all the usual questions?"

Robbie laughed and reached for her drink. They both laughed together.

Robbie was excited, and trying to hide her high. Fantastic publicity! This woman with a slightly foreign accent who had proved to be so nice and so friendly worked for Rufus Randall, who just happened to own—Christ! He was even bigger than Hearst in his heyday! Internationally. And she was *nice*— really nice and understanding.

"It's really a shame that they haven't asked you to the island, to watch some of the filming. After all, it *is* your book they are doing! I think I will have to talk with Mr. Randall."

It was Robbie's pet peeve, and she leaned forward, stubbing out her cigarette.

"Oh, would you? I'd really love that. Webb Carnahan's a friend of mine, you know. He promised . . . but I suppose they must be keeping him really busy!"

"Webb? Oh yes." Anna-Maria sounded uninterested. "But he is really not *that* busy, you know! I understand that he is spending this weekend with a friend of his in Pebble Beach. David Black—perhaps you know him?"

After that, it was easy. She had only to sigh and mention that she had been trying to get an interview with the so-busy Mr. Black for ages. She might have tried again this weekend, but unfortunately there were no accommodations to be found in Carmel—or in Monterey, for that matter—so she should be heading back down the coast.

Rising to the bait, Robbie said excitedly, "But I have a much better idea! Why don't you stay over with me tonight? I have plenty of room, and I'd really enjoy it! I could call Dave right now, and arrange it all for tomorrow—no, please! At least let me try!"

As Anna-Maria had expected, David Black's answer had been affirmative. She had received the impression that he, like Ms. Savage, was rather piqued at not having been asked to visit the film set. She might prove a useful contact.

It was convenient that she had brought an overnight bag with her, just in case she'd been lucky enough to obtain accommodations in Carmel.

Robbie fixed a steak dinner for them both, plying her with eager questions all the while. Were they sticking to the book in the script? What was this Anne Mallory really like? Had those rumors from London been just publicity or were they for real? She wanted to hear Inside Gossip in capital letters. Anna-Maria was careful to say just enough, while sounding noncommittal at the same time.

Webb. The bastard! What was he doing with that namby-pamby creature? Was he only using her, as Sal had suggested, or was it something else? He'd be surprised to see her tomorrow. She hoped that Anne Mallory would be surprised, too. And that sometime she could find the opportunity to have a girl-to-girl talk with Anne.

In Robbie Savage's guest bedroom, Ria stretched and yawned. Tomorrow was going to be a most interesting day!

It began with translucent gray fog, cloaking time. The drapes had been left open last night, to the stars and the moon. Morning was a time of coming back to reality, of shivering with cold in spite of the heated bed, because all the covers seemed to have disappeared.

Webb moved his body over hers, warming her flesh. At least that much. He was wide awake—there was nothing warming or comforting in his voice.

He attacked her before she had time to arm herself. Softly he said, "Hi, Annie. Feel better?" And then, his words an arrow-head striking through nerves and sinews, dead on target: "You don't have to worry about hidden cameras here, love. Or do you miss the replays?"

She wasn't ready. "Oh no! Webb, please, don't!" Fighting to get free, she found herself pinned down, as helpless as a butterfly. He'd been awake for some time before her, long enough to prepare his plan of attack.

"Why don't you tell me about it?"

"But you *knew*—I know you did. Why ask me? Danny Verrano—I suppose it was his idea of a joke on all his friends. Or kicks—or something—I don't care what it was! Why should you care? You're an exhibitionist and a voyeur, both. Aren't you? How often do you play your tapes back? And do you file us in alphabetical order?" She heard her voice rising and could do nothing about it. It was left to him to stop the swelling tide of hysteria in her.

"Oh *damn*, Annie! I guess I never learned to be tactful. Any more than I'm used to being patient—or being obsessed with a female the way I am with you."

Webb? Obsessed by any female? Obsession was *her* bag; she was the crazy one; the stupid one. Like a speeded-up film, images of Webb with other women flashed across her mind, a pitiful barrier against the present reality of his lips and his hands and the hardening, pulsating maleness of him, entering far too easily between her parted thighs.

Well . . . the thought was like a sigh, far back in her mind. At least he desired her. It was the one thing a man couldn't hide, or fake. And morning was the best time for love . . .

The trouble was that the contest—this game they were both playing with each other and against each other—wasn't finished yet. What would the end be? Sudden death . . . ?

Afterwards, Anne was to wonder why that particular phrase had flashed into her mind. But while she lay with Webb, his body locked into hers, there was only that old, terrible chemistry. Even at her moment of convulsion she knew with a sense of inescapable fatality that no matter what happened between them, whatever they did to each other, it would always be there. For him as well as for her. And her body had known it before her mind had sensed or accepted that fact.

It was her mind and her instinct for self-preservation that enabled Anne to get through the afternoon—starting with the moment when she walked downstairs with Webb into the almost blinding sunlight of the tennis courts.

She'd lain with him naked all night and into the morning, but she felt ridiculously naked and vulnerable in a too-short tennis dress that had belonged to Dave's wife.

"You ever play tennis, Annie? We take it seriously around here."

"In Switzerland I took lessons. At the school I went to. But not since then."

"Well, relax, baby. It'll be a change for me to be able to beat somebody."

No more serious "talking." Dave's houseboy had brought breakfast up to them—reminding her of the first night ever she'd spent with Webb. Scrambled eggs with hot muffins, champagne and orange juice.

And a truce between them—perhaps no more than an uneasy armistice; but at the time, she'd welcomed even that. Needing not to have to think, to be able to let go, relaxing in the sun.

The sunlight was an enemy, blinding her with its dazzle at first. The tensing of Webb's body beside her warned her before Dave Black's voice called out with forced cheeriness, "There you are! Jesus Christ, we were wondering if you two would ever decide to come up for air!"

We? Dave was sitting with two women. One of them—dark-haired, quite attractive—was looking at her with undisguised hostility. The other one was Anna-Maria. And she was smiling.

Dave was saying unnecessarily, "The ladies decided to come up for the afternoon. You know—play some tennis, take a swim in the pool later. And *this* lady wants to do a piece for a magazine." He touched Anna-Maria's arm, obviously attracted. She wore a maillot swimsuit that accentuated her almost too voluptuous curves. "Everyone knows everybody else, don't they?"

Anne felt herself propelled forward, while Webb said smoothly, "Hi, Ria. Hi, Robbie. I don't think Anne and Robbie have met yet."

Civilized games this time. Politeness cloaking jungle hostility.

What the fuck was *Ria* doing up here in the guise of a lady journalist? Webb met her eyes, and they were challenging, as if she dared him to say something. And as for Robbie Savage—she clung like a leech, making it only too obvious that they had been lovers. Damn Dave and his open-house policy. Damn his foolishness in bringing Anne here. But how had Ria known? Not that it mattered now; she was here, and up to something. And Anne had gone all stiff and wary, her eyes hidden behind sunglasses. Stretching out her legs to the sun.

He didn't know what he was going to do about Anne. Touching her seemed to light a short fuse somewhere inside himself.

When he brought her here, he'd meant to get all the information he could out of her. Anything he could use—using her, too, if he had to. She was Reardon's daughter. All changes and chameleon shapes ever since the first time he'd met her. What was real? Ria should have taught him.

Webb looked at Ria, his eyes measuring, more gold than yellow in the sunlight. She was smiling, talking to Anne. Hiro had brought drinks out to them; the prospect of a tennis game seemed distant with Dave playing the Happy Host and the girls having fun sitting around and talking.

His beer was getting warm—Roberta Savage reminded him of that, picking up the tall glass and handing it to him.

"Do tell me, how is the filming going? I've been wanting to come down, but my God! All the security . . . do you think I *could*, sometime? I'd love to watch. I mean, I've *read* the script. The changes they've made from my book won't upset me." He saw her glance towards Anne, not bothering to hide her resentment, even while she made her voice soft and sweet. "How's *she* doing? Anne Mallory. I couldn't really see her as *Glory*, do you know, but of *course* once I signed the *contract*, I *knew* I'd lost all the *rights* to my *characters*." She talked like *Cosmopolitan*, with an emphasis on every other word. But he smiled at her, and her heart did flip-flops when his eyes crinkled at the corners.

"Ah, she's doing fine. I'll talk to Harris Phelps and see if we can't arrange for you to come over to the island some weekend, maybe with Dave. See some of the footage we've shot already."

"I'd *love* that!" With enough persuasion, she was ready to forgive him Anne. After all, she'd read enough to understand how it could happen. She'd written all those very sexy scenes into her book, and the film script had left most of the sex in. Webb usually made love to his leading ladies, didn't he? It didn't mean a damn thing, and she had already sensed that Anne Mallory wasn't really his type. She was too quiet—too cold and withdrawn. And she'd pumped her new friend, the female reporter, who had hinted that she was Harris Phelps's girl friend, and had a romance going on the side with that handsome Egyptian actor who played the Mexican officer. If Webb was interested in her, it was only for the moment, and only for an occasional fuck. Robbie leaned closer to him.

"My next book is almost finished. Can I send you a copy of the galleys? My editor thinks it's the best thing I've done yet."

"Sure, I'd love to read it." He squeezed her hand.

Ria was getting up out of her chair, smiling at Dave. "Will you excuse us for a little while? Anne and I are going to—to powder our noses!" Her nose wrinkled, and she laughed when Dave patted her bottom.

Time for girl talk. What the hell was Ria up to?

Anne felt almost as if she were going to her own execution. "I think I must talk to you," Anna-Maria had whispered while the others were talking—Robbie Savage hanging all over Webb, and he enjoying it. They'd obviously been together before—she could almost smell it between them, and it sickened her. But what Anna-Maria—Ria—told her sickened her even more.

"I hope you don't think that I am jealous. Believe me, it's not that. Like you, I find he has a certain kind of fascination. I cannot deny it. But the difference is that I know him—and what he is. Do you remember when we were all talking one night with Dr. Brightman? He makes it easy to talk, to let go. I spoke of my past—it's something I hadn't spoken of before because it was something I did not wish to remember. But you have to know. Sal persuaded me to come here, and tell you."

The washbasin was turquoise, flecked with gold. Anne' fingers clutched at it for cold comfort while the other woman's voice went on, talking fast as if she needed to get it over with and done.

"I'm sorry. Except for the sex, it is over for me. But you see, he's my husband."

He's my husband. Husband, like husband-and-wife. Words pounding into her consciousness like hammer blows, Ria's inexorable voice, telling her things she hadn't known or guessed at, and didn't really want to know.

Webb had worked for her father once. Maybe he still did. (That would account for a great deal, wouldn't it?) Webb had betrayed his own wife—deliberately letting her go back to Cuba to face death or torture. Webb was connected with the Mafia —shades of Craig, his face serious as he warned her in Dunc's cluttered office. And Duncan Frazier was dead, just as Violet was. Coincidence or sick pattern? Hit man. Phrase out of a thousand novels, movies, television dramas. Not Webb! He was an *actor*, a bastard maybe, but the other was unthinkable.

"His profession is the perfect cover—don't you see it? Maybe I am telling you too much, and I could be killed for it, but I feel safer now that I have Sal to look after me. He sent me here to warn you. And whether you want to believe me or not, be careful. Please—be very careful."

Pieces fell into place. But was he her guardian or her executioner?

"I'm sorry," Ria said again. "I know what a shock it must be for you to hear all this. You must not let it show. And I understand the fascination. I feel it myself. When he makes love to a woman, it is as if there is no other woman alive. I was only seventeen when we married, and I am older than my age now, but I still feel it."

Anne felt as though she had sunstroke. All the symptoms. Her mind whirling into space—headache—nausea.

"No! How do you know . . . ?" Dunc—dead. Blown to pieces by a bomb. Violet—dead. Killed by person or persons unknown. But why, *why*? It didn't make sense . . . but then nothing made sense right now.

"You should ask Sal—or Harris. They will be able to explain it to you better than I can. All I know is that it has something to do with your father. I have already said too much, I think.

But there is a conflict going on. For control, for power. Two sides—hasn't he questioned you?"

It took her by surprise. Questions flooded into her mind—mostly *his*. Her face gave her away before she said in an unsteady voice, "Yes. And he knows about—about the hidden TV cameras. He knows I know."

"Then, if you know anything about survival, you will not let him know everything you know. Make him think there's more, that he might get out of you later. And you had better wash your face and put some makeup on—I have some in my purse." She said again, emphasizing the words, "Please, for your own sake, you will be cautious? You must go back out there and act normally. You are safe for the moment as long as you do that. And I would not like him to know that I have said anything to you."

Anne splashed cold water on her face. Color on her cheeks, lipstick—pale coral—on her mouth. She was *not* going to fall to pieces. Ria knew too much to be just a jealous woman. His *wife*! And he had called her "an old friend" without showing any emotion.

His body had claimed *hers*, his voice had been warm and husky like his lips and his hands. He wanted her—only this morning she had been able to console herself with that thought. She wanted him—desire was like a dark tide that ebbed and flowed between them. Blood-red, like the ocean at sunset. Would he really kill her or send her to death if he was ordered to? *Beloved executioner.* The words floated into her mind, stolen from the title of a movie or a book she must have known once. *Anne, you won't listen, will you?* Craig, his voice carefully controlled. And her father, the spider in the center of the web that threatened to trap her. *I have to protect myself too.*

PART FIVE

THE
PLAY

Chapter Thirty-nine

A POWER PLAY—or merely a shift of power? Oh, but she was really in it now, involved up to the neck since she had talked to Harris and Espinoza and Rufus Randall. And Webb was on the Other Side. The sunstroke feeling had not diminished, even after she'd gone back out to the tennis court with Ria, acting as if nothing had happened.

No, not much. Another old line from another old song. Why did she have to remember the times when he had been tender with her? All a part of the deadly role he was playing. That's what she had to keep in mind.

Outside, under the hot sun, it had been comparatively easy to pretend that nothing was wrong. Just the heat. Webb and Robbie Savage had decided to have a swim in Dave's enormous pool.

"You coming, Annie?" His voice sounded light and friendly. *Friendly!* Oh God—that was not the way to describe the force and the depth of the emotion, whatever it was, that kept bringing them together and pushing them apart. Love-hate. And she couldn't—wouldn't—spend another night with him.

Dave Black was flying back to Los Angeles the next day— he kept his private jet at the Monterey Airport. But he was talking about partying up tonight; his charm all turned on to Ria, who sat there smiling at him. They had discovered ac- quaintances in common in Monte Carlo. She talked a little, but

413

not too much, about her "friend" Sal Espinoza, and his love for dangerous sport.

"And you—where do you come from?"

"I carry a Nicaraguan passport. But I come from everywhere. Europe is more my home than South America, I suppose."

Anne tried to breathe deeply, to make herself relax. She needed to stay calm, especially when Webb and Robbie came back, laughing together and still wet.

The hardest part was for her to tell him she wanted to go back. Tonight, please. She thought she'd had too much sun, and she was tired. Tomorrow she wanted to study the script . . .

To her surprise, he was quite agreeable. "I guess I don't feel in the party mood tonight, either. Okay—what if we plan on leaving about eight? Excuse me for now, baby. I've got to call Leo, my agent."

Was he acting so goddamned polite and casual just to impress Roberta Savage, or was it for Ria's benefit? His *wife*— she couldn't get used to the thought. Thoughts were a jumble in her mind, which felt as if it had been turned inside out.

Plans for the evening were being made, and the sun was like a drug, helping to dull her senses. Roberta was going back to her house in Carmel to change, and then she'd be back. Ria wondered diffidently if she could get a ride back down the coast with Anne and Webb.

"Ask Webb. He's the driver."

"Oh yes, I will. When he comes back. Has he gone to change?"

"He said he had to call his agent."

"Oh, I see."

Small interchanges. And Robbie Savage, deciding not to be jealous, sat next to Anne and asked her questions. About her experiences being a model in Europe, how she felt about acting, about the movie.

Anne could have screamed. The woman didn't like her—her

manner, even now, was faintly patronizing. Damn Webb, and his women, and the games he played! And the aura of destructiveness and death he carried with him.

He drove like a speed demon on the way back. Ria, curled up in the cramped space behind, didn't seem to mind; but Anne, sitting next to Webb, was glad for her seatbelt.

It was only after they had returned, and Webb had parked the car in the underground garage, that the real reaction set in for Anne. She felt tired and shaken and sick, just as if the sun had really affected her. And she didn't want to meet Webb's eyes, turned on her now.

"Well, Annie? You going to come with me or go upstairs to join your friends?" He was ignoring Anna-Maria—she was his wife; how *could* he?

Quickly, she shook her head, negating the rush of emotion; aware again, now that she was no longer terrified for her life, of his nearness.

"I'm sorry, but I really don't feel very well. I'm going up to my room, to rest."

"Take your sweet-dream pills and pass out, huh?"

She forced herself to look at him directly. "Something like that. Thanks for—for taking me to town."

"Can I get out now?" Ria's voice sounded plaintive.

"I'll see you later, Annie," he said grimly.

She rode upstairs in the elevator, too tired for interminable steps tonight, hearing the sounds of music and voices on the way. And she wanted time to think—or at least to sort her thoughts out, but she wasn't given time.

She had been soaking in a hot bath, foamy with Joy, when Harris walked in.

"I tried knocking at the door, Anne. I'm sorry, but as soon as I learned that you were back . . ."

Harris looked concerned. Worried. He cared about her, and he wasn't a murderer. It was the one thing she had consciously tried not to think about. That Webb had put the finger on Duncan. That he might have known about Violet—or had that been part of an assignment, too? Sorry, "hit"! She must be spilling over into hysteria, and here was Harris looking at her, probably wondering why she hadn't said one single word to him.

"Carol's here. Just down for the weekend. But I know Caro can be rather overpowering, so you don't have to meet her until tomorrow, unless you want to. I told her you were gone visiting friends for the weekend."

"Did you tell her with whom?" Her voice seemed somehow detached, floating over the steam.

"She's not carrying a torch for Carnahan any longer. I think she gave up on him a long time ago. Jimmy Markham's here, too—a surprise visit. He's been golfing at Cypress Point. But, of course, that's not for official publication."

Her breasts rose out of the milky foam, and his eyes touched them. Her face was flushed. If he had been Webb Carnahan, he would have joined her in the tub, or taken her, all wet and dripping, on the rug beside it. He wanted to, but the time wasn't right.

"Anne, I didn't mean to intrude on your privacy. But I think it's time we had a talk."

She moved in the water; it sent ripples across her skin. She shouldn't mind Harris standing in her bathroom, staring at her. She'd been with him, naked in bed, before. "Ria and I had a talk—but you know about that, don't you? Would you mind handing me a towel, please, Harris?" She was reacting almost too calmly, considering the shocks she had been dealt; but conversely, that only made him desire her more. "You sent her to tell me, didn't you? Why didn't you tell me yourself?"

"I told you that you were free, Anne. I would have sounded like a jealous lover, and I didn't think you would listen. But then, I didn't think you'd let him carry you off like that—with not even a word to anyone. I sent Anna-Maria because I was afraid—for *you*, Anne."

Harris handed her the towel she had asked for and she wrapped it around herself as she stepped out of the tub.

Maybe it was the Valium she'd taken that made her sound so—unconcerned.

"Karim wasn't pretending for the cameras yesterday, you know. *Do* you know? Did you watch the rushes? Was it just another porno episode to be filed away and shown to a select group of friends, like the others I've seen myself? He—he hurt me. He put his fingers in me before he raped me. And then the others did, too. And nobody did a damn thing about it! They took pictures. *Cinéma vérité*. But I didn't enjoy it, Harris. Not one bit! I think I was in a state of shock when I let Webb take me away. At least I knew what he wanted—I *thought* I knew what he wanted . . ."

Her control slipped, and her voice cracked. When Harris put his arms about her, it was a kind of comfort.

"Oh, my God, Anne! I didn't know—I swear, nobody knew, not even Yves. But then, he gets so excited when he thinks he's getting something really good . . . Why didn't you say something? Cry out . . . struggle . . . ?"

"I *did*! I tried to, I think. But they were too strong for me, and it was supposed to happen, wasn't it? Maybe they thought it was all acting, or maybe they thought I was actually enjoying it! *Webb* did . . ."

"And yet he took you away with him?"

"Yes. And I went. And we spent a night together, and then this morning Anna-Maria was there with Robbie Savage. She told me . . . it's getting blurred in my mind, all the impossible, horrible things she told me. Tell me again—that's why you're here, isn't it?"

She didn't see Carol that night. Carol was too busy being entertained—and being entertaining. And James Markham had somehow gotten away from his lovely wife and his beautiful, perfect children to be here when she was. Well, maybe they really loved each other. At least Markham's wife was up front, everyone knew he had one. While Webb kept the fact that *he* had a wife under wraps. And he'd let her go to an almost certain death. Torture—how could Anne or any other woman who hadn't had to experience it *know* what it was like? Only from books that one quickly shut and put away as being too painful to read. But Webb, knowing, had sent his wife into it.

"I didn't know myself, Anne. Not when I signed him up for *Greed for Glory*. It was only afterwards, after I'd talked to Sal and Anna-Maria, and Rufus—he has his sources of information, you know. We thought that by bringing Anna-Maria here and confronting him with her . . . that he would become cautious, at least. But the stakes are high, Anne. The Mafia has its tentacles everywhere, and in this instance they're working right along with your father."

Her father. But why, why?

They explained it to her solemnly and a trifle pedantically, as if she were still a child.

"Power—and politics. We're supporting a popular, almost too popular, man for president. Jim Markham has all the charm and the charisma of the Kennedys. And he's liberal—a known antihawk. They don't want him elected. He's been too open about his views, especially about secret organizations that are answerable to no one, not even the President of the United States. Jack Kennedy and Bobby Kennedy were outspoken, too."

"But why is he here? Isn't it—too dangerous?" Her voice sounded faint.

"Frankly"—this time it was Rufus Randall who spoke, his cigar sending up spirals of smoke—"he's here because of Carol. The man's human, at least. But no one knows. Until he leaves, we can't afford to have anyone know."

"But why are you telling *me* all this? You know . . ."—her voice faltered—"you know that I'm . . . *his* daughter. For that matter, what am *I* doing here?"

"You're making a movie—and you're safe. Don't you believe in fate, Anne? I would never have allowed you to become involved in anything like this had I realized what might happen." Harris leaned forward and held her cold hands tightly. "But London was getting sticky, wasn't it? I wanted to get you away."

The whole thing was incredible, its implications almost too much for her too tired mind to grasp. But she *believed* that if she proved a threat, her father would have her put out of the way. And Webb—if he were given the order, how would he do it? With a kiss, like Othello? With his hands about her throat, choking off her breath even while he made love to her for the last time? Perhaps an "accident"—a fall off a cliff, a bullet fired by mistake. She had to be careful—very careful. Harris kept telling her that, even after the other two had left her room.

He went back briefly to his room and returned with a gun— a small, dainty-looking toy, althought he warned her solemnly that it was a lethal, deadly thing. He showed her how to use it, how to slip the safety catch off.

He put it for her in the drawer of the nightstand beside her bed before he left. It stayed there in her consciousness, even while she tried to get to sleep—like a poisonous spider, created for killing. But *could* she kill him, even to save herself?

Parmenter was skeptical. A handsome, suntanned man who looked the part of the successful tycoon, he let his skepticism and his disapproval show.

"Do you really think she'd use that on him? Judging from the evidence of those tapes you showed me, and the fact that she ran off with him to town . . ."

He didn't like having to work with men he considered amateurs, for all that they were rich and powerful and clever enough to have engineered this whole scheme, any more than he liked the fact that they knew that his cover of so many years was just that—a front.

"She tried to kill him once before—with a knife." Espinoza gave one of his grins.

"But that was different, wasn't it?" Parmenter said impatiently. "From what you tell me, this Dr. Brightman put her under hypnosis and gave her a trigger word—to help her become an actress. Unless"—one eyebrow went up interrogatively—"you mean to have her shoot him on the set. And I suppose you could have her think the gun was loaded with blanks. But something like that could cause this whole thing to blow up before we're ready—and you'd have the local sheriff and maybe even the goddamn feds crawling all over the place."

Parmenter didn't like publicity; it was an instinctive distaste.

"Harris thinks she needs protection—especially if he tries to snatch her, or to kill her himself." Rufus Randall's voice was devoid of expression, like his face. "There's always the self-preservation instinct to take into account, you know."

"His or hers? Now that she's told him everything she knows—" He broke off abruptly, still frowning. "And do you think it was wise to tell her as much as you did this evening? If he gets her off alone again . . ."

"I'm sure that Anne won't let that happen," Harris Phelps said irritably. He didn't care for Parmenter's officious attitude. "And we have him under surveillance, as you know."

"She told him about the video monitors," the other man pointed out. "He's going to be very careful—I doubt that we'll get anything out of him. And we don't know what all those phone calls he made today from Black's house were about, do we?" His face hardened. "It wouldn't do to underestimate Mr. Reardon."

"No one's underestimating Reardon. Or Webb Carnahan either. But"—and this time Harris Phelps let some of his inner triumph show for a moment—"I think we've come up with a very neat solution to a couple of our—um—problems."

"The further information that you have brought us helped to clarify our thinking greatly," Espinoza interposed smoothly.

He sat back in his chair, eyes heavy-lidded, while Harris went on to explain exactly what he had in mind. And this time the CIA man listened without interruption. But while Harris was talking, Sal Espinoza was thinking—very fast, very carefully. Fleetingly, he allowed himself to wonder if Parmenter had guessed that at this moment every detail of the lovemaking between Jimmy Markham and Carol was being recorded.

Chapter Forty

INTRIGUE AND CIGARETTE SMOKE had left his room hot and close. Declining to make an appearance at dinner, Webb Carnahan could hardly wait for Ria to leave.

He needed space and fresh air and time alone to think—and outside the air smelled clean and slightly damp. Cool, but not too cold. He shoved his hands into his jacket pockets and began to walk, feeling his muscles stretch with every long stride that took him away from the glow of orange lights and further into the moon-drenched night that yawned ahead between the cypress trees.

He began to smell the ocean as the dirt path snaked upward toward the cliffs, hear its incessant roaring more clearly over the other night sounds. The lopsided moon hung in the sky to his back; and ahead and above, the stars were like minuscule drops of mercury forming patterns against the backdrop of midnight sky.

He'd come out here to clear his mind of the clutter of emotion and blind instinct that had nothing to do with what his intellect told him he had to do; and he found himself not wanting to think at all. This was a night to go walking in the moonlight with a woman snuggled close against his side, with the only thought in both their minds the afterwards of a wood fire and cognac sipped slowly out of enormous snifters, the slow, long moments of making love that would follow. But he had had enough of Ria, and not enough . . . Angrily, deliberately, he choked off that other half-formed thought with a muttered expletive. Think about Lucia instead—his first and only real loyalty. Lucy, his kid sister, probably terrified and trying bravely not to show it because of the boys. And his telephone call to old buddy Peter, which had surprisingly ended with his being granted what amounted to a royal audience—a few minutes of stilted conversation with Reardon himself before Peter got back on the line.

"You're doing okay, old son! Old habits, and all that, huh? You haven't developed scruples during the past few years, have you? And don't worry, we'll be backing you up when you need it . . ."

Some dark night he'd like to get Peter the Wolf alone in an alley. Assassin against assassin. Remember things he thought he'd forgotten.

His thoughts were as black and twisted as the trees crouching behind him as Webb continued to climb the rutted trail that brought him suddenly to the edge of the cliff that dropped off to the ocean below.

A breeze that smelled and tasted of salt spray blew up against his face as he stared down at silver-white lace borders sucking greedily at the stretch of sandy beach, flowing easily between craggy-edged black rocks. Distant lights blinked against a moving, swelling horizon. A fishing boat, out late, or a freighter on its way from San Francisco to Los Angeles.

But he hadn't climbed all the way up here to look at the view. Webb let his long legs jacknife under him as he settled himself on a rock, flatter than the rest. He lit a cigarette, turning his back to the wind as he cupped his hands over the tiny flare of the match. The flame was there—and out. Like whatever it was he'd felt about Ria. The only warmth between them now that in their loins.

"Did I spoil your weekend for you?" Her voice had been innocent, but there was a quickly veiled hint of malice in her eyes. He had been watching Anne walk stiff-backed to the elevator, wondering why he'd asked her to come back to his room with him. Testing, perhaps—but himself or her?

Easier to concentrate on Ria and the battle of wills and wits between them.

"Did you mean to? And since you brought it up, maybe you can tell me why. You didn't tell me you're working for Randall now."

"Oh, that . . . !" She'd shrugged, trying to make it appear casual. "Well, I was getting bored, you know. And this woman Roberta Savage had been calling up, wanting to visit the set. It was really Sal's idea. He talked to Mr. Randall."

"Sure. Understanding guy, Señor Espinoza." He'd had her backed up against the side of the car, and his finger traced her jawline deliberately, feeling the tensing of her muscles. "And what did you tell Anne?"

"Nothing—why don't you ask *her*?"

"I'm asking *you*, Ria. If we're going to make our marriage work, maybe it's time we started leveling with each other, huh?"

He'd taken her by surprise, as he'd meant to. When he kissed her he saw the look of shock in her eyes replaced by one of calculation just before she closed them, letting her body lean wantonly into his. He thought he could almost read the thoughts that chased themselves about in her mind. Bring things to a head. Better sooner than later. He suspected that their thoughts ran on similar lines. Soon they would both gamble on how much or how little to tell the other to keep up the semblance of truthfulness and honesty.

Webb took one last drag on his cigarette and let it arc out into space. Somewhere to his left another cigarette glowed before it, too, went out. He saw a dark shape move towards him, moonlight glinting dully off a black leather jacket.

"*Buena sera*," Joseph Palumbo said pleasantly as he sauntered up. "It is a nice night, no?"

Sunday was one of the longest and most difficult days Anne had ever forced herself to endure. Sleep had not come easily the night before, in spite of the Valium. The setting moon shone into her room, and even after she had pulled the drapes together and had closed her eyes, she could almost imagine its cold silver light falling across her body. Dry ice—making her alternately cold and hot.

Don't think—don't think. If it hadn't been so late, she would have called Dr. Brightman. She tried breathing deeply, concentrating on making every muscle in her body relax, but when sleep finally brought the blackness she looked for, it was after five in the morning.

Harris let her sleep late, but she couldn't very well sleep all day long, nor hide away in her room. Consciously escaping, she tried to hide ugly memories behind the fog-bank of tiredness in her mind.

The sun shone in the late afternoon and everyone was talking about the drought and how much California needed rain. People who had gone to town for the weekend were drifting back in—including Sarah and Jean.

Anne met James Markham briefly before he left with his taciturn, unsmiling friend, who was such a contrast to Markham's smiling charm.

"I'm looking forward to seeing this film. Harris tells me you're fantastic in the part . . ."

And Carol was staying on for two extra days, to relax. No escaping Carol, and her bright, curious eyes.

"Darling, I watched some of the rushes and couldn't believe it was you. We have to have a nice *long* talk soon—to catch up on everything!"

How much did Carol know? Carol and Webb exchanging tapes . . . Karim glowering at her all through dinner . . . Webb and Ria coming in late without any apology, sitting very close together. Everything Harris had told her seemed absurdly melodramatic, perhaps because she wanted to keep on thinking so.

People and bits of dialogue flickered through her consciousness like pieces of glass falling together to make a kaleidoscope pattern. But once, while everyone else had been talking, Webb had looked across the length of the table at her and their eyes had met, fusing together for what seemed an interminable time and could only have been a mere instant. Long enough for Anne to feel the blinding truth like a sunburst of light flashing across her mind.

It's the same for him . . . the same . . .

She sensed it and knew he sensed it, too, even across the distance that separated them and would always separate them. Like animals that stalked each other in the dark, each one seeking to destroy the other and yet fascinated by the scent of the other. He would kill her if he had to, and she would kill him if she had to save herself, but even that knowledge couldn't change what was there between them.

The moment was there and gone, leaving her with a sense of fatalism that stayed with her through the rest of the night and most of the next day.

The script was now a jumble of multicolored pages that seemed to grow thicker and bulkier by the day. Pleydel, backed up by the director of photography, kept changing times and setting—sometimes even the dialogue itself.

Anne was in costume already—too many layers of petticoats under her skirts. She and Sarah sat in an air-conditioned room, leafing through the pages while outside the window the workmen swarmed about, setting up the next scene. There was iced champagne—Dom Pérignon, no less—in a silver bucket between them, and Carol, at loose ends since Markham had left, had drifted in and out.

She and Sarah knew each other—they had exchanged sweetened barbs already, while Anne had stayed neutral, sipping her champagne and wishing she could strip off her clothes and go swimming.

"You're not nervous, are you, darling? You've been doing just *marvelously*, everybody says so. You're going to be a superstar when this is finally in the can. Are you enjoying every minute?"

"It's too hot for all these layers of clothing. That's all I can think about right now."

Carol had laughed, running fingers through her magnificent mane of hair. "Do you ever think back to that time in Deepwood when you helped me out? All you had to wear *then* was my negligee, wasn't it? What a difference now."

Anne had managed to look directly into Carol's questioning, challenging eyes. "Yes—we're all very different now, aren't we?"

Carol was a basic bitch and she was getting to be one, too. After Carol had gone, Sarah gave a little sigh in her perfumed wake.

"You won't let her get you down, will you, dear?" She turned the air-conditioner up higher. "God! I thought it never got hot around here. I almost wish the fog hadn't been burned away. You're *not* nervous, are you? We don't have much to do this time, and Hal is really thrilled at the progress you're making in meditation."

They had had a late-morning session while Pleydel was supervising the shooting of some exterior scenes—mostly long-distance shots.

Anne had been relieved when Anna-Maria didn't appear, and annoyed when Karim, also up early, had tried to buttonhole her on her way back to the house.

"Why are you in such a hurry? You have been avoiding me, my little fair one. Is it because you are ashamed for having given yourself to me so freely?"

"Karim, I have a million things to do." She hated the feel of his fingers gripping her arm, bringing back the memory of the way he'd used her before. And she was also more than a little bit afraid of him.

"You always have things to do when it is *I* who ask for some of your time. But you would run off to spend a weekend with another. That . . ." She couldn't understand the string of Arabic words he used; fortunately, perhaps. And her meditation—the few minutes spent alone with Hal Brightman after the others had gone had really helped her. Better to block everything unpleasant out of her mind for the moment and exist from minute to minute. So she was able to look at Karim and force herself to stand still, not fighting the studied cruelty of his grip on her arm.

"I don't like being forced. Or tricked. Or hurt, either. And you're hurting me now."

"And I happen to know, also, that you are not always so icily controlled! Are you trying to drive me mad? Or is this your way of tantalizing me and leading me on? I thought you were different from most of these other women, especially the American bitches who think far too much of themselves and too little of their men. But now I am beginning to think that you are just like them—you act so independent, but like any bitch, you want to be taken and mounted and shown what a woman is meant for, don't you?" He shook her, his black eyes burning like coals.

At any other time she would have been frightened, but today her mind was numb—it had been dealt too many shocks already.

"Karim, you're all wrong. But there isn't time to talk about it now. Yves is probably looking for me already, and Harris . . ."

"Ah yes, Harris Phelps. Your protector, eh? But I do not think he minds too much. And as for your other lover—perhaps you'll see him in a different light before too long. And then you'll come crawling to me . . ."

"Ah, I beg pardon for interrupting, but they are looking for you both, you know!" Espinoza, strolling up the path towards them, wore his usual twisted, rather cynical smile. And why was it that they had happened to stop before the guest chalet that Webb occupied?

Anna-Maria, stretching and sleepy-eyed, came out the door, smiling as she came up without any embarrassment to link her arm through Espinoza's.

"So much noise so early in the morning! Hello, Karim. You look like a thundercloud." She added unnecessarily, "I promised that I would wake Webb."

And that had ended that—for the moment. With the others there, Anne had made her mumbled excuses and fled back to the house; and even now, sitting with Sarah, waiting to be called, she didn't feel like thinking. Especially not thinking back.

She looked down at the script on her lap.

. . . 189. EXTERIOR—COURTYARD—LATE AFTER-NOON.

"The light—the red light of the setting sun is most important. Very symbolic, eh? Crimson sunlight—torches on the wall—and shadows. We must take advantage of this unusual weather while it lasts, eh?"

Yves Pleydel. Part of his usual preliminary pep talk.

Sarah whispered, "I'm sorry that I am supposed to be so bitchy towards you in this scene!" That was before Carol had visited, bringing out the bitchiness in both of them.

Anne wished that they could get started and have it over with. In spite of her conscious efforts to relax she was beginning to grow tense. Sal Espinoza, looking undeniably handsome and distinguished in his nineteenth-century clothes, came in to join them; he poured himself a glass of champagne, with which he toasted "two lovely ladies." He added his apologies to Sarah's. "I am supposed to treat you harshly—I hope you will remember that I am only a clumsy amateur pretending to be a real actor!"

* * *

Was *she* real? Were any of them? Outside, the sun had started to go down, throwing the crimson light Pleydel had been waiting for against the fake-adobe walls of the courtyard. Long, slanting light, matched by the fire that had been built—adding its flickering flame to complement the flaring torches set in sconces against the walls.

Anne tried to keep her attention on the script. This was the scene when Glory's father had the man who had kidnapped and violated his daughter punished. But while he was testing Jason Ryder's endurance, he was also testing his daughter . . .

LONG SHOT. ZOOMING IN CLOSE, AS WE SEE . . .

No big crowd scene on this occasion. Private revenge. The Spanish governor's men, avid for vengeance. The turncoat Mexican officer who looked for the same thing.

The setting was real and the feeling was real; hardly needing Pleydel's call for "Action!" to set it all in motion.

"Watch closely, daughter. Revenge is no substitute for your virginity, but you should derive some satisfaction from it. You *were* abducted against your will, were you not?"

She stood as stiffly between them, hardly feeling the bite of his fingers over her wrist. Her father, and her stepmother. Don't think of them as merely Sal Espinoza and Sarah Vesper—it was her frozen expression that the cameras had to capture at this point.

Yves, mindful of the light, didn't call for too many takes.

"It'll do, it'll do!" he said impatiently, shrugging his shoulders.

They were all eager to get into the real action—Karim in his dapper uniform that suited him, somehow, standing across from them with the coiled-up whip tapping against his high, shiny boot top, glancing over at her with a strange, pent-up expression for all that his teeth flashed white under his thin mustache. Even Sarah seemed tense, like all the other watchers—even those who weren't playing an actual role in this torchlit drama.

"I would like to shoot this scene without interruption—that is why you see so many cameras set up. We are going to concentrate on facial expression, the reactions of everyone to what is taking place. So, we will all remember this, and the sunlight we cannot waste. Come, we will begin now . . ."

Carol Cochran, dressed in a forest-green pantsuit that complemented her eyes, let her lazy-lidded glance slide from Harris to Anna-Maria, who stood on his left, her teeth nibbling at her thumbnail.

"Yves is quite a perfectionist, isn't he? I wonder how long this is going to take? Because I'm beginning to feel very thirsty."

"Yves knows what he's doing." Harris sounded unusually short, and Carol raised one slim, arched brow as she lit a cigarette.

"Darling! No need to snap my head off. It just seems *different* to me, watching from the other angle, I suppose. And I must say that sweet, innocent Anne has begun to surprise me lately."

"What? Oh yes." Harris sounded abstracted, and Anna-Maria ignored her. Carol wasn't used to being ignored. She directed her next comment at the other woman, who hadn't taken her eyes off what was happening before the cameras.

"Webb really *does* have a nice body, doesn't he? In spite of being such a bloody bastard. Especially without a shirt on . . ."

Funny how some remnant of the old fires continued to flare up at the oddest times; even when she was hating him most. And it wasn't that Jimmy wasn't a good lover—only he *did* tend to become somewhat boring when he went on and on about his daughter! She had two whole days left to enjoy herself before she had to fly back to New York like a good little girl, and there hadn't been a single time before when she and Webb hadn't managed to strike sparks between them. Why not? It would put both Anne and this common Cuban bitch in their places.

Chapter Forty-one

"WELCOME. You have been made comfortable, I hope?" Karim's voice came from behind him, and for no real reason Webb could feel the muscles in his back tense. Had it been Karim's prompting that had made them tie his wrists so tightly to the crossbar that they had already begun to swell and grow numb? He could already feel the strain on his arms and shoulders; and damned if he hadn't suddenly begun to feel distinctly uneasy about this particular scene, especially in view of Pleydel's insistence on what he called *réalité*.

Wet rawhide strips—he tested them and there was no way he could get free. He heard Karim laugh as he ripped the shirt off his back—it tore with a convincingly loud sound. And now, mixed with the raging anger at his own unsuspecting foolishness, Webb could feel the nerves all over his body begin to crawl.

"How do you feel? I hope you are afraid. You have reason to be. It is not in my nature ever to forgive injury or insult, as you will soon find out."

The first explosion of pain was white-hot and unexpected, like the sting of a scorpion across his shoulders, and worse than anything he could have imagined. From somewhere outside himself Webb heard the breath escape from his lungs in a gasp.

Karim laughed jeeringly, the sound overlaid by the whistling swish of leather thongs cutting through the air before they bit deeply into his taut flesh.

Separate knife slashes of agony—hardly giving him time to

draw in his breath between. The sweat was pouring down his face and down his arms as he concentrated fiercely on *not* screaming, lips pulled back from his teeth in an animal rictus of agony as he clamped them together.

Karim, as if he recognized exactly what he was thinking, taunted, "Why don't you cry out? They say it helps. I will have you begging for me to stop before I am finished with you, my friend. And I think you know that, don't you?"

He tried to detach his mind . . . they said women could stand more pain than men could. Childbirth, the Resistance heroines of World War II. And this had all been planned, because Harris and his friends weren't exactly stupid. He should have guessed, should have . . .

Christ! How long before he *did* break? Was that what they were all waiting for? No escape—no exit until Pleydel yelled, "Cut," and that would probably be a long time coming.

Pain had limits—didn't it? He could feel the involuntary jerking of his body and tasted blood in his mouth, smelled blood—his own—in the humid air that seemed to clog his nostrils, making breathing difficult.

"You're more stubborn than we'd thought you might be, but soon . . ." Karim sounded out of breath.

Tongues of liquid fire overlapped each other, and there was a red fog of smoky agony in Webb's brain, almost dulling it, but not quite.

"Fuck you! I'm going to kill you, you bastard. With my hands . . ." Each word was a rasping torture that had to be forced out of his throat. Cling to the thought that it had to end—sometime. Because he couldn't take much more . . .

It wasn't real, of course. Somehow, this was all being faked. Special effects . . . But Anne could not help shuddering every-time she heard the whip crack against bared flesh, every time she saw the look of concentrated enjoyment on Karim's face, with the sweat trickling down it now. The same look he had worn when . . . God! Either *she* was crazy or everyone else was.

Acting . . . we're all supposed to be acting. Metronome thought in her mind. But how did they fake the blood?

She looked desperately at Yves, who kept squinting through his viewfinder. Took an involuntary step forward, to be stopped by a hand, gripping her arm.

"What—aren't you deriving some satisfaction from what you are witnessing, daughter? You should be smiling, but your face has gone quite pale. I am revenging all the brutalities this man inflicted on you while you were his—unwilling hostage. You *were* quite unwilling, were you not?"

Anne felt dizzy—the flickering torches on the wall and the blood-red sunset gave the effect of hell. The script—something in the script—but her legs didn't belong to her any more than the heavy long skirts Glory had to wear. It was like being suddenly trapped in a fog bank where lights reflected back at you and every tiny sound was magnified and the most familiar places looked unfamiliar and strange, and even time seemed to be suspended.

"No." The first time the word only echoed in her mind, hanging in silence while Karim's arm kept rising and falling like a pendulum that didn't tick, and nothing else moved and no one did anything.

"No!" This time she screamed it out loud, wrenching her arm free as she began to run. "Stop it—tell them to stop, do you hear? Has everyone gone insane? Can't you see that it's real—it's *real?*"

"Gloriana!" She heard a voice thunder after her, but she wouldn't stop. She stumbled over her skirts and kilted them up with one hand; not pausing, even when she heard the swell of murmuring voices all around her, or when Karim turned to meet her, an ugly smile curling his mouth.

"You want to see what good work I do close up?"

He stood in her way, and she felt her face contort as she hit him as hard as she could—all the pent-up hatred inside her behind her two fisted hands driving into his solar plexus. Something purely instinctive, learned long ago.

"You sadistic bastard!" That couldn't be her own voice, screaming the words like a virago.

And then she was up close, seeing the blood everywhere—real blood. "Webb?"

He didn't answer her, but she heard him suck breath into his lungs—a loud, rasping sound like a groan.

Webb heard the voices coming from a long way off. Anne's voice—he thought it was Anne's voice, before it was drowned out by other voices and the sound of the blood pounding in his temples.

Hate and fury kept him fighting to stay conscious, battling against giving in to pain that sank inexorably through his skin to paint itself on every nerve and muscle in his body. Pain he hadn't believed possible, reducing him to cringing anticipation of each fresh wave of agony while every muscle strained against what was inescapable.

"I'm afraid our friend Karim let himself be carried away. I'm sorry. You should have called out, said something. *Mon Dieu*, he really did a nasty piece of work . . . ah, here is the good doctor." Pleydel's voice sounded smug beneath his falsely commiserating shower of words.

Warning: *We're on to you* . . . Ria. Question-and-answer games.

"Goddammit, I don't need a shot . . ."

"But I'm afraid you do." Brightman's voice, sounding very professional. Pinprick of oblivion in his arm.

They were all being very nice to her—even Carol. Although —and in spite of the turmoil of her emotions Anne found her-self thinking cynically—Carol always carried a little needle even when she wore velvet gloves. Which was a strange, almost medieval turn of thought. Hadn't Carol played Lucrezia Borgia in one of her early movies?

"I'd watch out for that Karim if I were you, darling. His reactions are really quite primitive, aren't they? My God—I was like everyone else, caught up in the action . . ."

Had she been? Had Ria, who was now with Webb? Pleydel, who hadn't called a halt until the last minute? Anne didn't quite understand her own reactions, and she hadn't had time yet to sort things out in her mind.

Why had it happened? Why had everyone let it happen? There was a tap on the door, and Anne twisted around to see Harris, wearing a worried frown.

"Anne? Carol seemed to think . . ."

"*Why?* You knew, didn't you? You all knew . . ."

At least he didn't make excuses as the others had. He closed the door behind him, looking at her searchingly before he nodded shortly.

"Yes, of course. And you're not used to violence, are you? But violence is sometimes the only answer—the only message that is clearly understood by those who live by that particular code."

She gripped the edge of the dresser with both hands behind her back. "You're always *warning* me, Harris. I think I partly understand why. I remember when Craig, of all people, tried to—to warn me, too. In London. I wouldn't listen then. But . . . all *this* . . ." She swallowed hard and made herself go on. "If—if Webb is dangerous—then why . . ."

Harris came up close and caught her arms, the touch of his fingers subtly caressing. "I came here to explain to you. I know you've been held down and protected most of your life—I sensed that when I met you, when you were trying to break free, not sure where you ought to run! And I've tried to let you find your own way, in your own time. But you have to try to understand. What happened today—very well, what we *let* happen—was in the nature of a warning. If Carnahan realizes we're on to him, his instinct for self-preservation should make him cautious. I gave you a gun, but I didn't know if you'd use it—even if your life was threatened. And mind you, I don't blame you for it. You've never gone hunting, have you, Anne? You don't know if you'd ever be able to pull that trigger, knowing that gun that looks like a little toy can kill. But you must know that he would kill *you*. Acting is his cover; killing is his profession. Anna-Maria understands that. She's playing a dangerous game, but at least she realizes the risks—*now*. She had to learn about surviving the hard way. But you, Anne—" He shook her gently, because she was very still, staring at him as if she had been turned into a frozen statue. "For Christ's sake, do you comprehend what I've been trying to tell you? This isn't a game of patty-cake or a lurid television script—it's reality. We're fighting your father, and the others like him—those secret, shadowy behind-the-scenes figures that nobody quite believes exist. The manipulators, who aren't elected by the people, who send us into wars we don't need, who cold-bloodedly arrange for assassinations, connive with the Mafia—run this country! So far they haven't let anyone stand in their way—a president who thought for himself, anyone who spoke out or acted on their own. Do I need to remind you of what happened to the Kennedys, to Martin Luther King—not to mention the other killings . . . ?"

"Oh, Harris—don't!"

"I'm sorry, Anne. But you have to realize the scope of all this. Try to be objective."

"I think she understands," Harris told the others afterwards. If they weren't convinced, they didn't show it outwardly.

Randall merely grunted from behind his cigar. "How did he react to the sodium pentothal?"

"Parmenter warned us it might not work. Anyone who retires or resigns from the Service gets the full treatment. I understand it takes a couple of months. A process of tearing down and building up again."

"In other words, they fixed it so that he wouldn't talk under questioning."

"Brightman thinks it's only that they've made him immune in some way to answering questions under the influence of a drug—that consciously, his memory would be quite normal." Harris was frowning, his finger brushing at his mustache.

Espinoza broke in smoothly. "But, my friends, what does it matter, after all? We are on to him, and he knows that we are. It should make him more careful. In any case, he still has not found out very much, has he? It makes no difference what he *guesses*. Within a week, perhaps less, it will be too late for Reardon to do anything at all. When James Markham makes his speech on the Senate floor and breaks open the hornets' nest . . ."

Randall allowed himself an unusual guffaw of harsh laughter. "I must say I rather like your colorful turn of phrase, Sal! And you're right, of course. We might have been getting things slightly out of perspective."

"And, of course, while the hornets are buzzing and the attention of the media is concentrated in *that* direction, the discreet activities of our other friends in the Middle East and elsewhere should go unremarked. The energetic and far-seeing Senator Markham will have found new sources for supplies of oil and created a cordial entente with the rulers of several Middle Eastern states. The United States will once again enter a period of prosperity."

"You ought to start writing some of Rufe's editorials!" Harris commented rather sourly. He continued to wear a slight frown. "But I still think we ought to take steps to eliminate Webb Carnahan as a possible threat."

"Well—of course, we go ahead with what we'd planned earlier," Randall said, shrugging as cigar ashes scattered. He noted slyly that Harris Phelps's frown smoothed out, and wondered how much of the other man's insistence had to do with Anne Mallory.

Anne knew that she ought to rest—collect her thoughts and decide—but decide what, for God's sake? Rest, then. This time she wasn't going to run away. She was going to *stay* here, and finish the movie, and . . . she didn't have to think of afterwards right now.

She was safely in her room now—all the lights on, the door locked. Against whom, or what? Anne looked away from the door and saw her own reflection in the mirror. Her face looked pale and strained, with dark smudges under her eyes. Ghost face —wasn't that what the Indians used to call winter? And she felt just as cold, inside and out.

The telephone by her bed rang, startling her, and Anne could feel her fingers trembling as she picked it up. Anna-Maria's voice came sharply over the line.

"Anne? I'm sorry if I woke you up, but . . ." Anne felt her heart jump during the tiny pause. "Have you seen Webb? I had been sitting with him, you know, but when I saw he was asleep, I went to get some dinner and—he isn't in his room now."

Anne tried to fight the tiny shock waves that ran up her spine, stiffening it. She couldn't help looking at the door. Webb wasn't in his room . . . but why should his *wife* (remember that!) think he might have come to her?

She was amazed that her voice sounded steady. "He isn't here—and I haven't seen him since this afternoon. Perhaps he decided to go for a walk."

"You're sure?" Anna-Maria persisted, and then, as if she'd realized she might have gone too far, she let a sigh escape. "Oh—I am sorry! It's just that I became worried. Dr. Brightman gave him an injection of some kind for the pain. He warned me that it was pretty strong. I should not have disturbed you, but I thought I should . . ."

"That's all right. My door's locked, and I've already been warned. I won't be letting anyone in at this time of night." Anne drew some small, malicious satisfaction from hearing the other woman draw in her breath sharply. But then she spoiled it all by adding, almost without volition, "He's—I mean he must be all right, then? Do you know where Karim is?"

"I can only hope they have not found each other," Anna-Maria said grimly, before she hung up.

After a few seconds Anne put down her humming, empty receiver. She hated the thoughts that had suddenly started buzzing around in her head. Where *was* Webb? Looking for her—looking for Karim? She remembered his cut, bloody back and shuddered, as logic and common sense fought against raw emotion she couldn't help, even now. Each memory she tried to run away from came back like a whiplash to flick at the fringes of her mind.

She had been warned—she had been told what he was and what he had done—why didn't it make any difference? *I'm tired of running away from reality*, she thought suddenly, and she remembered again what he had told her of his past. She let memory wash her back to the more recent past, knowing with a sense of fatalism that she couldn't escape this time.

Face it, Anne, face it! And she got up from the bed and walked over to the mirror again, studying herself closely as if she hoped to find some clue there that would help her understand herself better. *And the truth shall set you free.* More memory. The truth was that she loved Webb Carnahan, and it brought her a kind of relief to admit it to herself. Even if they ended up destroying each other, and they might yet do so . . .

Strange, maybe. Sick. But from the beginning there had been a bond between them, and some primeval instinct that had nothing to do with reason told her that. It was the reason they couldn't stay away from each other—the monstrous *thing* that kept them coming back to each other. She had tried other men, but it hadn't cured her. She had fought, but it hadn't helped. If he came to her room tonight, as Anna-Maria had thought he might, she would open the door to him and let him in.

She had already changed for bed—into a nightgown that left her back bare and barely covered her breasts. Now, remembering the vigilant monitor that watched all of them, she moved around the room, methodically turning off lights.

Chapter Forty-two

SHE HADN'T TAKEN a Valium that night. "Sweet-dream pills," Webb had called them—had it only been two days ago?

She had locked all the doors, even the one that connected Harris's room with her own, and after the lights were out, there was only the moon to keep her company, shining through the French windows, and an electric blanket to keep her warm. The sounds of the ocean seemed very loud, and as she lay in bed she remembered her Dream. She hadn't had it again since Dr. Brightman—Hal—had put her under hypnosis and talked it away. Since then she'd caught him looking at her rather reproachfully on occasion. He was a nice man, and he'd helped her. She should talk to him again, join with Sarah and Jean in the daily meditation sessions. It was Anna-Maria's presence that had kept her away of late.

Anne turned on her side, facing away from the moonlight, too lazy to get up and pull the curtains together and too tense to fall asleep yet. She closed her eyes and listened to sounds. The ocean, that was constant. The screech of a nightbird. She thought she heard Harris try the door between their rooms, very gently, but when he found it locked, he must have decided to let her be. Harris was so patient with her, so understanding. And if it hadn't been for Webb, coming back disruptively into her life, she might have been content with him. She had been, for a while.

She thought she heard the helicopter come in, not as loud as it usually sounded, but it was far too late—after two in the morning, and who would be flying in or out at this hour? It was only thunder . . . thunder, with the moon shining? She must have been half-asleep, but a second distant rumble drove her out of bed and to the windows in time to see a cloud bank swallow up the sea-falling moon.

The freak storm wasn't close—somewhere to the east. She saw the sky light up for an instant, followed by another low rumble. And there were no lights anywhere below, so maybe they'd had a power failure as well. It used to happen quite often during the summers she'd spent here, and in the end her grandfather had had his own generator installed. Harris would know about it, of course. He'd have it turned on.

She was deliberately letting her thoughts ramble, while she was—waiting. She realized that fact only when she had started to grope her way back to bed, and heard her door open—and close. She hadn't shot the bolt on it—consciously or unconsciously? Anne felt herself freeze, trying to control the sound of her breathing. The bolt she had forgotten made a tiny, clicking sound, and she was locked in with terror, and the darkness pressing smotheringly against her. It was almost like drowning, like being back in the Dream. It was only when she heard his voice, a soft, husky whisper, that she could let herself make a sound.

"Annie?"

"I'm—I wasn't asleep. How . . . ?" The gun was still in the drawer of her night stand. But she knew with a feeling of despair that she could not use it.

"I learned to pick locks—a long time ago. Where the hell are you?"

A tiny beam of light flicked across her eyes and instinctively she blinked them shut. In the blackness that followed she felt his arm go around her shoulders, and realized only then, as he was holding her close against him, that she was shaking.

In bed, the darkness was no longer a black shroud but warm velvet, gentle against her skin, a curtain closing her into a private world where only she and he existed and no one could watch or hear.

He made love to her with an almost desperate urgency, and with hardly any words. Under his shirt, his body was swathed in bandages; they were sticky with blood. They found each other by touch and instinct; with mutual need, lost in the darkness of passion. She touched his hair and his face with her fingers, very gently and exploratively, and there was the wetness of tears on her own face. Everything had changed since the first time he had taken her and she had shed tears—and nothing had changed.

"Oh, Annie-love!" he muttered afterwards, his voice slightly slurred. "I'm stoned out of my head. I knew I had to get to you . . . there's not much else I remember. Not even how. I think they gave me sodium pentothal." He must have sensed her unspoken question, because he turned to put his lips against the hollow where her neck and shoulder met, and his voice sounded muffled. "Truth serum, baby. To make me tell everything they think I know. Only they know enough, and I couldn't have told them anything, anyway. The think tank fixed that. I'm brainwashing-proof, did you know that, hmm? Did they tell you?" He had her pinned down, somehow; she felt his fingers caress her hair, her temples, her neck, running gently over corded arteries. His laughter was very soft, as he nuzzled his lips against her ear. "You want to know anything, Annie? Why don't you ask me—every man's got a weakness, and you're mine, I guess. As long as you're alive . . ."

She stirred under him, and his fingers tightened, ever so lightly, until she could feel the pulsing of her arteries under his thumbs. She remembered suddenly what he had threatened her with once. Pressure on the carotid artery that carried the life-giving supply of oxygen to the brain, causing unconsciousness. Worse, if the pressure was continued.

"Webb . . ." The thunder growled outside and the room lit up and darkened again. And if he were the assassin they had named him, she wasn't going to beg. "I love you," she whispered. "And you? What's true and what isn't?"

"Christ, we're both caught up in the goddamned mechanism, aren't we, love? But what's true is right now, and *this*." His mouth covered hers in a long kiss that left her shaken. "And whatever they tell you, or you see, you've got to trust me."

How could she—how could she? Anne found herself persisting, in spite of everything her senses screamed to the contrary.

"I don't know what you mean. Webb, I've got to *know*! Are you—is it true that you—you *killed* . . . ?" She had to ask it, even if it meant condemning herself to death at his hands. Violet, Dunc Frazier. How many others? Oh God, no—no!

But—and maybe it was the drug they had given him—he answered her quite matter-of-factly.

"Yes. I've killed when I've had to—or been ordered to." He was talking now more to himself than to her, and she had to force herself to keep still. "They train you, like a killer dog. After a while, you act by reflex, and you stop thinking about it." He thought about Peter the Wolf, always smiling, enjoying what he did, and his body shuddered involuntarily.

Before Anne could ask any more questions he rolled away from her, wondering at his own weakness. He shouldn't have come to her. He had had other things to do, and the sudden power failure had helped, with everyone who was still awake running around looking for lights. He had heard Harris cursing as he searched for a flashlight.

"Where the hell is Palumbo? He'll know how to start the damn generator . . ." Piling out and scattering in different directions, they had left the door to the screening room unlocked, and that had been his opportunity to retrieve the tiny recording device, voice-activated, that he'd planted under one of the chairs when they'd been watching the rushes a few days ago. He should have gone straight back to his room, where Ria waited—sleeping soundly still, he hoped. If she wasn't—what the fuck, he'd been crazy, letting himself into Anne's room anyhow. But he'd been passing her door, and somehow he'd sensed her, had known that she'd be awake and alone. What he'd tell Ria depended on Anne, who had no idea of the time. The electric clock by her bed had stopped . . .

She had kept lying very still while he sat on the edge of her bed, dressing himself. Now she whispered, as if she'd been able to guess the dark direction of his thoughts, "Are you going back to *her*, to your wife?"

His head turned in the direction of her voice. She thought for a minute that he might not answer her, before he said, "Yes, I guess so." Blunt, bald statement that he didn't bother to qualify, and in a way she was relieved that he hadn't made excuses. Her mind was still numb. He'd *admitted*, he'd betrayed himself to her. Worse than that was the fact that it didn't seem to matter. She'd *known*, even before, hadn't she? And she had betrayed herself to him, by telling him that she loved him. That didn't matter either. There was a strange closeness between them at this moment.

"Do you still love her, Webb?" Or did he feel responsible? Had he been in part responsible for Anna-Maria's betrayal?

"I used to think I did, a long time ago. Then I thought she was dead. It takes time, adjusting to the fact that I have a wife. Oh Christ, Annie!" He had stood up, but now he bent down, holding her face between his hands. "Do you need for me to tell you the words?" He said harshly, "I'm crazy in love with you, baby, and you damn well know it, don't you?"

He released her abruptly, and left her without a kiss. She lay there for some time, trying to keep her mind blank, and then she got up and bolted the door he'd closed soundlessly, hearing the thunder accompany her all the way back to bed.

Anne was to think later that it was just as well she had had a few hours of sleep. An aftermath of the lovemaking her body had been craving. An escape from the answers to questions she should not have asked.

He had told her, almost unwillingly, that he loved her; and had admitted to being what she had been warned he was. An assassin—a man who killed by reflex, or because he was ordered to. He had *told* her, and that made her a threat to him. She was strangely calm, or maybe she had traveled beyond feeling. The same sense of fatalism that had overtaken her last night, while she had waited for him almost without knowing it, overcame her now. She remembered a movie she had seen when she was a child—*Duel in the Sun*. And remembered vividly the very last scene, when the lovers who had killed each other had crawled towards each other as they were dying, to hold hands. Would that be the ending for them?

Palumbo, that jack of all trades, must have started the generator going, or maybe Pacific Gas and Electricity had gotten on the ball. Harris was bound to have shares in the company.

It was the radio that had awakened her, and all they were talking of on every station was the damage that the freak electrical storm had caused. A fire in the vast national forest that was only a few miles up the road to the south of the island raged out of control, fanned by the winds that had sprung up. And the forest extended to *this* side of the highway. It could cut them off; but then there was the helicopter, of course. And maybe Harris would decide that they should all leave. They could finish shooting the movie somewhere else.

Anne brushed her hair mechanically. *I'm crazy in love with you, baby, and you damn well know it!* Was he? Did she? God, if only she could have slept longer!

Harris knocked at the connecting door, sounding anxious, and she had to let him in. He looked as if he hadn't slept at all, and his manner was more abrupt than she had ever known it to be.

"Anne. Thank God you're . . ." The radio was still on and he jerked his head toward it. "You know what that damned storm did? I've got to talk to you, before you go downstairs and hear it from someone else."

"We won't be filming today?" It was a deliberate ploy to keep from hearing whatever it was he had come to tell her, and she thought, watching his eyes in the mirror, that he knew it. He came up behind her and put his hands on her shoulders —she felt their pressure and flinched.

"I'm talking about Karim. You didn't see or hear anything of him last night, did you? He's disappeared, Anne. Not a damned trace of him anywhere. And Claudia's in hysterics, succeeding in making nervous wrecks of anyone who believes her story."

"What story? Claudia . . . ?"

"He'd been sleeping with her—on and off. Last night—well, last night I guess he was in an exceptionally bad mood. You humiliated him in front of everyone, Anne—not that I blame you, I suppose, but . . . I had to warn him myself to keep away from you, and he turned to Claudia." He was still holding her shoulders, and he must have sensed some movement, because he pressed down warningly. "No—please let me finish. He was with her, and he left her for a while, to go back to his room for—a joint. Hashish. That doesn't matter. The point is that he didn't come back, and when she got tired of waiting, and angry—you know what she's like—she went looking for him. She says it was just about the time that the lights went out, but the moon was still up. And she swears she saw two men, struggling together on the clifftop. Against the moon, she said. She has a way of dramatizing things, true, but . . . Christ, the worst of it is that he's not been found. The guards at the gate stayed alert and they say no one tried to leave. And I sent men down to the beach, of course, but they couldn't find anything. Claudia swears, though, that she saw one of the men go over. She keeps saying over and over, 'He broke his neck—I *saw* it. There was a sound.'" Harris shrugged, deprecatingly. "Damn, now I'm dramatizing, aren't I? But I'm sure you'll hear it from *her*, and I wanted you to be prepared."

After last night, the day could deal her no more shocks. Anne heard her voice, sounding surprisingly calm and steady. "What else are you preparing me for?" She twisted around on the stool to face him, and his hands dropped away so that he was no longer touching her, just looking at her, and she couldn't

447

read anything at all in his eyes, noticing how very shiny and opaque they were. "Are you trying to tell me that—do you think *Webb* killed him?"

It was out in the open, and why did she feel as if Harris were an antagonist? Still watching her, he said slowly, "He threatened to kill Karim. With his bare hands. It's on the soundtrack, Anne. And he wasn't in his room last night—Anna-Maria was quite frantic. She called you, didn't she?"

Again, without volition, she evaded answering him directly. "Where is he *now*? Webb, I mean. Or has he disappeared, too?"

"He came back very late—actually quite early, if you want to be technical. He told Anna-Maria that he'd been out for a walk because he needed fresh air and enjoyed storms. Quite frankly, I don't believe him. And if I hadn't made sure that both your doors were locked, I would have been extremely worried. You see, we had another visitor last night. Someone you know quite well. And he's helped establish for certain that Webb Carnahan is definitely working for your father. And that your father . . . I'm sorry, Anne; I meant to have Dr. Brightman break this to you, in his own way and his own time. But your father was responsible for your mother's death, you know. You saw it happen, as a child, and you blocked the memory out. That's why you kept having that dream."

Anne made an involuntary movement to put her hands over her ears. Was there pity in his eyes or something else? She brought her hands back down to her lap, fingers twisting together. "No—it's not true! How could you . . ."

"He put you under hypnosis, Anne. He regressed you back to your childhood, and once you'd released the memory you'd been trying to shut out, he brought you back with the command to forget. That's when you stopped having the dream. But being a methodical man, he had a tape recorder running. He also made notes. He gave me the cassette to store away in the vault for him—you realize the potential dynamite it contains? I knew about it because—I apologize if you consider it an invasion of your privacy, but I was concerned for you, so I watched and listened on the video monitor."

"You—"

He wouldn't let her finish. He went on inexorably, without pausing: "Webb Carnahan read his notes. We didn't catch that—you were asleep, and we'd switched to another room, I suppose. But he came in and took you back to his room that afternoon, didn't he? We *know* he read Brightman's notes because he telephoned the information he'd gathered to your father. And received his orders."

It was incredible, but it made horrible, ugly sense. She remembered her father telling her one night, in Deepwood, "You see, Anne, I have to protect myself, too." If she had to be killed, he wouldn't have any scruple against ordering her execution. To protect himself and the organization he'd built up. Just as he'd killed her mother. Love-hate—hate-love. Some other memory, just as deeply hidden as the one she'd revealed to Hal Brightman, nudged for an instant at the edge of her memory, and she started to say involuntarily, "No, he couldn't have," before it was gone. And Harris was shaking his head.

"Believe me, Anne, I would have spared you this shock if I could have. But if shock is what it takes to remind you that you're in danger . . ."

In danger—in danger. Words repeating themselves in her mind like a clock ticking away time. *Her* time. In danger from Webb, who was supposed to kill her and hadn't been able to—yet.

Harris was saying something else—she hardly heard him. She had gone alarmingly pale, and he felt a twinge of regret at having to tell it to her so abruptly. But Christ, everything was breaking too suddenly, and Craig Hyatt's arrival last night had brought things to a head with a vengeance. They had to move fast—at once—before Reardon did. The damned fire, sending its pall of smoke into the air and closing in fast, didn't help matters either. It was time to take the wraps off.

Chapter Forty-three

"I HAVE A MESSAGE for you," Anna-Maria said without any preamble. She had awakened him when she came into the room, but Webb had hoped, fuzzily, that she would think he was still sleeping and go away. He had swallowed two of the pain pills that Dr. Brightman had grudgingly allowed him before he could get to sleep—his back had felt, and still felt, as if it had been run over by an electric lawnmower. Shit! He couldn't have slept for any longer than two or three hours, and he wasn't in the mood for pacifying Ria, or answering her inevitable questions.

He grunted unintelligibly as she sat on the edge of his bed, wincing when she put her hand on his shoulder. "Don't pretend to be asleep. And you had better hear what I have to say, for your own sake."

Sunlight filtered through slats in the blinds, falling on her face and hair. There was something feline about her, with her slightly slanted eyes and that mane of tawny hair. A tigress, half-smiling as she looked down at him, but he noticed that her eyes were narrowed on him.

Webb sighed, trying to clear his brain. "All right, Ria. So I'm awake, and I'm listening."

"The message is from Espinoza. He would like to speak with you, in private."

"*Private?*" Webb pushed himself upright, running fingers through his hair. He cocked an eyebrow in the direction of the hidden camera.

"It's out of order—isn't that *strange*? Something must have happened during that freak storm we had last night—a shorting of some wires, something wrong with one of the circuits . . . There won't be time to have it fixed, though. Everyone is so scared of that fire they are screaming to Harris to get them away, quickly, quickly!"

"Seems like I've been missing out on all the excitement, doesn't it?"

She leaned forwards, so that her breasts almost brushed his chest. "Oh, but wasn't yesterday exciting enough for you? Did you watch the storm while you were—taking that long, long walk last night?"

He wondered how much she guessed. Not that it mattered. He had gotten quite a lot accomplished last night, as a matter of fact, including the job on the wiring.

He grinned at her, being deliberately provoking. "I started out looking for *you*, baby. Missed your warm body next to mine. And then all the damned lights went out and I got myself good and lost."

"You miserable liar!" She jerked erect and swore at him in Spanish, all but spitting the words at him. "Do you think we don't know . . . ah, you'd better think up a better story than *that*, especially if the sheriff should start asking you questions! Yes, you had better have a damn good alibi!"

Even through her anger, she felt a spark of exhilaration when she caught his slight frown, the almost imperceptible hardening of his mouth. Webb was as good at playing this kind of game as she was, but they would see who would win this time!

"Yes," she went on, "I hope for your sake that that woman Claudia's story was *not* true, or that Karim turns up alive. Otherwise you could be in quite a lot of trouble, couldn't you?"

Neat. Very neat. He could see that for himself, after Ria, shrugging skeptically, had explained exactly what she had meant. "And you *did* swear to kill him—'with my hands,' you

451

said, and that part was not in the script. It is on the sound tape."

"I see." His voice was flat. He watched her as she paced angrily around the room. "Well, I guess I could say I didn't know what I was doing, huh? After that shot our good doctor gave me, I went out like a light. Or *you* could alibi me, baby. Like a sweet, obliging little wife."

She turned on him, eyes narrow. "You bastard! You admit —oh, I suppose I am fool enough to do so, but I cannot. Too many other people saw me when I went to eat dinner. And after that I was with Espinoza."

All sewed up, Webb found himself thinking cynically. But he hadn't yet realized just how tightly—not until after he'd had a conversation with Sal Espinoza himself.

His first reaction was rage. He saw them watching him, Espinoza smiling sympathetically as he shook his head; Ria with her cat eyes narrowed, the way she stood by the window giving him the nerve-end impression that she was poised, waiting.

Thrown to the wolves—one of Reardon's chess moves? They knew—they knew almost everything. But why *tell* him? And why the secret talk with Espinoza?

"I'm listening," Webb said tightly, while his mind raced, finding alternatives and discarding them almost at once.

"Good, I thought you might be—open to reason," Espinoza said smoothly. He went on, his face bland, "Because, after all, we have many friends in common, you and I. It gives us, shall I say, a common cause in some ways? So, I will lay my cards on the table as a mark of *my* good faith. And I think that after you have heard me out, you will see the advantages of doing the same yourself. Because we also have a common enemy, eh?"

Reardon. Even Craig Hyatt, of all people, had finally turned against Reardon. Hyatt was the leak—and Hyatt knew where they were holding Lucia. If Webb cooperated, Espinoza himself would guarantee her safety and that of her sons.

"Only, you see, we have to move very fast. Before Reardon learns that his right-hand man is now on *our* side. Before . . ."

"Why?" Webb said tightly. "You know so damned much already, why suddenly decide to take me into your confidence? And what makes you believe Hyatt is on the level?"

"He's impressed by Markham, and getting queasy about some of Reardon's methods. But most of all, he wants to step into Reardon's shoes. Power, my friend, power! Haven't we all felt that particular hunger? And I would, frankly, much prefer to have you working *with* us. I don't want to jeopardize certain dealings I have with your—um—*family*. So?"

"That's all? And how's Harris Phelps going to take all this? You know, somehow I get the impression that Phelps doesn't like me—much."

"Harris is still a partner, of course. We have not had a falling out, if that is what you are thinking. But unfortunately . . ."

"He *used* to be the one who thought most clearly, and without the clutter of emotion to cloud his judgment!" Ria whirled on them both, her eyes blazing. "But somehow he has developed a stupid weakness for that whey-faced bitch! Reardon's daughter—the same one *you* go sniffing after! What is there about her that makes all you men so protective? She could not have survived for more than a few minutes what *I* have been through. She's weak, and Harris has been foolish enough to tell her too much. If our plans are to succeed, we cannot have any weak links, don't you see that? Would Reardon himself hesitate if she or anyone else got in the way?"

This was yet another Ria—tough, her voice almost strident as she stood before Webb with her hands on her hips, her chin thrust out defiantly. At last he was seeing her real self. She went on talking, while Espinoza, shrugging, let her have the floor; and it came to him with a sense of cold detachment, even before she had finished, exactly what kind of "insurance" he was to provide them with in exchange for Lucy's safety and his own immunity.

453

"Are you in love with her, too, Webb? Perhaps you'll change your mind when I show you certain videotapes—your sweet little Anne with Karim, letting him do anything and everything to her, and enjoying it—yes, enjoying it! Did you believe her little story of being raped by him in front of the cameras, eh? Did *you* ever have to rape her, even though she made a game of pretending she was unwilling? You men are all fools! And you went to her last night, didn't you? You had sex with her— I knew it as soon as I saw her face this morning."

"Shut up, Ria!" He spoke roughly to her, knowing it was the kind of language she understood best. "Sure, I dropped in on Anne last night. What the hell does it matter if I tell you *now* —I fixed that damn video monitor because I got tired of Big Brother watching me all the time. And I figured she might provide me with an alibi. But don't give me that crap about being in love with her, for Christ's sake. I'm not in the habit of falling in love with every broad I fuck. And"—he narrowed his eyes at Ria—"you forget, sweetheart, that she *is* goddamned Reardon's daughter, and I have no reason in the world to love that cold-blooded bastard. But when he arranged to have my sister and nephews snatched . . ."

"Then—kill her! Get rid of her, and prove it! You could make it seem like an accident—you could think of something, couldn't you? Both Sal and I would swear we were with you all the time, and even Harris wouldn't have to know. He'll come to his senses again once that bitch is out of the way."

"Look—" He made his voice cold, devoid of emotion. "Look, *you* figure out a way. You get your pretty little head to work on a real neat, tidy way to eliminate her, where I can be damned positive I have an alibi, and I'll take the contract."

Barstow was working late again, which wasn't unusual, especially when something really big was brewing. In any case, he had nothing to go home to. He'd never married. Wives—kids— they left you too damned vulnerable in his line of work. And when he needed a woman, it was easy enough to find one, especially in Washington, who was willing to be wined and dined and taken to bed. Not that he'd had too much time for even that small form of relaxation recently.

He heard the general clear his throat in warning, and looked up from the papers on his desk with an inward sigh. It was unusual for General Tarrant to be here so late, and he didn't like cooling his heels. He'd been stomping around the tiny office ever since he had arrived, bushy brows drawn together in a frown as he glared at the small red light that meant Reardon was on his private telephone, the Red Line, and was not to be disturbed.

Now he glared at the long-suffering Barstow instead. The general was in dress uniform, his neck above his uniform collar turning red, a big vein standing out on his forehead as it always did when he was angry. "All right, goddammit! You dragged me away from a reception for Markham, and I had a hell of a time getting away. *And* explaining to my wife. I've been waiting exactly ten minutes already, and you sit there shuffling papers while *he*"—here his stubby finger jabbed in the direction of the door leading to the inner office—"sits on the blasted telephone! What the fuck is going on? Has he told *you* yet? And where the hell is Hyatt? I'd have thought he'd be here, too."

Barstow leaned back in his chair and shrugged. He was tired; it had been a long day. And he was slightly worried, although he didn't like to admit that, even to himself. He supposed that Tarrant was entitled to some answers, before Reardon filled him in on the rest.

"Hyatt's in Monterey. Actually, on an island off the Big Sur coast." He forestalled the general's angry expletive by saying patiently, "He's the only one who has a damn good excuse for going there, after all. Anne Mallory's his ex-wife, and they're still on pretty good terms. He's also her attorney. I understand he called and got himself invited down. *They* don't know anything more about him than that, and since Carnahan thinks they're on to him . . ."

"Christ! I hope to hell there are no slipups! You've been reading those goddamn editorials lately, haven't you? And that snooping columnist fellow, with his hints of imminent exposures that will shake up people in high places . . . The reception I had to leave tonight was for Markham, you know! He's getting very sure of himself. Press all over the place, as usual, and he was hinting he was preparing a big speech that might shock a few people. Know anything about *that*?"

"Gentlemen." They both looked up, and Reardon stood in the doorway, his ascetic, unlined face showing no emotion at all as he courteously inclined his head. "If you'll come in . . ."

The chairs were padded and comfortable. Like a polite host, Reardon offered them drinks. Tarrant, unbending somewhat, had bourbon; Barstow declined. Reardon himself played with the stem of a wineglass that contained nothing stronger than chilled Perrier water with a twist. His fingers were long and elegant, but somehow they gave the impression that they could snap the thin crystal in two without a single splinter.

"Dammit, Richard, what's up? Markham's back from his rendezvous with his sideline sweetie, as you know. Surely if Hyatt were planning to go down there, he could have arranged to go while *he* was there! I still don't see why we've been holding off."

"I want you to listen to something," Reardon said, his soft voice cutting off Tarrant's angry questioning. "This tape was smuggled out this morning in Harris Phelps's own helicopter. Incidentally, it also brought Carol Cochran and Mr. Randall away from the island. He's back in town now, I understand. One of our men in Monterey flew out here with it immediately."

He pressed the button on a tiny tape recorder, calmly identifying voices that came through surprisingly clearly in spite of background noises.

"Harris Phelps. Sal Espinoza . . . that's Rufus Randall. Parmenter—CIA."

He'd already listened to the tape, and while the other two bent forward to hear, he allowed his mind to wander slightly.

They were closing in for the kill. And he could guess that Tarrant's first question would be: "Well? So when do we make our move?" Tarrant and Barstow believed that it was through Anne, and the publicity that would surround her after she'd made an extremely sexy movie, that they meant to expose her father and his real position. And that was partly true. But what he could not tell them was that there was that incident, far back in the past when he'd been young enough to lack the perfect control that he'd gained over all his senses since then. Helen, his wife. And Anne—the pale child who, grown up, reminded him too much of Helen. He should have been warned, perhaps, by the screaming nightmares of her childhood and the way she'd shrunk from him.

"She'll get over them. The trauma . . . shock to the mind of a child . . ." The psychiatrist had encouraged her to forget, and he'd been relieved that there was no need to see her too often. There had been a series of very expensive schools, and when she'd come back from Switzerland the last time, Hyatt had obligingly taken over. No need to worry about her any longer, he'd thought. But perhaps Anne was more like Helen than he'd thought, and not just in looks. There had been the divorce. Her surprising declaration of independence. Her lovers . . .

Helen's lover—or had there been others as well? He'd never managed to learn who the man was. After Helen's death it hadn't seemed important. But that, too, had been before he'd learned that everything was important. Every tiny detail. After he'd spoken to Webb Carnahan he'd had background checks run, and of all the people who were on that island, there were three who could have known that Anne had a held-back memory of her childhood that might be triggered under hypnosis.

Both Harris Phelps and Dr. Harold Brightman had been in or around the area during that time. And one other person as well.

"For Christ's sake!" Tarrant swore as the tape clicked to a stop. "So that's what all those reports we've been getting from our friend in Iran meant. And they sound damn sure of themselves, don't they? When . . . ?"

"We'll have to move very fast," Reardon said calmly. "You've heard of the big fire in the area? It seems to have thrown some of the movie people into quite a panic, although I understand that Yves Pleydel has persuaded Phelps to offer them extra pay to stay on a day or two extra to finish shootings. So I'd say that we have a little extra time."

"*And* a plan as well, I hope!" Tarrant snorted.

Barstow thanked God that Reardon at least was all reason and no emotion.

He unrolled the map that had been lying by the recorder as he nodded at the general. "That is why I particularly wanted to consult with you." His finger moved over contours. "Here's the coastline—the island—*this* area is where the fire is raging—and it's still out of control, they're having a hard time getting in there to fight it. Right here it's jumped the highway, and the telephone wires are down. They do have radio contact with the mainland, however, and their own generator . . ."

Chapter Forty-four

ANNE WAS DEAD TIRED in both body and mind. So tired she felt numb. Too many things, happening too fast, crowded in on her. She wanted nothing more than to get away—to run away. And Harris had promised her, soothing her. Then Craig, of all people, turning up to "protect" her, wearing the same air of angry patience she remembered too well from London. He'd been a little more gentle with her than he'd been then, putting his arm around her as he said, "My poor Anne! Look, I'll take you away with me if you really want to go! Phelps has no right to force you to stay here, especially in view of—" He'd bitten off the rest, but his meaning had been implicit.

Webb, she had thought. *He means Webb, of course.* And if she'd needed any more proof, Craig had given it to her. Harris had left them together, and she stood passively, letting Craig hold her while he explained in a rough, angry voice that *she* was the reason why he'd broken with her father, jeopardizing himself.

"I'm sorry, Anne! Until then, I just hadn't realized what he was like. I had him up on a pedestal, and I believed in what he was doing. But all *he* believes in is power for himself through manipulation. Not idealism, but cynicism. And Christ, to think that I went along with it all these years. I was patterning myself after him, without realizing it, and I didn't give *you* enough understanding, did I? Anne, I'd still like us to try again. I've never stopped caring about you, and this time I promise you

459

it'll be different. I don't give a damn about the past, or anything you've done."

She wanted to tell him that it was too late, she was too numb, she seemed to have lost the capacity for feeling all over again. But at that moment she was too tired to answer him. She had to fight the impulse to give way to tears.

And for once, Craig seemed to understand her silence. "You're still in shock, aren't you? You're hands are so cold, Anne! I suppose they've been making you work too hard. Look, I'll talk to Phelps, and to Pleydel. Why don't you lie down and get some rest? Do you want me to send the doctor up to you?"

After he'd gone, she stared blankly at her own face in the mirror, wondering who she was. Daughter of a murderer. Lover of a murderer. Victim of a murderer?

Webb's voice, whispering harshly out of the darkness, *I'm crazy in love with you, baby, and you damn well know it, don't you?* Another lie, meant to disarm her? Or the perverted truth?

She had begun to twist her fingers together, a habit from the past. Victim . . . she looked like a frightened mid-Victorian maiden from some gothic novel, standing here wringing her hands instead of *doing* something. No, dammit! She wasn't going to be anyone's victim! Cleansing rage made her snap her head up, as she sucked in a deep breath. *That's right, Anne. Fight back!* She didn't know if she was fighting for herself or for Webb—but she was sick of lies and subterfuge and intrigue.

She was dressed in jeans and a shirt, and now, not giving herself time to think any further, she snatched up a shoulder bag —blue denim to match her pants. She took the gun from the drawer and dropped it in. She wasn't going to hide in her room any longer, waiting fearfully for something to happen. She was going to make it happen herself for a change. She was going outside to find Webb, and face him with everything she'd learned.

Downstairs, everyone seemed to be gathered in the central courtyard. As Anne passed the open doors, she could hear Pleydel's voice; some kind of rally. Perhaps he was telling them that they were preparing to pack up and leave.

She hurried down the great, empty hallway and out into the open air. The sun was shining, beating down hot and bright. Late afternoon already. But as she started down the path to the cottages, Anne could see the pall of smoke that towered up into the sky in the east—an angry yellow-orange from the reflected light of both the sun and the fire itself. All those acres and acres of ancient forest—and the animals, poor things, who must be fleeing panic-stricken, not knowing in which direction to run. Like her—except that now she had her direction and her determination.

A sharp breeze blew up from the ocean; she should have tied her hair back. When she reached Webb's cottage, she didn't bother to knock. *He* hadn't knocked at her door last night.

Anne walked in, pausing to let her eyes become accustomed to the cool gloominess inside. His bed was unmade, the door to the bathroom stood open. A pair of faded levis lay on the floor and a bloodstained shirt on a chair. But Webb himself was absent.

Damn! Anne hesitated, biting her lip. He might have been in the courtyard with the others; she should have thought of that, shouldn't she? And then she heard a sound behind her and spun on her toes like a frightened cat.

"Hi!" Jean Benedict said pleasantly. She stood there with her fists dug into the pockets of her blue sweatshirt, her black hair blowing about her face. And she didn't show any surprise at all at seeing Anne there. "Looking for Webb? I talked to him just a few minutes ago, and he said he was going to take a walk on the beach, while everyone else was deciding whether they wanted to stay on and finish up the few scenes left to be shot here or not." Jean shrugged. "I guess we're going to stay—it means extra bread, and it'd cost a hell of a lot more to pick another location and do it all over, I guess! Me, I don't care one way or the other. I'm getting so I kind of like it here, you know? It reminds me of home—or where home used to be."

The beach, Anne was thinking. The beach! And all the time she'd been here she hadn't gone down there . . .

Aloud she said, "You're not afraid of the fire then? It couldn't reach us here in any case."

"Oh, I knew that from the beginning, and I guess everyone else is starting to calm down." Jean grinned suddenly, showing strong white teeth in her sun-browned face. "That's a relief, because, with Sarah coaching me, I was actually starting to look forward to that other small scene I've got coming up." She looked straightforwardly at Anne. "You going on to find Webb, or do you want to walk back to the house with me?"

She was wearing a "Jimmy for President" button, and Anne wondered how much the woman actually *knew*—not that it mattered any more than it seemed to matter to Jean that she'd wanted to see Webb. She still had to confront Webb, before her courage faltered. She didn't know which way Webb had gone. He might not know of the shortcut through the caves (why did a cold shudder go through her when she thought of it?) but if *she* used it, she'd get there before he did, probably. She had the gun to make her feel safe, and the thought—or was it an instinct?—embedded deep inside her mind that he wouldn't kill her, he couldn't, or he'd have done it before.

"I—I'd rather you didn't tell anybody that—I've gone looking for Webb," Anne had said hesitantly.

Jean merely cocked one dark eyebrow and said briefly, "Sure —okay, I understand."

There was no one in the underground garage either, not even Palumbo, who was always around.

Therapy. Going back in order to travel forwards. But Anne

had to force herself to move, now that she was so close. She wasn't a scared child any longer; she was an adult who understood the reasons for her childhood terror, her fear of the ocean and dark, damp, echoing places.

There was a door, standing slightly ajar, with a tide table tacked on it. Anne made herself study it. Low tide—the tide would still be going out. The sound of the ocean, when she opened the door, was muted. She wouldn't let herself hesitate now. The irrational terror was exactly that—irrational and ridiculous. A natural tunnel built by the ocean with a honeycomb of smaller caves and passages leading off it. Her smuggler ancestor had probably used it; her grandfather had as a boy. So had her mother . . . and brushing that thought away, so, no doubt, had Danny Verrano and his friends.

It was dark. She left the door open so that some of the fluorescent lighting in the garage could help her. And then, if she closed her eyes and felt her way, she would find it. She only had to remember that she was taller now. She mustn't run. Pocahontas . . . the game she used to play came back with a rush, and she almost giggled. Very well, she would be Pocahontas again. Looking for John Smith.

It wasn't a long way—not as long as she remembered it from before. She tripped on loose rocks a few times and almost fell until she reminded herself not to run. Walk slow. And then she saw the light and heard the deceptively soft hush-hush sound of the waves as they curled and flattened out hungrily against the sand of the beach, the far-off pulsing murmur of the ocean itself. She was able to picture it before she saw it— ruffled blue and white reflecting the sun, seabird sounds and salt smell. Infinitely better than the ugly, decaying kelp odor in the cave-tunnel. She could see the crimson kelp beds where sea otters hid, rising and falling with the swell, but the beach itself looked as if it had been washed clean by the high tides last night.

Anne stood savoring the freshness of the air and the feel of the sun on her skin. She was here, and it was as beautiful as she used to remember it. Not at all a place for nightmares.

The mouth of the cave was partially shielded by a rock formation that had always reminded her of an elephant. At this end, the beach started to narrow. To the south, it curved in against the uneven cliffs to form a beautiful crescent. There were tide pools she'd loved to explore. Was that what Webb was doing, or was he walking? Would he be surprised to see her—angry or glad? She had almost forgotten why she had come out here, conscious only of the need to see him and read the look in his sun-gold eyes when he first saw her. She had done something very stupid by coming out here alone to look for him, in spite of all the warnings she'd been given, but she was sick of warnings. She could look after herself.

The purse had grown heavy on one shoulder and Anne shifted it to the other before she stepped out from behind the rocks, giving her elephant a pat for good luck as she did. But instead of the stretch of wide, uncluttered beach she expected, she was brought up short by tall pilings, sunk deep into the sand. A *deck*? She looked up and saw that one end had been dug into the cliff itself—there were actually hewn-out steps leading down to it from the clifftop, cypresses shielding a wrought-iron fence with a gate that squeaked as it swung in the breeze. And the deck obviously doubled as a boat dock; she could see the winches, a canvas-covered shape of a boat directly overhead. Damn Danny Verrano, he was a vandal! This was *her* land now, and she'd have this monstrosity torn down . . .

And then she heard their voices. Soft, lazy laughter first, and Anna-Maria's voice sounding husky.

"I have always wanted to make love like this—in the open and under the sun. I am glad that we found each other again, *querido*. Aren't you?"

Listening frozen, as if she had turned into stone herself, Anne heard Webb say, "I wasn't at all sure at first, you tawny-skinned bitch! But now—I guess I never quite got over you, Ria."

"Is that why you never married again? Even after you thought I was dead? Did you suffer when you thought you had lost me forever?"

"Goddamn you, I almost went crazy. I should have killed you when I first set eyes on you again, instead of listening to your lies!"

"But they were not all lies, and you know that now. I suffered, too. And I know what they did to you when you refused to work for them any longer, those dirty capitalist assassins! But we shall both get our revenge now, hmm?"

"I haven't yet decided if I can trust you, Ria my love. Especially since you're mixed in with a bunch of capitalist assassins yourself." Webb's voice was dry. They were both unconscious of everything but each other as Anna-Maria raised herself on one elbow to look down into his sardonic face.

"But you can trust me. Didn't I tell you that I would give you an alibi for the time that Karim . . . vanished? And as for Harris Phelps and the other—pah, I spit on them! They are useful only to change the existing structure, and after that—no, you must listen to me and believe me, Webb. I am telling you all this, you see, because I know what you are! Yes, and I'll tell you something else, Harris knows, too. I was watching the monitor one night, and I heard him telling *her*. That bitch—that bastard Reardon's daughter. He was warning her against you, he even gave her a gun to use against you. I heard him say that you are a contract man, a man who will kill for pay. You killed some girl she knew in London, and a man called Frazier who was a CIA agent. And you are with a Mafia, sí? So what does one more killing matter? I will help you. I admit that I am jealous of her—I hate the thought that you have made love to her; I would like to see her suffer! And in any case"—her voice rose slightly, as she could read no expression in his eyes—"you can see now how dangerous she can be to *you*, as well as to the rest of us? I'll help you cover it up—it won't matter, we can make her disappear, too. You have to kill her to be safe, don't you see that?"

At last he sighed, putting his hand up to shade the sun from his eyes, its shadow like a bar across his face. "Okay, Ria. I guess you've got me convinced. But you'll have to tell me more about *your* plans, baby, You've got a little something of your own cooked up, haven't you? And if it's profitable, I want in. We're supposed to be a team now, remember?"

Anne had started to back away, one step at a time; not able to take her eyes off their shadows; the shapes of their naked bodies lying together on the slatted boards. She was shivering —with blind terror and reaction—and part of her mind still screamed no, no, what she had heard wasn't real, wasn't true. And the other, primitive unreasoning side of her wanted to kill them both—take the gun she carried out of her purse and aim it and fire through the boards, shooting until there were no more bullets left.

She *had* walked into a nightmare after all.

She almost cried out when she backed into the huge rock. Her elephant hadn't brought her luck after all. For a few moments she leaned against it, trying to still the sobbing sound of her breathing, afraid that they might hear it. There was the low murmur of voices—Ria's mostly, with an occasional comment from Webb. Once, she actually heard him laugh. The sound galvanized her into moving. He could talk about killing her and *laugh*, admiring the other woman's clever viciousness. Everything he had done with her and said to her had been calculated pretense.

The sun was slanting towards the horizon, and at any moment they might decide to leave. If they stood up, they would see her. Suddenly, all Anne wanted to do was to flee—as far as she could from the sound of their voices and the ugly truth. She slid around the rock, still with her back to it, feeling her way with her palms. Its rough, shell-encrusted surface stung her hands and snagged at her thin skirt. She felt very cold, with the wind biting through to her skin, and her legs felt weak.

When she reached the cave mouth it looked like the entrance to hell. It must be the smoke in the air—the sun seemed magnified, sending crimson rays all the way inside the tunnel, reflecting off salt-rime. When she forced herself to go inside again, Anne could see her elongated shadow running ahead of her. Running—get away, get away! The thought pounded in her head like the drumbeats of blood in her temples. She mustn't get lost. One more turn and she'd be safe in the darkness again, feeling her way back to safety and sanity.

Something tripped her, and she fell, sprawling. Fortunately, the floor of the cave was sandy here, so close to the ocean that had tunneled its way through what had originally been no more than a crack in the rocks. Anne lay there, gasping for a few moments, tasting sand and salt in her mouth. When her breath came back, she scrambled painfully to her hands and knees. And then she saw, her eyes dilating with the shock of horror piled upon horror, what had tripped her. An *arm*— bloated and turning blue with the shreds of what had once been a shirt clinging to it. A hand with swollen fingers, extended claw-like, gold signet ring glinting dully on one finger. She recognized the ring. The decaying odor she had taken for rotting sea-kelp assailed her nostrils, making her gag before she heard herself scream. It was involuntary; the sound was torn from her throat before she could stop it. Thrown back from the walls that enclosed her to reverberate against her eardrums and in her head.

Karim. She had found Karim.

Chapter Forty-five

"I'm BEGINNING TO FEEL COLD. Look at the sun! It looks as if it's going to burst." Ria stood up, stretching. Consciously proud of her body, she posed it against the sun. She wanted Webb to want to make love to her again. She didn't know how it had happened—perhaps it was since she had discovered that he had changed as much as she had changed—but she knew now that she wanted him for her own. He used to treat her tenderly and protectively, as if she were made of glass, but now he treated her as a woman needed to be treated—roughly and fiercely. She gloried in the fact that he was as ruthless and cynical as she was. The fact that he was an assassin, a killer for pay, only made her glad, even proud. She was sick of the effete intriguers she had had to cultivate and play along with; she had needed, all these years, to have someone like herself whom she could confide in and share with. And she admired him all the more for not having been taken in by her in the beginning. Now, at last, with all the cards on the table, they could work together.

He sat up, watching her, and she stretched again, provocatively. "Well? What shall we do now? Put on our clothes and our polite faces and go back to the others, or . . ." Out of habit, her eyes ran up and down the beach to make sure they were alone. Unbroken stretch of sand, marked only by the waves, except for . . . she cried out with sudden alarm and rage, "*Look*, Webb! There are footprints! They come up right here . . ."

And then they both heard the sound. A scream—a woman's scream, echoing hollowly. Followed by another, and another.

"Christ!" Webb swore. There were more precarious steps, leading down from the deck onto the beach, but he seemed to uncoil his body from its semiprone position as swiftly as a leopard, poised for an instant before he sprang from the edge of the deck onto the crisp sand below. He was already running when, after a moment's hesitation, Ria followed him. Before she had left Cuba she had been trained in guerrilla fighting, and her body was lithe and firm-muscled. Her hesitation had only been to snatch up the gun she always carried with her. It had a silencer fitted, and she knew how to use it.

It was too late to blame herself for having given in to hysteria; too late already when she pressed both hands over her mouth—as much to stop herself from gagging as to cut off her own involuntary screams. Anne knew it when she saw the shadow. She scrambled to her feet and tried to run, but again it was just as if she were living out one of her nightmares. The damp sand sucked at her shoes, and he caught her and spun her around all too easily.

"What the hell were you doing, spying . . ." He sounded out of breath and furious at the same time. She managed to wrench one arm free, scrabbling in her purse for the gun in a last-ditch attempt at self-preservation. She couldn't see his face, since his back was to the crimson sunlight, but she knew that he was still naked, fresh from lying with that woman. Hate combined with primitive terror, making her keep on struggling; fighting against his cruel grip on her wrist, beating and kicking at him; biting his arm and tasting salt blood in her mouth, until swearing, he twisted her around and the purse dropped from her shoulder with everything spilling out of it. He held her against his body now, with both arms twisted up behind her back. The pain became unbearable and she opened her mouth to scream, only to feel his hand clamp over her mouth.

The sun shone in her eyes, almost blinding her through the glaze of tears, and Anna-Maria was only an outline as she drawled, "It's a good thing you've got the bitch under control, *mi querido*. Otherwise I'd have enjoyed shooting her. And maybe that's what we ought to do—she knows too much to let her go. We can leave her here with her dead lover, and let the crabs and the ocean take care of her."

"You're far too blood-thirsty, my love. And not too practical. Don't you think we ought to find out just who knows she came out here—first?"

Anne began to kick backwards and struggle again until she felt he would break her arms; and then she sagged against him, feeling his body against hers in a travesty of what had been between them before. The tears had begun to stream down her face now, and she was ashamed of the display of weakness.

"But she's here, and she heard us talk—we can't let her go back and tell them! We could kill her now and stuff her body back in one of those little caves—where the tide last night brought *his* body. See where it has become wedged in?" Anna-Maria's voice was quite normal, even casual. She might have been talking of what to do with the dirty laundry.

"The difference between a professional and an amateur lies in covering all the possibilities before you act," Webb said coldly. He still held her fast, although by now he must have sensed she was incapable of any more fight. "I'm not having anything pinned on me. So we find a safe place to stash her away until we find out if she was sent here to spy on us or came on her own—and who she told."

"What difference does it make? And where would we put her? I think it's a waste of time." Anna-Maria sounded sullen. There was vicious hatred in the look she directed at Anne. But at the same time, she had been trained to follow orders, and Webb seemed to have taken charge. As long as he was being practical, and not soft . . .

Anne heard them arguing back and forth over her head, and it seemed unreal to hear herself discussed as if she weren't there.

"Ask her—ask her who knows she came out here. If she tries

to scream again, I'll fix her. And if she's reluctant to talk, I know how to make her—her kind is always soft, I can tell she's not used to pain or to rough treatment."

"Shut up, Ria! We haven't got time for that. We should be getting back and establishing an alibi for ourselves. You can restrain yourself for a little while. Afterwards . . ." The way he let his words trail off was both a threat and a promise, and Anne felt a trickle of ice run down her spine. There was death in the gun Anna-Maria carried, still pointed at her. Death and betrayal in the way Webb held her.

In the end it was he who came up with a solution. "The boat. It has a canvas cover. And it's hardly likely anyone would think of looking there. In any case, the tide's already starting to come back in, and it'll wash away all the footprints on the beach. If we can make it seem like she was scared and decided to run away . . ."

Anna-Maria's smile wasn't really a smile at all. A cruel curving of her lips that showed her strong white teeth.

"How very clever of you, darling! Yes, that's it. And I can tell we are going to work very well together."

Craig Hyatt had spent most of the afternoon watching videotapes. He knew that the monitoring system had broken down during last night's storm; but they had a couple of pretty good Sony machines that operated with any television set. Harris Phelps was downstairs with Yves Pleydel, trying to calm everyone down, and it was Sal Espinoza who was obliging enough to bring up a selection of tapes from the vault.

"While everyone else is busy, you might want to catch up on the action you've been missing," he said with one of his lazy smiles.

Tactfully, then, he had left Craig alone. And with reason. Apart from certain other episodes, they were mostly of Anne. Not the passive, cold creature he remembered from the days of their marriage. The woman he watched seemed to be a different being altogether—a wildly passionate, sensual female who gave as much as she took. Who seemed to have lost all modesty and reserve. He watched her with the Egyptian, Karim, hardly able to believe it was the same shy, inhibited girl he had married and taken as a virgin—tried to arouse. She seemed drugged with passion . . .

And then he watched her with Webb Carnahan, volume turned up, perversely. So that was how she could be—how she needed to be treated. Like a whore . . . His palms were sweating, and he felt an ache in his groin. So that was how he should have treated her, instead of trying to be patient and tender. She'd leaned against him, unresisting, when he'd offered to take her away. An act, or genuine?

Find out, his senses told him. *Find out!* Down one floor and down a short corridor. This big mausoleum of a house reminded him of an old hotel he'd once stayed in. Why did some people choose to build mansions to live in? And now all this belonged to Anne—through the generosity of Harris Phelps, who had made sure his room adjoined hers . . . Phelps hadn't seemed to mind his turning up. Maybe they had one of those modern arrangements that were so fashionable in some international circles. Craig Hyatt was a practical man who prided himself on his clear thinking, but he couldn't help the surge of purely primitive rage that swept through him for a moment. Damn Anne for a conniving, false-faced bitch! Obviously, she had learned to let go. Why couldn't she have done it with him?

He met Harris coming out of Anne's room, his face wearing a look of concern. Before Craig could speak, Harris said, "Hyatt, have you seen Anne? She told me she was going to rest, but she's gone from the room—and the gun I gave her is gone, too."

They had tied her up and gagged her and left her to suffocate—if she didn't die of a chill first. Anne heard herself moan with sheer terror, and the sound was muffled and hollow. She was lying uncomfortably on her back on the bottom of the small motorboat; the canvas cover was drawn tautly back into place so that it cut off the light and most of the air her lungs craved.

"Sorry, baby," Webb had murmured, leaning over her as he made sure the knots were tied fast. "But all's fair in love . . . you should have remembered what I told you last night."

Over his voice she'd heard Anna-Maria's jeering laugh. "All's fair in love and war, yes? And I am *not* sorry. I would like to see you suffer a little before you die—it will give you something to think about until we return for you."

The wind was blowing harder. She wanted to struggle and thrash about as she had when they had dragged and pushed her back out of the cave and up the steps to the deck. Anna-Maria had emptied out her purse; she had laughed contemptuously when she found the gun.

"So you had a little gun, huh? And you were afraid to use it, or too slow . . . it doesn't matter now."

If she struggled, the boat might go over the edge . . . the tide had started to come in already; Anne thought the roar of the waves was growing louder—and the sound of water sucking greedily around the wooden pilings that supported the deck.

It was hard to keep from panicking. She had told Jean Benedict not to tell . . . everyone would be looking for her and no one would know until it was too late. Sometime during the night one of them or both of them would come and lower the boat over the edge. Or perhaps they'd take her out with weights attached to her body and let her sink. So simple. She couldn't come back then, like Karim . . .

What made this worse than the Dream was knowing she wouldn't wake up—knowing that of all the ways in which he could have killed her, Webb, who knew of her hidden terror, had chosen this way.

"Sometimes she can be a headstrong, disobedient little brat!" From somewhere hidden in the deepest recesses of her memory, she heard her mother's petulant voice. "Look at the way she keeps *spying* on me!"

She had been spanked and sent to bed; the threat of being

sent back to Deepwood by herself if she didn't learn to behave had made her cry herself to sleep.

"Don't forget to say your prayers, Anne." Her grandmother's voice had always been gentle, even when she was reproving her.

"Now I lay me down to sleep." That one had always scared her, with its ominous suggestion ". . . and if I die before I wake." She didn't—couldn't—remember any other prayers she'd learned by rote so long ago. She was going to die—oh God, why hadn't he made it quick? Why hadn't he let Ria shoot her? She didn't want life to end like this—dying in slow stages by anticipation before the final end.

A fresh paroxysm of primitive, hysterical terror took hold of her as she fought the gag in her mouth, trying to scream, scared by the sounds that came from her own throat. She struggled, after all, and felt the boat rock slightly. Or was it the rising wind that had done it? Breathing became difficult when she started to sob.

She mustn't, she mustn't! She might drown in her own tears. If she didn't give in, if she tried to *think*—people had escaped from worse predicaments. Think of all the books she'd read, the movies she'd watched. Wasn't survival the primal instinct?

Anne forced herself to lie very still, concentrating just on that much, until the rising tide of hysteria had ebbed somewhat. She had reached the point when she had nothing left to lose—except her life. And she was still alive, they had left her here alone; she had a little time, at least. *Concentrate!* she told herself fiercely. *Don't give in, don't give them that satisfaction.*

She tested the knots that bound her wrists and ankles, and found them surprisingly loose. Her circulation hadn't been cut off yet, and the rope that had been lying on the bottom of the boat was old. Her wrists had been tied behind her back. If she could bring her ankles up to where her fingers could reach for *those* knots—it was worth a try at least. There was no convenient broken glass lying around, no old rusty knife she could use to saw through the rope. Just her fingers, before they became too chilled to use.

"Has anybody seen Anne?" Harris Phelps made the question sound casual. Yves Pleydel and the cameramen were still outside taking background shots of the unusual color effects the smoke from the fire had produced in the sky. Yves had let himself get too caught up in the goddamned movie itself, leaving "those other details" to Harris and Espinoza, since Randall had taken off. He had grumbled at the fact that no one was around when he needed them—meaning Anne, of course, and Webb Carnahan, who turned up belatedly with Anna-Maria, of all people, holding hands and acting for all the world as if they were on vacation—or a second honeymoon.

No one had noticed or remembered seeing Anne Mallory at all during the day. They'd all been too occupied with their own affairs—making up their minds if earning double pay plus a bonus was incentive enough to keep them here with a fire raging a few miles away. But by now most of them had realized there was no danger as long as they stayed on the island, and it had begun to seem like an adventure. After all, the winds were blowing the other way, and it wasn't as if they were actually marooned.

"I can't understand where she would have gone!" Harris said. His fingers brushed nervously at his mustache.

Espinoza shrugged. "Women! Who knows? Perhaps she felt in the mood to take a solitary walk. To think. Perhaps she wanted to escape from her ex-husband?"

"Where would she escape to? None of the cars is missing— I checked. Palumbo hasn't seen her either. It's starting to get dark, and if she isn't back . . ."

"You are both looking so grim!" Anna-Maria sauntered up. She had left Webb arguing with Yves Pleydel, who was furious because neither Webb nor Anne had been available when he needed them.

"What do you think—that you are being paid to be on vacation?" His accent became very pronounced when he was angry. But Webb could handle him, and she could find out from Sal

if little Anne had told anyone she was going down to the beach.
Then . . .

"But of course she'll be back," Espinoza was saying. He
looked relieved to see her. "Where have you been? Have you
seen Anne?"

She looked sunburned—and sated. He found himself wondering exactly what had been going on between her and Webb
Carnahan since he'd last spoken to them both.

"We've been sunbathing on the beach. And we didn't see
anyone. Why do you ask? Isn't she in her room?"

"No!" Harris Phelps looked annoyed. "And it's not like Anne
to just wander off on her own without a word . . ."

"Perhaps she went off with this Mr. Hyatt—her husband,
yes?"

"Hyatt's as anxious as I am." Harris's voice sounded stiff.

It was left to Sal Espinoza to interpose smoothly, with a
warning look at Anna-Maria, "He's on the radio right now,
is he not?" He gave a shrug as he explained to her, "Our tele-
phones no longer work—the fire, of course."

At that moment Craig Hyatt came outside, looking harried.
In a gesture quite uncharacteristic of him he raked his fingers
through his hair.

"I'm not sure what the hell's up. But apparently the coast
guard and the navy have been called in to help fight the fire,
along with personnel from Fort Ord. They say they might
need to billet some of their people here—it's a convenient spot
—I'm quoting the coast guard commander now—and they've
learned you have a helicopter pad here . . ." He let his words
trail off, looking from one suddenly still face to another. He
said distractedly, "Hell! I don't know if it means something
or not—any more than you do. It could be Reardon's Medici
hand at work, or it might not be. As far as I know he's sitting
tight until he gets more feedback. But . . ." And then quite
abruptly he cut his speech short when he asked, looking directly
at Harris, "Has Anne turned up yet?"

Chapter Forty-six

THE MOON CAME UP EARLY—an orange lantern hanging in a smoky sky. Very few people on the island noticed it. Harris Phelps was giving a lavish party for the cast and crew of *Greed for Glory*—an extra fringe benefit for staying on. Very few noticed that Harris himself wasn't present. The food was great and there was unlimited booze—who cared?

Yves Pleydel stood off to one corner, nibbling on a fingernail. The music had been turned up too loud—it blasted his ears. Sourly he watched Sal Espinoza, who positively oozed Latin charm this evening, playing surrogate host. He wished Espinoza would take his ex-wife Claudia off his hands. And he wished most of all that he hadn't become so carried away with the idea of finishing up the scenes that had to be done here that he'd persuaded Harris to keep everybody on. They should have all left while the going was good, and scattered in their various directions. Now —something was up. The coast guard and the military, tipped off by Reardon no doubt, might soon be crawling about everywhere, prying into things. He wondered angrily what Webb Carnahan had had to do with this latest move.

"Hey! I am still here; remember me?" Claudia pulled at his arm petulantly and Pleydel forced a smile. He almost felt sorry for the silly little bitch. In spite of too much makeup (why did so many Italian women insist on ringing their eyes with black?) she looked rather haggard. She had had a shock last night, and it had taken a clever combination of threats and bribery to keep her from pushing everyone else across the border into hysteria.

"*Petite*, how could I forget you?" She had never understood sarcasm, of course. It was one of her more fortunate traits. "And you have finished your drink. I'll get you another . . ."

She was already quite drunk. Another drink might make her pass out, and leave *him* free.

Claudia said with a pathetic attempt at dignity, "You do not have to treat me as if I am a child! I tell you that I saw what I saw! And I know a few things, too." She laughed at the look that crossed Pleydel's face. "Are you surprised? Do you think I am completely blind? In any case, Karim told me a few things —he asked me to come back to Egypt with him. Perhaps it was not him but the other person he struggled with who fell from the cliff—or perhaps he had to leave very quickly when he heard what has happened to his uncle."

"What? What are you talking about?" Pleydel grasped her by the arms, shaking her.

"Stop—you are hurting me. And we are not married now." Something in his eyes made Claudia tone down her indignation to mutter sullenly, "I heard it on the radio very late last night, or maybe it was this morning, I don't know. That his uncle —something about an attempted assassination. So then I thought . . ."

Yves left her with her mouth falling open and made his way purposefully towards Espinoza. At about the same time Anna-Maria slipped unobtrusively from the room.

The bottom of the boat was damp, and by the time she had worked her ankles free, Anne was chilled to the marrow and shivering uncontrollably. It was getting darker and darker. She could hear the sound of the tide coming in—waves covering the beach now, dangerously insidious sound of lapping water and an occasional big breaker that flung itself furiously against the cliff. *Oh God*, she thought desperately, *I've got to get myself free!* It was night, and they'd be coming for her. *No—don't think it, don't give way to hysteria now.* She'd have been missed, and Harris would send people to look for her. Jean— Jean knew where she'd gone, and she was bound to tell someone, especially when Webb turned up with Ria.

Webb! Tears came unbidden to Anne's eyes, stinging them. What a fool she'd been to come looking for him. The memory of his mocking words hurt her worse than the ache in her wrists and shoulders.

"You should have remembered what I told you last night, baby. All's fair in love . . ."

And Ria, finishing his sentence for him with a note of laughing triumph in her voice.

But that hadn't been what he'd said at all. He'd told her that he was crazy in love with her. He—Anne froze then, in midthought. Over the low thunder of the surf she heard another sound. The squeal of rusty hinges? Not yet, not yet, her mind screamed, and then she heard the vibration of soft footfalls along the boards.

She knew who it was. It was as if her nerve ends had sensed his presence even before he ripped the canvas cover away and leaned over her. She was seized by a feeling of inevitability, of déjà vu that made her still and unresisting when he lifted her up. She didn't even wonder at the fact that when he'd put her on her feet he held her closely against the warm, hard length of his body. He hadn't come here to kill her—it was to save her.

"Oh, Annie-love, I'm sorry!" he said softly against her damp, salt-sprayed hair; and she didn't even flinch when she saw the knife blade glitter in the strangely diffused light. He used it only to cut away the rope that held her wrists pinioned, and then he ripped away the gag, putting his mouth in its place for a long sweet instant.

The truth she'd spent so much time trying to hide from was that she didn't care who he was or what he was or even how many people he had killed. It was a terrible thing to know about herself, that she could accept everything he'd done because she loved him and he loved her. Leaning against him while he wrapped his windbreaker around her shoulders and started to massage her bruised wrists, Anne felt as if she'd been running against a strong wind for a long, long time and had just crossed the line.

"I see you were resourceful enough to get your ankles free! Can you walk? I hope to hell you can, because that moon's going to scale the cliff any time now, and it looks like a damned yellow searchlight!"

Anne was still shivering, trying to keep her teeth from chattering. She looked up towards the clifftop and felt Webb's fingers tighten over hers.

"Uh-uh. Not that way, baby. Because that's the way Ria will be coming if she decides to come looking. We're going to have to get wet, but if you remember your way back through the caves, we ought to make it before the tide gets much higher."

He hadn't asked her to trust him. Perhaps he knew he didn't need to. She nodded without speaking. Committing herself irrevocably. But hadn't Webb just done the same? He had gone against orders and expediency by coming back here for her, she realized that.

He pulled the canvas cover back over the boat, then he gripped her hand and started pulling her along with him urgently. Now was not the time to ask him questions, especially not about Ria.

Once she was out of the room filled with all those stupid, laughing people, all intent on getting drunk to show how much they were enjoying themselves, Anna-Maria slipped off her shoes. There was no indecision in any of her movements as she ran lightly down the deserted passageway that led to a room opening onto the garden. She paused only once, to retrieve the pair of rubber-soled shoes and black suede jacket she'd hidden earlier. Her dark-blue velvet jumpsuit wouldn't reflect the moonlight and would make her almost invisible in the darkness. Only the luminous dial of her watch glowed. She checked the time and smiled. It would take her less than ten minutes, if she ran all the way, to get to the little gate that was concealed by those twisted cypresses. She was athletic and slim, it would be easy to get there and back again without slowing down or losing her breath.

"Trust no one. And always make certain of even the tiniest little detail." As a member of the undercover terrorist organization known as the Red Guard, she had been trained well and had adapted to that training easily after her earlier training with the Cuban guerrillas. It had been her slight body and her innocent girl's face that had made them choose her for the assignment to the United States.

Anna-Maria smiled as she began to run, her feet making no sound on the path she followed. They had called her precocious as a child, and she had hated her parents for sticking her in a convent while they traveled. She had run away with the young man who seduced her and joined one of the guerrilla bands under Guevara, learning much more *there* than she could have under the tutelage of the nuns. Later, when she had come back crying to them with her pathetic story of seeing her parents shot before her eyes, the stupid cows had taken her in and smuggled her to the United States. Their contact there had arranged everything, including her job at the Languages Institute. It had all been very easy, until she had begun to fall in love with the man who was her quarry. Love was an emotion for fools! But still, a woman needed a man of her own who could be her equal. The Webb she had rediscovered wasn't the dotingly protective young man she remembered. He was harder, tougher, and more cynical. The fact that Harris Phelps had said he was an extremely clever contract man had decided her to take him, partially at least, into her confidence.

If he had been doing his part this evening, she would be

sure—but still, she wasn't going to take any chances. It was necessary that Anne Mallory, whom she hated as both a rival and a symbol of the typical spoiled capitalist-leech female, should die. Being what she was, Anna-Maria would not admit even to herself that there might be another reason she wanted the other woman to die.

She reached the top of the cliff, the gate, and paused there, checking the loads in her handgun. The moon, which had seemed to be following her, was still partially hidden behind the trees, and she let her eyes get used to the darkness, calling softly, "Webb? Are you there?" Only the ocean answered her, and now she could see the outline of the boat, its canvas cover still drawn tautly over it. The boards of the deck were damp from sea spray; it meant the tide was getting higher. Perhaps he had come as silently as she had and done what he was supposed to do. If he had, he should be back at the house to meet her by now. She had given him exactly twenty minutes before she followed him out of that hot, overcrowded room.

Perhaps, she thought. But just in case . . . A shaft of moonlight lit up the side of the boat, and she smiled as she leveled the gun, holding it across one wrist as she took aim.

"Good-bye, Miss Mallory," she called softly before she fired, emptying the clip, seeing the little holes spring up all the way across the top of the canvas in a pretty pattern.

The silencer and the crashing waves would cover any noise. She reloaded the gun with the ease and swiftness of long practice as she turned and sped back toward the house to look for Webb. She didn't notice what appeared to be the dim riding lights of a small fishing boat that rocked less than a mile out to sea, and if she had, she would not have paid it any attention. The moon, as it rose higher, still retained its jack-o'-lantern glow, framed by another more ominous glow in the sky to the east. The fire.

Harris Phelps prided himself on his detachment and resolution, his ability to meet and cope with any crises that arose.

But the goddamned fire! He hadn't anticipated that it would be allowed to run out of control until it had assumed the proportion of a national disaster. He found it easy enough to calm everybody else down. Espinoza and Plevdel had too much at stake not to cooperate when he had told them what he planned to do.

"So we put the ever-famous Plan B into effect, eh?" Sal had said with one of his infernal sardonic smiles.

"Something like that," Harris replied curtly. "You can understand why, at all costs, we must preserve an atmosphere of normalcy here? Once I've had time to pack away all those tapes and get them out safely, we can act without delay. And there will be nothing Reardon can do to stop the avalanche."

"And Reardon's daughter?" Espinoza said softly, noticing that Harris flushed with annoyance.

"There's no need for Anne to become too involved," he said stiffly. "I'm sure Hyatt will see that she's safe."

But then, soon afterwards, he couldn't find Anne. Her strange disappearance had both disturbed and distracted him, costing him valuable time.

Espinoza had been right, he was to think angrily later. He had come dangerously close to letting Anne become a weakness, disregarding all his father's warnings that had helped him shape his life so far. He would have sent a search party after her, if Sarah Vesper hadn't cornered him on his way upstairs.

"Harris darling, I know how very upsetting this all must be, but I thought you ought to know. *I'm* worried about her, too, you know! And so is Hal. So when Jean told me . . ."

He had been impatient enough to interrupt her. "Told you what, Sarah? For God's sake, it's getting dark, and . . ." He'd made light of it to Craig Hyatt, who had started to act far too proprietary since his arrival. And he was relieved that Hyatt, to keep busy, had volunteered to keep monitoring the radio. "Told you what?" he repeated.

"I was coming to that, Harris. She said she'd met Anne com-

ing out of Webb's room, and well—Jean told her he'd gone
down to the beach, so Anne said she might go to look for him.
She asked Jean not to tell anyone else, so of course she *didn't*.
Until Webb turned up with that Cuban woman he's taken up
with recently, and neither of them had seen her. I mean, if
she's had a fall, or got herself lost . . ."

A wave of rage had made Harris Phelps brush at his
mustache, giving Sarah a surface smile. If she'd gone chasing
after Carnahan again like a bitch in heat, disregarding everything he'd told her, all the warnings, she deserved whatever
she'd gotten into.

"Anne was born on this island, Sarah, and she knows every
inch of it. Actually, I suppose I should have mentioned it, but
with so many things happening at once—I found a note she'd
left, after I let myself get alarmed. She said she needed a very
long walk to calm her down—in the moonlight. I've no doubt
she's at the other end of the island by now, but I did send
Palumbo after her. You might pass the word around to the
others if you don't mind. And thanks for telling me."

He'd told Hyatt, noting with malice the look of angry dis-
pleasure on the other man's face.

"I thought you told me that was all done with? And especially after what both you and I told her . . . damn!" He'd
looked up at Harris, frowning. "Do you think . . . ?"

They both knew what he meant. Harris shook his head
thoughtfully. "Ria was with him, remember. She would have
said something. It could be she really did get lost."

"I wonder where," Hyatt said, almost to himself.

Harris, still angry, told him abruptly that he was going down
to the vault.

"Need help?"

"No. You'd better stay here and keep monitoring the damn
radio, I suppose. We want to know what's happening about
our threatened invasion." He gave a slightly twisted smile.

"Palumbo's getting the 'copter ready, and he's going to be waiting for me."

Now, he was almost done. All the tapes stacked neatly away in airtight containers were labeled, but it had been easy to pick out the ones he wanted, although he'd deliberately scattered them in with others. The important ones were numbered instead of titled.

Harris straightened his shoulders and allowed a sigh of satisfaction to escape him as he snapped the locks on his case shut. He looked around the vault and shrugged. Pleydel would watch over his precious cans of film himself. And Hyatt could look out for Anne. It was a pity that she had turned out to be so deceitful and ungrateful after all, but he had more important things to think about right now.

Harris had reached the entrance to the vault when he saw Anna-Maria come slipping down the side stairway. She had a gun in her hand, but she lowered it with a sigh when she saw him.

"Harris? Thank goodness it is you. I thought that Webb . . . have you seen him?"

He said sharply, "I thought *you* were supposed to be watching him!"

"I was with him all the time. But when I went to powder my nose and came back, he was gone. I thought he might be here, or upstairs."

"He's not upstairs—not in the control room, anyhow. Hyatt's there, and he knows enough to keep the door locked." He looked at her sharply. "Jean Benedict says that Anne told her she was going down to the beach—to find Webb. Are you sure you didn't see her?"

"Oh!" Her eyes widened as if she had suddenly recalled something. "We had been walking, you know, and we came back to the dock—the boat that is usually there, you know the one? It was gone. But we were busy with other things and did not think about it." She dismissed Anne with a shrug as her eyes went to Harris's case. "The tapes? It's very wise of you to take them away before all those other people get here. But how will you leave? Surely not by car . . . ?"

He felt annoyed with her for the first time since he had known her, but in spite of his questioning thoughts—the boat, Anne, any connection? why should she attempt to get away? —he forced his voice to sound polite.

"I'm going to take the jeep as far as the landing pad. Palumbo has the helicopter all ready to go."

Anna-Maria seemed apprehensive. Her teeth nibbled at her lower lip while she frowned.

"Harris, you are sure that Webb does not know this? That there is no way he could have found out? Please—let me ride with you. I have this gun and I am very good with it. I never miss. And"—her voice grew suddenly venomous, surprising him —"I would very much enjoy killing the bastard!"

He seemed to hesitate, then he shook his head decisively.

"No. You'd better stay here with the others. And I have a rifle in the jeep. Palumbo will be armed, too, and I really don't think Carnahan would have had the time to get that far. You don't have to worry about me, or these tapes. I'm going to make sure they're put to very good use."

Harris gave her an impatient wave as he climbed into the jeep, hefting the heavy case onto the seat beside him. He had reached for the garage door opener when he noticed that Ria had come up to him as if she had something else to say. He turned his head impatiently.

She was smiling. She kept smiling after she had shot him very neatly between the eyes and his body slumped backwards.

"But I think that I and my friends will put those tapes to an even better use, Harris *amigo*," she said softly as she reached over the still twitching body for the square black case.

Chapter Forty-seven

THERE HAD BEEN A MOMENT, when Anne felt the icy water swirling up to her knees as she slipped down the last few steps, when sheer terror seized her again. The receding wave sucked greedily at her, filling her shoes, like weights, with water. Not death by drowning, not this way. She could face any other kind of ending with courage, if it had to be; but her nightmare took her by the throat, making her struggle so fiercely that they both almost lost balance.

She heard a voice gasping hoarsely, "Please, Webb, please don't make me, don't . . ."

He swore under his breath, backing her up against one of the wooden pilings and holding her there so hard she could feel splinters dig into her back. He held her until her struggles stopped, with the weight of his body and his mouth against hers.

Another wave roared up and around them, flinging itself against the cliff with a shower of spray, trying to take her back with it. This time she clung to him, and the salty wetness on her face was as much from tears as the flying sea spray.

"Annie." She felt his lips move against her ear. "Annie love, this is the only way. Do you understand? The caves—you can find your way through them blindfolded, can't you? I don't have a flashlight, I didn't have time to find one. So it's up to you. You can't let go and become hysterical *now*, love. We've got to try it. I don't want anyone finding you but me."

She nodded, forgetting that in the blackness down here he couldn't see her. But he had sensed the movement of her head, his hands slid down her arms to grip her hands again.

"I—I'm all right now," she whispered. "I'm sorry I panicked, but it was—too much like the Dream, suddenly. I can find my way back through the caves." If only her teeth would stop chattering!

Another wave, smaller than the last. The massive wooden post protected them from the backwash. But when they had to leave its protection and make a run for the rocks? Don't think about it—hold on to Webb's hand, tight grip of his fingers twined with hers. Like that first time, when he'd held her hand fast and wouldn't let her escape him.

"Okay. After the next one . . ." And then she could feel him grow stiff.

She hadn't heard the gate hinges squeak this time, but he had. Goddamnit! Ria, this soon? Someone else?

"Annie, don't move. Don't make a sound." His voice was lower than a sea whisper breathing into her ear. He felt the tautening of her body; and putting his face against hers, whisker stubble and all, he knew she had clamped her jaws tightly together.

Webb heard Ria's voice then, calling his name softly. Somehow, he knew that Anne had closed her eyes. The water came higher. His pants were soaked through already. If Ria didn't go away . . . if she stayed to wait for him . . .

Anne flinched when the popping noises sounded directly overhead. Tiny vibrations, making the boat creak.

"Good-bye, Miss Mallory . . ." Had she heard that or only imagined it? If Webb hadn't come for her when he had, she'd be dead now.

It seemed as if they had been standing there for ages, with cold numbing feet and legs and hands and the wetness soaking upwards with its salt sting.

Over Anne's shoulder, Webb saw the dim glow of light from

a boat, somewhere out to sea. He waited, counting the seconds off grimly in his mind until he was sure Ria had gone. He had time to wonder what was happening at the house, and elsewhere. If Joe Palumbo had managed to radio that message without having it monitored. He wished he knew what the fuck Reardon was up to—why he hadn't acted yet—or if he was going to.

"Webb?" Anne whispered, pulling his thoughts back to reality. "Webb, she's gone, isn't she? Because I—I don't have any feeling left in my legs. I don't even know if I can walk."

He hadn't heard the damn gate again, but that didn't mean a thing. Ria might not have bothered to close it again. And if she didn't find him back at the house . . .

"You're not going to walk, baby. You're going to run. Both of us. And hang on to me, I'm not going to let you go."

Running, or even walking, was going to be sheer agony, he knew. His back, which he had almost forgotten about earlier, was a solid mass of stinging pain that helped, in a way, to keep his mind clear.

He timed the advance and retreat of the encroaching water, and then, grabbing her hand firmly, he pulled her with him and began to run, feeling as if he were becoming part of her recurrent nightmare himself as both wet sand and undertow slowed them down so that they seemed to be moving in one place, getting nowhere. He concentrated on getting as far as the cave mouth. When they reached the underground garage —*when*, dammit, not if—that would be time enough to think about what came next.

The locked case was heavy, but she was stronger than she looked—always had been. Anna-Maria set it down carefully beside her before she searched his pockets for the key. She found a keyring, was meticulous enough to fit the smallest one into the lock to make sure it was the right one before she slipped them all into her pocket. She wished she could have stayed long enough to welcome Webb, but there was no time. She thought about the waiting helicopter and smiled again. She caught Harris Phelps's sagging body by the ankles and tugged until it came free and thudded to the floor. Too bad; she had almost come to admire him. Now he might have been a stuffed dummy. Killing meant nothing to her; she had killed before and would kill again if she had to. For an ideal, a dream of a better world where everyone would be equal.

She glanced towards the door that led into the cave passage, and her mouth, full and smiling a minute before, became hard. She would lock it. Or—better still—place one of the tiny explosive devices she had in her jacket pocket against it. The slightest jarring when someone tried to open it, would set off an explosion. She should do that with the door leading to the vault as well—it would put everyone off.

"Did you have to kill him?" The voice sent Anna-Maria spinning around on the balls of her feet like a cat, her hand already reaching for the gun in her waistband. She found herself looking into another gun and froze.

"I don't know what you mean," she said cautiously, watching him as he walked softly down the last two steps. "I came here to find Webb, and found *him* instead—poor Harris! I was just going to . . ."

"Don't," he said softly, and she heard the hammer on his gun click back, freezing her in place. He continued in the same gently conversational tone, "I think I know what you were just going to do. Take that little black case full of incriminating tapes and take off. Did he tell you he had the helicopter waiting? The only other question that comes to my mind is—*why?*" He had moved, until his back was now against the wall and he could cover both her and the stairway at the same time. "Was this Espinoza's idea or your own?"

"I do not think you understand." She was watching his eyes and the gun in his hand; her tongue came out to lick her lips.

"When I found Harris dead, I knew that someone had to do something. Before Reardon's men come."

"Ah yes. As a matter of fact, that's why I came down. Harris had the forethought to install a very powerful radio, and it seems we should expect an invasion at any time now. I thought I'd warn him to hurry. Were you going in his place?"

"Yes." She swallowed. "Why don't you come with me?" The gun muzzle pointing at her midriff was unwavering. She looked at it and back into his cold blue eyes. "Why don't you? You don't trust me—I don't trust you. We can watch each other."

Surprisingly, he smiled, shaking his head slightly. "But I'm not afraid of Reardon. You see, I'm supposed to be working for him. That's why I'm here. At the same time, I have no objections to your leaving. Yes, and taking those tapes with you. There's nothing like having a foot in both camps, is there? I'm sure you'll deliver them into the right hands, won't you? I'll tell you what—you give me your gun, and I'll take the cartridge clip from it and toss it into the back seat of that jeep. I'll watch you until you drive off and close the garage door behind you. After that, if you mean what you say, you can drive like hell until you get to that helicopter. If you don't hesitate, I'm sure you'll make it. But I'd like you to answer a few questions for me first, just to get the record straight. What did you do with Anne?"

Craig Hyatt didn't let any feelings into his eyes or his face as he listened to her spill everything, becoming vituperative towards the end. Most of it he had already guessed. Reardon's training hadn't been wasted.

Espinoza was a useful cover—she actually despised him because he was too subtle, too slow-moving, and lived like a capitalist. Webb Carnahan had somehow managed to get under her skin, but now her hatred of him almost overwhelmed her self-preservation instinct. She was certain that he had gone back to rescue Anne, that they were even now groping their way back here through the caves.

"He's soft for her, that silly, whey-faced bitch! Like Harris, like you! I would not have trusted him for a moment if I had not learned what he was—an assassin, a contract killer for the Mafia."

Hyatt's smile widened while his lips thinned. He was quite a handsome man, standing there in a relaxed yet watchful stance with that businesslike gun pointed at her middle.

"Uh-uh. You got taken in by our story, didn't you? Carnahan had Mafia connections—still has, for that matter. But he was never directly involved. Harris and I cooked up that story to convince Anne. A pity you got fooled along with her."

"What?" She almost screeched the word. Hate and fury blinded her. The thought that he had been stringing her along, fooling her all the time she thought she was fooling him, was almost unbearable.

Hyatt's sharply uttered words snatched her back to her senses —and caution.

"Cool it! I have scores to settle, too, and I intend to settle them. You get those tapes out of here and take them to Randall; he'll know how to handle the rest. And in the meantime" —his teeth showed for an instant—"I'll stick around and do my part in covering up. When he's dead, Webb Carnahan can take the blame for Harris and Karim. I'll take care of Anne."

He didn't know—he thought she was still one of *them*. Ria's laughter was almost hysterical. If he still wanted his sniveling ex-wife, she was glad she hadn't told him that she might very well be dead already. But she wouldn't let that bastard Webb take the credit for Karim.

"I killed Karim." She said it proudly. "You know he had been trained by the PLO? But he had let himself get too soft, and had begun to talk too much. He wasn't expecting what he got from me. His neck was broken before he fell over the cliff. It was just bad luck that his body was washed into the caves and got stuck in there—we were supposed to find it, so that Webb would have been the one under suspicion." She laughed again, and deliberately turning her back on him, climbed into the jeep. "I will not give up my gun—and if you shoot me, all the little explosives I am carrying will go off and blow you to pieces along with me. So, shall we call it a stalemate and say *adios* for now?"

Craig Hyatt kept his gun leveled while she started up the jeep. The garage door opened noiselessly, and she gave him a careless, insouciant wave before she drove out. He admired the fact that she had the presence of mind to press the button again once she was clear, so that the doors closed again. She was tough and resourceful in addition to being a very attractive woman, and he could not help admiring her, even while he felt regret at what he had to do. When he was sure she had gone, he took the tiny transmitter out of his pocket and gave the signal. He got through almost immediately; and once he had passed on his message, he settled down to wait. It should not be long now . . .

They were together, at least. In a damp darkness that made Anne think about being in the belly of a whale, closed in and pulsating with the surf. Rushing in and pulling out, changing and unchanging at the same time.

She did not want to think about the effort that it had taken to get this far, every step like a knife-thrust. "The little mermaid," she had thought, knowing even then that she was close to hysteria. The ocean was as icy as the arms of a selfish, long dead lover, wanting to take her and keep her. And yet she had struggled and fought for every inch, every foot, clinging to black rock that bruised and battered her, finding her way back into the gaping maw of her most frightening dreams—flung forwards and tugged back like a tiny, bobbing cork.

Coldness, wet coldness, was like millions of tiny icicles working their way deeper and deeper through skin and flesh to penetrate all the way to bone. Each new breath a further pain.

"You have to go first, Annie. You know the way."

In spite of the now-enveloping blackness she closed her eyes —it made it easier for her to find the way. The only difference between now and before was that now Webb was with her, his fingers tightly laced with hers.

The cave sloped very gradually upwards and they would soon get to slightly higher ground. But in the beginning every time a wave came roaring in with a crash of splintering foam, it was like being caught in a gigantic washing machine. Stumbling, losing balance, clawing for handholds on slippery rock walls where there were none, Anne now knew why travelers in the snow had the overpowering urge to lie down and slide into an icy sleep. It had to do with a numbness that seemed to spread to the brain itself, bringing with it a sense of not caring.

Something bumped against them and she went down, swallowing water. She thought of Karim and tried to scream, knowing she was drowning, but again Webb yanked her upwards, shouting at her furiously over the thunderous sound of the rushing tide.

"Damn you, Annie, you're not going to give up now, hear me?"

"I can't—I can't!" She sobbed chokingly, coughing up salt water. "*You* go on . . ."

"The hell I will! And get myself lost in here?"

She kept shaking her head wildly until he slapped her.

"Keep moving, Annie. We're making headway, I can feel it. You just keep concentrating on finding the way back and I'll take care of the rest. Okay, *move*! I'm in no shape to haul you all the way."

Anne gritted her teeth. Even her face felt like a mask of ice, but his slap and the further goads of his words made anger banish the feeling of lassitude and hopelessness that had been creeping into her earlier.

She started forwards again. Bully! How dare he strike her? When they stopped running, after the next two bends, she would . . .

Only a few feet further! The water was no longer a menace and a monster but a wetness she hardly felt. It was only her legs that refused to move any faster when she wanted to run. They felt like blocks of wood that didn't belong to her at all.

Now the cave was more like a tunnel, widening. The sound of the pursuing waves seemed to subside into sullen, rumbling murmurs as the ground rose more sharply, becoming more rocky than sandy.

The door—suppose it was locked from the other side? There was no light, no sound except the incessant sea-murmuring and the sound of heavy, rasping breathing. The door should be right ahead. It was heavy, and well insulated around the edges to keep the moist air out of the garage. The door, too, was new. God, don't let it be locked!

Anne had been trying to run, driven on by a mixture of rage and desperation, feet moving clumsily in slow motion. She knew she had to stop and tell Webb about the door, and half turned her head, trying to find him behind her. She felt her wet, water-logged shoe slip on a loose stone, her ankle twist sickeningly.

There was no time and no way to stop herself from falling—sprawling heavily forward with the unexpectedness of it, bringing Webb crashing on top of her. She felt what seemed like an explosion in her head, red streaks of light, and then blackness.

Chapter Forty-eight

IT WAS ANNE'S SOFT BODY that had saved *him* from injury. He had still been holding her hand, but as they fell, he had put out his other hand, feeling the pain jar all the way up to his shoulder in spite of the numbness of cold. Almost immediately he rolled over onto his side, feeling for her; cursing steadily under his breath while he ran his hand over her, finding her neck and running his fingers gently under her wet, clinging hair that still contrived to feel like silk. He found the bump on her forehead, touched her closed eyelids, and put his ear against her back, listening, and praying while he listened, for the sound of breathing.

At least she *was* breathing. She had been knocked out by the fall, and would probably end up with a slight concussion. Forgetting all his own aches and pains, Webb turned her over, very gently, very carefully, and checked for any other injuries. Her pants were torn at the knee and he thought he felt the warm stickiness of blood. She was soaked to the skin, just as he was, and her flesh felt cold and clammy. He had to get her indoors and into dry clothes. They couldn't be far from the entrance now—she had tried to tell him so when she had stumbled and fallen. She couldn't be allowed to stay out here, which meant that he had to risk running into Ria or anyone else.

He tried to lift her but couldn't, weakened himself by their flight and his wounded back and their struggle against the tide.

496

As gently as he could, he managed to drag her limp body up further; he ripped off his shirt and folded it with fingers that shook, in spite of himself, with cold and put it under her head.

He touched the bump on her forehead—it seemed to have become larger—and felt with relief the flutter of her breathing against his fingers.

Dammit, he would have to leave her here while he went ahead and checked things out. And Webb swore again when he realized that all he had was a knife. The gun he'd shoved into his waistband earlier would be wet and useless now. He frowned, sitting back on his haunches while he massaged Anne's limp wrists, then her temples, very lightly. It was Ria he had to be careful with. But if he told her he'd gotten rid of Anne, and then had difficulty getting back through the caves . . . she might buy it. Slim chance, but one he'd have to take.

He's started to move away, feeling along the damp, rocky walls, when he heard her moan. "Webb . . . ? The door . . ."

"Hush, love." He came back to her and kissed her salty lips. "Listen, I don't want you to move, do you understand? You fell and hit your head, you probably have a slight concussion. Wait for me, I'll be back."

Without waiting for her incoherent murmur of protest, he forced himself to turn his back on her and go forwards again. "The door," she'd said. It had to be right ahead, if he remembered right.

It opened easily when he found it, and he almost fell inside, feeling warmth and light that made him dizzy and blinded for a while. Completely off guard. Bitterness seared itself across his brain when he heard the casual, almost friendly voice that greeted him.

"Hi, Carnahan. Thought I'd wait here for you. I suppose you know there's hell to pay?"

Hyatt. Instinct made him stand where he was, swaying slightly with exhaustion while he tried to blink salt-stinging eyes back into focus. He tried to act more dazed then he felt. "Christ, I didn't think I'd make it. What—where's Ria?"

Craig Hyatt's body wavered, blurred around the edges before Webb could see him clearly. And the gun he held.

"Ria? She was looking for you, you know. But she decided not to wait. She seemed rather perturbed—do you know why?"

Webb took a step forwards, risking it, and the gun muzzle lifted slightly.

"What the hell's that for?"

"Protection, naturally. Especially after what happened to poor Harris." Hyatt grinned. "I put him in your car. Your wife is a careless housekeeper. She just left him lying here, with blood all over the place. I'm tidy myself." And then, still in the same incongruously pleasant voice: "By the way, what did you do with Anne?"

Death looked out of Craig Hyatt's eyes, in spite of the friendly grin. Webb poised himself on the balls of his feet, hoping they would carry him forwards, even while he shrugged.

"I followed orders, that's all . . . And then, like an idiot, I got myself trapped by the tide, and lost my way in the goddamn caves. You ought to issue a road map." He let a note of bluster creep into his voice, hoping like hell that Anne would stay quiet. "Hey—why the gun?"

"As I just said—for protection. And persuasion." The mask dropped. Hyatt's face hardened. "I asked you about Anne."

"And I told you. You going to shoot me or let me go get some dry clothes on?"

He could only hope his bluff worked. No way of knowing what Ria had told Hyatt or where the man stood himself.

"I don't think I believe you," Craig Hyatt said softly. His voice hardened. "You have a gun. Drop it."

Webb shrugged. "It isn't any good anyhow. Got wet, like the rest of me." He pulled it out of his waistband and dropped it, keeping his eyes on Hyatt. "Would you mind telling me which side of the fence you're on?"

Craig's smile didn't reach his eyes. "Like you, I'm straddling the fence right now. But you see, I have the gun, so you'll follow orders. *My* orders this time. Walk over to that wall and press the button. When the doors open, get in your car and start it up. You're going to take our late friend for a ride and dump him. I'll leave the 'where' to your imagination."

"And after that?"

"After you've proved your loyalty and your—sincerity, I really don't give a damn. You can keep going, or join the others upstairs. In any case, the last radio message I got said the coast guard is on its way in. I read that to mean our mutual employer. And he doesn't like untidy messes, does he?"

The Ferrari roared out of the garage like a bat out of hell, the sound of the powerful motor reverberating off the walls.

Lying where Webb had left her, with her head throbbing and her whole body a mass of bruises she hadn't even begun to feel yet, Anne heard the sound, not quite understanding what it meant. And then the explosion of gunfire as Craig, taking careful aim, shot out the two rear tires.

The car seemed to take off into the air before it flipped over. He thought, with satisfaction, that he heard a scream of pure anguish before the dull whoosh of an explosion as it burst into flames. So much for Webb Carnahan. He hoped he'd had time to suffer before he died. But the screaming continued, and it came from a different direction.

Anne! So far he'd guessed right and calculated right. Now he had to find her. He hoped that at last she'd appreciate his cleverness.

Anne had managed to pull herself up into a sitting position with her back against the rock wall. She put her hands against her ears when the gunfire came.

They had killed him! She started to scream without knowing it, keening shrieks of pain and anguish that bent her double.

She rocked with agony until her throat closed up and she could only moan, like a mortally wounded animal.

Dead—he was dead. She wanted to die with him, she should have been beside him. She felt as if her heart had been torn out of her still-living body as she sobbed dryly.

"Anne?" Everything stilled inside her at the sound of the softly questioning voice. She lifted her head, very slowly; it felt as if it were bursting when she saw the tall silhouette framed against the light. Shattered pieces falling slowly into place as the long-buried memory came back.

Very long time ago . . . the same voice calling soft and cajoling, "Anne? Come out, I know you're there hiding. You shouldn't do naughty things like spying on your own mother . . ."

She'd stayed hidden in one of the little caves, curled up inside with her knees against her chin, her arms wrapped around her cold legs as she closed her eyes and pretended not to hear. It was the same voice that used to say, "Helen?" when her mother slipped out to meet him.

The survival instinct had been strong in the child she had been then. Strong enough so that her mind had blacked out certain memories. Now she didn't want to live because her life had no more meaning. If she'd had a gun herself she would have shot and killed him—the arch-traitor, her mother's lover who had made her his wife, who had killed the man she loved.

"Anne, you're safe now, my darling. You don't have to hide from *me*." Soft Judas voice behind a gun. Had he saved a bullet for her?

A strange calmness overtook her. With the backrush of memory, her sobbing had stopped. She was dead inside—the only thing still alive in her mind was hate.

"I—I'm right here Craig." She had to force herself to pronounce his name; her voice sounded husky and strained. "I've grown too big to hide away in little caves, you see."

Craig Hyatt felt a sudden tightening of his muscles. Her

words gave him an unpleasant shock, coming out of the darkness, sounding exactly like Helen's voice.

He took the flashlight out of his pocket and shone it ahead of him as he stepped forwards into damp darkness. She was sitting down, her back against a wall, looking at him, her eyes blue discs that didn't flinch at the light. Her face was bruised— Helen's face, bruised by her husband's slap. And time slid back in that instant as he heard her voice again, and was eighteen again.

"I'm *sorry*, darling, but don't you see? If he actually *hit* me, it means that he still cares. And I married Richard because I was in love with him—now I know he isn't quite as cold and detached as he pretends to be. You're sweet, but you'll get over me, you know! This has been a kind of experiment for both of us, hasn't it? And I'm sure you'll find someone else . . ."

Cheating, patronizing bitch! But he'd shown her, hadn't he? Anne looked like Helen, but she was a ghost, a paler, washed-out version of Helen who had smiled pityingly when he'd pleaded with her. He had *loved* her, been obsessed by her with all the fervor of an eighteen-year-old. Until she'd shown him what she really was; and once he'd seen, she'd soon stopped smiling. He'd held her face underwater, waiting patiently until her body had stopped its futile thrashing before he'd let her go; giving her up to the ocean tides for their plaything.

Now Craig looked at Anne, who looked like Helen but hadn't any of Helen's warmth and sexuality. Not with *him*, anyhow, and that was the most unforgivable thing of all. She had been his revenge—his precious, ironic revenge on Helen and on Reardon, Helen's husband, his father's friend. Marrying Helen's daughter—possessing Helen all over again. But Anne, like Helen, had betrayed him. He'd tried, but she'd rejected him for other lovers—like Webb Carnahan, like Harris. And they were both dead. He wanted her to know that before he killed her, too. But, above all, he wanted to see her frightened, begging and groveling, before he took her back to the ocean and held her face under the water, shallow water. Just as he had done with Helen. And no one would know! He was cleverer than all of them—even Reardon himself. No one had known, no one had guessed. How could they? He had been eighteen, a college freshman on vacation. Shy and rather serious until Helen had seduced him. Bored, beautiful Helen with a husband who stayed away too long. But he would have given her everything and anything she desired if she hadn't rejected him. Anne could have shared in his final triumph if she hadn't turned out to be too much like her mother.

Poor Anne! That was what they would all say afterwards. They would believe that it was Webb Carnahan who had killed her. Another beautiful irony, that. And only he would appreciate it. Too bad!

He moved forwards, and the flashlight at waist level, shining upwards, made his face look like a death's-head to Anne. He was smiling strangely, his voice still soft and meant to soothe and disarm.

"My poor darling! What did he do to you? But you mustn't worry, I got rid of him for you. They died together, Webb and Harris. They were both bad for you, surely you can see that now? You should have trusted me and let me look after you."

He was standing over her now. He had turned off the flashlight and was a silhouette again with the light from the garage behind him, reflecting dully off the gun he held.

"Get up, darling, you're safe now. You have to come with me, I'm going to make sure the others don't find you."

I got rid of him for you . . . they died together, Webb and Harris. Each word a spike driven deeper and deeper like hammer blows. The agony in her voice was real. "I—I can't move. I think I've broken my ankle. You'll have to help me, Craig."

Whimpering bitch! He hesitated, annoyed; but he believed her. He prided himself, as he always had, on being clear-headed. Better that she die without a bullet wound in her. He came closer, reaching out his hand, and she grabbed for the gun, screaming like a wild thing as she did.

The gun went off, sound splintering into a million echoes in the hollow space. At almost the same instant Webb Carnahan, looking like an apparition out of hell itself, threw his knife. It caught Craig Hyatt between the shoulder blades, and his body poised and leaped like a dancer's before it started to slump forwards. He screamed once as the knife was pulled out to rise and fall again and again.

When he'd gunned the motor to drive out of the garage Webb had expected Hyatt to pull something. He'd had the door on his side unlocked, holding it with one hand while he'd pressed his foot down on the gas pedal. Just beyond the garage doors there was an embankment blanketed by ice plant, and he'd counted on the soft resiliency of the succulent to break his fall when he threw himself out of the car at about the same instant that Hyatt shot the tires. He'd fallen and let himself roll, arms over his head, as pieces of burning metal had scattered all around him. And then, when he'd got his breath back, he'd gone to find Craig, crawling part of the way because his legs felt like rubber under him.

Anne—waiting for him, trusting him. He'd known Craig would try to find her, he'd prayed he wouldn't be too late. The door leading to the caves had been open and he'd begun to run, stumbling; not knowing how he managed to stay on his feet. The sound of the gunshot slammed into his ears, and Hyatt's back made a blurred target as he threw the knife he'd carried strapped to his calf. Anne—he thought of what she must have gone through before the rotten bastard had fired his gun at what must have been point-blank range and he was driven by cold, killer rage that made him want to stab and slash at the man's body long after he was dead. He'd killed before—in war, to defend himself. But never like this, out of a blind urge born of despair and hate and frustration. Hyatt's body lay on its back now and he slit his throat. If he had lived a century ago, he would have taken the scalp as well, as a symbol of bloody vengeance.

Sweat poured from him, dripping into his eyes. Anne was a still, huddled heap on the floor of the cave. Sickly, in the light that poured in from the garage, he saw the stain of blood trickling down her outstretched arm.

When he dropped to his knees and took her in his arms, Webb didn't know if he was praying or cursing. "Oh Christ! Annie—"

Her face was cold and damp, her lips were like ice. But they parted under his urgent, despairing kiss, and he felt the faint flutter of her breath, as warm as life and hope.

PART SIX

CURTAIN CALL

Chapter Forty-nine

"IT's ALL FINALLY wrapped up then?" General Tarrant questioned. An inveterate golf addict, he owned a ten-room "cottage" overlooking the golf course at Cypress Point, where he was a member. The question was almost rhetorical. Richard Reardon had flown down this morning, and of course that had to mean that everything was settled. But he was still curious about certain rather puzzling things. The loose ends.

Reardon turned away from his contemplation of the view. "Quite. No scandal, no publicity. Randall—and the others—proved extremely cooperative, as we had expected. And by the way, I owe a great deal to your idea that we use navy frogmen to get into the house through the caves." He almost smiled. "A good thing your friend Admiral Stuyvesant feels the same way we do."

"Well . . . !" Tarrant cleared his throat to cover his pleasure. Reardon seldom paid anyone a compliment. And, damn him, right to the end almost, he'd been too damned secretive. Almost too slow to take action. If anything had gone wrong . . .

He looked at Reardon with his bushy eyebrows shooting together as he said gruffly, "Well? I've been patient for a long time, you've got to admit. And now, dammit, I think you owe me some answers."

Reardon moved away from the window, turning his back to the view of rocks and blue water. The sound of seals barking filtered through the heavy glass. Almost absentmindedly he took the glass his old friend proffered him and began to turn it around in his long fingers.

Tarrant couldn't understand how the man could remain so calm and coldly rational while his daughter was lying in the hospital suffering from the collective effects of exposure, concussion, a gunshot wound and God knew what else. She'd been in pretty bad shape, he'd understood. He wondered, as he often had, how a man like Reardon could once have been married and had a child, like any ordinary man. If he'd ever felt with his gut instead of his head.

Craig Hyatt—now there was the most puzzling piece of all! Bringing his mind back to the facts he wanted to hear, Tarrant leaned slightly forward. He said almost querulously, "What I can't figure out is what Hyatt hoped to gain—and how you got on to him."

"I'd begun to wonder about him," Reardon said obliquely. "That business in London, for instance. Too many coincidences there."

Hyatt had been responsible for that nasty business. He'd romanced Violet Somers for the information she passed on to him, which in turn was passed on to the unfortunate Karim's uncle, who headed a league of the smaller oil-rich states. When the Majco "cover-up" story was deliberately leaked to the British press in order to implicate Anne and make her more amenable to Harris Phelps's plans for her, Violet had to be eliminated. And Duncan Frazier in his turn, because the poor devil had been in love with Violet and was beginning to have suspicions. After that Hyatt had laid low and been extra cautious, although *he* had been the one to keep Phelps informed of Reardon's moves. They'd known all along that Webb Carnahan had been coerced into working for his old organization, and if Carnahan hadn't been smart enough or desperate enough to have some cards of his own to play . . .

Tarrant let out a gusty sigh. He was frowning. "We were just plain lucky, weren't we?" he grunted. "Why did you let Hyatt go down there at all?"

"To make sure." Reardon said it without inflection. "Making sure" had almost cost his daughter's life. Tarrant wondered grimly if he'd taken that into account.

"What about the rest of them? We know what happened to the Egyptian and Phelps, and that Cuban woman—Carnahan's *wife*, or ex-wife, eh? Must have been quite a little Peyton Place there, what with that fun machine Danny Verrano had set up to spy on his friends at play."

"The de Leone woman had all the really incriminating tapes with her—that's what she killed Harris Phelps for. We've just learned she was a Red Army member. It's just as well the helicopter she took off in was headed off by our own men."

Anna-Maria had almost spoiled all their plans. Palumbo, who owed his first loyalty to Vito Gentile, was supposed to have taken care of that angle. When he landed the helicopter at Monterey Airport so that Phelps could transfer himself and his briefcase to his Lear jet, those tapes were to have been taken over by Reardon's own men. But Anna-Maria had shot Palumbo and taken off in the copter herself. When she'd headed away from the coast guard planes that came after her, she'd gone straight for the smokescreen that the fire provided, taking a chance that had failed when a downdraft sucked the small craft into the maw of the flaming forest.

Espinoza and Pleydel, as soon as they realized what had happened, had shown nothing but surprise, concern, and a desire to help. In private, Espinoza had been more talkative.

"So . . ." Tarrant flexed his shoulders, already eyeing the trimmed greens over Reardon's shoulders while he calculated how many hours of play he might squeeze in before it became too late. "I guess with Randall deciding to play it cool and cautious, everything *is* damn well sewed up, eh?"

He wondered how Richard Reardon could manage to look so detached, just as if it had been a successful chess strategy they had been discussing instead of a clever plan that had almost been pulled off, that would have involved and changed millions of lives—not to mention the delicate balance that now existed between the international powers. Reardon was an enigma, and always would be. The man was almost inhuman. There were people who whispered, although never in his hearing, that he had not been born but manufactured.

He also seemed to have an uncanny knack for reading minds, and catching his rather quizzical look, Tarrant could feel his neck reddening. He stomped off to his elaborate mahogany bar to pour himself another drink, muttering over his shoulder, "Well, thank God that's that! What about the movie people? Suppose they start spreading stories around . . . ?"

"I had a talk with Randall this morning before I came down. They're going to finish shooting the movie at a later date. In Spain, probably. He thought it might be released as a rather toned-down version of what had originally been planned. And, of course, there'll be hints of a jinxed production—Pleydel seems to think that might prove good publicity. In any case"— his voice turned bland; the general turned around sharply. "—the upcoming election is what's on most people's minds right now. Randall and I agreed that James Markham is almost certain to win."

"Huh!" Tarrant's bushy eyebrows flared as he waited for the rest of it.

"I think he'd make a good president," Reardon went on in his quiet voice. "He's young, of course, and—to quote the press —charismatic. He's also quite intelligent, I understand. With a Democratic majority behind him in both the House and the Senate, I'm sure he'll achieve a lot of good things for this country."

Reardon never underscored his words, but to Tarrant the meaning behind that enigmatic little speech was implicit. Jimmy Markham was intelligent enough to conform, especially since he had been rather indiscreet.

Anne saw the headlines on a two-day-old newspaper:

TRAGIC HELICOPTER ACCIDENT TAKES LIVES OF THREE
Multimillionaire movie producer Harris Phelps and two
companions were killed last night when the helicopter
which Phelps was piloting himself went down over the fire.
Phelps's companions were identified as Craig Hyatt,
prominent Washington, D.C., attorney and Anna-Maria
de Leone, constant companion of racing driver Sal Espinoza . . .

The letters danced and blurred before her eyes before she
closed them again, not understanding why she felt so sleepy,
still so numb all over. The nurse must have been reading the
paper . . . she vaguely remembered someone sitting in the chair
by her bed, she had thought hazily it might be Webb, but of
course it couldn't be because he was—was . . . her mind closed
itself against the thought and she slept again, unwillingly slipping back into a black box—or was it a cave?

She rediscovered that blackness had shades and textures and
shapes, and her dreams were like a miniature movie screen in
the darkened theater of her mind. She wanted to keep dreaming to keep away the nightmares. Sharply etched picture of
Craig, silhouetted against the light, calling her Helen.

Anne stirred uneasily, moaning, and the nurse, reentering
hurriedly, checked the IV in her arm before she sat down
again and picked up the newspaper. She shook her head. Bad
luck—they shouldn't try to finish this picture. All those people
dying or having accidents, including *this* pretty young woman
who was her patient. Poor thing—imagine being trapped for
hours in an underground cavern with the sea reaching up to
take you . . . she shook her head again, frowning slightly when
she remembered the bullet wound she wasn't supposed to
mention—not to anyone. Who could have wanted to shoot

Anne Mallory? Had it been another accident? Ah well, perhaps her patient would feel like talking about it when she recovered consciousness. She'd had a close shave. Good thing the coast guard had gotten in there in time to fly her out.

Anne moved again, uneasily. She felt as if she were encased in steel, or ice. Perhaps she'd drowned? That's what Craig had planned for her. She remembered the triumphant sound of his voice, remembered that she'd wanted to kill him—had tried. Ugly sound of gunshots coming back to echo in her mind. Terror and pain and the desperation of no hope at all, nothing left. She'd *wanted* to die, slipping into the black waters of oblivion and nonfeeling.

Until the nightmare changed into a not entirely unpleasant dream. Webb's voice—even though she had heard the shots that killed him, and Craig had laughed, boasting a little. Webb was pulling her out of the bad part of the dream, whispering to her, "Annie? Jesus Christ, Annie-baby, Annie-love, you're not going to die on me, damn you! I'm not going to let you . . ."

Oh God, she wanted that to be true, to be real. Please . . .

Anne woke up to the sound of her own voice saying "Please . . . please . . ." She was back in the room she remembered vaguely. Full of sunshine and flowers arranged in big bowls. Patio doors open onto what looked like a forest. Even piped-in music. Hospital. Nurse. Newspaper. She hadn't dreamed that, had she? Harris was dead, Ria was dead. Craig was dead—he must have left her then, to run away. She frowned, and the nurse bent over her, voice determinedly cheerful.

"Well, good afternoon, Miss Mallory! Isn't it a beautiful day? Dr. Stein will be very pleased. He's been in and out all day, checking up on you."

"I can't move my legs . . ."

"That's because you've got your ankle in a cast, dear. But it's only a crack in the bone, you'll be up and about in no time.

And we'll take the IV out this evening, if you'll promise to eat." The nurse, a middle-aged, smiling woman, looked arch as she leaned over to take Anne's pulse and adjust her covers. "In fact, you're well enough to have a visitor this evening. Won't that be nice?"

Anne felt her heart leap, and then fall back hopelessly. Not Webb. Never again. The unbearable agony of loss made her eyes sting with weak tears she couldn't stop, and the nurse began cluck-clucking.

"Now, now! Didn't you just hear me say everything's fine? Why, in a week or two you'll be able to leave and go home. But you must make up your mind that you're going to be well. All your bruises are going away . . ."

"I—I'd like to see the newspapers, please."

"Of all the strange things to ask for!" Nurse Dunn told the doctor later, shaking her head. "I didn't know what to do—the poor little thing, she looked so lost, you know? With the tears just streaming down her face. It didn't strike me until just that moment that Mr. Hyatt, the one who died in the helicopter, had been her husband."

Anne had almost snatched at the newspapers the woman had handed her unwillingly. Skim-reading—not in that one, no mention of Webb at all. Merely a brief announcement towards the end that the cast and crew of *Greed for Glory* had been flown off the island. Hints of a "jinxed production." *She* was mentioned as lying critically ill in the Monterey Community Hospital, suffering from the effects of exposure and a broken leg. She grimaced, looking at her bandaged right arm, which had begun to throb abominably. And the effort she'd made had tired her out, so that when the nurse came hurrying back into the room to say the doctor was on his way and she mustn't overexert herself, Anne was forced to ask her to read aloud from the next day's paper.

"It just says the same thing, almost. And a little bit about

513

the backgrounds of the poor souls who were killed in that crash. Funeral arrangements—you can't be thinking . . ."

"Do they say anything about—about the other people who were taking part in the film? Are they all right?"

She thought the nurse gave her a peculiar look and didn't care. She had to know. For sure. Kill or kindle the hope that had started to make her pulse race.

When Richard Reardon came in to see her late that evening Anne was sitting propped up in bed. They looked at each other, and Anne could feel that her face was as stiff and devoid of emotion as his. Reardon. She couldn't think of him as "Father." Father-figure. Symbol of everything she didn't and would never understand.

"Anne, how do you feel?" He sounded as gravely formal as she remembered. He didn't come near her, choosing to stand by the patio doors instead. He didn't look changed at all since the last time she'd seen him. God, had it really been almost two years ago? And there was still nothing between them except a mutual wariness. They might have been strangers—and were.

"Hello. I'm fine. Hasn't the doctor told you? He says that if I behave myself and follow orders, I should be . . . out in a few weeks." Out, not home. She had no home. No safe, familiar place to go back to, feeling the roots of old memories hold her fast.

She couldn't keep a certain amount of hostility out of her voice. What did he want of her? Why had he bothered to come? Fleetingly, Anne wondered if he had really ordered her killed. She'd been told so many things . . .

"I'm returning to Washington tonight." His back was to the light, and she couldn't see his face any longer. "I thought I'd look in on you before I left."

His voice remained politely detached, as it always had been on the few occasions when he'd had reason to speak to her.

Anne felt a wave of irrational anger wash through her, staining her pale cheeks. She moved impatiently against her pillows. Why should she let him escape her before he'd answered some of the questions that hammered away in her mind, giving her a constant headache? He knew, of course, that she would have betrayed him and everything he stood for, but she didn't think it made any difference to him. She'd been a gullible, easily manipulated tool—and he'd managed in spite of her to "protect himself," as he'd promised her so long ago.

She had to swallow before she could force herself to ask him. "Before you go, there are—some things I'd like to know, please. All I've seen is the newspapers."

He nodded gravely. "Of course. That is part of the reason why I decided to come by this evening. It's better that you should hear the truth from me than from—any others." Almost imperceptible hesitation there. Had he meant—Webb? *Not yet, Anne,* she warned herself. *Come to that later.* She wondered whether this cold stranger actually knew who his wife's lover had been—or that he'd murdered the mother and married the daughter. Or if he knew, whether it mattered to him.

He surprised her then by sitting down in the straight-backed hospital chair that was placed some distance from her bed.

At least he didn't try to prevaricate or stall her with evasions. He told her everything she needed to know, answering her stammered questions calmly and quietly—without hesitation. Suddenly, all the little pieces in the ugly puzzle fell neatly into place. And she could ask the one question she had kept until the last. The one most important to her.

Chapter Fifty

MADRID AIRPORT BAKED under the hot Spanish sun. All Anne had brought with her was one suitcase, small enough for carry-on baggage. It was heavy, and she was nervous. Damn Webb! All she'd had from him, all these weeks, was a postcard in his almost unreadable scrawl that said something innocuous like "Wish you were here." Why had he even bothered?

Three weeks—and she'd spent them wavering between moods of irrational anger and despair, especially when she'd read that he was making another movie in Spain because the final shooting of *Greed for Glory* had been postponed for some months. She'd gritted her teeth when she'd learned that Carol, of all people, was his co-star again. Did he want her? Didn't he? Perhaps he'd changed his mind, perhaps . . .

There had been times when she felt she might go mad, cooped up in the hospital with her private nurse for company. Hating the two black eyes (soon turning purple) her concussion had left her with. Hating being forced to hobble around and have her daily physical therapy while the other patients tried not to stare. They'd all read the newspapers—she was an object of curiosity, if not pity.

And then there had been the well-intentioned visitors to cope with. Sarah Vesper, beautifully dressed as always, her perfume the same. She was on her way to a well-deserved vacation in Greece. "You must come and visit, Anne. It's exactly what you need. Taki always lets me use his villa. It's magnificent!"

Jean Benedict came, too, but separately. All the nurses in the wing made excuses to pop in, just to get a look at her.

Everyone but Webb—and by the time his card arrived, Anne might well have torn it up in a fit of jealous frustration if Sal Espinoza hadn't turned up, smiling his friendly-tiger smile, all strong white teeth and tanned skin.

Anne had looked at him mistrustfully, hardly able to feign politeness, even when he'd kissed her hand. "I had to come and see you before I left. You're looking very well."

"No thanks to you," Anne wanted to retort nastily, but she managed to say politely, "Good luck with your next race." And then, hastily: "How is Yves? Is he very disappointed about the film?"

"Ah, he plans to reschedule shooting as soon as he can get everyone together again. And when you are well enough to come back to us." He shook his head. "It was terrible, what happened, was it not? You must put it out of your head—I'm sure the doctors have told you so. Life goes on for those of us lucky enough to survive, eh?"

"I suppose so." She wished he'd go. Too many memories, most of them unpleasant.

And then he came out with it. "I mustn't tire you, I suppose. But I had promised Webb I'd look in on you—he was like an absolute madman that night, you know! I was afraid those men from the navy might shoot him. And there was another man there who called himself an old friend, a man who grinned constantly. Webb did not seem to like him at all, especially when this man—Peter, yes, that was his name, I believe—told him he would have to leave with the rest of us. In the end, they went off together. Hmm!" He looked thoughtful for a moment and than shrugged. "Ah well—have you heard from him?"

"A postcard," she'd said tightly, to cover the illogical fluttering of her heart.

"Some men don't care to write. But you really should visit

Spain as soon as you are well enough to get about. You need some sunshine and warmth. A vacation, yes?"

A vacation—maybe. In spite of the heat, Anne felt her hands become cold and clammy with sweat. She'd waited until the very last moment to send him a cable. Perhaps he hadn't been able to tear himself away. Perhaps he hadn't wanted to. Had she ever really understood Webb, in spite of all that had been between them? Would she ever learn?

She didn't see him. She'd carried her case, which seemed to grow heavier by the minute, past customs, out into blinding sunshine. *And now what, Anne?* she asked herself. She saw him suddenly, standing in front of her—looking sun-browned and disreputable in his faded levis and carelessly unbuttoned shirt.

Anne felt as if she had lost her voice. She knew suddenly that she had been crazy to have come here chasing after him. The case she had been carrying dropped unheeded between them, and he kicked it aside with a muttered expletive before he pulled her enormous sunglasses off her nose—and took her into his arms.

He hadn't bothered to shave, and his whisker stubble scratched her face atrociously when he kissed her.

"I'll have you know that embracing in public places is frowned upon in Spain," Webb told her roughly as he hefted her suitcase, still keeping hold of her hand. "And I had to double park. Come along, before we both get arrested."

Anne felt so lightheaded with happiness that she giggled. "But they'd forgive us, wouldn't they? Because we're two crazy Americans."

"You're damn right, we're both crazy. And damn your eyes, Annie, for keeping me waiting this long! I only got your cable a few hours ago and took off in the middle of filming." He grinned down at her suddenly, sun wrinkles crinkling at the corners of his sun-gold eyes. "Last I heard Parelli was tearing his hair out and yelling that I was suspended."

"Oh—good!" she said happily, and he laughed outright. She couldn't remember having seen him really laugh before.

They both laughed a lot in the month that followed. And made love. With urgency, and without. With time stretching ahead. And when Webb had to go to work, Anne lay in the sun, not thinking of time at all while her body turned golden and the hollows in her face filled out.

Webb had rented a small pink-washed, sun-splashed house that overlooked the beach, not far from where they were shooting the movie he was in. There was a housekeeper to go to town for supplies and to cook enormous, fantastically spiced meals, and Anne didn't really care if she went to town or saw anyone else at all. Once, when the woman obligingly brought up an American news magazine, Anne learned without surprise that James Markham had won the presidential election. There was a picture—Markham grinning triumphantly, hands clasped over his head. He was flanked by his smiling family, and there were a few nondescript faces in the background—none that the public would readily recognize. But one of them was Richard Reardon.

Anne put the magazine aside and rolled over onto her back, closing her eyes against the sun. Suddenly she was remembering the hospital room—the sunlight fading outside. And just before he'd left he'd turned on a light that took the shadows away from the corners of the room. As if he wanted her to see him clearly for the first time and the last time maybe—exactly as he was. He'd turned to go then, and she'd asked him one more question.

He'd hesitated at the door.

"Why?" she'd asked him compulsively. "Perhaps I don't have a right to ask you, but I'd still like to know. You've told me about everyone else—their motives, their ambitions. But you —what about you?"

"What about me?" He sounded as if he were rediscovering

519

something for himself as he answered her quietly. "I guess I'm a patriot, Anne. And I suppose that word in itself is something your generation would call 'corny.' But I happen to love this country and all it stands for—more than I am capable of loving or caring for anything else. There's no room in my life for divided loyalties. It's as simple as that, Anne."

That simple. The answer to the puzzle that was Richard Reardon.

Anne found herself frowning—and then she sat up quickly, when ice-cold drops of liquid spattered over her. Webb stood grinning down at her, deliberately holding a bottle of champagne tilted.

"Webb, no! You can't waste our last bottle of Dom Pérignon!"

He squinted his eyes at her wickedly. "Who said it's going to be wasted?" And then, dropping down beside her onto the warm turquoise tiles, he dropped a letter onto her bare stomach. "I thought we should celebrate the last day of filming—and a letter from my sister Lucia. She sends her love, and thinks I ought to marry you if I intend keeping you around. We're an old-fashioned Irish-Italian Catholic family, you know. So"—While she held her breath he leaned down and licked champagne from her navel. "Dammit, Annie my love, I guess I'm going to have to marry you and keep you pregnant every year. And I'm not asking you, I'm telling you, hear?"

"If you'd listen," she whispered, "you'd hear me say yes."

And then she turned her mouth up to his and there was no need to say anything else.